WEREWOLF
COP

WEREWOLF COP

A Novel

ANDREW KLAVAN

PEGASUS BOOKS
NEW YORK LONDON

WEREWOLF COP

Pegasus Books LLC
80 Broad Street, 5th Floor
New York, NY 10004

Copyright © 2015 by Amalgamated Metaphor

First Pegasus Books cloth edition March 2015

Interior design by Maria Fernandez

Library of Congress Cataloging-in-Publication Data is available.

ISBN: 978-1-60598-698-2

10 9 8 7 6 5 4 3 2 1

Printed in the United States of America
Distributed by W. W. Norton & Company, Inc.

KENNEDY

This book is for
Ellen, Faith,
Spencer and John

WEREWOLF COP

PART I

A LEGEND OF
LOVE AND DEATH

1

TASK FORCE ZERO

L ots of bodies. Lots of blood. So much disassembled humanity lay strewn from one end of the fourth-floor railroad flat to the other that even the veteran detectives surveyed the puddled gore with chalk-white faces. Even the men and one woman of the Crime Scene Unit refrained from making the kind of ironical remarks they had learned from watching TV cop shows. They went about their business in near silence, literally counting heads to determine just how many souls had been dispatched into the mystery.

One uniform—not a particularly young or callow patrolman, either—was outside in the alley next to the building, vomiting. In between bringing up his breakfast bacon-and-egg sandwich in painful spasms, he was trying to figure out what he was going to say to deflect the ridicule of his fellow officers, which was sure to follow. A female uniform who had been the second officer on the scene—and who *was* young, and a delicate-looking blonde as well—was sitting alone in a patrol car, crying uncontrollably. She knew there was nothing she could say to stop her colleagues from believing she was a weak girly-girl, prone to hysteria. The fact that department policy would prevent them from saying this out loud only made it worse. Sitting there in the squad-car passenger seat, no longer trying to stop her unstoppable tears, she didn't think she wanted to be a police officer anymore and wondered if she might have a future in the legal profession.

Outside the car window: a forsaken city street. An empty lot, strewn with rubble, to the left. A hollowed brownstone to the right. And in between, the six-story apartment building of grimy white brick that housed the crime scene.

Upstairs, in one blood-washed room after another, the grim forensic work, the terse remarks, the crinkling of plastic bags all continued in an atmosphere of increasing anticipation. A squat balloon-gutted bulldog of a character with the clichéd cop name Muldoon had caught the case and was lead detective for now, but no one expected that to last very long. Muldoon was a good man to have when your typical gang-banger-wannabe made his bones by firing a 9mm slug into the brain of some honor student. But this was not that. This was not an angel-dust-and-buzz-saw family quarrel either, or even a showy act of vengeance on the blacks by the Russians. This was big. Big. This was something outside the purview of your workaday murder-man like Muldoon, something entirely off the local map of his imagination.

This was Big—and Someone was Coming. Everyone in the railroad flat knew it. Maybe it was the FBI, or Homeland Security, or the CIA—but Someone was going to take this case over.

So everyone went about his business and everyone was waiting. Muldoon dutifully dispatched his minions to canvass the neighborhood for didn't-see-nothing lies. The Crime Scene Unit dutifully tagged and bagged the hunks of meat that had lately been some mother's son or daughter. The patrolman in the alley puked and the patrolwoman in the squad car cried. And everyone waited, because everyone knew: This was Big and Someone was Coming.

Sure enough, less than half an hour after Muldoon arrived, a dark blue Crown Victoria pulled in haphazardly among the official cars blocking the street below. Muldoon felt a complex brew of emotions—relief, excitement, resentment, and admiration—as a buzz of murmuring reached his ears:

"It's the Zero boys."

"*Really* big."

"The Cowboy and Broadway Joe!"

Moments later, there were footsteps on the stairway and then in the hall—and, finally, into that makeshift charnel house, with casual yet unmistakable authority, walked Agents Martin Goulart and Zach Adams.

They were the two chief detectives of Task Force Zero, and Adams was legendary. The Task Force itself was practically mythic, since no one knew exactly where it had come from or what it was for. Its official name was Extraordinary Crimes—though whether it was a division or bureau or agency was uncertain. The federal Department of Homeland Security had assembled the group six years ago by quietly hiring some of the finest detectives away from some of the biggest police departments in the country. Why they had done this, no one would say. In fact, no one had even admitted E.C. existed—until an emergency called it into action and thrust it into the public eye.

This was three years ago. An angelic, bright-eyed five-year-old girl named Emily Watson had been kidnapped from her bedroom in the little town of Clyde, Ohio. The kidnapper was a flamboyant psychopath named Ray Mima, already wanted for three sadistic killings in Oklahoma. For the next five days, Mima proceeded to taunt the law and tantalize the media by broadcasting his plans for his little hostage on social media. His plans were horrifying, brutal—and irresistibly readable. The country—much of the civilized world—was mesmerized, rigid with suspense, as the days went on and the ugly messages kept appearing on the Internet.

Enter—seemingly out of nowhere—two cinematically mismatched law dogs from something no one had ever heard of called Extraordinary Crimes. Zach Adams was a former Houston homicide detective who spoke with a soft country twang. A tall, slender man in his late thirties, he was the very image of a western hero: blond-haired, blue-eyed, with a lean face that would have been boyish had it not been weathered by the elements. Martin Goulart, on the other hand, was former NYPD and pure Brooklyn, a slick and swarthily handsome man, solidly built and fit, with a full head of jet-black hair and an arrogant smile women fell for.

The two had somehow traced Ray Mima to a hundred-year-old farmhouse, an abandoned wreck standing in noble isolation amid the Flint Hills of Kansas. While backup was racing to the scene, Zach and Goulart entered this quaint piece of decaying Americana on their own. There, on their own, they confronted the kidnapper.

The way the world heard the story that evening, Zach and Ray Mima stumbled on each other in a narrow hallway. Zach shouted a warning. Mima opened fire at him with a monstrous hunting handgun. The big weapon's kick sent the kidnapper's arm flying and a .50 cal missile went screaming past Zach's ear. Whereupon Zach, steady as steel, put three 9mm slugs in a tight group in the center of the psycho's chest and sent him promptly to hell.

What happened next: one of a dozen local cops, just pulling up out-side, saw the two feds exiting the building and snapped their picture with his handheld. The photo showed Zach holstering his weapon as he strode from the farmhouse with Goulart right behind him, cradling little Emily—miraculously unhurt—in his arms. The image flashed around the world—the picturesque farmhouse, the rescued child, the two grim cops—a Texas Cowboy and a Broadway Joe—a happy ending. It became iconic.

And for a day or two, the media wanted to know: what was Extraordinary Crimes exactly? When had it been established, and why? What department was it in? Who was it responsible to? What was its brief? The answers were so vague, the proper authority who could even give an answer was so hard to find, that one TV commentator dubbed the group Task Force Zero, a federal law agency that didn't exist. The name stuck.

Then some new event that was more or less newsworthy happened and everyone forgot the whole business. Except other law officers. Especially in the major cities. Where every now and again, the Cowboy and Broadway Joe—or two other similarly mismatched but expert detectives—would show up and take a case over for no reason anyone could pinpoint.

So yes, there were mixed feelings in the cop-like heart of Muldoon when Zach and Goulart arrived on the blood-drenched scene.

Muldoon, forty-six years old and only a couple of years away from possible retirement, was not as ambitious as he used to be. He would have liked to take the lead on what was going to be a high-profile case; but if he was going to lose the spot to the feds, well, it wasn't so bad to lose it to the Zero boys, who tended to remain invisible and let the local law take the credit. Plus Zach Adams was a celebrity hero with an unmatched reputation. He was said to be modest, relaxed, soft-spoken, hardworking, honest, and a great detective. It would be something for Muldoon just to be able to say he had worked with the Cowboy.

"Marco Paz," he told the two agents as they approached. As they all shook hands, he gestured with his head to the carnage around the room. "Sometimes called MP. He owns this building. This is his apartment. And he's one of the vics. A major-league fence. All the truck-jackers use him. Used him. High-level burglars. The mob. Just about everybody got him to sell their stuff, launder their money, whatever. He had a good rep. Played fair. Discreet. No muscle, no gunplay. Just an honest criminal peddler, basically."

Zach and Goulart nodded. They stood silently shoulder to shoulder near the center of the living room. Hands in their pants pockets, they surveyed the slaughter with practiced eyes. After a moment, Muldoon saw them exchange a knowing look. This made the detective want to add something, to show that he was knowledgeable too.

He said: "They didn't use a buzz saw, I don't think. Russians and Cubans go in for that shit. This looks more like an axe or something. . . ."

"A sword—longswords," said Broadway Martin Goulart—and the woman from the ME's office, on her knees beside a torso near the far wall of the living room, glanced up and nodded.

"Looks like the handiwork of the BLK," Zach explained in his soft drawl. And Muldoon appreciated this: information sharing; including him in the case; none of the usual federal bullying. "They like to use these old-fashioned longswords. It's like their calling card."

"The BLK." Muldoon shook his head. He'd never heard of them.

Goulart said: "The Brüderlichkeit—the brotherhood."

"German mob originally," said Zach, ambling away casually toward the far wall.

"German and Russian," Goulart went on. "They had their beginnings in the Russian gulags after World War II. Nazis guarded by

Communists, right? They all turned out to be natural pals once they stopped talking politics. Natural killers and black marketeers, the lot of them. They got along famously."

Muldoon nodded as if it was all clear to him, which . . . no.

Zach, meanwhile, squatted down next to the ME's woman and the bloody torso she was working in the corner. "Hi," he said. "Name's Zach."

She glanced up from her work. "Molly." She was a petite, coffee-colored woman. She smiled, but only briefly. Her smile—and her figure, hidden under the baggy ME windbreaker—were her best features, and she worked hard not to deploy them while on the job. Especially to guys she found attractive. Which she definitely found Zach Adams.

"Hi, Molly. How many bodies we looking at here?" he asked her.

"Five, I'm guessing," she said. "There are five heads, anyway. That's what I'm counting so far."

"Marco Paz and . . . who else? His family? His crew? What do you think?"

She wagged her head, uncertain. "Some family. But some crew too, that's my guess. Definitely Paz and probably his woman and then a teenager, who was maybe their son. Then two other guys, both strapped—holsters, no guns. The guns gone. They were probably crew."

"Thank you kindly, Molly," said Zach. He stood.

Molly allowed herself a glance down the back of him as he strolled into the next room over. He had good manners too, she thought.

After a while, Goulart came up next to him. "Tell me nobody in the building heard this going down," he muttered out of the corner of his mouth.

The two stood shoulder to shoulder again while a CSU guy and another ME tech worked the blood-stained room behind them.

"Right. Or that no one saw a whole dadgummed army of bad-men with longswords parade into the building," said Zach.

Goulart's head went up and down once with noiseless laughter.

Now Muldoon stepped into the doorway and began to say, "They apparently took the duct tape with them after—"

But Goulart silenced him with a raised hand. Goulart knew his partner, and he'd come to recognize when Zach had gone into what

Goulart liked to call "hyper-focus mode." The Cowboy's body had gone still and the crow's-feet crags at the corners of his eyes gathered. He peered down into what seemed nothing more than another thick splotch of blood on the chipped paint of the rotten floorboards. Pulling a pair of rubber gloves out of his back pocket and working them onto his hands, he crouched over it. He reached into the sticky mess and plucked from it . . . what? What was it? Zach held it up before his eyes and turned it this way and that in the light. Goulart crouched down beside him and squinted until he could see it more clearly: it was a piece of fluff of some kind with, perhaps, a thread attached to it.

"Say there, people?" Zach called out.

His tone was casual—as if he were about to ask someone to help him recall a name he had forgotten—and yet something in his voice brought Molly hurrying to one doorway and some CSU guys peeking in at another. Zach held the piece of fluff up to all of them.

"Any of you folks find a little plastic disc—or maybe a glass disc—about the size of a button, maybe designed to look like half an eyeball? An eyeball for a stuffed animal?"

"I found that." This was from the CSU man right behind him, a roundish young fellow blinking with surprise through misting glasses. "I already tagged and bagged it. You want me to—"

But Goulart raised his hand again and cut him off as he had Muldoon.

Because now Zach, still squatting, was turning on his toes, turning his head in a slow-motion swivel that panned his narrowed gaze from one end of the room to the other. Not only Goulart, but Muldoon and Molly and the rotund CSU guy and the other ME techs and CSU's stopped to watch him—and all of them tensed internally when his eyes came to rest on what (he later explained to Goulart) was the faintest smear in the dust of one section of wall. It was only just barely visible in the space beneath an arc of blood spatter and beside a low built-in knick-knack shelf in the corner.

"Well, look-a-there," Zach murmured.

He stood. He strode across the room and crouched again—crouched this time before the low knick-knack shelf. The shelf was empty. Its clutter of ashtrays, baseball caps, magazines, broken watches, pens, and spare change had already been cleared away by the forensic team.

Taking hold of the edge of the shelf with both hands, Zach tugged—and then tugged again.

Molly said "Oh!"

Muldoon cursed.

The shelf came away from the wall, bringing a section of the wall with it to reveal the hidey-hole secreted behind it. Muldoon cursed again and one of the CSU guys cursed too, and the shocked Molly covered her mouth with her gloved hand.

The late Marco Paz had been a fence, a trader in stolen goods, an expert in converting hot valuables into cash. Naturally, he had needed a secret place in which to hide that cash, and so he had fashioned this shelf-and-hole dodge for the purpose.

But it wasn't the 275 thousand dollars in neat stacks of small bills that brought forth the gasps and curses of the investigators.

It was the child. Six-year-old Mickey Paz. He was huddled beside the money stacks. He was kneeling and stooped to fit into the cramped hideaway. He was trembling with terror, sucking the thumb of one hand—and clutching in his other hand a bedraggled Teddy bear with one eye missing.

2

DOMINIC ABEND

Women make crap detectives," said Martin Goulart. "The only good ones are lesbians—you ever notice that? Lesbians and fat black women. I don't know what that's about. I'm thinking of that two-ton Negro broad—what was her name?—Susie—used to work the one-seven. She was all right. But for the most part, being a detective, what is it, right? Reason, unemotional observation, a sense of responsibility, guts—why would you hire a female to do a job like that? It'd be like hiring me to do sensitivity training."

This was typical Goulart. He was always saying stuff like this. He'd been called on the carpet for it a dozen times, sent to—speaking of sensitivity training—sensitivity training himself, twice. Didn't help. He was incorrigible. Nothing changed him. An all-American mongrel of French, German, Italian, and Scottish extraction with some Jew in there somewhere, he was a bubbling cauldron of urban energy, a walking flashpoint on the lookout for a flame. In service to that quest, he felt it was his duty to say just about anything that would offend just about anybody, just about anything you were not supposed to say.

It was April Gomez who had gotten him started today. Plus the fact that he was bored. He and Zach had been standing in a storage-slash-observation room of the city's one-six precinct for the past half hour. Slouched amidst file boxes and broken computers in their habitual shoulder-to-shoulder position. Gazing sleepily at the monitor which was now showing live video of NYPD Detective April Gomez interviewing little Mickey Paz in a language neither agent understood. Which April had been called in to do because the little boy had been traumatized and because children generally responded better to women and because April was proficient in the Castilian dialect common to Venezuela which, in his traumatized state, was the only language little Mickey could remember how to speak. So Goulart felt it was necessary to explain to Zach that April Gomez had only been promoted to detective in the first place to fulfill some sort of minority quota because she was Hispanic and female—and the rest of his diatribe followed from that.

Zach, as usual, could only roll his eyes and shake his head. Some people were shocked by Goulart's rants and some secretly agreed with them, but Zach just found them comical and ridiculous. Goulart could say whatever he wanted about women—or blacks or Hispanics or homosexuals or French-German-Italian-Scottish-maybe-Jews, for that matter: Zach took none of it seriously. For him, there were only two kinds of people in the world: sinners and criminals. If you were the former, he considered himself your brother and protector. If you were the latter, he considered himself the flawed but relentless instrument of a just and terrible God.

Goulart's nonsense was obnoxious at times, if Zach bothered to pay attention to it. But, on the other hand, the New Yorker was one of the best detectives he had ever worked with. Goulart had an instinctive sense about people that was almost like mind-reading. He was funny. And generous, for all his blabber. Basically, a good partner all around.

And there was this, too: despite all the hogwash the Brooklyn hardass spewed out, there was always a bit of truth mixed in. April Gomez *had,* in fact, been promoted to detective because she was a Latina and because some loud-mouthed pol and the media had complained about the absence of Latina detectives on the job. She was a sweet girl and by no means stupid, but she had as much business being called to a crime scene as a vase of carnations. Everyone in the department who knew anything about it knew that this was true.

That said, April was doing a good job with the boy right now. The kid seemed mesmerized by her gentle sisterly gaze. Still clutching his one-eyed Teddy bear, he was speaking to her in a fluid half-whisper.

So when Goulart started up again: "It's like we're all supposed to pretend that women are what they aren't and if we pretend hard enough that's going to somehow make it true. Which is the opposite of police work, when you think about it. Which I mean is, what? It's figuring out what's true no matter *what* you want it to be. Take the Muzzies, for example . . ."

. . . Zach lifted a finger and said, "Turn your face off and listen."

Goulart's voice trailed to silence, and the two of them focused on the monitor, standing just beneath them on an old conference table.

"I think April just asked him if he heard any names mentioned," said Zach.

The boy's tremulous voice continued, only just audible—and suddenly April Gomez, assuming the detectives were watching her, glanced up, startled, at the video camera hanging in one corner of the ceiling above her.

And simultaneously Goulart said, "What?"

And simultaneously Zach said, "Did you hear that?"

April apparently couldn't believe it either, because she turned back to the boy and asked him to repeat himself: *"Dijo* Abend?"

The boy nodded solemnly. In a corner of the room, an older black woman from Children's Services looked on with her hands folded on the skirt of her purple dress. Even she seemed to understand that something important had happened.

"Si," said Mickey Paz. "Señor Abend. Señor Abend." Then he went off into another musical strain of something akin to Castilian.

Zach and Goulart listened, leaning their heads forward as if that would help them understand.

"Are you getting any of this?" said Goulart. "What exactly did he say about Señor Abend?"

Zach, who knew just enough Texican to avoid a bar fight, said, "I think he said one of the men was named Abend, that someone called one of the killers Señor Abend."

"You gotta be kidding me," said Goulart. "You mean, as in: Abend was there himself? In the room? Standing there while they're hacking these people apart? You think that's even possible?"

"No," Zach murmured. "I don't. Sure ain't likely, anyway."

"But that is what he's saying?"

"Near as I can make out. Have we found any security footage from the scene yet? Anyone who took a picture with a cell phone? Any pictures at all?"

"Last I heard, they were still canvassing," said Goulart. "But I'll go check."

He detached himself from Zach's shoulder and left the room. Zach stayed where he was, still gazing down intently at the monitor. He remained like that, in hyper-focus mode, for another few seconds; but as the boy was now rattling on much too rapidly for him to comprehend, his mind eventually drifted. To Dominic Abend. Who was said to be the chieftain of the BLK. Which had wafted out of the post-World War II gulags to infiltrate every level of Soviet tyranny; and had then become the very medium of Eastern Europe's post-Communist gangsterocracy; and had then, with the fall of the Iron Curtain that had once contained it, spread like a miasma over the free nations of Western Europe, infecting every organized crime operation on the continent and in Britain, transforming all of them into mere agents of itself.

Now, these last few years, the Brüderlichkeit was said to have traveled here, to the U. S. of A., breathing a new, poisonous, unifying zombie-life into the homeland's beleaguered organized crime operations—Cosa Nostra and Yakuza, the black Disciples and the Mexican mob, and the Russian Bratva, which had never been more than a tendril of the BLK anyway, and all the rest.

Back in Europe, journalists and academics had heard of the Brotherhood, though no one had yet seemed to grasp its pervasive dominance. But the fact that the organization had now come to America—this was unknown to the media and the professoriate alike. Evidence, testimony, reports, and statistics simply did not reflect the BLK's mushrooming influence in the U.S.

But law officers in all the major cities sensed it nonetheless, the way family doctors sense a new, more drug-resistant strain of an old disease. Coast to coast, the law dogs confided in one another: criminal operations were proceeding with heightened brutality and smoother efficiency. Gangs were harder to penetrate, their transactions harder to detect. Old capos, lieutenants, and muscle-men were vanishing without a trace. Suspects who once would have betrayed their mothers for a plea bargain suddenly preferred to take the fall. A new silence seemed to underlie the tips of even the most reliable confidential informants. None of the cops was certain, but they all felt it: a new cancer of corruption was eating into the country. The underworld was on the rise.

All of it was linked to Abend. In lawman legend, at least, Abend was the source and controlling genius of the invasion.

Dominic Abend was a German-Russian billionaire of unknown occupation and murky antecedents. He had gone invisible after the USSR collapsed, and then risen into the consciousness of Western law enforcement as more shadow than light, as an empty Dominic-Abend-shaped space at the center of what little information they had about him. There were a few old photographs of him. A few mentions of him in criminal testimony. Some hints from tipsters here and there. An occasional sighting. And, most recently, a digital snapshot taken by an ambitious plainclothesman working the crowd at Times Square on New Year's eve one year back. That last suggested Abend, like the BLK, might himself be in the country.

So little Mickey Paz's statement that Abend—the international criminal mastermind—had been personally present at the scene of a mass murder turned Zach Adams's blood hunter-hot with excitement. Because Abend and the BLK were the reasons Task Force Zero had been formed in the first place. Finding them—stopping them—destroying them: this was Extraordinary Crimes' underlying commission.

Zach's mind was called back to the moment by his phone buzzing in his jacket pocket—a text message, judging by the length of the vibration. He began to reach for it but stopped with his hand hovering in front of his sternum as something new developed on the Observation Room monitor.

The little boy in the Interview Room had begun speaking English. He had slipped into it unconsciously, it seemed, as April Gomez's warmth and gentleness slowly soothed and relaxed him.

"They kept saying to him again and again, 'Where is it? Where is it?'" said Mickey Paz, the fingers of one hand absently massaging his Teddy bear's ear as if to comfort it. "But Papa didn't know. He said, 'I don't know. I swear.' He kept saying that to them, but they wouldn't listen."

"Where is what?" said April Gomez, who slipped into English just as smoothly as the boy in her effort to keep him comfortable. "What were the men looking for, Mickey? What were they trying to find? Did they say?"

Zach noticed the little boy's eyes shift to the left—which might possibly mean he was trying to access an auditory memory. Zach also noticed that the kid went on fiddling with the Teddy bear's ear—it was touching; pathetic.

Then, haltingly, the boy said, "Stu . . . stu . . . stupe bassard . . . stum . . . they said a word I don't know. Stoomp bassard. Bassard."

"Bastard?" suggested April Gomez. "Stupid bastard?

"No!" whispered Zach urgently to the empty room. "Don't tell him what he's saying, April."

The boy thought about it and then gave a strong and certain nod. "Bastard. Yes. Stupid bastard."

Well, sure, thought Zach. *Now that you put it in his head.*

April Gomez sat back in her chair, glancing up at the video camera with an air of satisfaction. "Stupid bastard," she repeated.

With a flicker of annoyance at the corner of his mouth, Zach reached for his phone again to check that text. But he was interrupted—again—as the door came open fast and Goulart charged in after it.

"Look at this."

He slapped two pages onto the desk and Zach moved closer, leaned in over them for a better look. Two printed photos, two blurry images. Goulart pointed at one, then the other.

"That's the one the uncle took on New Year's eve, right?—the one the feds think is the guy Interpol lost track of in Brussels five years ago. And that—is from last night, from a security cam Paz himself had placed in his building. The killers took out the cam above the door, but this one was hidden in the super's basement flat and trained up at the door through the window."

"Because Paz knew they were coming," said Zach, "and wanted to make sure we got a picture of him."

"Maybe. Or maybe it was just to foil the neighborhood vandals."

Zach turned the second photo this way and that under his fingertips as he studied it. Neither this image nor the other was very clear. The New Year's eve shot—which he'd examined many times before—showed a man standing absolutely still at the edge of a dense and roiling Times Square mob. The man was fifty, or maybe fifty-five or a fit sixty. Tall, square-shouldered, wearing a long dark overcoat, his hands in the pockets. He had a shaven head, a bulbous nose, and thin lips. And his expression. . . . Possibly Zach projected this onto him—probably—the shot was so grainy, how could anyone tell for sure?—but the man's expression seemed predatory, the smile sadistic, the glint in the eyes likewise cruel. It was as if the man were eyeballing the humanity massed around him and trying to decide how he would best like to have it cooked for his supper.

The other photo—the one under his fingertips—the one from just before the Paz slaughter—showed four men hustling through the autumn darkness toward the front door of Paz's grimy white-bricked building. Three of the men were hunched over, their chins sunk into their overcoats, their hands gripping black dry-cleaning bags in which, Zach assumed, they were hiding their sheathed longswords.

The fourth man—the man surrounded by the others—was, as near as Zach could tell, the same man as the one in the New Year's eve photo: tall, broad, shaven-headed, European, cruel.

"If that—" said Goulart pointing to the Paz shot, "is the same man as *that*," pointing now to the New Year's eve photo, "and *that* is the same as the guy Interpol lost track of in Brussels. . . ."

"And if the guy in Brussels was in fact Dominic Abend. . . ." Zach added.

"Right. If he was."

"Well, then," said Zach with a wry smile, "we are on his trail for damn sure!"

Broadway Joe Goulart grinned, nodding with that silent laughter of his.

Whereupon Zach's phone buzzed again—which is what it did if he didn't read a text soon enough after the first buzz. He glanced at the monitor on the desk. The lady from Children's Services was standing up out of her chair now, apparently bringing Mickey's interview with April Gomez to a close. Zach reached into his pocket, drew out the phone, and called up the message.

"What's the matter?" said Goulart casually. It wasn't that Zach had gone pale or anything like that. He'd barely changed expressions at all. It was just that Goulart was that good. He could read faces like he was reading a street sign.

Zach shook his head as he slid his phone back into his pocket. "Nothing," he said with a quick frown. "Just—the usual flapdoodle."

He didn't for a minute think Goulart believed him, but that was beside the point. Whether Goulart believed him or not, there was no possibility Zach was going to tell his partner what had been in that text, or who had sent it, or that he had been dreading just such a message for weeks and weeks, and that now that it had come, the low boil of suspense that had been robbing him of sleep in the small hours of more nights than he cared to think about was bubbling over into a sour and sickening certainty that the worst mistake of his life had come back to haunt him.

3

GRACE

Driving home through darkfall on the out-borough streets, Zach listened to the news on the radio—or, that is, he set the radio to the news station and drove without listening at all. The radio reporters—one reporter after another—described the second day of looting, rioting, and arson fires in London, Berlin, Paris, Madrid, and Athens far away. The urgency in their voices, at once pompous and terse, became a wordless drone, part of Zach's aural ambience, along with the sea-like sough of tires on pavement and the hoarse rush of air from his Pontiac's vents. He gazed out the windshield at the twilight streets—at brownstones and supermarkets, at white headlights and red taillights, at brown-skinned women pushing silver shopping carts under Chinese restaurant marquees and Spanish grocery awnings—and half to himself and half to God, he cursed the day that Margo Heatherton had found him.

She *had* found him. He knew that now. She had seen—well, everyone had seen—the photograph of him after the Emily Watson kidnapping, the famous Cowboy shot of him holstering his nine as he swaggered out of the Flint Hill farmhouse where he'd out-gunned Ray Mima. She had set her sights on him and sought him out. But, of course, he hadn't realized that at the time.

At the time, there were a lot of things he didn't realize. He was not a man who thought about his own emotions much. They came and went, a distraction more than anything. As far as he was concerned, emotions did little more than distort the shape and color of the landscape of events, turned it gray when he was down, turned it bright when he was feeling good. Which was all only in his mind, because the landscape of situations and events remained unchanged no matter how he felt, no matter how his feelings colored it. Best to keep his eyes on the world and out of his own shirt pocket, that was his philosophy. Let his heart feel what it would, it made no difference to the facts of the matter.

At the time Margo found him, Zach's wife, Grace, normally sweet-natured, cheerful, and efficient, was feeling low and disoriented after their move to New York. She missed her mama and her sisters and her church people back in Houston. She was harried with relocation details and, though she never said as much, Zach sensed that she resented the long hours he had to spend on the job. For the first time in their marriage, she gave off an air of sweat and weariness when he approached her. Meanwhile, he himself was coming down from what he hadn't even realized was the excitement of his year-plus of fame, suffering delayed withdrawal from the drug-like thrill of the chase and the gunfight and the public triumph afterward. He was lonesome and bored.

Not that he considered any of this an excuse for what happened. Zach Adams never excused himself for anything. He carried in his mind a precise catalogue of his moral errors going back to the age of three, and he lost sleep over all of them. It was not about excuses—it was just that he realized now, looking back, how restless and dissatisfied he'd been, whereas at the time he hadn't given it a thought. It was only emotion.

Margo Heatherton had had a friend in the governor's press office and had gotten his e-mail address from her—that's what she said. She wrote to him asking if she could interview him for background to a novel she was writing about a kidnapping. That sounded different, anyway. After a month or two of back-and-forth, Zach had arranged to have lunch with her. She was a poised, elegant 25-year-old with long, silky blond hair and fine rose-white features. She had a sympathetic air and a mischievous wit. Not the usual class of woman he came into contact with: she had an aura of high society.

He cursed the day.

The Pontiac now veered from the crowded commercial streets onto a grid of neighborhood back roads. The heavy-hearted Zach traveled from stop sign to stop sign until he reached his home territory: green lawns divided by front walks leading to front steps rising to the front doors of two-story red-brick houses with white bay windows below and gray cross-gabled roofs above—one after another of them.

He pulled into his driveway. As he was stepping out of the car, his five-year-old boy Tom came banging through the house's storm door. He shouted "Daddy!" and dashed to Zach across the lawn. Zach's two-and-a-half-year-old daughter Ann, gripping the wrought-iron bannister, was carefully negotiating the cement steps. Grace was right behind her, bending forward to shepherd her down. They were this way every evening when he came home, as excited to see him as if he were returning from an ocean voyage of many months. He put his arm around Tom's shoulder and hoisted Ann up into the crook of his other elbow. The boy chattered to him about the day's heroics and the girl showed him her crayon picture. Grace met him on the walk and kissed him, her eyes smiling. She had a scent, he would have sworn, a sort of atmosphere about her that, even now that they were nine years married, gave him a yearning feeling deep down.

This was all the love life Zach had ever wanted. Despite his romantic good looks, he had never been much of a Romeo. Maybe it was his religious upbringing, but the sexual pursuit of strangers had never inspired him the way it does some men; a lot of men. He had had a few flings in college. A few longer relationships afterward. But there had always seemed to him something vaguely—what was the word?— *disfiguring* to his sense of himself—even *corrupting*—about being naked with—being asleep in the arms of—being physically *inside* somebody he didn't much give a damn about.

He had found Grace in church, as he liked to joke in his slow drawl. He had started going to church again when he began to feel it was time to somehow "get serious" about his life. His own ideas about God were a bit more amorphous than anything he read in scripture, but he'd always found church a suitable place to go think good thoughts for an hour, if you didn't take any of it too literally. First day there, and out she came to collect the four- and five-year-olds for the Sunday school. He took, as they say, one look at her. . . . Practically brimming over with tenderness for her little charges. And the eager way they clustered around her. And the spilling ringlets of her honey hair, her sweet face so kindly, her figure sturdy and full.

She was then, and remained now, a mystery to him. He was not a sentimental man. He knew she could not be the perfect Proverbs 31 wife he thought she was, or the cornball angel-of-the-house he thought she was either. But damned if he could catch her with her angel mask off or her Proverbs guard down. She was religious in the same beat-by-beat scriptural way his own mama had been, the way he assumed a good woman was supposed to be. And, also like his mama, she gave herself to being a housewife and mother with what seemed to him an almost feral ferocity. She gave herself to him that way too, devoted herself to him, attached herself to his life and submitted herself to his authority so completely that it simply baffled him. He did not have such a high opinion of himself that he could ever imagine he deserved such devotion, so what the hell was she thinking exactly? Day to day, he was never really sure.

But never mind. He loved his wife. This was no mere matter of emotion to him. It was a profound fact of his existence. He might feel any which way about her at any particular moment, sure. But as long as creation endured and ever after, Grace's good was his good, her suffering his. Even his love for his children was somehow an extension of his love for her. Even his love of his own life. When the psycho kidnapper of Emily Watson had fired that 500 at him in the farmhouse, his primary emotion—aside from the adrenaline rush—had been righteous indignation on his wife's behalf. How evil could Ray Mima be that he would risk causing Grace to grieve? That was how much he thought of her.

At that first lunch with Margo Heatherton—this was maybe eight months ago—Margo had interviewed him as "research" for her "novel." She had been flattering him, he realized now, but it was subtle and at the time he hadn't noticed it. She had simply let him do the talking and occasionally admired his expertise. Then, after a while, she had told him about the troubles of her young life—her desire to go her own way rather than succumb to pressure from her father. Which allowed him to dispense a bit of easy wisdom to her, which also flattered him. Which, again, he didn't realize until much later.

After that—for the next month or two—she did little more than e-mail him from time to time. She'd ask him some new interview question or send him an article she thought might interest him. Every e-mail had her photograph attached. That was just a feature of her e-mail program. But he found himself searching for other pictures of her online. He found two. One in particular showed her at a fancy New York debutante ball, wearing a gown that made her look like a princess. It fascinated him.

Once, after about six weeks, she arranged to bump into him on the street outside the NYPD's 16th precinct, where Extraordinary Crimes was housed. He bought her a cup of coffee at a nearby diner. She somehow ended up telling him about her problems with her on-again, off-again boyfriend, a medical student. He felt jealous, though he didn't quite recognize that that's what it was. She invited him to a party later that night. "Bring your wife!" she said. "I'd love to meet her." But he knew Grace wouldn't be able to get away, and wouldn't like it much if she did. He refused Margo's invitation to go on his own. He liked the look of disappointment in her eyes. All of this, he had now come to believe, had been calculated on her part, a well-planned campaign to draw him in.

It worked, too. She got into his mind. He began to think about her. There were things that she said and ways that she looked when she said them that kept coming back to him during the day. By this time, Grace had started to rebound from her mild depression. She still missed Houston, but she'd found a church she liked in Queens and the kids were pretty well settled in their red-brick home. She was almost back to her cheerful and generous self. As for him, his work on the

Task Force was still slow and frustrating, but traces of the BLK were starting to emerge—they were making progress.

None of this mattered. The only thing that mattered was that she, Margo, was in his mind. Otherwise, he would not have been so vulnerable to the final phase of her seduction.

She invited him up to Westchester, where she lived. To a café where she said she was going to give a reading of some of her novel. He did not go there to have sex with her. He went, though he didn't realize it then . . . he went on the chance of feeling flattered again. Maybe he'd hear portions of their research interview underpinning her prose, or maybe he'd find that her book contained a character like himself, or a better version of himself. Maybe he'd just get the chance to give her some criticism on her writing while she listened to him, all serious and sophisticated and doe-eyed the way she was.

He did not go to have sex with her, but he didn't tell his wife he was going to see her either. So later, he understood that Margo had played him expertly and that he had been a country fool, two acres dumber than dirt.

Of course, there had been no reading. There was no novel, as he later came to believe. *He* was the novel. He was the story she was telling herself. Margo—as he now understood her—was a fantasist and a manipulator. The emotionally disturbed daughter of a wealthy businessman, she was spoiled, unemployable, and idle, nothing but time on her hands. Most of that time she spent on the Internet. She had been taken with him, charmed by his famous picture, and had conceived this romantic drama for them to play out.

The café was closed when he got there. She was waiting for him on the sidewalk outside. She had some long excuse about why the reading had been canceled at the last minute. This included a story about why she needed a ride home. Which, of course, he gave her.

By then, he should have been suspicious about who she was and what she was—even more so after he saw the house she lived in. It was nearly a mansion to his eyes, with acres of landscaped garden in front of it and a local forest preserve stretching down into a gorge behind. But she asked him to come in with her until she got the lights turned on, and then she pretended to be upset about the canceled reading so he stayed for a drink. Until the moment he felt the shocking satin of her skin beneath his hand and the shocking sweetness of her kiss against his lips, he had imagined he was a man more or less in control of himself.

Tonight, after he read his son a story and sang his daughter a song, he sat at the kitchen counter with a beer. He watched his wife finish cleaning the kitchen, and he told her about his day. She had advised him to do this—to tell her—from the start of their marriage. She had warned him not to become one of those cops who keeps the horrors of the job to himself—either out of some misguided sense of chivalry, or out of the conviction that no civilian could possibly understand—and so ultimately becomes more intimate with his partner than his spouse. He didn't give her all the gory details, but he told her about the murder house and about the child in the hidey-hole and about the nearly unbelievable possibility that Dominic Abend had at last made a fatal error.

"Y'all aren't thinking he was there himself, are you?" she asked. "At the murder? Himself?"

Grace was standing at the sink polishing the spots off a glass with a dish towel. Her hair was shorter now than when they'd met, but there was still a spill of honeyed ringlets over her round cheeks. Her eyes were still a church girl's eyes, bright and full of faith in heaven and earth and, yes, in him, her husband. Zach knew full well that no one was innocent, no one was pure, but he couldn't stop feeling that she was, she was. This willingness of hers to take an interest in his world of unholy bloodshed and wickedness—it was so touching to him that he wanted to . . . to more than make love to her, to meld her with himself, to protect her by making her part of his own strength and indestructibility. He wished he had died—died—before he had ever laid eyes on Margo Heatherton.

"Now why would he go and do that?" Grace wondered, still shining the glass absently. "Why wouldn't he just send his henchmen?"

His henchmen. God, he loved her. As if Abend were a villain in one of the old black-and-white movies she watched on TV. These, along with religious and homemaking websites, were almost the only media she looked at.

"It does seem kinda unlikely," Zach murmured into his beer bottle—which was pretty much what he'd said to Goulart too. Only now that he'd had the time and quiet to think it over, Grace's question struck him as a good one. If Dominic Abend was personally on hand while Marco Paz and his family and his crew were being hacked to pieces—*why* was he? Why would he expose himself like that after living out of sight for so long?

"The little boy said the killers were looking for something," he told her. "They kept asking 'Where is it?' That's what he told April."

"Did he say what it was?"

"He did not. But it wasn't money. There was plenty of cash lying around, and Paz would have given it up if they'd asked."

"Then what?"

"Well—it could make sense, you know, if you think about it. If these killings had just been about money or revenge or punishment or some kind of territory or power play, Abend could've sent his crew to do the job. But if he was looking for something else, something important . . ."

". . . maybe it was important enough, he wanted to make sure he found it himself," said Grace.

"That's right. Maybe he wanted to make sure none of his crew got there ahead of him."

"There you go, then," she said. "This could be your big break."

Big break. Like in one of her old movies.

"*You're* my big break," he told her.

"Oh, yeah?"

She gave him that look she gave him, and he was achingly aware just then that she had never given it to any other man, that it had not even been in her look repertoire until after their wedding night.

Upstairs, in bed with her, he was able to forget for minutes at a time about the threat hanging over him. And afterward, with her head on his chest and that scent or atmosphere or whatever it was coming off her and into him with every yearning breath he drew, he was even able to doze off for a while. But an hour later, he was awake again, wide awake and in a cold sweat of anxiety and remorse.

We need to talk.

The remorse had begun at once, the very instant he was finished with Margo. It was terrible, way beyond any sorrow he had ever felt before, even his grief at his mama dying. Margo's hips were still hoisted in his hands, her arms around his neck, her back against her living-room wall. Her blouse was dangling down from the waistband of her hiked skirt, her bra gone, her body still desirable even as the desire drained out of him—and all Zach wanted to do was detach from his solid self and reel back from his own flesh in revulsion. How many times in how many places had this idiot scene played out in the history of men and women through the ages? How small and stupid a little incident it was, when you considered it that way. Yet, now that it had happened to him—to him who had never so much as broken his word before this, not even the word he'd given to some murderous bad man who had fallen into the clutches of his justice—now that it had happened to him against all his principles and expectations, it seemed to undermine the very foundations of his self-image and self-respect. Adultery! What had he been thinking of, for Christ's sake? What had he *not* been thinking of? Grace. Tom. Little Ann. An unwanted pregnancy. Disease. Divorce. The children's faces when he told them he was moving out. . . . Ten seconds after the climax of what had seemed his need for Margo, he couldn't even remember what it felt like to want her, what it felt like not to be repelled by the very sight of her.

He let her slide slowly, slowly down until both of her delicate feet were on the floor. He leaned forward to put his forehead against the wall, as his hands fumbled to arrange his clothing.

"We should not have done that," he said.

"Don't say that, darling," said Margo Heatherton, with her fingers feathery on the back of his neck. "It was meant to be."

In his sudden, depressing clarity of mind, those words—the triteness of them, the *written-ness* of them, their mawkish melodrama—revealed everything to him. *Don't say that, darling. It was meant to be.* Meant to be! Was she kidding him? As if this were some sort of sweeping romance with background music, and bubbling hearts and morning-after flowers—instead of a nauseating, sordid betrayal of all his promises to the only woman he loved, the triumph of dick over soul.

"Meant to be," he said, turning away from her, buckling his belt.

She clung to him, hugged herself to his back. "We were meant for each other. I knew it the minute we met."

He made a noise of derision, turned his face so she could see his sneer. "What are you talking about, Margo? I have a family. A wife, children, a life. This was a mistake."

He pulled gently away from her, but her fingertips kept contact with his shoulders, with his arms, as she said, "We don't have to tell them right away. We'll make sure they're taken care of. But, darling, this isn't something we can just forget about. It's too powerful. You know it is."

It was like waking from a nightmare into another nightmare. The e-mails and phone calls that followed. The urgency, anger, and pathetic pleading of Margo's make-believe love. And he—even he heard the naïve stupidity of his replies. Trying to reason with her, trying to explain, as if she didn't already understand, as if this hadn't been her script from the beginning, as if she weren't simply playing out the scenes she had already written in her own mind. As awful as his remorse was, he could not even experience it because he was too steeped in the fear that she would expose him, the woeful woe of having this crazy woman slither her way into the most intimate reaches of his life.

Then, about a month ago, a little over a month ago, maybe six weeks, it stopped. The e-mails. The phone calls. All of it. Over. Suddenly, completely. On her last call, she had even said to him, "All right, darling. All right. I won't ever bother you again. This is good-bye forever."

Good-bye forever! More trite melodrama. Maybe he should not have allowed himself to hope. But when he heard those words, and the silence after she disconnected, he clutched the dead phone in his sweating hand, shut his eyes, and thought, *Thank you, Lord.*

Margo had, in fact, let him be. Day after day went by without word from her. It was as if a deluge had ended. The floodwaters of fear and self-pity slowly drained from inside him until there, revealed beneath, was the underlying moonscape of remorse. What now? Should he tell Grace? Hell, no. He might just as well beat her, might just as well beat one of the children into the hospital before her eyes—it would have been that devastating to her sense of the world, to the underpinnings of her joy in life. And what purpose would it serve? Confession might relieve his torment of guilt, but why should his torment of guilt be relieved? It was his guilt, after all, it ought to be his torment: that's how he saw it. He just had to live with it, that's all. Take the medicine. Go to church. Never mind if the ceremony and scripture and Jesus Christ of it all is a little out of your spiritual line at this point. Just go, Cowboy. Get down on your cheating knees. Pray for solace and forgiveness. Swear to become a better man, the man you used to think you were. These were the only answers he could come up with.

And somehow, after a while, he began to find his way across the interior desert. Oases of relief appeared. Whole hour-long gaps in his self-flagellating misery. Occasional minutes in his wife's arms when Margo didn't curse and witchify his imagination.

Then, just as he thought he might have crossed the Shame Sahara, might have spied the Land of the Living at the far horizon (well, of course; because this was her original calculation, the timing of her mind-novel)—just as he was beginning to think he might recover from his mistake, her text came this afternoon:

We need to talk.

Grace was breathing rhythmically against his body now. He slipped out from under her, slid from her embrace. He wasn't going back to sleep, that was for sure—not for hours, anyway. The doze he'd had after their love-making had only made things worse. It had given him just enough rest to keep him awake. Might as well get something done tonight, take his mind off things, maybe catch a nap tomorrow.

He went downstairs. He set his laptop up on the living-room coffee table. He perched on the edge of the sofa cushion in his Jockeys, bending over the keyboard. He called up the video of April Gomez interviewing the boy, Mickey Paz.

What were the men looking for, Mickey? What were they trying to find? Did they say?

Stu . . . stu . . . stupe bassard . . . stum . . . they said a word I don't know. Stoomp bassard. Bassard.

Bastard? Stupid bastard?

Bastard. Yes. Stupid bastard.

Only not, thought Zach. Because he *did* know that word—"bastard." Zach could tell by the way the boy seized on it when April made the mistake of suggesting it to him. He *would* know that word, young as he was, hanging out in that den of thieves. He'd know that word and plenty worse.

Stu . . . stu . . . stupe bassard . . . stum . . . they said a word I don't know. Stoomp bassard. Bassard.

He called up his search engine. It would spell-check and make substitutions, which might make some sense out of what the boy had said. Zach searched *stupe bassard.*

Did you mean stupid bastard? the search engine asked.

He searched *stump bassard.*

Did you mean stump busters?

He scrolled through a few stump removal services, then tried again: *Abend bassard . . . Brüderlichkeit bassard . . . German bassard. . . .*

That seemed to get him somewhere: *Did you mean German bastard sword?*

He shifted a little closer to the edge of the sofa. "I might," he murmured to the living-room shadows. He was thinking of the longswords the BLK preferred to kill with. "I might mean that."

The French épée bâtarde as well as the English bastard sword originates in the 15th or 16th century . . . irregular sword of uncertain origin. . . . The German langes schwert ("long sword") . . . as opposed to kurzes schwert ("short sword") or half-sword . . . hand-and-a-half sword later called bastard. . . .

He skimmed through it, but could see nothing meaningful, no connection to his charnel-house crime scene. Could there be some valuable old sword Abend was looking for? Something with some important history or symbolism maybe . . . ? *He who pulls this sword from this stone shall be crowned mob boss of the Western world. . . .*

He put a fist against his kidney and stretched his back, trying to figure it out.

We need to talk.

He shook the thought of Margo off, literally shook his head to make it go away. No sense worrying about it in the dead of night. Nothing he could do now. But, of course, he *was* worried—very.

He leaned forward again, resting his fingers on the keyboard, staring over the top of the monitor into the darkness, uncertain where to go from here.

Experimentally, he typed: *stupe sword.*

Did you mean stone sword? State sword? Stun sword? Stupid word?

He typed: *stump sword.*

A couple of video-game sites came up: *The Stump and the Sword. He who pulls this sword from this stump. . . .*

He was about to try some other combination when he noticed, at the bottom of the page: *Stumpf's Baselard.*

He remembered Mickey Paz: *Stoomp bassard.* . . .

"Stumpf's Baselard," he whispered into the quiet of the sleeping house. "What the hell's a baselard?"

The search engine displayed the first two lines of the entry: *By Gretchen Dankl. This abstract explores the history and legend surrounding a missing 15th-century dagger.* . . .

A missing 15th-century dagger. . . . He tried to keep his mind easy, but he sensed that he had hit on something. More than that, the semi-accidental way he'd hit on it had an aura of providence about it, like it was a Meant Thing. Wouldn't be the first time. Every cop depended on such heaven-sent coincidences. Hunches. Random chains of discovery. Nothing mystical about it, just something that happened from time to time. Every cop had a collar with a story like that attached.

Zach hit the link.

The page you have requested is no longer available.

He was midway through a curse of frustration when a new e-mail appeared, and he clicked over to the e-mail page and saw it was from her, from Margo.

Darling. I know you got my text today. I need to talk to you. Please don't ignore me. Not after what we've meant to each other. M.

His whole body recognized her old fraught style. His whole soul soured at it. *What we've meant to each other.* It was black-magical in its power. Zach could picture her, in her Westchester mansion, sitting in her dark living room as he was in his, sitting at her computer as he was at his, pressing SEND. *What we've meant to each other.* Like casting a spell on him from a distance. The familiar melodrama of her diction seemed to suck him out of his life into a vortex that pulled him down, down, down. . . .

"Zach?"

His breath caught as he looked up and saw Grace on the stairway. Wifely in her flowery nightgown. All the love life he had ever cared about or wanted.

"You all right?" she asked.

"Yeah, baby, I'm okay," he told her. Margo's e-mail glaring at him from the laptop monitor. What if Grace came over and sat beside him, laid her head on his shoulder, saw? "I just couldn't sleep, thought I'd get some work done. You go on back to bed."

"All right. But come to bed soon. You need your rest."

"I will."

He deleted the e-mail even as she shuffled sleepily back up the stairs. As full of rage as his heart was, as full of fear and woe as it was, he couldn't hate her—Margo—only himself.

He slouched back against the sofa cushions. Stared at the empty screen, his sick soul leaden.

His thoughts went random. The name Gretchen Dankl swam back into his mental ken. The woman who had written the article about Stumpf's Baselard. He leaned toward the computer again. Typed in Dankl's name, thinking, *Could she be pregnant?* Meaning Margo. But no, it had been six months since they had been together. Too late now for her to run that game on him.

Did you mean *Gretchen Kunkel? Gretchen Runkel?*

But underneath the suggested substitutions was a bona fide hit: *Ludwig Wilhelm University, Freiberg. Gretchen Dankl, adjunct professor, literature. GDankl@umail.com.*

Dear Professor Dankl, he wrote to her. *My name is Agent Zach Adams. I am a United States law enforcement officer with Homeland Security's Extraordinary Crimes Division based in New York City. I am writing in connection with a murder investigation here, and looking for any information you might have about Stumpf's Baselard. . . .*

When he was finished, he snapped the laptop shut. With the monitor light gone, the living-room darkness was even deeper. He sat in it—the darkness—for several silent seconds—leaning back again, his arms stretched out on either side of him, rested along the tops of the sofa cushions—just sitting there with the whole Margo disaster a dead weight in his gut. He was unable even to muster a puling prayer for help he knew he didn't deserve.

Then he made a noise of angry dismissal, pushed off his knees, and stood. He slung the laptop under his arm. Trudged wearily up the stairs. He hoped he was tired enough to sleep at last.

And he did sleep, eventually. But first he lay beside his wife for some unknowable eternity, breathing that mysterious air that came off her, that atmosphere that was weirdly like a memory, but like a memory of something better than he'd ever actually known. He lay there and yearned for her touch and love and comfort. But he would not wake her. So he lay alone and wallowed in a looping replay of that irretrievable split second of decision: Margo against the wall, her blouse off, her legs around him, him grunting in her, stupid, predictable, clownish, a human punchline in the Great Running Joke of the World.

Ridiculous. It was all so ridiculous.

But it had ruined everything.

4

REBECCA
ABRAHAM-HARTWELL

ext morning, Goulart slapped Zach on the shoulder. "The Bitch Goddess wants an update on Paz."

By the Bitch Goddess, he meant Rebecca Abraham-Hartwell. She was the director of Extraordinary Crimes, their boss. Goulart hated her. She'd come up through the ranks as a lawyer, not a cop. That was one strike against her, in his book. Plus she was a woman—that was the other two.

Zach was at his gunmetal desk in Task Force Zero's New York squad room. It was the usual broad common room of desks and cinderblock walls, corkboards covered thick with fliers and venetian blinds striped with a view of some side street. Zach was at his computer, searching *Stumpf*. Finding Stumpf the philosopher. Stumpf the banker. A couple of guys in the law-enforcement databases named Stumpf. A con man. A chop-shop guy. All of it garbage. Dead ends. Nothing.

He sighed and rolled his chair back. Stood.

"Waste of time," Goulart was muttering—about their meeting with the director, not about Stumpf.

He looked especially sharp today, did Goulart. Light blue suit, white shirt, red striped tie, black hair combed to a fare-thee-well. A slick hook-up artist, was the thought that flashed through Zach's mind. He reflected morosely that his partner's marriage had ended in the typical cop-style divorce, complete with rage, hatred, guilt, recriminations, and one night when Goulart had waved his gun around so that an NYPD domestic incident report had to be discreetly shredded. With droll self-pity, Zach congratulated himself that, if Margo Heatherton had her way, he and Goulart would soon be able to sit around bars together trading ex-wife stories. Something to look forward to, ha ha ha.

"Abraham-fucking-Hartwell," Goulart sighed as he and Zach walked together down the shabby-tiled hall to the elevators. "What is that, anyway? Abraham-Hartwell? Is she Abraham or Hartwell? I mean, make up your mind, right?"

"Hartwell's her husband's name."

"Some high-priced mouthpiece for Wall Street dickheads," said Goulart, stabbing the elevator button with a stiff index finger. "Hartwell," he said, drawing out the 'a' to make it sound hoity-toity. He and Zach waited there, shoulder to shoulder. "What, she doesn't want a Jewish name anymore? Hey, I'm not passing judgment, but make up your mind. You wanna pass for WASP, dump the Abraham. Just be Rebecca Hartwell. You wanna assimilate, I say: go for it. Am I right?"

Zach looked down at him. Goulart was broader and thicker, but Zach was taller. "'Are you right?'" he said. "Are you seriously asking me that?"

Goulart silent-laughed. Which was one of the things—along with his being a great cop—that made it impossible for Zach not to like him: he'd laugh at himself the same as at anyone. "Hartwell," he said again. "What the hell is *he* thinking? I'd rather get a blow job from a rattler than touch that skank."

They weren't alone when they got in the elevator. There were two people in the little box with them: a clerical, female, and a uniform, male. Did that stop Goulart? Shoulder to Zach's shoulder against the back wall, he went on.

"These fucking meetings, too." Muttering, but loud enough for the whole box to hear. "S'what I mean about women in positions of power. Gotta talk about everything. Bah-de-ba-de-ba." He got an over-the-shoulder glance from the clerical. He smiled good morning at her until she turned back around. "We could be hunting these savages down but no, we have to *discuss*. We have to *process*. It's hormonal, I'm telling you."

Zach couldn't help but snort—it broke out of him—which only encouraged Goulart. The clerical woman was shaking her head at the elevator door. Luckily, it opened now. She and the uniform both got out. One of the local detectives got in. Stooped, silver-haired guy. Nodded respectfully to the two Zero boys.

The door closed and Goulart muttered, "I mean, look: women—they can't even go to the bathroom by themselves. One gets up, they all go, right? Like a flock of sheep. They gotta be directed. That's their nature."

The silver-haired guy looked at Zach. Zach rolled his eyes. The local detective grinned.

"Rebecca—I'm not saying she's not a nice person, all that. Whatever," Goulart continued. "I'm just saying: she's not a leader, that's all. All these meetings—everything she does—it's all about what the bosses think of her, what the press thinks of her. She's over-responsive to authority, what I'm saying. See, a woman, if she doesn't have *a* man to tell her what to do, then she's gotta have *the* man tell her what to do. Makes life a misery for all of us."

And again, this was the thing about Goulart—about him and his whole belligerent say-the-unsayable routine: crazy as he was, there was always just enough truth in what he said to keep it interesting. Because in the wake of the Paz murders, there was, in fact, a media frenzy (SLAUGHTERHOUSE! was the headline on the *Post*'s website) and there was, in fact, pressure from D.C. and Rebecca Abraham-Hartwell. . . .

Well, Zach liked Rebecca. And he respected her. She was smart, clear-eyed, and well-intentioned. But Goulart had a point: she *did* worry too much about what the media thought of her and what her bosses in Washington thought of her and even what they, Zach and the other agents, thought of her. And she *did* waste their time with too many meetings, too. But then she was the one who had to answer to the federal bureaucracy, not Zach.

"You look like shit, by the way," Goulart said as they came down the upstairs hall to her office.

"Thanks."

"Not sleeping?"

"I had a bad night, yeah."

"That text you got yesterday, I'm guessing."

"Just a lot of things," said Zach, with no hope of fooling him. "Personal crap."

"Woman trouble?"

"Right," said Zach with a laugh, as if that were an idea too absurd to contemplate. "I got 'em running hot and cold, that's me. Can't sleep for fighting 'em off." Try to keep a secret in a building full of cops. . . .

The Director's office door was open and her secretary nodded them in—then Rebecca Abraham-Hartwell herself waved them in from the far end of the room. It was a distracted gesture. She was standing over the flatscreen TV on her wall, holding the remote in her hand, staring down at the images. She had one of those modes working that showed four different channels at once: all news, it looked like, all shots of burning buildings and running mobs and cops in riot gear.

"Crazy," she said. "London. Paris. Berlin. Look at that: that's the Acropolis," she added, pointing to one of the fires. "The Louvre—look at that. Eesh." The sound was on low. Reporter's voices murmuring: *Unions . . . Islamists . . . Fascists. . . .* She muted them now. "Sit down, sit down."

She pointed them to the sofa, then took her place in the armchair in front of her vast wood-veneer desk, her thin legs crossed. The men sat shoulder to shoulder on the oversoft cushions, looking at her where she was framed in the glare of day from the big window behind her. The gleaming right triangle that topped the Citibank office tower was wedged into the gray autumn sky out there. The flaming images on the TV set were half-visible on the wall to their left.

Rebecca Abraham-Hartwell was small and taut and wiry. Hair short and wiry. A big nose on a long face—looked like a depressed pony,

Goulart once said, a description Zach could never quite get out of his mind. She always wore pants suits, always dark colors—dark blue today—with something bright for contrast—a bright green jacket now. Zach imagined she had gotten this fashion strategy from some magazine article about "Power Dressing" or something. But that was just a guess; such things were beyond his ken.

"So, where are we on Paz?" she said. She addressed herself to Zach. She loathed Goulart. No big surprise. It wasn't as if he was discreet in expressing his opinions about her. And he was just the sort of swinging dick she generally hated on sight anyway. So while she prided herself on her objective appreciation of his professional skills, blah, blah, blah, she would have loved to reassign the guy to a school crossing somewhere.

"Still canvassing, looking for any more videos," said Zach—while she peered at him with her big, dampish eyes in a very intent *I-am-all-business-Buster* sort of way. "Waiting for the ME prelim, though I've got a hunch our vics died from being chopped into pieces. Our main lead is the boy. He says Abend was looking for something."

"Something or someone," Rebecca Abraham-Hartwell corrected him brusquely. "He said Abend was asking about a 'stupid bastard.'"

Zach didn't want to undercut April Gomez—and didn't want Goulart to open *his* big mouth and undercut her—so he disregarded this and pushed on.

"Since Paz was a fence," Zach said, "we're going on the theory that what Abend's after is likely some item of stolen merchandise that passed through his hands—or something Abend believes passed through his hands. Whatever it is, if the boy is right, Abend was willing to show up personally to torture Paz into telling him where it is. We figure he either got the information he wanted out of Paz before he killed him, or Paz didn't have what he wanted, so he killed him as the perfect end to a perfect evening. Either way, we figure if we find out what Abend wants, we have a chance of finding Abend."

"Ideas?"

And what's with all her clipped one-word, two-word sentences? Goulart sometimes ranted. Is that supposed to make us understand just how tough and efficient she is? Talk like a human being, for Christ's sake!

"We're trying to run down who Paz was doing business with," Zach went on. "And any storage facilities where he might've been warehousing the hot goods."

"Good," said Rebecca Abraham-Hartwell. "Follow up on that."

No, Zach knew Goulart would say later, *we thought we'd just let it lie there like a lox.* Which was a particularly irritating thing about Goulart: the way he got in your head so you would actually think the things he was going to say later. You basically ended up saying them for him as if to save him the trouble.

"There's something else," said Zach. "Could be nothing, but. . . . The boy said Abend was asking about 'stoomp bassard' or 'stupe bassard' or something. I turned up something online called Stumpf's Baselard. According to the dictionary, a baselard is a kind of sword or dagger folks wore in the 14th and 15th, maybe 16th, centuries. And Stumpf's Baselard—well, we're not sure. It seems to be a dagger that's gone missing. Maybe valuable or something. Anyway, some professor in Germany wrote an article about it and I'm trying to track her down."

"Interesting," Rebecca Abraham-Hartwell said. She looked from one to the other of them, waiting for more. That was all they had worth telling. "Okay." She practically leapt out of her seat in that *I'm-all-business* way she had. "Back to work." But then, as Goulart started for the door, she said, "Give me a second, Zach, there's something unrelated I wanted to ask you about." Adding a look at Goulart that said: *Zach alone.*

Goulart hesitated, but what was he going to do? Throw a tantrum? "I guess I know when I'm not wanted," he said with a show of good humor.

"Good," said Rebecca Abraham-Hartwell. "And if you don't mind, close the door on your way out."

When he was gone, when Zach was seated on the over-soft sofa again, she brought her chair around the side of the little coffee table and moved it in close to him, her knees near his. Blocking his view of the TV set, of the smoke and fire on the screen, she jutted her long face at him.

"We need to talk about Goulart," she said.

Zach managed not to groan, but only just. If there was one thing he hated, it was office politics. He considered it girly kindergarten stuff: *If you're friends with him, you can't be friends with me.* Goulart didn't like Rebecca Abraham-Hartwell, Rebecca Abraham-Hartwell didn't like Goulart. So what? Deal with it. Catch bad guys. Do your job.

"We have reason to believe he's dirty," said Rebecca Abraham-Hartwell.

Zach was completely blindsided. He reacted before he could stop himself. "Oh, come on, Rebecca!"

"I know." She held up a hand. "I know. He's your partner—"

"It's not that—"

"And I know what you're thinking. I know how Goulart feels about me. Or about women in general. Or about his ex-wife, whom he projects onto women in general, or whatever it is. I know you figure that must mean I hate him back. Well, I won't pretend he's on my Christmas list. But truth is true, right? That's the whole thing about it. Eyes open or eyes shut, it's just the same. Things happen or they don't. People are what they are. You have a lead, a clue, you follow it, you find what you find, like it or not. The truth is true. We know that."

Zach's narrow, wind-weathered face had turned to craggy stone. She was right, of course. The truth was true. But she was also right—it was also true—that Goulart was his partner. And unless Rebecca Abraham-Hartwell could prove what she had said—unless she had recordings or pictures—real money shots of Goulart receiving a brown paper bag full of Benjamins in a drug-den men's room—Zach would stand by the man who had walked into that Kansas farmhouse with him three years ago—and his feelings for Rebecca Abraham-Hartwell would turn as stony as his expression.

"There's true—and then there's proving it," he told her tersely.

She leaned in even closer. Zach could smell her bath soap, feel the heat of her breath. He caught a glimpse of the flames dancing around a marble façade on the TV set behind her.

"You remember that cargo ship we had the Coast Guard stop last month?"

"The *Chevalier*, yeah. What about her?"

"Supposed to be carrying—"

"A container of sex slaves out of Eastern Europe, yeah, only it wasn't."

"Only it was. Only it might have been, anyway," said Rebecca Abraham-Hartwell. "A sailor off that ship was busted for killing a hooker in New Orleans last week. He was looking for a deal, so he told the cops there that they'd been tipped off—on the *Chevalier*—they were tipped off that the Coast Guard was coming for them. He says they took the girls out of the container, cut their throats, and threw them overboard. Raped them first, made a party of it."

Zach flinched at the image, but he said, "What's that got to do with Goulart?"

"Sailor says they got the tip on the Wednesday. That's before we even contacted the Coast Guard. On the Wednesday, no one knew we were onto them but you, me, and Goulart."

". . . and the CI who tipped Goulart off in the first place. And whoever told *him*."

"The sailor says the tip-off came from law enforcement."

"The sailor also rapes and kills women. That raises some questions in my mind about his character."

There was a flash of irritation in Rebecca Abraham-Hartwell's green eyes. Irritation—and anxiety, too. Well, yeah: she worried about what people thought of her, and Zach—Zach was the Cowboy—honest to the ground and universally respected. If she lost his good opinion, she'd lose the support of every agent in the division. They'd mutter to one another about her behind her back whenever she passed by. So this was getting tense for her now. She couldn't afford to alienate her best man.

She broke eye contact. Stood. Went back to her desk, around her desk. Zach avoided watching her. He gazed stonily at the TV where some rioters were throwing bottles at some big old church, it looked like.

Rebecca Abraham-Hartwell yanked a desk drawer open, yanked a manila folder out, her motions tight and brisk: more of her *I'm-all-business* routine. Zach just about never lost his temper; but he was, all the same, getting good and angry at her now.

She gauntlet-slapped the folder down on the desktop. "We've put key captures on his work computer. Taps on his desk phone and cell. A trace on his cell."

Zach stood up. He didn't say anything, but the way he stood up, the way he glared at her, let her know that she was close to losing him entirely. Bugging his partner's phone and computer? She better be right. She damn well better be.

"Why just Goulart?" he asked her. "Why not me? I knew about the *Chevalier*. So did you."

"Because I know you didn't do it. And I know I didn't. Just hear me out, okay?"

"I'm listening."

"Goulart has been making multiple calls to burners, untraceable phones."

"Probably to CI's."

"He's made several night visits to an abandoned mansion up near Rhinebeck. Windward, it's called. We think he's using it for some kind of message exchange."

"To meet a source, more likely."

"And he's got an alias drop."

"Probably . . . some girl. Or some case or something." But even in his anger, Zach knew this was suspicious, hard to explain. An alias drop—the old trick where you set up an e-mail account under a fake name, then leave draft messages for your contact to pick up—it was pure dealer stuff, pedophile stuff, a ruse meant to cover the trail of your communications.

Rebecca Abraham-Hartwell saw Zach waver. She seized on it, pressed her advantage. "When we monitored the drop? The receiving end? An untraceable IP. Pinged around hell and gone until we lost it. Very sophisticated. Someone who really-really didn't want to be identified and knew his way around a computer."

"You read any of the e-mails?"

"They were mostly in coded language. 'I may go out walking later.' That sort of thing. One said 'Contact you later.' He kept changing the drop, and we think he was also using a laptop that wasn't on the warrant. We didn't get much but, come on, just the fact of them. . . ."

This didn't sound good, Zach admitted to himself. But it wasn't enough to overcome his loyalty.

"Broadway ain't dirty," he drawled. "I'd know if he was."

If Rebecca Abraham-Hartwell had been married to the man, she'd have recognized that drawl. Grace knew it well. It meant Zach was digging in, end of conversation. He was—as Grace often whispered in frustration as she swished from the room—stubborn as a mule in cement when he wanted to be.

But Rebecca Abraham-Hartwell was deaf to it. She kept at him. "Dominic Abend knows we're after him, right? More than that, he probably knows we're the only agency that *is* after him in any meaningful way. Makes sense he'd want someone inside. Doesn't it? Goulart's vulnerable. He has the divorce. The lawsuit on his old house. We know he just applied for a twenty-thousand-dollar loan. . . ."

Which he wouldn't need if he was on the take, Zach thought—but he was so disgusted with all this now, he wouldn't even grace it with an argument anymore. He knew why Rebecca Abraham-Hartwell hated Goulart. Everyone in the Bureau knew. Goulart wouldn't keep his mouth shut about her, and some of what he said was true. That would get you in Dutch with any boss. But to call him dirty. . . .

Rebecca Abraham-Hartwell could not keep the tension out of her voice anymore, or the gleam of anger out of her big eyes. This had not turned out the way she had hoped or imagined—and she was so desperate at this point not to lose Zach's respect that she wouldn't let it end, wouldn't let him go. She was too insecure to realize that that would have been her best move—or, if she did realize it, she couldn't get herself to do it.

"Look, I swear to you," she said, "this is not personal. This is not about him and me. All I'm asking: keep an eye out. Make sure. See something, say something. We have a line on Abend now for the first time. That's the only reason I bring this up. Otherwise I would have waited till we had more proof. But I don't want Abend to slip away like that container ship just because we didn't do due diligence. . . ."

There was a light, brisk knock at the door. It clicked open a crack and Rebecca Abraham-Hartwell's receptionist stuck her round, dark, pretty face in.

A flash of green-eyed annoyance from Rebecca Abraham-Hartwell. "What?"

"There's a call for Detective Adams," she said. "From overseas. A Professor Gretchen Dankl. They sent it up here because she says it's urgent."

"I better take that," said Zach. He didn't bother to disguise the subtext: *Plus I've had enough of this crap.*

Rebecca Abraham-Hartwell could only nod, pressing her fists to her hips, deflating with a long sigh.

"All right," she said, and then added more or less pathetically: "We good?"

"Yeah," said Zach, meaning *no*. "We're good." Meaning: *You're on my shit list for certain.*

He strode toward the face in the doorway. "Put it through to my cell," he told her.

His cell phone buzzed in his pocket as he stormed angrily down the hallway toward the elevators. He snapped it out.

"Agent Adams," he said.

The voice on the line was an eccentric cocktail of qualities. It was deep, almost masculine, but vulnerable and womanly, tremulous like a damsel's in distress but at the same time somehow also strong, grimly determined. She spoke rapid-fire. A thick German accent but perfect English.

"Detective Adams. This is Professor Gretchen Dankl. I have received your e-mail."

"Yes, Professor. Thank you for getting back. I wanted to—"

"It is Abend you are looking for. Dominic Abend. It is he who has butchered these people."

Zach slowed to a stop, a live wire of excitement snaking in his belly. He was near the elevators but turned his back on them, narrowing his focus to the voice on the phone. "You know Abend?"

"I know him. I know everything about him, more than you do. He will do worse than this, much worse, before he is finished. You cannot understand how bad. You must come to Freiberg. You must come talk to me, listen to me, see what I have to show you. You must find Stumpf's dagger before Abend does. Otherwise all is lost. *All* is lost. Your city. Your country. All the world."

5

THE WEREWOLF'S DAGGER

M *odern Europe began and ended in Germany, was born when Martin Luther shattered the unity of Christian truth, and died amidst the atrocities of the Third Reich. At the beginning and at the end, at the birth and at the death, was Stumpf's Baselard.*

When the jet lifted off, Zach had just begun reading the translated article Professor Dankl had sent him: actual printed pages she had sent him by overnight mail, strangely enough. She had refused to e-mail him any kind of electronic file. He glanced up from the words, looked out the window, saw the Newark runway let go its hold on the 767's retracting gear, saw Manhattan's jagged density of soaring stone fill the twilit window, the scene distant and unsteady as an old silent movie—and he was startled by his feeling of relief, startled by its strength and sweetness—startled, but not entirely surprised. These last two days on the earth below had been nothing for him but round upon round of trouble and unease. He suspected he had argued so forcefully for this trip to Germany in part because of his eagerness to get away. He likewise suspected that Rebecca Abraham-Hartwell had freed the two grand from E.C.'s budget as a way to get back in his good graces after her accusations against Goulart. Well, fine. He was damned glad to be airborne whatever the reason, glad beyond telling that for the next eight hours—all night long—he would be out of reach by phone or e-mail, out of touch with the troublesome world.

He lowered his eyes to the pages again:

The man who would become known as Peter Stumpf was born Peter Griswold in the village of Epprath near the country town of Bedburg in the electorate of Cologne. Though records of his birth were lost during the chaotic bloodshed of the Thirty Years War, the date was doubtless some time in the mid 1500's.

The son of a well-to-do farming family, young Griswold was said to have devoted himself to sorcery and evil from an early age. After "acquainting himself with many infernal spirits and fiends" (according to his trial transcript), the necromancer managed to raise the Devil himself, who promised to give him "whatsoever his heart desired during his mortal life," presumably in exchange for his soul. Griswold's request of Satan was that "at his pleasure he might work his malice on men, women, and children, in the shape of some beast, whereby he might live without dread or danger of life, and unknown to be the executor of any bloody enterprise which he meant to commit." The Devil agreed, and gave him a magic belt which, when worn, transformed Griswold "into the likeness of a greedy, devouring wolf, strong and mighty, with eyes great and large, which in the night sparkled like brands of fire; a mouth great and wide, with most sharp and cruel teeth; a huge body and mighty paws."

Even now, airborne and all, Zach found it difficult to concentrate on the paper. Those accusations against Goulart were still on his mind, for one thing. Words that couldn't be unsaid, thoughts that couldn't be unthought, following him up into the stratosphere. Rebecca Abraham-Hartwell had motive to slander his partner, yes. But that didn't make her wrong. She was insecure and desperate to establish herself with her masters in Washington—who included, as near as Zach could tell, the Attorney General, the director of Homeland Security, some sort of FBI liaison, and about seven or eight congressional oversight committees—but that didn't make her wrong either. If Goulart's opinion of her got back to D.C., it could ruin her; if Goulart was dirty and she nailed him—well, that could make her name. But none of that made her wrong. Goulart had either gone over to the dark side or he hadn't. The truth was true, no matter who spoke it or why. So after his meeting with Rebecca A-H, Zach found himself watching his partner more closely, combing their conversations for clues, even giving Goulart opportunities to confess, to come clean—and hating himself for it, and hating Rebecca Abraham-Hartwell for getting him started.

He let out a long breath to clear his mind—to try to, at least. Returned his eyes to the pages in his hand.

For twenty-five years, Griswold the werewolf roamed the countryside around Bedburg, wreaking havoc and spreading terror. At first, he limited himself to taking revenge on anyone who displeased or defied him, but as his anonymity stoked his confidence, he felt freer to indulge his worst impulses. As a man, he would waylay maidens in the lonely meadows and deflower them—then devour them in the form of a wolf, escaping afterward undetected into the deep forests. At last, he descended into every kind of cruelty and depravity. He committed long-running incest with his daughter and enticed her into complicity in his murders. He seems truly to have loved his son and "yet so far his delight in murder exceeded the joy he took" in him that he slaughtered the boy and "ate the brains out of his head as a most savory and dainty delicious means to staunch his greedy appetite."

In all this, he escaped detection—escaped even suspicion—by changing from a wolf back into the shape of a man when his crimes were done. So even as the countryside was gripped with terror, the killer remained incognito.

Enter a local executioner, whose full name has been lost to history, but who is sometimes referred to in later documents by the generic name of "Hans." A dishonorable outcast because of his bloody profession, Hans longed to establish himself in the community as a respected hero and thereby win the love of Margarethe, a farmer's daughter. Convinced that the monster who had been terrorizing the countryside for so long was no mere wolf but some kind of demon, Hans devised a plan to catch him. He armed himself with a baselard—a short sword or dagger—which he had confiscated from one of the murderous highwaymen whom he had lately beheaded. This weapon he had now gotten blessed and anointed with holy water by a local priest. Hans believed these solemnities would redeem the dagger from its sinful history and transform it into an instrument of godly justice.

The executioner set up a blind near a local meadow where the werewolf was known to roam. He lay in wait for three consecutive days, spying on the maids who came here to do their washing in the river and then lingered to gossip as the daylight waned. At last, on the third day, just as sunset approached, Hans discerned his quarry: an enormous wolf prowling through the trees hard by, sniffing for the blood of innocents. Before the beast could launch an attack on the young women gathered at the riverbank, the executioner leapt from his hiding place and confronted him. Though the werewolf's claws tore across the executioner's chest, Hans nonetheless managed to strike back, slicing the creature's foot off with the sanctified dagger. The wolf swiftly limped away, howling in agony, and the wounded Hans followed its trail of blood until it led him, lo and behold, to the home of Peter Griswold. There, it was discovered that Griswold's left arm now ended in a bloody stump, so that he was known ever after as Peter Stump or Stumpf. On this evidence, Hans assembled the locals roundabout into a posse, and had Griswold bound and brought before the authorities.

It was Hans himself—now recovered from his wounds—who laid Peter Stumpf on the rack for interrogation. Fearful of torture, the werewolf confessed to everything, a whole lifetime of demonic crime. On All Hallow's Eve, 1589, in keeping with the sentence of the court, Hans brought Stumpf to the place of execution known as the Raven Stone. There, he pulled chunks of Stumpf's flesh off with red-hot pincers (a practice known as "nipping"), broke his legs and arms with a wooden axe, and finally cut off his head with a sword.

And then, of course, there was the whole Margo fiasco, Zach thought. Which was even worse than the Goulart situation, much worse. Rebecca Abraham-Hartwell's charges against Goulart were sure to bring trouble down on the Task Force one way or another, but Zach could live with that. Margo, though. . . . She could lay his life waste. Break his wife's heart. Destroy his children's home. Condemn everyone he loved best to a grief he couldn't even bear to think about. And what other outcome—what good or even less-horrible outcome—could there possibly be? She had texted him again yesterday. *What do I have to do to get you to pay attention to me, darling?* He could practically hear the rising hysteria in her tone. A sizable part of his relief at wangling this trip to Germany derived from the fact that it enabled him to put a message on his phone and text and e-mail saying "I will be out of the country for the next few days and unable to receive communications." Which would electronically make his excuses to Margo and maybe give her a chance to calm down or reconsider or be fatally hit by a car. It would give him a chance to think things through as well.

"Thank you," he said with a brief smile as the stewardess handed him a double bourbon. Thirty thousand feet in the air with a drink—it was practically like being in paradise after these last few awful days. He hoped this jet would never land.

But what the hell was this crazy thing, this report he was reading, anyway? A 16th-century werewolf? A magic dagger? This better have something to do with Dominic Abend or he'd have two thousand dollars' worth of explaining to do when he got back to the office, along with his other troubles.

He sipped his drink, set the plastic receptacle down on the fold-out table, and read on.

After doing his duty in the torture and beheading of Stumpf, Hans the executioner all but disappears from history—although B. F.

Korchinski maintains that a reference is made to his memory in the fictional picaresque account of the Thirty Years War, A Christian's Progress, written shortly after the 1648 Peace of Westphalia. The sardonic narrator is describing the aftermath of a battle:

"The surviving women having been raped and disemboweled in the most Christian fashion imaginable, their still breathing bodies were tied with ropes and dangled from the branches of nearby trees so that the defenders of Our Most Gracious Lord could amuse themselves with their death throes. It was when I went out in the dark of night to see if I could bring relief to any of these poor creatures that I spotted the enormous wolf ranging among the dead and dying. Such a beast was he that had never been seen or even heard of in this region—twice the stature of a man, with flaming red eyes and teeth the size of daggers that glistened in the light of the full moon—so that I was certain I was witnessing a demon who had been summoned from hell by the wickedness that had been perpetrated here. After gorging itself on the bodies of the dying women, the thing retreated. My curiosity overcame my fear and, thinking I might witness some demonic marvel, I followed at a little distance. What then should I see as the full moon crossed the meridian, but the hideous beast transform itself into the likeness of a man! At first, I thought this must be the devil himself. But no. As I watched, this poor sinner, naked and covered in gore, sat himself down upon the grass atop a little ridge and, holding his face in his two hands, began weeping piteously and crying out, 'My love! My love! It is for you I am become an abomination!' Father Jacob [a local priest] later explained to me that this was the wandering spirit of a medicine man, who had rescued his lady from a werewolf only to be himself transformed into such a beast by the creature's bite."

Though the transformed wolf is referred to as a "medicine man," Korchinski points out that many executioners doubled as healers, their medical skills enhanced by the anatomical knowledge they had acquired in the torture chamber and at the gallows. This and the fact that "poor sinner" was a common locution for referring to a victim of capital punishment indicates, according to. . . .

Zach was chewing on his ice at this point, his bourbon gone and he a damn sight more relaxed than he had been on takeoff—and he was thinking *What the hell is this? This Dankl dame must be crazier than a bull-bat!*, shaking his head at the pages on the fold-out table. He had to remind himself of Professor Dankl's phone message—how she'd known about Dominic Abend—her academic credentials—her tone of urgency—Mickey Paz with his "stoomp bassard"—in other words, all the stuff he'd brought to bear when arguing for this trip in the first place. He had to remind himself that there really was a good reason for him to be traveling four thousand-some-odd miles on the taxpayer's dime. Because otherwise, he'd be forced to admit that this thing—this paper or report or whatever it was that Dankl had sent him—was the screwiest and most irrelevant load of bull slop he'd ever read. Werewolves. Executioners. The Thirty Years War, whatever that was. What the hell did any of it have to do with a murdered New York fence and a German uber-gangster?

From here on, he began to skim the pages:

> But while Hans the executioner faded from memory, not so his dagger. . . . Weapons used by executioners commonly thought to possess magical powers . . . mixture of werewolf's blood with holy water on the blade . . . transforming the blood of human sacrifice into a panacea, curing every disease, and retarding the aging process . . . its owner slowly gaining magical powers over beasts and insects . . . mind-control abilities . . . a sort of black communion with demons or perhaps the devil himself . . .

Zach snorted. And then there was this:

> . . . dagger referred to in the journal of several executioners during the witch panic of the early 17th century . . . half a dozen reported appearances of the dagger during the Thirty Years War . . . legend that Mozart witnessed the use of the dagger in a secret Masonic ceremony . . . long period when the talisman was forgotten . . . interest in the legend revived among the Nazis . . . Nazi fascination with the supernatural . . . Hitler's desperate attempt to recover the dagger and enlist its demonic powers on his behalf. . . .

Zach's chin began to sink to his chest. His eyes began to sink shut. He forced himself awake. He didn't want to fall asleep. He wanted to have another drink. He wanted to enjoy as much of this time in the air as he possibly could . . . far away from his worries . . . from Margo's outstretched claws. . . .

The meaning of the dagger is intertwined with the political-religious implications of the Stumpf trial. During the period of Stumpf's worst crimes, the electorate of Cologne was torn by Catholic–Protestant warfare. The wealthy farmers sided with the Protestants and converted, but the Catholics ultimately won back the area. The public exposure of the werewolf's depredations would have made a vivid example of . . .

The jet lurched. Zach woke up—sat up—startled. Dawn was suddenly breaking at the portholes: pale-blue sky over dark-blue ocean. The jet was beginning its descent into Germany. He'd dozed off and slept through the night.

Muzzy, he blinked and stretched and looked around him. There lay the soporific report on the fold-out table. It was turned to the last page, the final paragraphs. His eyes passed over the words, though his befogged mind barely grasped their meaning.

The legend of Stumpf's Baselard is the legend of Europe's great moment. In its blade lie both the continent's murderous savagery and its striving toward the holy, its sinful debasements and its yearning for redemption, its beastliness and its incomparable cultural beauty. The desire to lay hands on this artifact is the desire to take possession of a legacy that may have only been imaginary and yet was well worth the imagining: a history of blood sanctified by the mind of faith, the will to sacrifice, and the spiritual instinct to renounce vengeance in the name of love.

Who holds the dagger, therefore, owns the distilled energy of a dead past and thus lays his claim to the life of the future.

Who holds the dagger, therefore, holds power beyond telling.

6

PROFESSOR DANKL

L ooking back on it later, Zach was never sure when he lost his grip on reality—or when reality, rather, lost its grip on him. It could have been that moment when he fell asleep with his head full of stories about werewolves and magic daggers. He certainly woke up unclear and befuddled. He dozed on and off through the landing as if he were in a fever. He walked through the airport at Frankfurt feeling distant and discombobulated. The place was mobbed with travelers—his cop eyes noted their worried faces, their furtive glances at the television sets hanging here and there from the ceiling. On the screens he saw the images of cities on fire, mobs in the streets. And yet it all seemed very far away and fantastic.

The fact that he had never been to Europe before added to the weird and dreamy atmosphere. He'd never been farther out of the U.S. than

Mexico, which didn't really count as a foreign country where he came from. He found it disorienting to be surrounded by people chattering in a language so completely incomprehensible to him. *Ichten flichten richten schtickten.* What the hell were they talking about?

"Looks like some kind of mass exodus," he said to the woman behind the counter at the coffee shop, gesturing with his head at the crowds streaming through the concourse. It was his first attempt to make a connection with one of the locals.

The woman behind the counter was brown-skinned and wore a scarf over her head. She looked at him with wide, frightened eyes. Said nothing. More weirdness, as far as Zach was concerned. He took his coffee from her and fought his way back into the crowd.

For the rest of the ninety-minute layover, he kept to himself, dozing in the waiting area by his gate or walking past the airport shop windows to stretch his legs. Trying to clear his head without much success. Then he boarded the plane for Dresden.

In Dresden, after the mob scene in Frankfurt, the airport seemed bizarrely deserted. Same pictures on the TV sets—the fires and mobs—but they played to empty rows of plastic chairs in the waiting areas. Carrying his overnight bag toward the exit, Zach had the nagging sense that he was wandering farther and farther away from the world he knew.

He made a brief, grateful connection with the lady at the rental-car counter. Trim and pert with short brown hair and the warm, patient expression of a young mom, she could've been any girl anywhere. That gave Zach the courage to talk to her—that and the fact that she spoke almost impeccable English.

"Y'all seem to be having some real troubles over here," he said, by way of making conversation. He leaned his elbow on the counter while she worked her computer.

"Ach, it is terrible, the riots," she said, her eyes never leaving the monitor. "Usually it is one or the other—the immigrants, the unions, the fascists—now it is all together, so I don't know what will happen." She handed him the car keys.

"Well," said Zach. "Good luck to you."

So all of this was a bit bewildering, but—again, looking back on these events later on—he sometimes thought it was during the drive to the university that some essential connection, between himself and the world as he had always known it, had been severed. The scenery along the way seemed whimsical and out of time. His sporty red Sebring, modern enough, cruised twisty mountain roads with ancient rocks and ancient walls looming over them. Inside, there was temp control and radio music and an English-speaking computer lady giving him directions from the GPS. Outside, it could have been the world of Peter Stumpf. It could have been the Brothers Grimm. Rolling fields and milling cows and autumn forests on misty hills. Startling veins of pastel lacing the pale green of vaunting firs and junipers and pines against clouds in an afternoon sky he'd seen in old paintings. The villages he passed: all so strange, so foreign and old-fashioned and unreal. Half-timbered buildings and churches with onion domes and ruined structures of maybe Roman stone and curlicued hilltop castles that seemed to have been imported from Disneyland. Really, the whole place seemed like something out of Disneyland.

Then—in his memories—or maybe even at the time—there came a city nestled in some past century. Red rooftops and chimney pots and church towers in a yellow valley surrounded by October hills. It seemed like the GPS lady was calling to him from the present day as he wound down the slope into the storybook past.

Finally, there was the university. He parked the car in a lot here. He continued on foot, bowing under the branches of an oak tree gone shockingly orange. He came into a grassy quad surrounded by great brooding temples of brick—what looked to him like courts and palaces, guarded by twisted verdigris statue-gods from some tribal age. Like the airport, the campus was nearly deserted. He saw only one student—a pert, slender girl with short black hair—wandering along an asphalt pathway under yellow lindens. To find the building to which Gretchen Dankl had summoned him, he had to break away from the main area and head down the slope of a small side path until he reached a stalwart stone lodge standing all alone in a grassy cul-de-sac.

When he pushed the heavy front door open, the snap of the latch seemed to echo through empty halls. His footsteps likewise echoed on what might have been marble as he stepped into more unreal, out-of-the-past eeriness: a towering hallway lined with stony saints. That was all that was there: Zach and two long rows of bowed apostles on their pedestals—oh, and gargoyles hung up high, dragon-faced drains grinning down at him at intervals from the top of the walls.

An echoing door echoed his, echoing footsteps echoed his, and he looked down the long gallery of statues to see that a woman had entered through the farthest door. She was small, slumped, wearing a misbuttoned gray cardigan and a wool diamond-pattern gray skirt that even Zach knew was out of fashion. She wasn't short but seemed small, slumped, narrow, frail. Her hair was drabbish silver—what woman let her hair turn such a color nowadays?—and her face was pouty and pinched like the face of an anxious monkey. She was smoking too. That in itself was startling to the American. In a public building, a museum like this? She had a filter cigarette scissored between two overlong fingers of one wrinkled hand.

She came toward him unsteadily in the pale daylight from the Catherine windows between the gargoyles.

"Agent Adams," she said—and Zach recognized the deep, sure, yet somehow trembly and feminine voice of Professor Dankl from her phone call. She gestured vaguely with her cigarette at . . . something. He wasn't sure what. "Do you believe?"

Zach blinked, confused—as he had been ever since he fell asleep on the plane coming over. "In werewolves?" he said.

Her anxious monkey face went lopsided with a world-weary grin. "In God, I meant."

"Oh, in God." She had been gesturing at the statues. He made as if to consider them. "Yeah, sure."

"'Yeah, sure.'" She planted her hand over her mouth and took a long, hissing draw of her cigarette. It seemed to Zach a somehow decadent, Old World procedure. "A very American response," she said, the smoke tumbling out between her lips. "You look very American. Like a cowboy."

"Well," said Zach. "I guess I am. American, I mean. Not a cowboy." Not knowing what else to say, he offered her his hand. "Zach Adams."

The professor went through an elaborate, careful series of movements to transfer her cigarette from her right hand to her left. Then she took his hand and shook it. "Come," she said, with a quick motion of her head.

Their combined footfalls set up a complicated reverberation as they walked together under the blank stone eyes of the apostles.

She said, "If you believe in God, the evidence of Him is all around you. But if you do *not* believe, no evidence can ever be enough. Here, we do not believe."

"Here in Germany, you mean?"

She made what seemed to him another Old World gesture, circling her cigarette hand in the air between them. Zach thought this was meant to answer his question, but he had no idea what the answer was supposed to be.

"We see the violence now, the riots, the burning, and we think 'Ach, it is destroying us,'" Gretchen Dankl continued. "But no, this is not the case. It is not the violence. It is the peace, the too-much peace that came before. We were already destroyed—inside, you know—before the rioting began. You see, where there is no spirit, there is only flesh. Where there is only flesh, there is nothing but pleasure and pain. Where there is nothing but pleasure and pain, who would choose pain? Who would choose conflict? Who would not choose peace?"

"Well, peace . . . peace is always a good thing," said Zach because he thought he ought to say something, even though he hadn't the slightest clue what they were talking about. The whole conversation already seemed surreal to him—which was almost funny when he thought back on it later, considering how surreal it was about to get. This was Surreality Amateur Hour, compared to what was coming.

They reached the far door of the gallery—the glass-and-metal door through which the professor had come. She paused with her hand on the handle, the cigarette sending a zigzagging line of smoke up from between her fingers. She gave what seemed to Zach a Germanic shrug. "Peace would be wonderful, the most wonderful thing," she said, "if only there were no God. Then there would be no good or evil, nothing to fight over. But there is, you see. There is good and there is evil. And if you will not fight for the good, if you will not suffer for the good, if you will not accept pain even unto the pain of your own damnation for the good, then there is only evil. This is what Dominic Abend understands. This is how he has triumphed over us."

With that, she pulled the door open sharply. Zach held it for her while her hunched, weary-looking body hobbled through. He was glad of the mention of Abend—glad she had gotten to something real, something solid, something he could hold on to. This whole

57

experience—this whole trip—had grown way too febrile and phantasmagorical for him. He had come to investigate the murder of a fence—so what were they even talking about?

Also, where the hell was everyone? Professor Dankl and he were in a long hall of offices now, and still there was not another human being in sight. Dankl led the way past display cases full of stone fragments, past one closed door after another.

"After the Wall came down, after he escaped from the East, he took over everything here," she was saying, smoking, gesturing over her shoulder at him, walking in a way that suggested it was difficult for her to keep her balance, staring at the floor as if she had some kind of spinal complaint that forced her to bow her head. "The politicians, the churches, the criminals, even the people—all became the agents of his power-madness and corruption. He knew we would not fight him."

She stopped at a thick wooden door. Brought a heavy ring of jangling keys out of her cardigan pocket. She selected one and held it up to Zach—as if she wanted him to take it, he thought at first, but then he realized she was just pointing it at him, like a finger.

"We would not fight him, because we did not believe." She looked up at him with unnerving steadiness, her eyes set deep in her pinched simian features. "For us, there is only flesh and pleasure and pain. And who would choose pain? Who would choose conflict? We would rather become what is evil than dare to oppose it. This is what Dominic Abend understood."

She unlocked the door and pushed it open, and again Zach held it for her as she went in. She turned on the lights and moved to crush her cigarette in a cheap metal ashtray resting on a cabinet.

"You have read my paper that I sent you?" she asked.

Zach stepped in after her. The door slipped from his fingers and slammed shut loudly. "About Stumpf's baselard? Yes, I did. Pretty wild story."

They were in a small, cramped book-lined room. The air smelled sour with old smoke. No space here for anything but the three pieces of furniture: the uncomfortable-looking wooden visitor's chair and the desk chair and the desk between them, a square desk of scarred wood. The desktop was smothered in papers and books. The computer and printer were drowning in them. There was a window, small and square like the desk, four frames of glass looking out on a patch of grass and a linden tree.

Professor Dankl hobbled around the desk, lifting a finger back at him. "I show you."

With a few quick gestures, she brushed some papers aside and lifted a manila envelope that had been hidden underneath them. From this, she drew an old photograph which she then slapped down on a large book. The book was propped sloppily on a desk lamp, so the photo almost slipped off. She had to slap it again to keep it in place.

"You see?" she said.

This was another moment he considered—later, when he thought back on it. Like the moment when he woke up in the plane, his mind saturated with old German legends—like the drive here through Grimm Brothers fairyland—like this weird conversation—like the moment the case began, in fact, the moment he had walked into the slaughterhouse aftermath of the Marco Paz murder—this moment now, when he looked at the photograph Gretchen Dankl slapped in front of him, later seemed to him a candidate for that decisive instant when his life detached itself from the gravity of natural things and floated into the deep space of the uncanny.

It was a black-and-white photo of several Nazi officers—thirteen of them, it would turn out when he got the chance to count them. They were arrayed around some sort of old jeep, at once relaxed and formal, leaning on one another's shoulders in a collegial manner and yet unsmiling, staring into the camera lens with grim purpose.

And in answer to the professor's question, yes, Zach did see—he noticed right away the soldier on the far left, a man of around thirty or thirty-five with crewcut hair, thin lips, a bulbous nose, and eyes that gleamed with unmistakable cruelty.

"*Unternehmen Werwolf*—Operation Werewolf," Professor Dankl said. Then, seeing the uncertainty in Zach's eyes, she asked again, more urgently, "You read my paper, yes?"

Zach dismissed his first thought at the sight of the young Nazi's face—because it was ridiculous; impossible—and forced his attention back to her. "Operation . . . ?" Embarrassed, he realized he must've skipped over this part of her paper as he drifted into a snooze. He tried to remember what he could. "Hitler tried to recover the dagger, you said. . . ."

Her long haggy finger with its long haggy gray nail tap-tapped the photograph. "Now the historians say the operation never happened. They say it was just a desperate dream that Goebbels had—a guerrilla underground to get behind the Allied lines as they closed in for the kill. It never materialized. But that—the underground resistance—that was just a ruse, a cover-up for *this*—" tapping the photograph—"a core of SS men sent to find Stumpf's Baselard, Hitler's last hope of saving himself, saving the Reich. They say they named the operation after a novel about the Thirty Years War: *Der Wehrwolf*. A clever—how do you say?—*inside joke*, you see?"

She tap-tapped the photograph again, drawing Zach's eyes back to it—back to where her long, gray nail was spearing that very same man he had noticed, the SS officer on the far left.

"So . . ." he said. "What? Your paper didn't tell what happened to the mission." He remembered noticing this, even as he dozed.

"*Nein!* No. Of course not. Of course not! What good is it to send a warning no one will believe? I hoped only that others would follow the evidence, see for themselves. That is the only way they would understand. Ach, it is too late for Europe now anyway. . . ."

"I'm sorry. What are we talking about here?" said Zach. "Are you saying they found it? Operation Werewolf. They found the dagger?"

Professor Dankl's simian features bunched together in her intensity as she stabbed the photograph yet again. "I'm saying *he* found it. It had been removed with the other works of art from the Zwinger Palace in Dresden when the war began. Somehow he traced it, found it—and, realizing that the Nazi cause was lost, he buried it before he was captured by the Russians. Fifteen years later, when he was released from the gulag, he returned to dig it up. By then, he had helped to form the Brüderlichkeit—the Brotherhood—the criminal organization, yes?"

"I know it."

"And with the dagger in his possession, he took complete control. Complete control."

"And so now you're saying . . . ?"

The professor gave what looked to Zach like a heavy Germanic shrug. "He must have lost it again somehow. Or misplaced it. This is what I believe. This is why he has killed your people in New York. He has lost the dagger! It is the one thing, the only thing, that would bring him out into the open like this. It is the chance, the only chance you may have to find him, to stop him before he does to your continent what he has done to mine. You must find the baselard, Agent Adams! You must find it before Abend does."

"Wait. . . ." Zach began, leaning over the desk, peering down at the picture, trying not to let his voice sound too droll or skeptical. "What are you telling me here? You telling me that that's Dominic Abend? That there in the picture?"

"That is Abend, yes. Though he had another name then. Heinrich Dietz. But it is Abend."

"Well . . . Professor," said Zach, forcing down a smile. "That man there must be at least thirty-five, forty years old in that photo if he's a day. Why, he'd be well over a hundred by now. Well over."

"I know what you're thinking."

Zach couldn't help it then: a curt, riffling laugh broke out of him. She couldn't possibly know what he was thinking. He was thinking he must have fallen asleep on the jet coming over and that everything after that, including this, was a dream. Or if it wasn't a dream—he was thinking—if it wasn't a dream, he had just traveled four thousand miles to hold a parley with a woman who'd been thrown off the hay-wagon one too many times.

He straightened his long body from the table and stood towering over her. "Look, professor, I want to thank you for your help with my case. . . ."

Her hand shot up from the photograph. She gripped his wrist with surprising strength. She was staring fire at him. "Do you think I brought you all this way to tell you what I knew you would not believe? No. No. I brought you here to *see*. You must see—and *then* you will believe."

7

IN THE BLACK FOREST

He wanted only to go home now. He realized—what he had known in his heart before but only now accepted—that he had come to Germany, traveled all this way, to escape. He couldn't kid himself about it anymore, not after that mad meeting with the nutty professor. He had come for no other reason than that—to escape what was, of course, inescapable: himself and his troubles. The case, the lead, his hunch about the baselard, the professor—all were excuses, distractions designed to disguise his true purpose, to hide his true purpose from his own mind. Even the unpleasant office politics between Rebecca Abraham-Hartwell and Goulart—even that was a distraction. It was all about Margo, that was the truth. He had come here to escape Margo, to escape the consequences of having been with—having had sex with—having committed adultery with—Margo. And from those consequences, he realized finally, there was no escape.

He checked in at his hotel, a quaint pink-stucco building on a cobbled side street, one of the red roofs he had seen as he drove into town. He made his way up crabbed stairs to the top floor, to a small but pleasantly modern room. Dropped his bag on the shiny parquet and plunked his butt on the narrow bed. He sat there hunched in a beam of afternoon sunshine that streamed down through the skylight in the sloped ceiling. His mind, he noticed, was clear now. That fog of unreality he'd been immersed in all day—he understood that it had been a thing of his own making, the psychic symbol of his self-deception. Now that he had fully acknowledged why he had come on this excursion, the fog was gone.

The fog was gone, and he saw what he had to do.

He turned his phone on long enough to pick up his e-mails and his messages. She had phoned him—Margo. He had suspected she would.

"Oh, you're away," she said—and the sound of her voice brought her back to him, brought back the uptown New York aura of elegance and sophistication with which she'd gulled the West Texas rube still inside him, brought back her magazine-shiny presence and her scent, brought even the silken touch of her flesh back to his palms and fingertips. "Well, listen . . . I need to talk to you. I'm serious, Zach. Don't make me out to be the bitch-devil here, darling, really. I just want to talk. Please call me when you get back. All right? Please. I mean it. Love you. Always. Call me."

He would. He would call her. He would talk to her; confront her. If she would not agree to leave him alone for good, he would confess everything to Grace. The thought of hurting his wife like that was agony to him. The thought of losing her was nigh on unbearable. But he wasn't a man to go on living with lies and he wasn't a man to hide. He wasn't going to be blackmailed. He wasn't going to be controlled. He had done what he'd done—that's where the source of the trouble lay. There was no taking it back, no erasing it. If he could protect Grace from the truth of his infidelity, he would. If he couldn't, he wouldn't make it worse by adding deception to deception. He would confess everything.

Using his phone, he dashed off a few quick e-mails. He wrote to Rebecca Abraham-Hartwell and Goulart and told them that the meeting with Professor Dankl had been a waste, a dead end. He wrote to Grace and told her he loved her. He wrote to Tom and Ann and told them that Germany looked like Disneyland and Daddy would be home soon. When he was done, he lay back on the bed and closed his eyes and said a quick prayer for strength and guidance. He slept for an hour. Then he got up and got ready to go.

He had agreed to meet Professor Dankl one more time, at a quarter to five, at sunset. She had given him directions to the spot. She had said he would see and then believe. Okay. He'd come all this way. He might as well give her the chance to show him whatever else she wanted to show him.

But what exactly was she expecting to get him to believe? That Dominic Abend was Heinrich Dietz? That he was some kind of warlock kept supernaturally young by the magic of an old dagger that had been used to kill a werewolf? What exactly could she show him that would make him believe that? Whatever it was, if it worked, hell, it'd certainly make this trip more interesting! So he thought anyway, smiling with one side of his mouth, as he drove out of the city in the late afternoon.

The sky was gathering toward sunset, the drifting clouds red behind the silhouetted church tower in his rearview mirror. But oddly, or maybe not so oddly, the drive this time had none of that fairytale sense of unreality that had suffused the drive in. The traffic of trucks and small European cars was certainly real enough. So was the sleek but somehow miniature freeway with the scrubby trees by its side. Even as he broke out of the more urban areas, wound back through rolling farmlands dotted with forest, and even as the first dark blue of oncoming dusk turned the scenery distant and two-dimensional, as pockets of thick mist settled into the valleys among the distant hills, it all still looked real enough to him, like any farmland. It might have been parts of upstate New York he'd seen, except for the foreign street signs and the strange, quaint shapes of some of the barns.

If there was any sense at all that he was journeying out of the everyday world, any omen of the supernatural, any warning of what was going to happen next, it came when the professor's directions took him away from the main thoroughfares. Then the misty twilight did begin to transform the scenery. The trees edged toward the sides of the road like tall phantom sentinels taking up their night positions.

The forest grew eerie with the oncoming night, the trees clustering thicker and the low sun sending final flashes of orange past the naked trunks of the junipers and pines. A canopy of oak and maple and linden branches folded over him so that the dark grew even darker and their yellow and red leaves turned gray. Tendrils of mist threaded through the woodland spaces in the middle distance all around him, like spirits following his progress toward their secret homes.

He switched on the Sebring's headlights. Where the hell was this woman dragging him? What the hell was it all about?

Following her instructions, he turned the car onto a dirt road. Suddenly he found he was in the middle of nowhere, deep in the *Schwarzwald*, the Black Forest.

The sun was still stretching fingers of dying light through the towering conifers. There were still patches of gold and red where the oaks and maples caught the fading glow. But the trees' high crowns were melding into the deepening indigo of the sky. Second by second, the forest around him was becoming dim and hazy—so dim, Zach nearly missed the place where the road ended. He had to stop sharply to avoid planting his fender in the gruff trunk of a pine.

He sat there in the car, the engine running. He hoped he would spot the professor in his headlights. A bird, frightened by the motor noise, shot out of a far tree. It flew the length of the windshield and vanished into the woods. After that, nothing moved.

Zach shut the car off. Climbed out into a fine autumn chill. He felt the earth soft under his shoes: this was no road anymore. He took a few steps toward the edge of the forest, peering into the trees. He was aware of a watchful tension in himself—the same sort of feeling he would have had entering a house where a suspect might be hiding. His hand made a move toward the place beneath his windbreaker where his gun would have been, had he been wearing one—then it fell to his side.

Professor Dankl had told him there would be a trail, and yes, there, he spotted the head of it, a thin dirt path snaking deeper into the forest. He walked it slowly, his footsteps whispering over the fallen leaves, crackling on the dead twigs. The trees gathered closer around him. The beams of sunlight narrowed and flattened and began to fade. The darkness settled down through the crown cover above him and crept in around him through the gnarled branches. A bird cried out as he approached. A stream gurgled. The underchatter of frogs and insects waxed and waned.

The sun went down. Its hazy beams dissolved. The trees blocked the horizon light. The trail sank out of sight. He had a flashlight on his keychain, but it didn't help much. It barely picked out the next few feet of the way.

He wound around a bend and came into a flat clearing. It was brighter here. A circle of tall conifers surrounded him. Tortuous oak and maple branches, silhouetted against the last blue of dusk, pressed in behind them. Zach stood and listened to the croaking frogs and twittering crickets and the underlying silence.

A wooden door shut nearby. He tensed. He heard footsteps on—what?—wood?—stairs—a porch, yes. Now he heard the steps whisper and crunch over the leaves. He saw another flashlight bobbing through the trees.

"Ah, good. You came. And just in time," the professor said—her familiar voice in the shadows, low, heavy, but with a certain energy that had not been there before.

He had to squint to pick her out of the gloaming, just the shape of her behind her flashlight. Then she stepped from the forest tangle, moved through the encircling evergreens, and came into the clearing with him. He saw that she was dressed as before, in the nondescript skirt and cardigan, only now she also had a dark overcoat thrown cape-like over her shoulders against the cold. She was carrying something under her arm, but the wing of the coat hid it from his view. She hobbled toward him with her strange half-crippled gait, her flat shoes shuffling through the carpet of leaves.

When she was closer, only a few yards away, he could make out her worried-monkey features. He saw fresh depths of pain and sorrow in her bright eyes. It came to him again just how crazy she was, a couple of tacos short of a combination plate.

She stuffed the flashlight in a coat pocket. Drew out the object she had under her arm: an ornate box of some kind. His own flashlight picked out portions of the carving on it. It looked machine-done to him. Cheap wood, stained to appear fancy. Some sort of souvenir box from a tourist shop.

"Here, take this. Open it," she commanded.

"This is what you brought me out here to see?"

"Open it."

He pocketed his own flashlight. Took the box. Opened it. Even in the thickening forest dusk, he could see that there was a pistol inside.

"What's this?" he said.

He put his hand on it. Drew it out. An old .38 Smith and Wesson. He tried to make sense of it. Was she going to tell him it was a relic of World War II . . . ?

"Do you know why the bullets are silver?" she asked him.

"What? Oh. Silver bullets. For, like, a werewolf." Now he got it. It was a magic gun to kill Dominic Abend with. Great.

"Silver is the metal that conducts the best. Heat. Electricity. But not just that. More. More mysterious things too. It is not the bullets that will do the death-work, you see. It is your 'Yeah, sure.' That. The silver conducts that as well."

"Right," said Zach, with a sarcastic drawl. He gripped the gun in his hand and turned it this way and that, from professional habit mostly: he couldn't see it well. "And you want me to have this. To protect myself from Abend. Is that right? Well, I don't know if I can get it back through customs. But thank you kindly for the thought."

Even the details of her features were sinking into the darkness now, but he thought he caught a glimpse of some strange tenderness in the sadness of her smile. She reached up and briefly gripped his elbow, as if with true affection. Then she turned away. Turned her back on him.

"You know the word *liebestod*?" She could not have seen him begin to shake his head, but she went on anyway before he said *no* aloud. "Love-death, it means. A song or story about lovers who must together die. Romeo and Juliet—these you know, yes? But Americans do not tell such stories. Each one is everything to himself there, so I think. And always they believe they will make for themselves the happy ending. They do not know about *liebestod*."

A wind moved, the fallen leaves rustling on the ground, branches creaking overhead. Zach shivered and looked around him. The woods were now draped in such sable night that the trees beyond the conifer circle had vanished into a general black and twisted thickness. Even the nearby evergreens were becoming mere suggestions of themselves. In such full darkfall, Zach's eyes were quick to make out the odd star-like gleam that had appeared on the far rise to his left, to the east. In the moment or two that he watched it, wondering what it might be—an airplane? the evening star?—it expanded into a brighter blast of radiance, and then took shape: a curving silver crescent, the top edge of the rising moon.

"And yet it has been like that for me and my country," Professor Dankl went on, her voice still deep and hollow but full of feeling too, full of a world-weary fondness that struck Zach as somehow particularly European. "*Liebestod.* I have sacrificed even my immortal soul to defend her—to defend her from evil and from death—to chase them through the centuries of unbelief, alone in my understanding of them. *Umsonst.* For nothing. I have failed and she is gone. My country . . . my continent . . . my culture. . . ."

Zach stood fascinated by the moon as it rose and rose, as it became a half circle illuminating the romantic silhouetted skein of branches and forest vines beyond the clearing, and then still kept rising from behind its far hill. He felt Professor Dankl glance over her caped shoulder at him, and looked at her—but she had turned again, was facing away from him again, and he went back to watching the moonrise, only half listening to her mad ramblings.

"Now she is gone, I cannot bear what I have become for her. Why should I fear what I must now do? Why should I fear hell even? I am *in* hell."

Taking another quick look her way, Zach saw her shake her head at the earth beneath her feet. From where he was, she was little more than a shadow, frail and hunched. He turned his eyes to the moon again. It had crested the rise. It was full and glorious. The forest was magical with its glow. The deep interweavings of the branches had grown mysterious and fantastical.

"My love, my love," said Professor Gretchen Dankl. "It is for you I have become an abomination."

Zach stood for one more second appreciating the beauty of the moon and the moonlit forest. Then he drew a deep breath, resolving that he was finished here. He had humored the loony old woman enough. Enough.

He turned to her and began to speak, but before he could, she made a sound—and it was such a sound as he had never heard before.

Animal in its rumbling depth and savagery but human in its grief, it was a cross between a feral growl and a low moan of mourning.

"Professor? Are you all right?" he said.

He took a step toward her. Had an instant in which to begin to realize that she was changing—that she *had* changed—but it was only an instant, and he only *began* to realize, because the truth of it was too impossible to imagine.

Then she spun round and tore him open with unimaginable speed and violence.

He was flying backward, his torso shredded, even as his mind was forming the image of what he could not in all reason have seen: the small, hunched shadow of the woman in the dark transforming into the great, hunkering beast of a thing that pivoted toward him quicker than the eye could follow. Its massive, blackly furred arm was still expanding, still bursting from its sleeve as it whiplashed through the night at him, its dagger-long, dagger-sharp claws slicing away his jacket, shirt, and flesh in one slashing sweep. The gun and the box it had come in flew from his outflung hands. Then his back smashed into the earth with a force that would have knocked the air out of him if he had not already gasped it all away.

He felt the life-blood spilling from his core. He choked on the blood rising in his throat. It coughed up out of him and spilled over his chin, and he was full of the primal knowledge that he had been wounded in some deep, essential way, maybe unto death. He did not even have to think this; he just knew it—he had a single second in which he knew it. . . .

Then the moonlight broke into the clearing in a broad and radiant beam—and the beast rose up above him, raging in the silver glow.

On his back, bleeding and in an agony more of shock than pain, Zach gaped up at the thing as it continued its metamorphosis. With sounds like the tearing of fabric and the splintering of wood, its muscles and bones were breaking out of themselves and the last traces of its humanity were molting from it. Shreds of what had been its clothes were flying and falling away. Its limbs were lengthening, its core thickening, its face—like some nightmare flower—was blossoming into a fire-eyed, snouted, snarling mass of bared and dripping fangs.

Another instant and its transformation was complete. It was no longer the little German professor at all. It was a massive monster, rampant against the moon.

Rearing on its huge hind legs, it raised its forelegs, its talons flashing. It howled—*howled!*—its muzzle tilted to the sky. The sound sent such an ancient and unholy terror through Zach's whole body that it seemed to curdle his sinews into milk. Any courage he had, any strategy, any hope, was blasted out of him by that high, primeval cry. The oldest instincts of his brain informed the rest of him that life was over. He was prey. He was food.

If the beast had fallen on him then—as he was sure it would—he would have died and been devoured like any rabbit paralyzed by a predator's glare. But the creature hovered above him in the moonlight another long second. He couldn't tell why. It almost seemed to be pausing, to be relishing its expectation, snarling and slavering and staring in anticipation at the feast spread before it on the ground, its guttural noises full of hunger, nothing but ravenous hunger in its fire-yellow eyes.

In that moment of the animal's hesitation—whatever its cause— Zach's inner man rallied. The soul of a hero cop broke through his age-old mammal-shock, and he thought: *the gun.*

He didn't know where it had fallen. It had been in his right hand. It must have flown off to the right. He didn't know if he could find it. He didn't know if he could reach it. He didn't know if he could move at all, with his midsection torn apart and the gore still burbling out of him. Even his cry of effort gurgled with blood—but he did cry out—and he rolled.

The monster roared. It sprang at him. Zach reached desperately across the clearing's floor, his fingers scrabbling blindly through the leaves. The beast was on him. Its huge claws sank deep into the flesh of his lower leg, spearing his calf through and through. Zach shrieked in wild agony—and his palm touched metal. His fingers clutched the .38.

The wolf-beast dragged him across the earth. He twisted his bleeding body round. He saw its eyes—enormous, and a color like no other thing: viscous yellow depths of extinction. The beast's mouth was wide, its fangs were bared and ready to clamp on Zach's throat. Its other paw was already swinging down to swipe the last life out of him.

Zach brought the gun to bear. He didn't even know he was pulling the trigger until the third shot fired and the fourth and fifth. He screamed in pain again as the beast's claws were wrenched out of his leg, ripping away chunks of him—and the enormous creature staggered back, reared up again, and wavered in the broad, mellow swath of moonlight.

Zach steadied his gun hand with the other and fired his last bullet, aiming center mass. The monster took one more faltering step backward, then stood still and swayed. It looked down at the meat-man on the earth beneath it. The great yellow eyes blinked, and Zach thought for all the world he saw some recognition in them, some bizarre ecstasy of feeling that he couldn't begin to name.

For what seemed forever, the beast swayed there above him. He thought it might—he thought it must—pounce on him again, and him now weaponless. Finally, though, it began its slow collapse. It sank down almost gracefully, one hind leg bending under it until the knee-joint planted itself in the leaves, one forepaw bracing itself against the earth. It panted rapidly, its huge tongue hanging over its fangs.

Coughing up some last bits of something—some essential organic matter from his deep entrails—Zach pushed himself off the forest floor, propping himself on one hand, so that, for a second or two, he and the beast were in almost the same position, the man rising, the creature sinking down. Their eyes met on a level, and Zach could've sworn that he saw something human there, some tenderness or gratitude in their savage depths.

Then the great wolf fell, toppling onto its shoulder with a thud that Zach felt in the ground underneath him. The creature made a high, weak, and sorrowful noise like the yip of a wounded dog. And as Zach watched—too badly wounded, too badly shocked, too thoroughly amazed to think much of anything—the thing began to change again.

Its substance seemed to shrink into itself. It made a strangled noise of human anguish. The sounds of tearing muscle and splintering bone repeated themselves in a weird inversion—a damp congealing noise—a clattering of reconstruction. The black fur of the beast seemed to retract into gray, aged, naked flesh—until, in the shadow and moonlight, there lay the old professor, Gretchen Dankl, her wrinkled white body settling onto its back, her old dugs sinking into the outline of her ribcage, her taut, anxious features pointed at the sky.

The wolf-creature was gone as if it had never been there at all. Zach could only stare at the professor, his mouth open, his mind in a muddy fever of denial: this was not happening. This could not be happening. Had he killed the woman?

Gretchen Dankl's lips moved weakly. She whispered up into the air—to no one—to the forest night: "*Liebestod.*"

She seemed to smile a little, then her final breath rattled out of her for what seemed an impossibly long time. Her naked old frame sank into itself so that it appeared to Zach to grow even older—and then he realized it was—it *was* growing older, aging even as it died, as if the life inside had somehow kept time at bay, and now that the life was gone, the hindered years were returning to claim their due.

The body grew old, and even older. The face caved in at the cheeks. The eyes grew large and round in their widening sockets. The dead woman shriveled to an ancient corpse, and then to something like a mummy, its flesh wrapped tightly around the bones protruding from beneath. Then even what flesh there was grew darker; grew thin—paper-thin—and turned to ashes. The ash drifted down into the skeleton so that only the skeleton remained—the skeleton, skeins of sinew and the eyes still staring out of the skull. Then the staring eyes liquefied and drained away.

In his shock and disgust and confusion, pain and fear, Zach gagged. He hung his head and coughed at the earth, thinking he would vomit up the last life inside him. But the gagging subsided. With a heavy breath or two, he recovered. Still panting, he lifted his head and looked at the old woman's bones.

The sinews dissolved and the bones began to crumble. The ribs clattered onto the spine. The skull collapsed into itself. The whole structure disintegrated, atomized. The dust pattered down upon the leaves, and was gone.

Breathing hard, Detective Zach Adams looked around him with mad, white, rolling eyes.

He was all alone in the clearing.

The gun fell from his hands, and he dropped down into the leaves to die.

8

ALL THE WAY HOME

Z ach had little memory of what happened next: fragments and flashes of memory like pictures in a museum, each isolated in its frame, separated from the one beside it. He remembered, for instance, lying on his back with his hand on his middle, the sticky, slippery feel against his palm of the blood and gore smeared all over the core of him. White-hot agony screamed from the wounds there and in his gouged leg, and the cold knowledge seeped through him that this really was the end, that he could not lose that much of himself and still survive.

He remembered—again in flashes, in fragments—moments of trying to make sense of what had happened to him. Was it a dream? Had he gone mad? Had he just killed a woman? Had he killed a wolf? Was he even here, or was he somewhere else, sleeping? He must have passed out between questions and come to later, asking more questions. A good deal of time must have gone by. He remembered lying on the forest floor at one point in a sickness of complete unknowing, unable to imagine any plausible explanation for his being there at all.

Then—as if it had happened later, but how much later he couldn't tell—he had a very distinct recollection of suddenly becoming conscious in the night, of taking a deep, deep breath, what he thought might be his final breath, and finding instead, to his confusion and surprise, that it had actually become *easier* for him to breathe somehow, that he actually felt *less* pain than before, had *more* strength than before—less pain and more strength, bizarrely, than he'd had when he'd first fallen.

He remembered crawling on his belly through the leaves. A sense that he must be leaving his guts in a bloody trail behind him. An even stranger sense that, no, he wasn't, that he wasn't leaving anything behind at all.

There had been a cabin—hadn't there? He had an image in his mind—an image that included himself as if he were outside his own body looking at it. He was lying on dirt, in a cleared space on the forest floor. He was half-lifted on his elbows in a spill of blue moonlight. He was at the base of a set of porch stairs—yearning up at the front door of a wooden cabin as if he knew he would never find the energy to climb to it.

But somehow he must have done it. Because he had another memory: he was inside the cabin. He was in a bare room. There was a metal bowl of water. Chains—this part couldn't be right, but he did remember it—there were chains in the wall—chains and manacles like in some old dungeon. Crazy, but that's what came back to him.

More clearly, he remembered the taste of the water as he guzzled it thirstily. He remembered the cool, cool sensation of it as he splashed it over his wounds . . . over what he'd thought were his wounds . . . what had to have been his wounds . . . but he also remembered, or thought he remembered, how he'd sat propped against one rough, untreated wood-plank wall, his chin on his chest as he looked down at himself in stupid amazement, as he pawed through the bloody shreds of his shirt and jacket to see his torso, to find that his stomach was not wounded at all, but whole! His chest was whole! His leg—though his pants too were gory and torn—his calf was whole, completely unharmed!

Everything after that was fever and dream. An image of himself staggering through the woods. An image of himself in the Sebring again, on the road. A sense that he had driven on nearly empty highways in the dead of night, fighting to keep his eyes from sinking shut, his head from pitching forward onto the wheel. He did not remember returning to his hotel, but he must have because he had obviously retrieved his overnight bag. He had brought his bag back on the planes with him—his bag, but not the clothes that he remembered wearing, the clothes that had been ripped to blood-soaked rags. Those, he must have left behind somewhere.

The misery of the trip home came back to him in blurred flickering snatches. Jostling crowds at the airport. Grim faces, frightened eyes all around him. People pounding on countertops. Someone shouting in English in a German accent, "Zis iz madness! Zis iz madness!" over and over again. It was: madness. TV screens showed pictures of fire. Pictures of chaos, shaky-cam anarchy on city streets. Weak but grimly determined, he fought his way onto the plane. Sat on the plane covered in sweat, hot with fever. His head rested against the window. Sleep fell heavy on him, smothering sleep like a woolen shroud.

The last thing he could recall was waking up after the landing at Newark. Feeling slightly refreshed. Cooler. Thinking: *Thank God.* Thinking: if he could just get home, just take a couple of aspirin and crawl into bed. . . .

He never made it. He had no memory of this at all, but, according to witnesses, he had come out of the plane walking steadily, carrying his bag. He had looked pale—very pale, nearly gray and damp with sweat—but had seemed alert and strong. He had continued quickly through customs to the airport exit. Stepped out into the gray autumn weather. He had then stood as if considering which way to go. He had taken a deep, appreciative breath of the cool air.

Then, as if checking the weather, he had lifted his face to the sky. His mouth had fallen open and his eyes had rolled up into his head until only the whites were showing. The bag had dropped from his slack hand and—"as if he'd suddenly turned into a piece of string," one witness said—his body sank in a wavering line to the sidewalk, and he spilled across the pavement, unconscious.

The doctors said he must have been traveling on pure willpower, sick as he was.

PART II

A DREAM OF
GOOD AND EVIL

9

THE GRETCHENFRAGE

A sickly yellow fog lay over the headstones. It twined like a cat around the bases of the monuments. A statue of a cowled mourner gazed into its depths. A marble child, staring with blank eyes, appeared and disappeared as the mist blew and shifted over her. Inscriptions spoke and fell silent as the fog revealed or covered them. Here lies . . . Beloved mother of . . . What I once was. . . .

The mist felt cold on the back of Zach's hands as he moved among the markers. With a low frisson of fear, he realized: he *knew* this place, this cemetery. The dead here—the dead were not dead. Some were walking near him—very near him—hidden in the fog. Some were even closer than that, running through his bloodstream, racing through his brain, as near as his own thoughts.

He paused beside the statue of the cowled mourner. He felt it staring down at him. He raised his eyes to it.

Good God, it wasn't a statue at all! It was a woman. He knew her from someplace. . . .

He looked around him. Ah, now he understood! This was a dream! He was in a dream. Yes, look. There, up ahead. A shadow in the mist: the shape of a scaffold—a platform framed by rising beams. . . .

He did not want to draw closer to it, but it was a dream so he couldn't help himself. He stepped toward the structure. The thick fog parted like a curtain. The figures standing on the platform emerged, tendrils of mist hanging off them like rags. An executioner in a frilled collar stood holding a sword—a strange sort of sword with sharp edges but a rounded end. Another man knelt in front of him, his back straight, his shirt pulled down over his shoulders to expose his neck to the executioner's blow. His arms were tied together in front of him, and Zach could see that one of his hands was missing, cut away, the ragged stump of his wrist obscenely naked and putrefied.

The kneeling man looked up. He called out to him—to Zach. "Do you believe?"

"*Ja*," said the executioner heavily. "*Ja, das ist die Gretchenfrage.*"

Zach heard a soft footstep behind him. He turned and saw another figure approaching him through the fog. The cowled mourner from the grave! She was pushing the cowl back off her head as she moved between the stones to expose her face . . . the face of a corpse . . . rotting flesh on a grinning skull with strands of gray hair hanging around it . . . Gretchen Dankl!

The thing reached out for him. Her damp fingers closed around his wrist. "It is for you that I have become an abomination," she said.

And Zach realized: *This isn't a dream! This isn't a dream at all!*

He woke up with a gasp of fear, his heart pounding hard. He was lying on his back, staring up at a white ceiling. He turned his head and saw Agent Martin "Broadway Joe" Goulart slouched in the wooden armchair beside his bed. His partner was wearing one of his fine, fancy suits—a pinstriped gray—and a tie just the perfect robin's-egg blue. He was playing with his phone, tapping and swiping the screen with his thumb. He barely glanced at Zach, but he said "The Cowboy awakes!" Zach was about to ask him *Where am I? Why am I here?* but before he could, Goulart added "In the hospital. You had septicemia."

Zach turned a muzzy-headed gaze down toward his wrist. There was a needle stuck in the vein there, a tube running out of it. Near the entry point, the wet imprint of a woman's fingers was just now evaporating. . . .

It wasn't a dream.

"Wanna know how I knew what you were gonna ask?" said Goulart, still tapping away at the phone. "It's because this is the third time you've woken up and asked me. The third time today. You did it twice on Tuesday too. Same questions. A week, by the way. That's your next question: 'How long have I been here?' A week."

"What's a *Gretchenfrage?*" Zach asked.

"That's a new one! What's a *what?*"

"A *Gretchenfrage.*"

"A French girl with a German name? Gretchen Frog? Just guessing." He gave one of his silent laughs as he went on playing whatever game he was playing on the phone.

"I've been here a week?" murmured Zach faintly.

"Now we're back to the script. You collapsed outside Newark airport right after you got back from Deutschland. Doctors say you would have died if you weren't such a tough guy. Your whole body was infected."

Zach shut his eyes hard, trying to clear his mind. But the graveyard came back to him. The fog. The scaffold. The headsman. *Das ist die Gretchenfrage.* How could someone use a word in your dream if you'd never heard the word before? And then that creature approaching him . . . the dead professor. . . .

He opened his eyes again quickly before he could picture her face. "Why?" he said softly to Goulart. "How? How did I get so sick?" He had already remembered the answer—no one knew—but he asked anyway, to distract himself from the memory of the dream . . . or whatever it was. . . . That graveyard. He shuddered. Where the dead were not dead.

Goulart shrugged. "They don't know. Said it could've been some small infection, like a urinary thing or something, that just suddenly flared up. Or maybe something you picked up overseas. None too surprising with all the hairy scumbags running riot over there, burning things down and whatnot. You know the government of France resigned yesterday? The whole government! I didn't even know you could do that. They're saying the new president wants that Islamic Sharia shit added to the legal system. What could possibly go wrong with that, right?"

Zach groaned. Brought his right hand to his forehead—which was no easy task; there were needles and tubes in his right arm too. "You're giving me a headache, Goulart."

"You should've woken up half an hour ago. Your wife would've been here. She's been here practically the whole time—s'why I'm spelling her for a few minutes. Bad timing on your part. She's a much nicer person than I am and with far superior tits. On the other hand, I bet she never scored fifteen million at Temple Run 4. Plus she can't bring you up to date on the Paz murders."

The Paz murders. Dominic Abend. It came back to him. Zach tried to sit up.

"There's a button. . . ." said Goulart, gesturing sideways with his chin so he wouldn't have to stop playing the game on his phone.

Zach found the button and raised the head of his bed. "What's new on the Paz case?"

"Nothing," said Goulart. "Or nothing much. We've been trying to locate any properties Paz owned, anyplace he might've stored his stolen goods, you know, so we might be able to find out what Abend, if it was Abend, was looking for, if he *was* looking for it. . . ."

Zach got a whiff of something—a smell—it was coming off Goulart—just for a moment, then it was gone—but in that moment, Zach thought: *He's lying.* And with a sour feeling in his stomach, he remembered what Rebecca Abraham-Hartwell had told him: *We have reason to believe Goulart is dirty.* Was his partner hiding something from him—or had Rebecca Abraham-Hartwell just managed to plant her foul suspicions in his head?

"And you haven't found anything?" he asked.

"We found a warehouse in Woodside under a shell company we think was Paz's. But someone must've gotten to it when they heard Paz had been murdered. It was cleaned out by the time we got there. What about you? You come up with anything in the old country?"

Zach said: "That woman . . . in Germany. . . ." It was all coming back now. The museum. The double row of stone apostles. The hunched professor hobbling toward him, cigarette in her hand. "Gretchen Dankl . . . it was a dead end. She was crazy."

"Yeah, well, I figured," said Goulart. Then he let out a curse. He'd lost the game, the one on his phone. He shook his head with annoyance and slapped the plastic rectangle against one thigh. "Fucking thing. Anyway, I figured. I tried to contact her after you got back. No one at the university has ever even heard of her."

"What?"

"It's hard to get anyone on the phone over there right now with the apocalypse going on and all, but we've had some e-mail contact. No one's ever heard of a Gretchen Dankl. She sure as hell's not on the staff."

"The paper she wrote . . . on the baselard. . . ."

"No one's ever heard of her paper either. No one's heard of Stump's Baselard, or whatever it was. Looks like you got punked, brother. I don't know why. My guess is she's some sort of Dominic Abend groupie or something. You know, like one of those women who marry serial killers in prison. If I'd only known that was the best way to get laid. . . ."

Now Zach remembered something else. A clearing in the moonlit woods. A noise—a noise unlike any other he had ever heard—a moaning growl half animal, half human. . . . He shook his head quickly to make the thought go away. Must've been a fever dream. To keep from thinking about it, he asked again: "What's a *Gretchenfrage*?" He gestured at Goulart's phone. "Look it up for me, will you?"

Goulart tapped the word in with his thumbs. "'A compound of the name Gretchen—a diminutive of the name Margarethe—and *frage*, meaning *question*. In reference to . . .' I don't know how you pronounce this . . . 'Goth? Gothe? Goth's *Faust*, a play first published in 1808, in which Gretchen asks Faust, who is in league with the devil: *What do you think of religion?* Hence it is any question that gets to the core of an issue, especially one with a difficult or unpleasant answer. A question about a person's religious beliefs.' There you have it: *Gretchenfrage*. Let's move on to Obscure Words for 200."

Zach shook his head, mystified. "I never heard of any of that," he said. That wasn't quite true: the name Margarethe rang a bell, but he couldn't quite remember why. But the rest: Goth, Faust, *Gretchenfrage*. . . . "How could that have been in my—"

But before he could finish, the door banged open. His children shouted "Daddy!" and rushed across the room to him. His wife came in behind them, smiling through her tears, calling out to warn them, "Careful, kids. Gently."

The children obediently pulled up short and did not launch themselves on top of him—their original plan. Instead, they rested their elbows on the edge of his mattress and gazed at him raptly with their scrubbed and rosy angel faces.

Zach was not prepared for the strength of the emotion that welled up inside him, not prepared for the size of it, which seemed too big for his body to contain. He caught a whiff of his blue-eyed boy—the brown-sweet scent of his flesh—and a whiff of the silken shampoo blonde of his daughter's hair; and then Grace sat down beside him, and that mysterious atmosphere that always surrounded her, that always made him yearn for something that was beyond her but that he could only somehow get to through her—all of this filled his nostrils, his lungs, his body head to toe, and a feeling welled up inside him that was beyond anything he could remember experiencing. It was as overwhelming and savage as lust, as primordial, but it was not that. It was his love for them—for his woman, his boy, his girl. It was the very thing that bound him with them as completely as the cells of his own flesh were bound together.

He had to touch them. Had to. Had to put his palm against little Ann's cheek and ruffle Tom's hair, and then he had to reach up a weak arm trailing intravenous tubes and draw his woman—his mysterious Grace, whose inner life was a riddle to him—draw her down to his chest and press her close, press her into that spot where she fit beneath his chin. He kissed her hair and kissed her cheek and smelled . . . he could smell her very blood pulsing inside her, pulsing through the artery in her white throat. He could smell her blood—and his own blood seemed to mingle with it through the love he felt for her so that they seemed spliced together into a single living system.

A guttural noise came out of him, a low growl of passionate attachment. "God, it's good to see you, Grace," he whispered into his wife's ear. "I could eat you up."

10

ON THE HUNT

There were cheers and applause when he finally swaggered back into the Task Force Zero squad room. There were cards and flowers on his desk and even, courtesy of Janine in Records, an oversized plastic cowboy doll from some cartoon movie: "Welcome Back, Cowboy." Much shaking of hands all around, some bumping of fists. Many jovial remarks on how pale he was, how thin, practically invisible if you tried to look at him from the side.

He'd been there five minutes when the Director's receptionist summoned him upstairs over the in-house phone. Which would've been fine—he would've figured it was just a welcome-home from the boss—a rueful postmortem of his wasted trip—except that the receptionist added "Just you, Agent Adams. Not your partner." He remembered his last meeting with Rebecca Abraham-Hartwell, how she'd tried to enlist him in her vendetta against Goulart, how he'd walked out angry. Now it seemed they were going to take things up where they'd left off. So he went up in the elevator with a sense of foreboding.

It was fifteen days since he'd gotten back from Germany, eight since he'd come to his senses in the hospital. The events of his trip and the dreams of his long fever had blended together in his mind so that he wasn't sure anymore which ones were which. There were some things he felt fairly certain about. The drive to Freiberg through the fairytale landscape, the meeting with Gretchen Dankl, or whoever the hell she was, in the hall of stone saints—these, he was sure, had actually happened. Then there were other things that *seemed* real enough but that *couldn't* have happened. The professor's transformation into a raging beast, the fatal wounds that magically healed—these must have been the hallucinations of his illness.

And then . . . then there were the mysteries. Things in between.

There was the report, for instance: the paper Gretchen Dankl had written, which he had read on the plane. If that had been real, where was it? The pages she had sent him were gone, though he had no memory of discarding them. The link to the abstract that he had found on the Internet that one time—it too seemed to have vanished. And yet, if the report had not been real, if it had been some kind of fever dream or hallucination, where had the information come from? There really was a Peter Stumpf, it turned out, accused of being a werewolf in 16th-century Germany, and there really was a Thirty Years War in the 17th century and a Nazi operation code-named Werewolf—but Zach had never heard of any of them before. He could not have made the report up, in other words. So it must have been real—right?—but where the hell had it gone?

And then there was that dream, that dream he'd had in the hospital. The graveyard in the mist. The scaffolding. The executioner. *Ja, das ist die Gretchenfrage.* Again, there really was such a word, but he'd never heard it before the dream. And the sword the executioner had held—the strange sword with the rounded blade that had no point—that was real too. He'd looked it up. Medieval German executioners had actually used such swords—what would they need a point for?—but Zach had had no idea. All of which was not to mention those damp fingerprints just fading from his wrist when he'd awakened. That had to have been some sort of illusion because . . . well, because things like that didn't happen, that's why. Still, it just didn't make any sense that he could see.

These matters bothered him, but he had tried to push them to the back of his mind. Work to do. Returning to family life. Regaining his strength. Catching up. Too many other things to think about. . . .

"Welcome back," said the chief's receptionist as she nodded him through the half-open office door.

"Zach! You look good," said Rebecca Abraham-Hartwell, striding from behind the great desk to greet him with a brusque handshake. She was as she ever was. Wiry, wound-up. Navy blue pants suit. Power jacket, red this time. The long depressed pony face set in its *I'm-all-business* expression. She gestured Zach to the oversoft sofa and took a detour to turn off the flatscreen on the wall. All four pictures showed some Arab-looking guy addressing a cheering crowd.

"Christ," said Rebecca Abraham-Hartwell as she marched to her armchair. "First Greece and Italy turn into gangsterocracies. Now France. . . . Pretty soon we'll be the only free country left in the world."

Zach suppressed a flashing memory of Gretchen Dankl leaning toward him urgently through the smoke from her cigarette . . . *stop him before he does to your continent what he has done to mine.*

"So—the German trip? Total write-off?" She was planted in the chair across the coffee table from him now, leaning forward, her arms draped over legs crossed at the knee.

"Professor Dankl, or whoever she was, believes Dominic Abend is an immortal warlock who destroyed post-war Europe with a magic dagger and is now coming after the U.S.," Zach told her.

"Great. So we move on. Have you had time to catch up?"

"I just got in."

"But you've talked to Goulart. Impressions?"

"Well, the Paz case seems. . . ." Zach paused to choose the word.

Rebecca Abraham-Hartwell barked it at him: "Stalled. Completely. What do you make of it?"

Zach already knew what she was getting at. He could smell her anxiety—or sense it, anyway. She knew she had lost him last time. She knew she needed his support in the bureau. She didn't have the patience to let it ride, so she'd been waiting all this time for the chance to win him back. He was thinking wearily: *This again.* He had no patience for playing political games with her, so he spoke right out. "Come on, boss! You gonna try to tell me Broadway's dogging it 'cause he's on the take?"

"He tell you about Paz's warehouse? Emptied out? Like someone knew we were coming."

"Well, someone *would* know, Paz being hacked to pieces and all."

Rebecca Abraham-Hartwell drew herself erect, unsmiling. "It's like a game we play, Zach. I point to something suspicious, you rationalize it away."

"Because Goulart's *not* on the take," Zach drawled—that set-in-stone drawl that made his wife crazy with frustration. "He's not working for Abend. If you've got proof otherwise, show it. If not. . . ."

Rebecca Abraham-Hartwell's sinewy frame uncoiled from her chair in one tight, swift movement. "You think it's personal? You think it's just that I don't like him because he's a sexist loudmouth who calls me an idiot behind my back?"

"I would understand if you found those particular character traits less than endearing," said Zach.

She did smile at that, or one half of her mouth lifted anyway. "Goulart's not my favorite person. I admit it. But no matter what he thinks, I am a professional. I wouldn't accuse an agent of turning rotten just because of that."

She pinned him with a challenging gaze and waited for his reply, but he let the silence grow awkward. The truth was, he believed this about her. She *was* a professional; she *wouldn't* accuse Goulart out of personal animosity. But on the other hand, when a fellow gets under your skin, it's easy to start seeing things in a certain way, to see corruption and evil where there's just . . . who knows what? Bad luck. A tough case.

Rebecca Abraham-Hartwell was on the march again, striding back toward her desk, framed by the big window, the white skyscraper against the blue sky. "While you were gone, Isaiah Medina moved away."

"The pimp? Moved . . . ?"

"From Yonkers to the bottom of the East River—that's my guess. It's Dominic Abend—the BLK—taking over the brothels all the way up to Westchester. And we've had high-level drug dealers disappearing for six months. Abend's moving in there too. And yesterday I got a call from the U.S. Attorney's office. Someone is investing heavily in the next city election."

"I know all this, Rebec—"

"All invisible. All untraceable. All untouchable. This son of a bitch is spreading through the city like a virus. And the one time he shows himself—the one time! Stalled? Come on, Zach! Look at this."

She had snapped a drawer open, snatched a page out of it. Was marching around to the front of the desk, thrusting the paper at him.

"I told you we were monitoring Goulart's computer, right? This came in last night. Another Paz shell company. A storage unit in the Bronx. Did your partner happen to mention this to you?"

Zach took the paper silently. Goulart hadn't mentioned it.

"What do you think he was waiting for?" said Rebecca Abraham-Hartwell as his eyes ran down the page. "Maybe he wants to make sure someone else gets there before we do."

Zach's anger was the stony—not the fiery—kind. His face could've been on Mount Rushmore as he rode the elevator downstairs. He was right back in the thick of it. All that nastiness between the Director and Goulart. Hell, if she had something on Broadway Joe, why didn't she just bust him? And why hadn't Goulart told him about the damned storage unit in the Bronx?

He had just reached his desk, when Goulart—returning from the coffee machine to the desk across from him—said "I got something."

Zach dropped sullenly into his chair. Goulart plunked a butt cheek on the edge of the gunmetal and perched just above him, sipping from one of the mugs they'd stolen from NYPD.

"I think I've found another Paz shell company, another storage place," Goulart said. "A unit in the Bronx this time."

His jaw set, Zach lifted a chin to his partner. "When'd you find out about this?"

"Last night, but I just now confirmed it was Paz behind it. What?" Goulart added, seeing the look on Zach's face.

But Zach just shook his head. He hated having Rebecca Abraham-Hartwell's suspicions stuck in his brain like a bad song. "We better get up there before it gets cleaned out like the warehouse."

"I sent a black-and-white over to stand guard."

Goulart made as if to savor his coffee, but Zach got to his feet. "Let's just go," he said.

The whole time Zach was piloting the Crown Vic up the eastern edge of Manhattan, he was brooding on the business, thinking, well, what if they got to the Bronx and the storage unit had been cleaned out—what then?—was he supposed to assume Goulart had given Dominic Abend a heads-up, a head start? And Goulart, meanwhile, riding shotgun, was oddly quiet, oddly missing out on the opportunity to go into one of his anti-female or anti-black or anti-somebody rants.

Then Zach felt his partner's eyes on him and Goulart suddenly said, "Listen, partner. Who's Margo Heatherton?"

The usual four-letter words flashed through Zach's mind, but he managed to keep his face impassive. He said, "A woman I know. A writer. She was writing a book. I helped her with the research."

"Uh-huh," said Goulart—which was as much as to say *And you were boning her, right?*

"Why? She get in touch with you?"

"She said she'd been calling your cell, but kept getting the message that you were away," Goulart said. Zach had been hoping this wasn't true, but he'd figured it was. There had been a lot of calls on his cell when he came out of his weeklong fever, a lot of them were blocked numbers, no messages. He had hoped they weren't from Margo, but he knew the truth deep down. "She said she was worried about you," Goulart went on. "You devil, you."

Zach gave a puff of air, a sound of dismissal. He knew Goulart wouldn't buy it, the dismissal, but what could he do? He felt a cold sweat breaking out on his scalp and could only hope it didn't show.

"Listen," Goulart said again. "I'm not saying anything, right?"

"There's nothing to say. For Christ's sake."

"Right. That's why I'm not saying anything. But I'm just saying: with the texts and the phone calls and I'm-worried-about-you . . . if there *is* something, if you got yourself in a situation here. . . ."

"I thought you weren't saying anything."

"I'm just saying I'm gonna keep your six, that's all. I mean, I know what Grace and the kids mean to you. And I know from personal experience that getting a divorce is like having a spiked baseball bat shoved up your ass."

"What the hell, Broadway? I just helped the girl with some research. I don't think Grace'll divorce me for that."

"I. Will. Keep. Your. Six," said Goulart, emphasizing each word. "That's all. Message delivered. I will keep your six because that's what partners do. *Verstanzee?* I'm there for you. You're there for me. That's how it works."

"You finished?"

"Yes, I am."

"Good. There's no problem. I just helped her with some research."

"Excellent. Glad to hear it. Truly. Joy throughout the land."

Zach made a show of shaking his head and rolling his eyes. Then he drove on in silence. But he hadn't let it go, not by a long shot. Goulart might have just been being nosy—friendly—the usual partner stuff. Still, as they crossed the bridge above the steely Hell Gate water, Zach was wondering what else he might have intended by it all, by all that *you-got-my-back-I-got-yours* crap. Could it have been blackmail? If you expose my corruption, I'll expose your affair? Or was it just a pointed reminder of where Zach's loyalties lay? As in: I watch your back with Margo, you watch mine with Rebecca Abraham-Hartwell. Either way, Zach didn't like it, didn't like being pressured, didn't like being in a position to give a damn. He resolved again to get straight on this, to confront Margo face to face, have it out with her, and take the consequences either way. Bad as that might be, it would be better than this, better than compromising his integrity to keep the secret, better than living a lie. What a tangled damned web we weave. . . .

When he thought enough time had passed, when he thought Goulart wouldn't make anything of it, he ran a hand up through his hair, pretending it was a casual gesture, but really wiping away the last of his cold worry-sweat. He was pretty sure Goulart knew exactly what he was doing, but he went through the elaborate pretense anyway.

There was a uniform waiting for them at the storage facility, sure enough. Sitting bored in his cruiser outside the white brick building on a shabby warehouse block in the shadow of the Cross Bronx Expressway. He was visibly relieved when Goulart waved him on his way. The kid was tired of riding his backside and eager to get back on patrol. Shoulder to shoulder, Zach and Goulart continued on into the building.

A burly red-headed tough guy named Chaim ran the place. Friendly but businesslike, used to cops. He led them from the front office into a concrete bunker, past rows of metal roll-up doors. He unlocked the padlock on number seventeen, and up the door rumbled. He stepped aside to let Zach and Goulart have a look inside.

Ransacked, but not emptied. Boxes of jewels and electronics were spilled all over the concrete floor of the little bay. No two boxes had been left stacked against the corrugated metal walls.

Zach thought: *Shit*. His stomach soured. He had been hoping the place would be untouched, clearing Goulart of any suspicion that he had tipped Abend off, given the gangster time to search the place before the law arrived. He was thinking . . . and then he stopped thinking. His breathing slowed. His eyes narrowed.

"We're gonna need security cam video and records of who used the access code," said Goulart behind him. "You got a man on-site?"

"Me," said Chaim.

"But you didn't see anything suspicious."

The guy hoisted both heavy shoulders high. "Nah. Nothing."

Goulart was about to say something else, but he stopped himself when he saw what was going on with Zach. The Cowboy had gone into his legendary hyper-focus mode again. He was standing very still, scanning the trashed unit with that squinty gunfighter gaze that made the crow's feet bunch at the corners of his eyes.

"Look, I don't keep a record of every—" the storage guy, Chaim, started to say—but Goulart silenced him with a raised hand. He waited.

"The warehouse was cleaned out, right?" Zach murmured slowly after another moment. "The other place Paz had. The place you found when I was in the hospital?"

"Yeah," said Goulart. "It was emptied."

"Like someone ripped it off, maybe."

Goulart shrugged. "Could be."

"Like someone—one of Paz's crew, maybe—heard the boss was dead and . . ."

". . . figured it was bargain days—why not? Could be."

"Because this place . . ." said Zach. "This place was tossed. Searched."

Now Goulart understood. "Right. Because Abend is looking for something specific. He's not some garden-variety nitwit, hamburgering warehouses."

Zach was working his rubber gloves on now. He crouched down amidst the strewn treasure. He lifted a dented loving cup out of a tangle of emerald and pearl necklaces. Held it up in Goulart's direction.

"You remember that series of mansion burglaries out on Long Island?"

"Yeah, I remember reading about it, sure. Bunch of them. Last one maybe . . . what? Couple weeks ago?"

"East Beach Yacht Club," Zach said, gesturing with the cup.

"Lot of gangster summer homes on the Guyland," said Goulart. "Wide-open spaces. Nice and private."

As Zach stood up, he let the loving cup fall from his gloved fingers. It dropped into a pile of jewelry, making the gems rattle. He moved out of the bay toward where Goulart was standing at the edge of the entrance.

"Let's say Abend's got a place out there . . ."

". . . and he got ripped off in the burglaries," said Goulart.

"Maybe intentional, maybe just an accident. Either way, they took something—something private or even secret—something he valued. . . ."

"And they fenced it with Paz."

Zach turned his head back toward the storage bay. Considered the mess in there. He drew in a deep breath of the warm, stale air. Faint images and sensations came to him like distant music. Sea breezes. Potpourris. Children squabbling. And something else, something closer, more recent, more real. A dark, hot, male aroma. Rage.

"Whatever it is, I don't think he found it here," he said.

"How do you know?"

"I just don't think so." He could not account for his sense of the atmosphere. "Call it a hunch."

As Zach drove the Crown Vic back to Manhattan, he said, "I'm thinking you should rustle up the Guyland inventories, find out what was reported stolen where. Then we go out there and canvass the homeowners, see if any of them happen to be a cue-balled German gangster."

"And you, meanwhile?"

"Thought I'd go chat with—"

"Don't tell me," said Goulart. "With Fatboy Mooch."

"If anyone knows who pulled those mansion heists, he will."

"He will. But that is one evil Negro. You think he'll talk to you?"

"I have a feeling he will, yes."

"You sure you don't want me to come along and be the bad cop."

"Well, you are a bad cop. But he won't meet up with you around. Somehow he's got this idea you're a racist."

"Moi? Why? Because I call an evil Negro an evil Negro?"

"It's your tone," said Zach. "I don't think folks say *Negro* anymore."

"No fooling? Do they still say *evil*?"

Zach laughed. The first time today. It was hard not to laugh when Goulart got started on this crap.

"You're laughing," Goulart said, delighted with himself, happy to get back to their old rapport. "I'm a dying breed, right?"

"You are. The Loud-Mouthed White Male Asshole."

"We were overhunted. Now we're practically extinct."

Zach laughed again. He wished the damn storage unit hadn't been ransacked.

"You'll miss us once we're gone," said Goulart. "Mark my words. The truth dies with us, my friend."

Abend could've tracked the unit down the same way they did, Zach thought. He just might've gotten there first, that's all. There was no evidence of a tip-off from Goulart.

But still. He wished it hadn't been ransacked.

11

INVISIBLE WAR

Funny thing about Fatboy Mooch: you never saw him indoors. Zach never had, anyway. He always met with him on street corners—in cafés—in parks. Today it was in one of those little pocket arcades with the waterfalls: the butter-bellied thug liked to meet in such venues, to sit at one of the tables amidst the white folks and honey locust trees and nibble delicately on a croissant from the snack bar while he talked pure wickedness. Zach wondered if this was some form of ironic street theater or something like that. Or maybe the point was just that the Mooch wasn't hiding, wasn't scuttling around to protect his rep. Dealing with law dogs was part of doing business in this city, so why not do it in the open? Or maybe the Mooch was just claustrophobic, who could say?

"Do you even *have* a place to live?" Zach asked him.

"The foxes have they holes," said Fatboy Mooch, "and the birds of the air have they nests, but Fatboy Mooch got nowhere to lay *his* head."

"That's a sad story."

"You wanna see sad? I'll show you sad. Come with me, Agent."

Fatboy Mooch was fat all right, but he was big and carried his lard spread collar-to-jockstrap so he was shaped more like a bomb than a beachball. He favored T-shirts with slogans on them like KILLER, or a picture of a .38 with the caption WELCOME TO NEW YORK. Which was more or less truth in advertising because, despite his imitation-civilized raconteur veneer, there were all sorts of stories about what he'd done to guys with his bare hands. Most of the stories ended up with the Mooch's enemies liquefied and hard men losing their lunches left and right at the sight of what remained.

"You know this corner? You see this corner?" he asked Zach after a while.

They'd been strolling west and north together, talking baseball and the weather. Fatboy had been laying down a running commentary on the Yankees' chances in the postseason, with glosses on Houston's crap-ass pitching to try to get under the Texan's skin. But they stopped now, on the northeast corner, looking to the northwest, and Zach took in the panorama with a cop's eyes: the school playground down the block to his left, the rundown brownstones directly across from him, the empty lot, the scaffolding in front of the grocer's shop. He could guess at the location of the dead drop where the drugs would be hidden. He could guess where the corner boys would have been stationed—dealer there, steerer there, runner there—if there had been corner boys, which there were not.

"I see it," said Zach.

"You know whose corner this is?" Fatboy asked him.

"I'm a *federale*, Mooch. Which dirtbag is poisoning children where—that's local stuff. Not my beat."

"You see it, though. You see it with that inward eye that is the bliss of solitude."

Zach nodded. "It's your corner, sure."

"It is my corner, Agent."

"But where's your corner boys?"

"Where indeed? Pretty soon, those third graders gonna be let out for recess, where they gonna get their re-up at?"

"Goddamned city. Nothing runs right."

"You know where I think my corner boys is at?"

Zach drew his gaze slowly off the scenery and turned to show his baby blues to Fatboy. The two men were about the same height—Mooch maybe half an inch taller—so it was a direct hit, stare to stare. Zach wanted the gangster-man to read him: he knew all this—everything the Mooch was about to say—he'd guessed it, anyway—or seen it with that inward eye that is . . . whatever Fatboy said it was—that's why he was here in the first place.

"I think they be at that land from which no traveler returns," said Fatboy, straight at him.

"You think your corner boys are dead."

"That's my deduction. You know how I deduces that? I deduces it because one of them—a young brother go by the name STD—he wear a ring on his finger with a gold skull on it, have some diamonds for the eyes, you know. And that very ring was still on his finger when his hand showed up in a paper bag at my park bench where I eat my morning burrito."

"Does sound like a clue."

"The bad man uses a sword, I heard."

"He does."

"Put me off my damned breakfast."

"You shouldn't eat that crap anyway. It'll turn your heart to stone—although maybe that warning comes a bit too late."

"They an invisible war going on out here, Detective. I'm getting that you already know that, don't you?"

"I do."

"We ain't fighting against flesh and blood no more. We're fighting against principalities. And powers. Against spiritual forces in the heavenly places. This is a battle between good and evil going on, Agent Adams."

"Which one are you?" Zach couldn't help asking.

"Me? Why, I bring the gift of laughter to a sorrowful world!" Fatboy Mooch protested, as if his feelings had been hurt. "No one *has* to give me money to get they self high. Reality is free. Ask yourself who deals out *that* shit. I'm a better man than God, when you come to think about it. I make you feel better than He does, anyway."

You cannot survive as a lawman unless corruption amuses you at some level. Otherwise, it'd be a life with no laughs at all. Zach was amused by Fatboy Mooch, and Fatboy Mooch was pleased by that and smiled to himself as he surveyed what had, until very lately, been his domain.

"What if I told you I had a lead on Dominic Abend?" Zach said. "That I could bring him down with the right intel? Get you your corner back so you can go on killing those children with your drugs."

Without another word, Fatboy Mooch began to walk again—to walk along the school fence, the empty playground at his shoulder. Zach hesitated only a moment, then followed after him until he caught up, until he had a view of Fatboy's profile. He could see the gangster was doing a nervous scan of every face that came toward them on the sidewalk.

Fatboy noticed that he'd noticed and murmured low, "A world full of faces—and every face a face to meet the faces that it meets."

"Someone stole something from him," Zach answered, side of the mouth. "Abend. By accident or on purpose, I don't know. But whatever it was, he wants it back. Wants it bad enough to show himself. We think he was there in person when they sliced and diced up Marco Paz."

The street was noisy. Traffic; sirens; truck panels rumbling as tires hit potholes. Even the sound of footsteps on concrete was loud. Voices could get lost—intimations and innuendoes could get lost. Nonetheless, Zach heard the Mooch's breathing change, or sensed it. He smelled . . . *something* coming off the man. He smelled him thinking the situation through. He smelled him putting the pieces of the puzzle together. Apparently that had a smell. Who knew?

"The Guyland heists," said Fatboy then.

Smart, thought Zach. Say whatever else you would about him, the gangster was smart.

Fatboy Mooch continued: "Out in Gravesend near Avenue U, near a red brick building across from Moody Square, there's a dumpster in an alley with a black plastic bag inside. And in that plastic bag there is a moldy old mess of shit that looks like papier-mâché before it dries. You ever seen that?"

"Papier-mâché before it dries? In school when I was little, sure."

"Well, good. Then maybe you will be able to tell the difference between what that looks like and the remains of Billy Grimhouse, which is what's in that bag—all that's left of him after that devil was done."

"And Billy Grimhouse is? Or was . . . ?"

"The brother of Johnny Grimhouse. Which made them the Brothers Grimhouse. The pair of fools who did the Guyland heists."

Now it was Zach's turn to make the connections—a whole series of them rattling into place in his mind like dice coming up Yahtzee. These Grimhouse clowns had been doing mansions out on Long Island. They had taken something from Dominic Abend. Dominic Abend had traced some fenced merchandise back to Paz, tortured Paz to get to the Grimhouse brothers, tortured Billy Grimhouse. . . .

"How long ago was this?"

"Don't know," said Fatboy Mooch. "Two days. Three. A week at most."

Before the storage unit had been tossed. So Billy didn't have the answers and Abend still hadn't found what he wanted, Zach thought. Which raised a new question: If Billy was the Guyland thief, why *didn't* he know where Abend's merchandise had gotten to?

"If you were up on all this," Zach asked the Mooch, "why didn't you drop a dime and let me in on it, give me a head start?"

"'Cause that German mo-fo already owns half the cops in town. And though Fatboy Mooch is wiser than the children of light in his generation, even he isn't wise enough to know which half is which."

This sent another twinge through Zach's anxiety centers re: Goulart. Was Goulart one of the fifty percent of cops Abend already owned?

"But I figure . . ." Fatboy Mooch went on. "I figure if you're asking me, you want to know. And if you want to know, maybe you ain't yet been body-snatched. Maybe you're still clean."

If, thought Zach, annoyed to think it, cursing Rebecca Abraham-Hartwell because she had made him think it. *If* you want to know. . . . Did Goulart want to know? Did he really? Or was he just helping Abend stay out in front of Task Force Zero?

Zach and the Mooch were stopped at a corner, at a red light. They didn't have the schoolyard on their flank anymore, so there were pedestrians on every side of them. Yellow cabs and panel trucks and cars whooshed past them from every direction. Fatboy Mooch's head was swiveling, eyes watching everything at once.

And Zach, when he spoke, spoke in a secretive mutter. "There's still Johnny Grimhouse, then."

"Last I heard."

"And I'm guessing Johnny Grimhouse is on the run."

"All men fear death," said Fatboy Mooch.

"Of course if Abend could find Billy, he can find Johnny too."

"Johnny the smarter one."

"All the same."

Fatboy Mooch's *Killer* T-shirt rose and fell and rose and fell while he considered whether to trust Zach with what he knew. At last he spoke into the middle distance. "You trying to tell me *you* the only hope of saving Western civilization?"

"You trying to tell me you're Western civilization?"

"You was expecting maybe Mozart?"

The light turned green, but the two big men stayed right there at the sidewalk's edge while the other pedestrians streamed past them, while Fatboy Mooch made his decision.

"Johnny got a hole I know in Long Island City," he said then. He murmured an address. "And was I you, I would hie me hence with wings as swift as meditation or the thoughts of love."

Zach had already pivoted on his heel, was already hurrying away.

12

GRIMHOUSE

Z ach was about halfway across the 59th Street Bridge, the Crown Vic doing twenty in steady traffic, when a wave of fever hit him. The world turned suddenly distant and unreal. The criss-crossing bridge supports surrounding him became a sort of graph superimposed on the surface of the scenery beyond, making it all seem two-dimensional. The gleaming pinnacles of Manhattan in the rearview—the drear flatlands of Queens in the windshield—the alien reaches of Roosevelt Island at the windows—looked to him all at once like territories on a map of themselves, drawings on one of those old brown maps with sailing ships and whales in the sea-spaces and monsters in the vast unknown beyond the borders.

Zach felt sick and started sweating. The cars ahead of him blurred. Their red bright taillights smeared themselves across his field of vision.

His sudden sense of unreality—this image of New York as a map of itself—a hand-crafted picture of a place—a cartoon cityscape through which he was all too mysteriously passing—reminded him so much of his drive through Germany that he was only somewhat surprised, only somewhat nauseated, to see the executioner from his dream standing impossibly on one of the bridge's low stone towers just up ahead. Both the executioner's hands were resting on the hilt of his long sword, and the sword's round end was pressed into the concrete. He watched Zach drive by beneath him with what could only be called a tragic smile.

My love! My love! It is for you I am become an abomination!

With that, the wave of fever—the sense of unreality—receded. The bridge was the bridge and the city was the city again, after what had to have been less than half a minute. Nothing remained of the incident but the high-sea-rolling of Zach's stomach, and that was already subsiding as well.

Still, the moment left him worried—weak and worried. Since returning home from Germany, he had come to believe that his dissociation during that weird drive out of Dresden must have been the first symptom of the septicemia that ultimately brought him low. He was worried that this—this moment on the bridge between Manhattan and Queens—was a sign that he hadn't fully recovered, that he was in danger of having a relapse.

Which, in turn, made him think that he should have brought Goulart along on this excursion. He should have called Goulart, at least, and arranged to meet him in Long Island City. Of course he should have. He *would* have, at any other time, and he had no idea how he was going to explain to him why he hadn't, why he had come out here alone. But if there was any chance of getting to Johnny Grimhouse before Abend did, he had to take it. And if there was even the slightest chance that Goulart might have gone bad, that he might give Abend a warning call, he couldn't risk it. Damn Rebecca Abraham-Hartwell for putting these thoughts into his mind; but now that they were there, he couldn't ignore them. He had to do this on his own.

His head was more or less clear again as he pulled the car up to the curb on a desolate gray block beside the railway yards in Long Island City. He stood out of the Crown Vic into the cool clear autumn weather. He still felt a little hollow and fuzzy in his gut. He breathed deep in an effort to restore himself, but even the air was dead here. He looked around him. There was a dirt construction site with an abandoned tractor sitting idle by a half-dug pit; there was the ruin of an old concrete plant, the aluminum siding half-stripped off its water tower; and there was the building Fatboy Mooch had sent him to find. It was six stories—red brick—blackened red brick—and had held apartments once, but was gutted now. The big windows were dark. The glass in some of them was broken. The brick was smashed around some of the frames. There was a lopsided scaffold rotting around the building's base, and a construction screen draped down one corner, roof to sidewalk. It looked as if a restoration project had been abandoned halfway through.

A train rattled across the yards, one level below the street. Zach was about to start away from his car and cross toward the building—but his breath caught and he stiffened as he spotted a movement at one of the windows. Unconsciously, he raised his hand in the direction of the gun under his arm. He stared hard at the window, a tall intact rectangle of black glass up on the fourth floor. Nothing. No movement now. His hand slid slowly back to his side. Maybe it had been an optical illusion. Or more fever stuff.

Still, he kept his eyes on that window as he walked across the empty street. He scanned all the windows but kept coming back to that one until he reached the sidewalk, reached the building, and stepped under the scaffolding to reach the front doors. The doors were two majestic slabs of carved mahogany, sadly scratched and weathered. There was no padlock on them—no lock of any kind. Zach pulled the handle on one and, sure enough, it opened.

He stepped through into the foyer. He caught a glimpse of ruin. A shattered mosaic on the floor, lacerated walls, a lopsided balustrade rising with the stairs. Then the door swung shut behind him and the place went dark. Not full dark—there was gray light from the window of a gutted ground-floor apartment against the far wall—but dark enough, the shadows hanging like drapery. Zach smelled brick dust and emptiness and . . . something else. A heat at his nostrils. A whiff of something alive. Someone. . . .

He drew out his flashlight. Panned it from one wall of the foyer to the other. He moved behind the beam to the stairway and started up.

The treads moaned grievously as he made his ascent. He paused on the second landing. Moved the flashlight over the hallway from the far corner on his left to the near corner, just to his right. Everything was silent. No movement anywhere. Still that smell—the hot smell of life—had grown thicker as he climbed.

On the third landing, some unthinkable creature suddenly skittered across the floor, out ahead of his light. Not a rat—too jittery and insectile—but if it was a cockroach, Christ, he didn't want to think about the size of it. He was from Texas and he'd seen a toe-biter or two in his time, waterbugs the size of your forearm that would take a chunk right out of your foot given half a chance. He hadn't liked them on the prairie; the thought of something that size here, full of the filth of the city, roiled the waves in his stomach again.

Whatever it was, it was gone before he got the beam on it. Just as well. He didn't want to see it. He stood where he was and caught his breath and let his heart steady. Then he reached for the shattered orb of the newel post and was about to head up to the fourth floor, the floor where he'd seen that movement at the window.

But before he took a step, somebody screamed.

It was ugly—an ugly scream. A man's scream—the sound wrenched out of him as if someone had rammed a hand down his gullet and ripped it up out of his belly. A gurgling death scream.

Zach had his gun in his hand—his gun and flashlight in his two hands braced together—and was chasing the flashlight beam up the next flight before the sound faded away. He swung around the landing balustrade—saw the assassin waiting for him down the hall—a robed, hunched, monkish, rat-featured man with long greasy hair. Zach fired and dove and rolled behind the cover of the corner before the blast of the killer's giant pistol made the walls quake around him.

Plaster pattered to the floor. What the hell was that bastard shooting? A Dezzy, Zach figured: a gangster's Desert Island .50 cal.

Zach rose to one knee. He shouted, "Drop that heater, you son of a bitch! I'm a federal officer!"

No answer. Not even another shot. Zach pressed his body against the wall, whipped his gun-and-flashlight around the corner in front of him, and peeked out behind it. He caught a quick glimpse of the killer scuttling around the corner at the hall's opposite end, gone before he could get a shot off. He climbed to his feet and was about to go after the guy when another gunman—this one goateed, grinning, and satanic—broke through a doorway and fired another Dezzy cannon—*boom! boom!*—twice, running, shooting wild. Zach let out a strangled curse as he pulled back into cover—then immediately swung out around the corner again, gun and flashlight first, and squeezed the trigger. The jolt of the 9mm went up his arm and glass shattered somewhere, but this second killer had turned the corner too and gotten away.

Zach held the gun and flashlight steady, trained them on the open door. Edged down the hallway.

Suddenly, a black blast went through his mind, a quaking jolt of pure nothingness that filled his heart with terror. He thought: *What? What? What just happened?*

And Dominic Abend stepped out into the pale white of the flashlight's beam.

He was a looming presence in the gray light and gunsmoke: even taller and broader than he seemed in the photographs, his shaven head large and powerful, his eyes vital and flashing. He held a longsword, the hilt out from his side, the blade half lifted across his body, so that the line of the bright metal slashed the dark spill of his black overcoat.

"Drop the weapon, Abend!" shouted Zach, approaching him slow step by slow step. It was the excitement of the gunfight that made him shout, the confusion of that dark jolt he'd felt. "I want you alive, but I'll take you dead. Drop it."

Even in the shadows, he saw Abend smile—that thin, cruel, damp, and somehow ancient smile of his. He saw it just before he felt the pain—the excruciatingly deep burn—like being stabbed in the ankle with a blade of fire.

Zach looked down and saw the horror that had locked on to him—a tremendous cockroach—an insect at least a full foot long—its legs scrambling clackety-clack over his shoe as it twisted its beak into his flesh.

He shouted and, with an instinctive spasm, tried to kick it off him. As he did, he caught a glimpse of the other one on the wall, just as big—bigger!—right by his face. He glimpsed its searching mandibles—its weirdly human expression of gleeful hunger. Then, with a wet flutter of wings, it sprang at his eyes.

Zach reeled away, batting at the thing wildly so that the light from his flashlight jerked over Abend's grin—up over another bug on the wall, and another nearby it—and up over the ceiling where five or six more of the monsters had crawled out from under the chipped plaster trim.

The flying waterbug dropped to the floor beside the other, the one Zach had kicked away, and amidst two more that were scrabbling toward Zach's feet quickly. Zach staggered back away from them, his flashlight lifting over the corridor—and in its wavering beam, he saw them all.

There were dozens of them. Roaches and waterbugs of mind-boggling size—impossible, preternatural size. They were racing toward him over the walls. Swarming toward him across the floor. The hall was filled with their hungry chittering and with the eager skidding patter of their legs. His light went up and—oh God, they were above him too, on the ceiling. Even now, one dropped onto his shoulder. He knocked it off with the flashlight—and another dropped into his hair.

Zach let out a scream. Writhing, he had to put gun and flashlight in one hand so he could tear the clawing creature off his head with his fingers, drag its wriggling legs and searching beak out of the tangle of his hair. For a moment, he caught sight of its gleeful hungry human eyes staring into his. He felt its six legs clawing for purchase in his hand. Then, his gorge rising, he flung it down onto the floor—and saw that there were so many of them now! A swarming brown mass flowing toward him as one.

Afraid of Abend and his sword—the unseen swipe of steel across his throat—he sought the gangster in a panic, waving the flashlight beam all around him. Where the hell was the man? There! Right where he'd been. Grinning in amusement. Turning calmly now. Strolling quietly away, tapping the longsword's blade against his leg in an easy rhythm.

Teeth gritted, Zach made to chase after him. But the bugs crunched and exploded under his shoes, and he tripped on them and slid in their goo. Two more were climbing onto his pants legs. One took a lacerating bite of his calf that made him cry out. As he fought them off, he nearly toppled over, nearly went down—and the image that flashed through his mind—himself on the floor, the creatures swimming up over him, devouring him, tearing him apart—filled him with nausea and terror.

He saw the back of Abend's overcoat as the gangster vanished around the corner, but he had no chance of going after him now. All he could do was struggle to keep his balance. The floor, the walls, the ceiling—they were one great moving carpet of enormous roaches, swarming up him, falling on him, bent on bringing him down.

He had to get out of here. The door. He had to get to the door. Get into the apartment.

He let out a roar of fury and kicked a clutch of the giant, chiggering creatures out of his way. He stumbled forward, feeling waterbugs gathering in a rising pool at his feet, catching glimpses of them as they tumbled over one another to get their huge mandibles into him. He crushed one of them underfoot—his shoe sinking in yellow gunk— and he fell sideways against the wall so that the swarm there snapped at his face. One fell onto his neck, its quick feet scrabbling at his skin there. He gave another scream and knocked it off.

He reached the open door. Charged through it. Kicked it shut behind him, spinning into the room, pulling another squirming monster off his shoulder. The bug went skittering away out of sight, and Zach, in a full panic, desperately passed the flashlight beam over his body— and screamed out "Fuck!" as he saw one of the insects clinging to his thigh by its mandibles. He struck it with the butt of his gun. It would not let go. He struck it again, hard. It lost its grip, fell to the floor, and scurried away.

Gasping, Zach passed his hands over every part of himself, feeling for more of the insects. There were none. He began to gag, acid coming into his throat. Then, quickly, he realized his danger and stopped himself. He turned his flashlight on the room, here, there, scanning for any other killers. A man with a gun—or with a sword—any of Abend's thugs could already have killed him three times over. But no, there was nobody in sight. He was alone here.

His shoulders sagged. He staggered slowly out of what had once been the front hall into the main apartment. Bright light from the windows here showed a gutted wreck of a room. In that first moment, it seemed empty. But then, trying to steady himself, Zach drew a deep breath—and the thick, rich, coppery, overwhelming scent of violence washed into him. He knew full well what he was about to find.

Johnny Grimhouse. The thief was strung up naked, his wrists tied high to a beam in a broken wall, his bare heels scraping the ruined floor. With his body stretched out like that, his wounds showed plainly. He had been sliced to ribbons, mutilated head to toe. His mouth was gaping and his eyes were wide—he seemed to be horrified by the sight of the half dozen or so foot-long roaches that were feeding on him, like piglets nursing at their sow. But that expression on his face—it only *seemed* to be horror, Zach knew.

Grimhouse was beyond all mortal horror. He was clearly dead.

13

HAUNTED

Later that evening, six-thirty or so, Zach sat at his dinner table watching Grace coax a meal-time prayer out of little Ann: "Thank you, God, for our dinner." He thought they looked like angels from heaven, the two of them. Really. Grace, with her cheerful plump cheeks and bright faithful eyes framed by her honey ringlets, smiling across the table at the child. The child bowed over her clasped hands, making her earnest effort to shape the words that she could barely speak. The boy, too, Tom, with his head bowed and hands clasped too and his eyes closed: beautiful. So patient with his sister's efforts—though when it was his night to pray, Zach knew he would take such pride in showing her how it was done. Just look at them, he thought. And okay, he knew he was being mawkish. But all the same, there they were: the most mawkish greeting-card drawing of mother and children could not have done them justice, truly. He felt an aching hunger of love for all of them, almost an anguish of yearning, as if they were somehow beyond his reach: off in a sweet world of ideal and innocent goodness that he could only see far off from where he was, mired deep in the hellish images inside his mind.

"Very *good*, sweetheart," said Grace when the little girl's prayer was finished.

They began to pass the meatloaf around. The meatloaf and the mashed potatoes and the greens. Good food in great abundance, Zach thought sentimentally—and the very fact that Grace had made this meal for them, that she had stood in the kitchen and cooked it for them, wife-and-motherly, struck him just then as a thing of impossible beauty, impossibly beyond the dark country of his thoughts. There, out there, was the family dinner, bright and far away. And here, in here, was Abend grinning at him through the gray light and gunsmoke. The swarming roaches on the walls and floor. The chattering hum of them and the wriggling touch of them—especially that one that had gotten tangled in his hair. He couldn't forget the feel of that. And Johnny Grimhouse—he couldn't forget the sight. The bloody body; the gaping mouth; the eyes staring at the insects . . . like piglets . . . Christ!

Little Tom had been patient long enough. He wanted to tell Daddy about his day now. He wanted to tell about the autumn leaves his kindergarten class had collected and pressed into a book. Zach managed to make the appropriate noises, nods, and smiles. He did the best he could, but he always suspected that children, his children at least, could tell when their father was really listening and when he was merely going through the motions. Or maybe that was just his guilt talking. He would have given the world to be fully present for the boy, his son whom he loved. He longed to slog up to him out of the gut-muck of ugliness inside him. But he was stuck down there in the dark, in the memory of those long minutes before backup arrived, long minutes when he had been alone in the room with Grimhouse's mutilated corpse and with the smell of death and with the sounds, the awful sounds of those insects feeding on him.

It wasn't just the gruesomeness of those minutes that held him. It was also their morbid mysteries. How had he known the things he knew, standing there? Sure, his senses were heightened—he'd always had that ability to go into what Goulart called hyper-focus mode, that elevated level of perception that helped him spot things in a crime scene other investigators missed. But just how heightened could his senses be? How could he smell the fading aroma of Johnny's *helpless* agony—and understand that it was helpless agony because Grimhouse hadn't known what Abend wanted him to tell? How could he not only smell Abend's frustration at being interrupted mid-torture, but *remember* that smell, match it to the smell of frustration he had picked up in the storage bin? Abend hadn't found what he wanted here either—Zach knew that. And he knew that Abend had been in such a hurry to get out without being seen that he had left a fingerprint on the doorknob. Zach would tell the Crime Scene Unit to search for it and they would find it sure enough. But how did he know? It wasn't normal. Nothing was normal about him anymore—he was different— he had been different ever since he'd come back from Germany, ever since he'd awoken from his fever.

"Did you collect leaves when you were in school, Daddy?"

Zach caught the questioning tone just in time, and went back through his mind until he could remember what the boy had asked him. "I did," he said. "I remember doing just that thing. We glued them in a big book with colored pages."

"That's what I'm going to do," said Tom. "Mommy, can we get colored pages so I can glue the leaves too?"

And while she answered him, Zach returned compulsively to his memories like an addict to his drug. He remembered the roaches on Grimhouse's body fleeing as backup arrived, clattering away into the broken wall as the door burst open and the uniforms charged in. The roaches were gone from the hallway too; that whole sea of them had receded, and there was no sign of them anywhere. No trace that they had ever been there except for the bites on his calf and ankle, the only bites that had really broken through the skin. He had gotten one of the EMS guys to disinfect them for him.

What the hell did that?

Some sort of gigantic cockroach or something.

These buildings, man. The stuff that comes out of them. I swear, there's things been growing in the walls here since dinosaurs walked the earth.

Maybe so. But that didn't explain the way they'd attacked him, the way they'd poured out of their secret places, scrambling toward him, scrambling in his direction only, while Abend walked calmly away. It was as if the bugs were acting in service to the gangster's will, as if they were instruments of his malice. Zach knew that could not have been true, and so he felt it must not have been true, that he must have imagined it. And yet, though he kept going over and over it in his mind, he couldn't bring his memories into line with the requirements of reality. He told himself it might have had something to do with his fever, might have been an aftereffect of that wave of fever that had hit him on the bridge. But he wasn't convinced. He had seen what he'd seen—it was no illusion. And if the bugs had been real—if the malice of their attack had been real—what else was real that couldn't be, what else was real that he had chalked up to the fever? What about that impossible executioner standing on the bridge? What about that meeting with Gretchen Dankl in the clearing in the woods? He had let that memory slip away as dreams slip away, but if the attack of the roaches in the hall was real. . . . What the hell? What the hell was going on?

When he put his boy to bed, Zach lay down beside him. He read him *The Cat in the Hat* while Tom snuggled up on his chest. Even when the book was done, Zach continued to lie there with his arm around his son. He knew the boy was breathing him in, whether the boy himself knew it or not. Zach's own father had died when he was only eight. A Green Beret missing behind enemy lines in Afghanistan—Zach could never learn much more. He still remembered the smell of the man when he would tuck him in at night. You got to get the smell of your father in you when you're little, he thought, lying there until the boy was snoring softly. It's what makes your spine grow strong.

He found his wife, as usual after the children's bedtime, washing the dishes at the kitchen sink. He came up behind her and put his arms around her and held her close.

"Oh my," she said, leaning back against him.

"Oh my," Zach breathed into her ear.

She turned around in the circle of his embrace. She reached up to touch his cheek with her wet fingers. "I heard on the radio they found a body that might be connected to the Paz murders. They're saying it's some kind of gang war or something. Were you part of that?"

"I found the body."

She studied his face, concerned. She was already worried about him, back at work so soon after his fever.

"I thought you seemed kind of far away tonight," she said. "Well, you sit down now and tell me all about it."

It was the last thing he wanted to do. He didn't even want to *think* about it anymore, though he knew he couldn't stop—and he definitely didn't want to talk about it. It was too much effort, and there was too much he would have to leave out. The roaches—he couldn't tell Grace about that, could he? She'd think he was hallucinating. She'd insist on his going back to the doctors. And he wasn't going to end their evening with a description of Grimhouse either, the body hanging from that beam with the creatures crawling on him.

But this was their arrangement—that he would tell her about his job—so he sat at the kitchen counter with a bottle of beer and said what he could. He told her about the thugs blasting away at him with their cannon-like Dezzies and about his confrontation with Abend.

"He was right there in front of me," Zach said. "That close, but . . ." he added, vaguely, "I was pinned down and couldn't go after him."

As quickly as he could, he got to the part about his confrontation with Goulart in the aftermath. That was good gossip—a woman would like that, he figured. It would distract her from the inexplicable strangeness he'd carefully omitted from the rest of his story.

"Broadway was sorely P.O.'d I hadn't brought him with me. I can't rightly blame him. He was sticking his finger in my chest. Whisper-yelling, you know, so the NYPD detectives wouldn't hear us going at it. 'Why didn't you call me? What did you think you were doing coming out here alone?' I told him I thought it was a bum lead and I didn't want to waste his time. Pretty lame excuse. I never even called him."

"Well, it's just not right of Rebecca to put you in that position," Grace said. "You can't work with a partner you don't trust."

"I know it."

"She's just trying to enlist you against him, because she hasn't got the courage to stand up to him on her own and she knows everyone respects you. That's weak leadership." She plunked a glass in the dishwasher with an extra fillip of indignation. "If those gangsters had blown your head off, it would have been partly her fault for making you feel like you had to go there with no backup 'cause you couldn't trust Martin."

"No, it was my fault. It was a dumb play."

"Well, now that she *has* put you in that position, you're gonna have to decide one way or the other. Either y'all can trust him or not, either he's your partner or not. You can't go on like this, baby, you'll get yourself killed. Stupid woman!" she finished, meaning Rebecca Abraham-Hartwell.

Zach tilted the beer bottle to his lips and let a taste of the foam touch his tongue, but really he was watching her over the top of the brown glass. It suddenly occurred to him that she was upset about the gunfire, about the thugs blasting at him. Well, of course she was! It went to show how little insight he had into her inner life, that even an idiotically obvious thought like that struck him with the force of revelation. Sure, he knew a cop's wife worries all the time and has to be strong and so on—he knew it theoretically. But most of the time he didn't see it realistically. He didn't think about it from her side, didn't think about the effort involved, or the actual anxiety she must feel. Grace was always so cheerful and gentle and good-tempered that it didn't often occur to him that she might have to struggle to be that way, to fight down her worry and her flashes of temper. He imagined her praying over it. He assumed she did, but now for a moment he actually imagined her on her knees ardently begging God to give her the strength and patience she needed to do her job as his wife. It occurred to him that if she did pray like that, she never told him about it. She never even mentioned it.

"What do *you* think?" he asked her, letting his bottle hand sink down to the counter.

She was using the faucet hose to wash scraps down into the garbage disposal. She was watching the swirl of the water fiercely, intensely—probably focusing on that so he wouldn't see how upset she was about the gunplay.

"What do you mean?" she asked him. "What do I think about Martin? I think Rebecca ought to get herself some proof before she goes on ahead and opens her big mouth."

Zach nodded slowly. "But do *you* think he could've gone bad?"

She watched her own hand—fiercely, intensely—as she waggled the hose back into its hole. When she was done, she plucked her hair from her mouth with her fingers and blew it from her eyes, giving her something else to do besides meet his gaze.

"Well, baby, I don't want to make things any worse for you," she said.

"But you think he might've, then."

"Well . . . I think he *might've*," she said. And when he flinched, she said, "Oh, baby, I know how much you like Martin. . . ."

"Well, he's saved my life more than once, Grace."

"And God bless him for that, for sure. For sure. And I know how you like how he says all those rude things other people won't say. . . ."

"Well, it brings out the ugly truth sometimes, that's all."

"I know it does. I know. And a man doesn't like to be told what he can and can't talk about, like he's in church all the time. It goes against his natural grain. But . . ." She searched for the words. ". . . I mean, anyone can say a true thing by being mean on people. Can't they? We're all sinners, after all."

"We are. That's for certain. Still. . . ."

"I know," she said. "I know. And I don't mean to talk Martin down. It's just. . . ."

"What, then?"

"Well, baby, you got a goodness in you he doesn't have. No, it's true, anyone can see it," she said, in answer to the look on his face— because he was grimacing at the memory of that night he'd betrayed her with Margo, he was thinking he had no goodness in him at all. "You got a—integrity in you he doesn't. Probably 'cause your mama put The Word in you."

"Oh, there's plenty of fine folks without religion, Gracie, you know that."

"I know," she said, though she didn't sound convinced.

"You've always been judgmental on Broadway 'cause of his women and the divorce, and all that."

"It's not that. . . ."

"That's just his way, that's all. He's suffered for it, Lord knows."

"It's not that," she insisted. "It's just. . . . Well, there comes a time in a person's life when doing wrong just makes perfect sense to him. And if he hasn't got . . . well, *something* in him—" He knew she was going to say *The Word* but had amended it to suit his more broad-minded view. "If he hasn't got *something* in him that makes him say 'Well, I don't care what sense it makes, I'm not doing wrong anyhow,' then that's when the Enemy can make his move on him."

"And you're saying that's happened to Broadway—"

"No. I'm just saying it could've. It might've. It wouldn't . . . you know, shock me if it had."

Zach had an awful nightmare that night. He couldn't remember it later, not all of it, but it had something to do with one of those war documentaries he liked to watch on television sometimes—only, in the dream, he was inside the documentary, walking through its black-and-white scenes. He was in one of the Nazi death camps—he remembered that. There was a bulldozer pushing through a pile of corpses—so many corpses—hundreds and hundreds of marble-gray bodies. They were drained of all color and spirit, but their eyes were still open, their stares lifeless yet somehow accusatory. It was as if they were watching him as he watched them being collected by the 'dozer in ghastly piles of murdered flesh. The stench of offal and rot was overwhelming.

Dominic Abend was not in the scene himself, but Zach sensed him there—sensed in that horrible nightmare way that if he turned around, the killer would be standing right behind him, wearing his Nazi uniform and grinning in amusement as he'd grinned in the hallway just that afternoon. Zach was afraid of that grin—that's what the dream was about, he realized later. He was so afraid of the mind behind that grin, and the black world inside that mind, that the fear threatened to unman him. He had sensed that black world for a moment in the hallway. He had felt the jolt of its utter emptiness just before Abend had stepped into view. It was a world, it was a mind, in which conscience was the discarded custom of lesser men, in which cutting a child's throat and nursing a baby were of equal value, depending on what you felt like or who got the benefit. It was terrifying to him.

In the dream, Zach struggled against the compulsion to turn and face the gangster—and so he went on watching the hundreds of bodies being bulldozed—and that's how he came to focus on one pair of eyes among all those staring corpse-witnesses—a young woman's eyes—staring directly back at him—until she blinked!

Sweet Jesus, she's still alive!

Whereupon he woke, with a little gasp, his heart hammering.

He lay on his back, taking steady breaths to calm himself—and, as he did, a tendril of that death-camp stench wafted into his nostrils.

He sat up hard, searching the darkness, the thudding flutter of his pulse loud in his ears. But he was in his bedroom, just in his bedroom, and the smell was dissipating with the dream. Relieved, he was about to lie back down.

Then he saw something—someone—in the shadows.

A figure was sitting in the armchair in the far corner by the dark window, a frail, childlike figure, slumped in a posture of defeat. Zach glanced over at Grace, to make sure she was still in bed with him and, yes, there she was, curled on her side right by him, turned away, breathing lightly.

And the figure was still there in the chair. A woman, he saw now as his eyes adjusted to the dark. The death smell coming off her was faint but unmistakable. She lifted her hand. She lit a match, making Zach recoil from the glare. She held the flame to the cigarette bobbing between her lips. Her face in the orange match-light was more horrible than anything Zach had ever seen, because she was so obviously dead and yet alive.

In the low, heavy German accent he remembered, she said, "It's history, Agent Adams. History is in your blood now, and the sins of history. All your American ignorance can't save you. You do not have to remember to know." Then she waved out the match and her features sank back into the shadows.

"What?" murmured Grace. She rolled over to face him, lifting her head. "You say something, baby?" And before he could tell her *no*, before he could tell her *go back to sleep*, she rose up farther, propping her elbow on the mattress, and said, "I smell smoke."

Staring at the figure in the chair in the corner, Zach reached out blindly for the bedside lamp. He turned it on.

The chair was empty. The figure was gone.

"Do you smell cigarette smoke?" said Grace.

He placed his hand on her hair, her curls soft and springy beneath his palm. "It's all right. Go back to sleep."

"What's going on?" Her eyes were open, but she settled back down under his touch.

"I think someone just passed by outside smoking, that's all. I smelled it too."

"Are the kids all right?"

"They're fine. I'll go check on them. Go back to sleep."

She didn't, of course, not until he came back from the children's bedrooms and reported, "They're fine."

She was sitting up in bed now, blinking in the light from the lamp. "Something still smells in here," she said to him.

"I'll open a window."

"What is that? It smells like something's rotten."

"It does, doesn't it?" He was at the window. As he pushed it up, he glanced over at the chair in the corner. From here, he could see the slight indentation on the floral seat cushion, as if someone had just been sitting there. His pulse was still racing, and the dreadful sight of Gretchen Dankl's face in the match-light still haunted him, making him faintly nauseous. From here, he could tell that the smell—the smell of the death camp—was plainly coming from the chair. Then the cool, fresh autumn night air blew in through the screen and swept it away.

"You think something went bad in the fridge?" said Grace.

He paused, breathing through his nose, testing the atmosphere. Then he shook his head. "No. It's gone now. It's all right."

But his pulse was still racing, and he was sick with knowing what he was only just beginning to know.

14

THE GUYLAND HEISTS

Three days later, shoulder to shoulder, Zach and Goulart pushed out through the doors of the one-six precinct, and Goulart asked "Is that her over there? Is that your Margo Heatherton?" Zach couldn't stop himself: his head jerked up and his mouth opened and his eyes widened as he followed his partner's gesture. But then he said, "No. No. I don't know who that is."

"She sure had her eyes on us. And look at her take off."

The woman had, in fact, been watching them from beside the entrance to the parking garage across the street—and she was, in fact, hurrying away now that Goulart had spotted her. But Zach was telling the truth: he didn't know her—though he did have the vague sense that he had seen her somewhere before. It definitely wasn't Margo, anyway. This was a slender, pretty, bird-like woman in her twenties with short black hair and a turned-up nose—nothing like the blond and glamorous Margo. Plus she was wearing a belted purple woolen thing over a pair of jeans, the sort of tatty stuff even Zach knew you bought off the rack in some department store. Not something Margo would ever wear.

"You sure that wasn't your girlfriend?" asked Goulart. He gave Zach an insinuating look over the top of the Crown Vic just before he lowered himself into the passenger seat.

Zach rolled his eyes at him and got in behind the wheel.

"Just wondering," said Goulart. "Now that we're keeping secrets and all. . . ."

"We're not keeping secrets, Broadway. Damn, man!" Zach made a show of shaking his head and sighing loudly as he put the car into gear and headed into the morning traffic. Goulart was still giving him hell over going to Long Island City without him, without even calling him. They'd been busy writing reports and making phone calls for two days and hadn't really had the chance to work the bad feelings out between them. As Zach guided the car among the weaving yellow cabs on Second Avenue, he said, "I made a mistake not calling you. I told you that. I already told you I made a mistake. I've been sick, all right? Maybe I wasn't thinking clearly."

Goulart was turned away from him, though, looking out the window, tapping one fingertip against his knee, something on his mind, still eating at him. He didn't say anything until they were on 42nd Street, going by the rising silver slab of the United Nations, the gray-blue sky reflecting off its mirrored windows. All he said even then was, "You hear about that guy in England got assassinated?"

"It was on the news this morning as I was coming in. Some anti-immigrant politician or something?"

Goulart shook his head. "Bunch of savages. They just gun him down, cut his throat while he's lying there. And now the lunatic lefties are saying it served him right 'cause he was a fascist. And what's worse, he *was* a fascist! And now his guys are on the streets with torches practically, looking for any poor schmuck of an immigrant who happens to be walking by. First France, now this. You mark my words: they're finished over there. The whole continent is going down the drain—and we're next, if we're not careful."

The car dipped into the Midtown Tunnel. The underground whoosh and rumble made them both fall silent again. The grimy yellow walls went rushing past. Goulart's words had gotten Zach's mind working. He was trying not to think about the specter on his bedroom chair, trying not to consider the possibility that his meeting in the woods with Gretchen Dankl had actually happened, had not been a fever dream.

She is gone. My country . . . my continent . . . my culture.

You mark my words: they're finished over there. The whole continent is going down the drain—and we're next, if we're not careful.

They broke out of the tunnel's end into the grayish light of day, and Goulart rounded on him and said, "She thinks I'm on the take, doesn't she? Rebecca. Abraham-Hartwell. Is that what she thinks? That bitch. She does, doesn't she?"

Zach had not been expecting this at all, but Goulart had such a great detective mind, it actually didn't startle him much. He decided on the spot he wasn't going to lie about it, not to his partner, not for Rebecca Abraham-Hartwell.

He nodded. He said, "She does."

"She got you spying on me?"

"She's on your phone, your computer. Says you've been calling burners—"

"Big surprise. I got CI's—"

"And setting up e-mail drops. And—what else—oh, yeah, visiting some deserted mansion somewhere in the dead of night."

"Jesus." Goulart shook his head, disgusted. "She show you anything? She got anything? Anything real?"

"Circumstantial stuff," said Zach. He kept his eyes on the highway, on the gigantic movie-star faces smiling from the billboards, the ashen expanse of the factory flatlands beyond. "She says the *Chevalier* was tipped off that the Coast Guard was coming for them, that they killed Abend's girls and dumped them overboard because they got a tip."

"Oh, and she thinks *I* did that? I tipped them?"

"And she's . . . concerned, you know, about the way Abend stays ahead of us. The warehouse. The storage bin. The Brothers Grimhouse."

"So you went out to Queens without calling me," Goulart sneered. "So I wouldn't tip him off."

"Fatboy Mooch told me Abend's got half the force on his payroll. I thought if there was any chance you'd gone rotten, I better go it alone."

"You think that lowlife Kraut piece of shit has enough money to buy me with? Fuck you too. Partner."

"Yeah. I deserve that," Zach said flatly. "I let Rebecca get in my head."

"The bitch." Goulart frowned out the window, but he nodded to himself at Zach's apology. You had to say this: the Cowboy was a straight-up guy and everyone knew it. He made mistakes like everybody, but he was a man about it and never dodged the consequences. After he'd had a few minutes to chew on it, Goulart made an offering. "Your head's probably all messed up over that Margo Heatherton piece blackmailing you or whatever she's doing," he said.

Zach laughed. Goulart. "That's probably it."

Goulart laughed too. Nodded out the window some more. Tapped his knee with his fingertip some more. Then he said "I'm sick, Cowboy."

Zach glanced over at him. "What do you mean?" But he could tell by the look on his face exactly what Goulart meant. "You mean like sick-sick?"

"Might be." Goulart let out a long sigh. "That's why the e-mail drops. Been communicating with my doctors that way. Even staying clear of the 'Feeb' plan till I'm sure. You just never know who's listening in. As we see. And I didn't want anyone telling me I had to stand down, that I wasn't up to the job, whatever."

Zach took his time finding the right tone to answer with. Not pity—Goulart would hate pity. They were both men, and death was death. "It's bad then," he said.

"Might be, might be. They just don't know yet. They're doing, you know, tests."

"How bad? Might it be."

"Bad like you might as well drop me off right here."

They were driving past a vast cemetery, endless crowds of graves, stones and steles rising—when Zach glanced up at them in the sideview mirror—rising against the backdrop of the Manhattan skyline, so that they seemed a small, visual echo of the city towers—as if the vaunting monuments of the living were reflected by the dwindled markers of the dead.

"Man!" Zach said. "Man. I'm sorry, partner."

"Eh."

"I'll pray for you. I'll get Grace to pray, better yet. God's more likely to listen to Grace."

"Well . . ." said Goulart, shrugging it off. "Just figured you should know, at this point. Where all that circumstantial crap is coming from. All the skullduggery on my end. That's why."

Zach nodded, his lips in a tight frown. He wished now he'd told Rebecca Abraham-Hartwell to go to hell.

They drove on in silence.

They had a list of homes that had been hit in the Grimhouses' Guyland Heists. Thirteen of them, from garish mansions in Kings Point to grand old estates way out beyond the Hamptons. They had no clue what they were hoping to find in any of them, so it seemed a waste of time to phone. But they thought: maybe if they went out there, talked to the homeowners, saw the crime scenes with their own eyes . . . well, maybe something stinking of Abend would jump out at them.

Anyway, it was the best lead they had at this point. The Frenzies—the forensic teams—were still combing the Grimhouse murder sites for clues. They had what was left of both brothers and were dissecting and weighing and pondering the scraps. Other Task Force Zero agents were out canvassing underworld informers. In the wake of Zach's face-to-face with Abend in Long Island City, there was excitement in the shop, an unspoken hope that for the first time, they had their all-but-invisible quarry in sight.

And yet . . . yet for all that, there was an underlying sense throughout Extraordinary Crimes that they had hit—if not a dead end, then a dark alley with a brick wall waiting in its shadows. Suddenly they were hearing silence on the streets, an epidemic of silence. The sort of thing a lawman sensed but couldn't prove. No one knew anything. No one said a word. Which was the sort of crap that didn't actually happen too much anymore, not at the upper reaches of corruption at least, not since wiretaps and conspiracy laws had broken through *omerta*, the code of silence that used to keep gangsters mum. Nowadays, much of the time, thugs had no honor and everybody talked.

But Dominic Abend was no ordinary thug. In fact, it was beginning to seem he was not even a gang-leader, not in the usual style. There seemed no center to his organization. No headquarters, no crew, no specific turf. Rats and rivals never knew which shoulder to look over to spot the threat. He was like a flu-bug or a heat wave or maybe like an idea whose time had come—one day it was business as usual, and the next day he was the air you breathed and you were dead of him. No one wanted to talk about him, not even in general, not even in theory. Even Fatboy Mooch, who would talk about anything, had reached his limit and was nowhere to be found.

But if Abend was in fact searching for something that had been ripped off by the Grimhouses in one of the Guyland Heists, then it stood to reason one of the houses hit in the heists was his or was connected to him. So Zach and Goulart were heading out to the Island in the hope of escaping the Abend Fever of shut-uppery that seemed to have struck the five boroughs and their under-city.

They interviewed homeowners and housewives.

They asked: "What was the most valuable thing you lost in the robberies?"

"Well, as I already told the other detectives. . . ."

They casually examined the mansions as the owners spoke, looking for telltale signs of their man.

"Was there anything special about the jewelry that was taken—any heirlooms, anything with a history?"

"My mother's necklace. She bought it on her honeymoon. . . ."

They searched for anything German, anything European, anything just out-of-place.

"Did you happen to own a dagger of any kind, or a ceremonial sword?" Zach asked at each location.

"No . . . no . . . nothing like that."

"Would you look at this picture? The bald man at the edge of the crowd—he look familiar to you at all?"

"Never seen him."

This went on for more than a week. The travel was what slowed them down. The first four houses took them all the way out to Huntington, at which point they had to head back. Then there was the day NYPD uncovered a couple of storage units owned by the Grimhouses. They'd already been ransacked, of course—the brothers would have given up everything under Abend's torture.

And then there was the weekend before they could go out to the Island again.

Mostly, the entire enterprise felt like a big fat waste of time; but there was one house—all the way out near Westhampton Beach—one of the last houses they went to—where Zach, at least, felt as if they had touched on something, though he wasn't sure what.

The place was a three-story shingled mansion, right on the water. The sort of house that had a name. Its name was Sea View. You approached it by a driveway lined with perfectly manicured, perfectly spaced cypress trees—until you reached a fountain in a circle of flowers on the rolling lawn. There was a curtain of black oaks protecting the long, gabled façade. The curtain opened in the middle to reveal the white portico before the front door.

"How much you think a place like this would set you back?" said Goulart as they stepped out of the Crown Vic—both of them sorely aware of how paltry the junker looked parked beside the silver-blue Bentley in the raked, pristine gravel of the cul-de-sac.

"Twenty-five, thirty million," Zach guessed. "How the hell should I know?" It was the sort of conversation they'd been having for days so as to avoid talking about the results of Goulart's medical tests, none definitive yet, but each so far more ominous than the last.

Shoulder to shoulder, they walked to the door, their shoes crunching on the gravel.

Sea View was the home of one Angela Bose—the first name pronounced with a hard G, the way the Germans do it, which right there had both detectives on the alert. According to newspaper reports of the burglary, Miss Bose was an eccentric and reclusive young beauty, already at twenty-seven a leading donor to local charities, who single-handedly supported many of the homeless shelters and rehab centers between Montauk and Queens. The local gossip was that she had retired from the wayward party-days of her teens about a year and a half ago. Chastened by suffering, she had come here to live with her father, a European businessman, likewise reclusive. But when Zach called her on the phone, she told him "Come out anytime, I'm here all alone."

"She had a slight accent—could've been German," he told Goulart—and again, alert, they exchanged glances.

125

A maid answered the mansion door—a pretty Spanish girl in a black maid uniform with a frilly white collar and apron. She told them she would fetch Miss Bose and left them in the foyer.

"You think her boyfriend spanks her in that uniform?" Goulart asked as he watched her go.

Zach cracked up. "Would you shut up, Broadway. God Awmighty."

"Look at this place."

Zach did. They'd seen a lot of fine houses these last few days, but this had to be one of the finest. No flash, just clean elegance. Persian rugs over parquet floors with walnut inlay. A straight-through view from the foyer to the tumultuous surf visible through the picture windows in the grand back room. A switchback staircase with a white balustrade and a walnut banister going up to one balcony and then another. Gold designs painted straight into the white, white walls.

It sure is purty, Zach was about to drawl aloud, but before he could get the words out, he caught a whiff of something—something dark, fulsome; offensively organic. The word *blood* went through his mind, and he thought of a great red, thick, rancid pool of blood, before he shook the word and the image off and told himself to stop this crazy nonsense—whereupon Angela Bose appeared from around a corner and said "Welcome, Detectives. Come this way please."

Was this another symptom of his fever: this maddening patina of the uncanny that lay over ordinary things? Moment to moment, Zach was not sure whether Angela Bose was one of the most beautiful glamour-queens he'd ever laid eyes on, or the product of some sort of artifice—makeup or plastic surgery or something—disguising a face and figure that would otherwise have appeared withered and unpleasantly overripe. She seemed to change even as he looked at her—which could've been a trick of the beach-light pouring through the wall of windows in the back room, catching her at different angles as she turned gracefully from one of them to the other. Or maybe, even at twenty-seven, she had simply reached that precise second when a woman's perfect youth trembles on the brink of ending. . . .

Or maybe he was just going loony.

Whatever it was, Zach got the idea in his head that, despite the strong and chiseled and regal features beneath her shoulder-length auburn hair, and despite the sleek figure in her white blouse and white slacks, Angela Bose was secretly a shriveled cadaver that had somehow been inflated to a semblance of vitality and loveliness as a tick is bloated with blood. He kept catching the aroma of blood in the room. And the aroma of corruption.

The maid placed a tray of coffee and china on the low table set among the cushioned wicker chairs, but Angela Bose poured for them herself. She spoke without condescension or self-consciousness, but Zach could see that her manners were elegant and ladylike as if she were, as he put it to himself, highborn.

"Could you tell us if the thieves took anything really valuable?" he asked her.

"There was a gold brooch that I was quite fond of, handed down from my great-great-grandmother," she said. "Of tremendous senti-mental value, though the insurers only assessed it at eight or nine thousand dollars. And they stole a drawing by Bosch that I do believe is worth something. I suspect they made off with that by accident, though, because they took a lot of worthless prints and watercolors besides—probably for the frames."

"Excuse me asking, but what sort of accent is that you have, ma'am? Is that German?" Zach said. He sipped his coffee from a cup decorated with roses.

"Dutch, actually. My family has been in the Netherlands for some four hundred years. What about your accent, Agent?"

"West Texas. My grandpappy was a moonshiner and that's all I know."

She smiled graciously—though damned if there wasn't something skullish and awful about it too. Or was this just more creepy stuff from his imagination?

"You ever hear of a fellow named Dominic Abend?" said Goulart, leaning forward with his elbows on his knees.

"No. No, Agent, I don't believe so."

Goulart unfolded the photo from his jacket pocket and showed it to her. She looked it over—and Zach could have sworn she recognized it, but at this point he didn't trust his own instincts.

"No," she said. "It is not a very good picture, of course. But I don't think I've ever seen this man."

Outside, on the beach through the picture window, a green wave rose against the blue sky and crashed down upon the yellow sand.

The white froth of the surf seemed to be reflected by the thin white clouds above.

"You live here with your father?" said Zach.

"No. Pa-pa lives in Amsterdam. He visits me from time to time, and the house is in his name."

"Which is?"

"His name? Herman Bose. Von Bose, actually, but he doesn't like the aristocratic pretension. He owns a shipping company. I'm curious why you should ask."

Zach gestured with his coffee cup. "This Dominic Abend we're looking for is German. I'm just casting around for any possible connections."

"Of course." She smiled again—politely this time—and her bright blue eyes went up and down him. It was not a mere sexual appraisal, he thought. She seemed to be taking his full measure. When she was done, she inclined her chin slightly as if to say she knew him now, she knew who he really was, deep down.

"There wasn't any kind of weapon stolen, was there?" he asked her. "A dagger. A sword. Something like that."

Her eyes were still lingering on his face so that when she lied—and Zach felt sure she was lying, sure enough that his heart raced—he thought he could see a look of irony in them. She seemed to be sending him a message that went something like, *Forgive me, but now I must lie to you, even though we both know I am lying. It is simply what must be done.*

"No," she said aloud. "There was nothing like that. I *have* given a full inventory of what was stolen to the local police, you know. I'm sure they would happily share it with you."

Driving back into the city, Zach spoke only after the Crown Vic was on the expressway, only when he felt he had put some distance between the rear fender and Sea View, as if he was afraid Angela Bose would overhear him.

"You get the feeling she was lying?"

Goulart rounded on him in surprise. "No! Did you? I thought she was being totally straight with us."

"Really?"

"Well, yeah. I mean, the whole accent and everything had me on the lookout, but there's a lot of these European types out here. Especially recently, with all of them escaping from the apocalypse and so on."

"I thought I saw something in her eyes when she looked at Abend's picture. Like she recognized him."

Goulart shrugged and shook his head: he hadn't spotted it.

Which bothered Zach. Because Goulart was such a mind reader. And he, Zach, had thought it was so obvious. But then he'd also thought he smelled blood and corruption. He also thought he'd been attacked by malicious giant cockroaches and that he was being haunted by a German college professor. . . . So, yeah, maybe Angela Bose *was* lying and maybe Goulart was on the take and covering up for her, or maybe Goulart was just not at his observational best because he was distracted by his medical problems, or maybe Goulart was lying about his medical problems too. . . . Or maybe Zach was just going out of his ever-loving mind. Hard to say at this point which scenario was more likely to be true.

"Can I ask you something?" he said after another while.

Goulart grunted. "Sure."

"Not sure how to put this exactly, but . . . all you been going through? The medical stuff and all."

"Yeah?"

"You ever give any thought to the big picture? God and the supernatural and like that."

"You're not gonna preach to me, are you, Cowboy?"

"No, no, not at all, I'm just . . . curious, I guess."

He heard Goulart take a deep breath in and out through his nose. "Well. . . . Who the hell wouldn't give it some thought, right? In my position. The way I see it: sure, maybe there's a god, and maybe not. But maybe the thing is: it doesn't make any difference. You ever think of that? I mean, maybe there's a god and this is all just his train set or something. Maybe we're like a TV show he watches in his spare time. Because he likes the sex scenes and the car chases. 'Nuclear war? Yeah, that was cool. Great special effects. Wonder what else is on.'"

"Well, what about . . . ?" Zach stopped.

"What? No, go ahead. This is good. We're sharing. It's like we're partners. Gives me a warm glow. Kiss me, you beautiful son of a bitch."

Zach gave a crooked smile, but he pushed on too. "Well, to be honest, I was thinking about the practical side of it. You think there could be . . . supernatural stuff? Here on Earth, I mean. Evil stuff.

Or even supernatural good stuff. I mean, Grace, she's always talking about miracles and God's will and the Enemy's schemes and all that. Angels. Demons." He eye-checked Goulart to see if he would laugh at that, but he only gave a small snort. "I know, but she really believes in it. My mama did too. And they weren't stupid, either of them. I mean, sure, women, you know, are crazy and all that, but they're not always wrong about things. And Grace—well, she knows people. She understands the world, in some ways. In some ways better than I do. She gets a lot of stuff right."

"Hey," said Goulart in a broad-minded tone—because you never disrespected your partner's wife, and he'd always liked Grace, all the guys did. "It's as good a way of describing things as any. There may not *really* be a devil, but the world behaves exactly as if there was. So if you believe in that stuff—yeah, you'll never go far wrong."

Zach grunted thoughtfully in response, but in fact the answer wasn't much help to him. Was it possible there were ghosts and magic daggers and marauding cockroaches, or not? That's what he wanted to know.

The sun went down beyond the windshield, and the blue of the sky began to deepen. The expressway street lights came on, and so did the oncoming headlights, and so did the diamond-like gleams of house windows that were splayed to the left and right of them in the Island towns.

"The thing is," said Goulart, "when you look into the abyss. . . . 'Cause that's why you're asking me this shit, right? 'Cause let's face it, I'm looking smack dab into the abyss."

Zach answered with a gesture so he wouldn't have to lie—because, of course, that wasn't why he was asking at all.

Goulart went on: "All I can tell you, pard, is that from where I'm standing? The abyss is awful abyssy. You know? Awful dark. And in all that dark, who the fuck knows? Right? Could be angels and demons playing checkers with our souls. Could be dirt and nothing all the way down."

"What the hell is taking them so long with those tests of yours?" Zach blurted out, because he really did care about the New Yorker and wanted him to know it.

"Ah!" said Goulart and he waved the question away.

Once again Zach had to push down the thought that his partner was hiding something. Or that he knew more than he was telling. Or that the whole sickness story was a deception. Because if any of that was true—if any of his instincts and paranoid suspicions and weird feverish perceptions were accurate—then what about the rest of it? Those giant cockroaches? The executioner standing on the bridge? The corpse smoking a cigarette in his bedroom chair? And that night—in Germany—in the Black Forest. . . .

He had to be crazy, had to be. His mind had to be messed up by fever. There was no other reasonable explanation. But then how the hell was he supposed to be a cop—how the hell was he supposed to be a human being—if he could no longer trust his own observations? If he no longer knew what was real and what was madness?

It was full night when they parked in one of the angled spaces outside the one-six. Shoulder to shoulder, the two detectives walked wearily across the street and up the three concrete steps to the precinct's front doors. Goulart pulled one of the doors open and went through first—and Zach caught the edge of the door with his hand and was about to follow when he felt someone's eyes on him.

He paused. He turned, the door still in his hand. He saw that woman again—the woman they had spotted watching them days ago, the slender pretty girl with short black hair, wearing her belted purple sweater. She was back. Watching them again—watching Zach, anyway—from just down the sidewalk now, only a couple of dozen yards away.

She didn't hurry off this time. She went on standing there, a little outside the glow of a street lamp. She went on staring at Zach, so that Zach realized she had meant for him to feel it, that she had been beckoning him silently.

Zach called into the building after Goulart, "I'll catch up to you," and let the door swing shut. He walked back down the steps and headed toward the woman.

She waited for him to reach her. She stood with her hands in her belted purple sweater-thing, her shoulders hunched, her chin tucked in. Maybe she was simply huddling against the cool of the autumn night, but Zach thought she looked nervous too. He felt a little nervous himself, come to think of it. He had that sense again—that sense he had had earlier—that he had seen this woman somewhere before, and that it mattered.

He stepped up to her and before he could say anything, she said, "It's odd that we can do that, isn't it? Feel someone staring at us. Scientists say it's just a superstition but . . . I find it really quite odd." She had a clear, bell-like voice and a distinct British accent.

"You wanted to speak to me?" Zach said.

"You are Mr. Adams? Mr. Zach Adams?"

"Agent Adams—I am, yes," Zach said. "And you are?"

"Forgive me—Agent, of course. My name is Imogen Storm. I'm a journalist. I work for a website called *Bizarre!* It's important that I speak with you."

"*Bizarre!*" Zach repeated, deadpan. He did not know whether to be amused or alarmed. "What do you want to speak with me about?"

The woman drew a deep, unsteady breath. She really was nervous. She said, "I want to speak with you about Gretchen Dankl. The werewolf."

15

STORM WARNING

S he seems to have vanished," said Imogen Storm.

"She seems to have never existed," said Zach.

They were sitting at a square blond-wood table in a coffee shop on a corner near the precinct. Sitting by the window with the homeward-bound pedestrians rushing past in both directions on the other side of the glass.

"Oh, she existed all right," said Imogen. She leaned forward, the fingers of both hands wrapped around her cardboard coffee cup. "She murdered my fiancé."

Zach raised his cup to his mouth but didn't drink from it. He was using it to cover his expression. He didn't want her to see his unbelief or his eagerness to believe—either of them. On the one hand, he was excited and afraid at hearing her speak the impossible thing he had barely allowed himself to think. On the other hand, two people con-firming each other's delusions were still deluded—maybe twice as deluded. He wanted to be certain she wasn't simply as crazy as he was before he told her anything about his own experience.

"It's true," said Imogen, sensing his skepticism. "She tore his throat open. While in her wolf mode, of course."

"In her wolf mode, sure," said Zach. "What did you say the name of your website was again? *Incredible?*"

"*Bizarre!*" She took a card from her purse and pushed it toward him. She had scribbled a New York address on it. "We used to have a dead-tree edition as well, but we've gone fully digital now."

"Congratulations."

Imogen Storm heard his droll tone clearly enough, but she would not be baited. She was used to this. Skepticism. Sarcasm. Teasing. She always rebuffed it with a composed and professional air. Any sign of agitation only encouraged the hecklers.

"We cover—well, all sorts of things," she said. "Anything, really, that smacks of the uncanny. We follow up on reports of UFO sight-ings, strange creatures, hauntings, other paranormal events and so on—and we describe them to our readers in objective, unemotional prose, without sensationalism."

"So you mean you take them seriously . . . ?"

Imogen weighed her response. "For much of our audience, our dispassionate approach gives our stories a rather cutting-edge tone of irony. Because the subjects are so outlandish, you see, the proofs generally so meager, the witnesses . . . well, they're so eccentric that we only have to describe them accurately for them to seem a joke to many of our readers."

"I get it."

"But now and then, it's different. Now and then, we hit on some-thing—something unusual."

"Like Gretchen Dankl." Zach had left his cup on the table now, but he was still hiding his mouth, propping his chin on his thumb, draping his index finger across his upper lip. "You're telling me she's really a werewolf?"

Imogen had turned her head to look out the window. Her profile struck him as elfin, what with the boy-cut black hair and the kiss-curl sideburns and the cute turned-up nose and bright brown eyes. Elfin— and yet wistful for a girl in her twenties, or she seemed wistful at the moment as she gazed out at the rushing New York pedestrians and the yellow cabs bunched up together under the traffic light with the white beams of their headlights crisscrossing.

"It's all so normal here," she said. "You can't know how odd it seems, coming from where I do." She faced him. "You've heard what's going on in my country—all over Europe?"

"What I catch on the news, yeah."

"I wonder sometimes. I turned on the television today to see what they were saying about it, and all I could find were stories about a child trapped on a cliff face in North Dakota or somewhere."

"We're a big country. We've always got plenty to talk about right here at home."

"The fact is, there may not be an England when I get back. There may not be one now, for all I know—I'm not sure how one tells when a country is gone, how many of its institutions can be transformed before it's no longer the place it was. It's not like it all collapses outright or anything, is it? Nothing of it that doth fade but doth suffer a sea change and all that. Myself, I think that England—that all of Europe—died in World War II, the spirit of it anyway. It's just the corpse rotting now, the maggots devouring the flesh. Rather overwhelming to think about, when I *can* think about it. A whole civilization—Western civilization—Shakespeare, Newton, Mozart, Michelangelo. . . ."

Fatboy Mooch, Zach couldn't help thinking.

Imogen flicked her fingers off her thumb to indicate a puff of smoke. "Gone like that."

"You've lost me now, Miss Storm. What's this got to do with Gretchen Dankl?"

"She approached us. Or, that is, she approached Bernard, Bernard Albright, my fiancé, our then-editor-in-chief. This was more than a year ago, before all the troubles started, but it was already pretty clear which way the wind was blowing. She told him there was a gangster named Dominic Abend who was behind it all somehow—the currency collapses, the strikes, the corruption, even the Islamist terrorist attacks. She said he—Abend—was an immortal warlock in league with the devil in some way. Bernard didn't tell me all that much about it. It was just the sort of usual thing we cover."

"Immortal warlocks in league with the devil."

"Oh, yes, we must get two or three calls about them a month."

Zach finally lowered his hand from his mouth to reveal his faint smile. "So . . . just so we're clear. You're telling me this in your—unemotional, objective way, but I'm supposed to catch the cutting-edge tone of irony, is that right? What you're trying to say is that Gretchen Dankl was insane."

One corner of Imogen's mouth lifted. It was an attractive mouth, Zach noticed, the glossed lips thin but inviting in their prim, self-certain English way. "I forgot. Americans don't have a sense of irony, do they?"

"It's a national handicap, no question."

"Can't be helped. Mustn't grumble," she said briskly—and Zach began to like her now. He sensed real intelligence in her; he sensed she was trustworthy. "How if I simply give you the facts and you can decide for yourself, all right?"

"Fair enough," he said.

"Gretchen Dankl rang up my fiancé Bernard with her story about Abend, and he was intrigued enough to agree to a mysterious evening meeting with her in the New Forest—about two hours outside of London. He never came back from that meeting. They found his body the next afternoon. His throat, as I say, had been ripped open."

"I'm sorry."

She didn't acknowledge his condolence at all. She merely continued: "The police were noncommittal, but the tabloids chalked it up to a panther attack, of all things. *Bizarre!* covers quite a lot of those: panther sightings. The Beast of Bodmin Moor and all that. We even get an occasional fuzzy picture of one, like the sort you see of Bigfoot or the Loch Ness Monster. I don't believe there's ever been a proven case, though. We cover a lot of sightings of ghosts as well."

"So y'all don't believe it, in other words."

"When I went through Bernard's computer afterward, I found some notes he'd taken during his phone conversation with Dankl. I gather she told him a rather convoluted tale about a line of werewolves who had allowed themselves to become beasts in order to fight off the evil threatening Christendom or suchlike. The idea seemed to be, you know, that evil can only be thwarted where people are willing to sacrifice themselves to fight it—to sacrifice not only their lives but their very souls."

"By becoming wolves."

"There you are."

"And you think . . . ?" Zach began—but then said, "Well, what do you think?"

"Bernard was an older man—older than I am, at least," said Imogen. "But he was in absolutely top condition and an accomplished martial artist to boot. I doubt a woman the size of Gretchen Dankl could have done much damage to him."

"Except in wolf mode."

"Mm." Even as she spoke of her fiancé's murder—perhaps because she was speaking of her fiancé's murder—Imogen had become distracted again. Her elfin face had grown wistful again, and she was gazing past Zach's shoulder at the busy scene outside. Zach glanced at the window too. He could see there was something cheerful and comforting about the sight of the people hurrying home through the cool weather. Even the sight of the jammed traffic had a festive and vital air about it. He'd read somewhere that it was bad in London now. People hiding in their houses, afraid to go out. . . .

The young woman shook herself as if waking from a trance. "You've heard the term *lycanthropy*, I suppose."

"Uh-huh. It means being a werewolf."

"Or being convinced you're one. It's been recognized as a mental disorder at least since the 16th century. Some even say it was the form of insanity that afflicted King Nebuchadnezzar in the Book of Daniel, when he went off to live with the wild animals. That was back in the 6th century before Christ. But the 16th century, that does seem to've been the . . . lycanthropical high-water mark, if you will. Between 1520 and 1630, there were as many as thirty thousand people condemned for being werewolves in France alone. Those sorts of numbers indicate something beyond mere superstition—or they do to me, at least. In fact, there's a professor at the University of Maryland who claims that a fungus, ergot, infected the bread eaten by French peasants, causing them to have hallucinations and delusions, the effects similar to those of LSD. In any case, there have been documented cases of lycanthropy from then on, right up to the present: people who believe they can change into wolves or other animals. Shape-shifters, in other words. Nowadays, many psychiatrists think it's a form of schizophrenia."

"And you think Gretchen Dankl was suffering from lycanthropy. The mental disorder."

"Well, if she was suffering from it, she may be still. She's vanished, as I say, but I have no particular reason to think that she's deceased."

And now, with a feeling in his mind as if a three-dimensional puzzle piece had been dropped into place, Zach remembered where he had seen Imogen before—which, in turn, answered the other question that had been nagging at him: how had she made the connection between Gretchen Dankl and himself?

"You followed her," he said. "After your fiancé was killed, you started trailing her. I remember now. I saw you on the campus in Freiberg, walking under the trees."

"You must be a very good detective," said Imogen Storm without, apparently, any irony at all—though, as an American, he couldn't be sure. "Yes. I did follow her. After reading Bernard's notes, I theorized that she suffered from the delusion that she was a werewolf. And I thought it quite possible that she had killed Bernard in one of her fits, her madness giving her extraordinary strength as madness sometimes does. The police were not convinced, not even interested. My profession made me suspect, for one thing: a kook working for a kooky website and all that. On the record, they claimed to be certain that Bernard had been killed by an animal. A dog or boar, if not some sort of wildcat. Off the record, one of the detectives indicated that they were afraid there was terrorism involved. They didn't want to stir up headlines and trouble. They told me what hotel Dankl had been staying at, but that was as far as they would go. She was long gone by the time I got there, of course. But I was able to pick up her trail and, over the next year, I chased her across four countries. No mean feat, if I say so myself, especially as I had to keep the website going all the while in order to pay my way. It was only last month that I caught up with her in Germany, in Freiberg. She was selling cigarettes out of a kiosk there."

"A kiosk," said Zach, slowly shaking his head. This confirmed what he already assumed: that his meeting with Dankl at the university—her office there and so on—was all a setup, all a sham. "And you were trailing her the day I met with her."

"I was. Your arrival was the first thing that had happened that was out of the ordinary. I was excited. I wanted to find out who you were. I knew where Dankl was staying, so unfortunately I made the mistake of following you back to your hotel. Thinking, you know, I'd be able to pick Dankl up at her flat when I was done. Well, I got your name and address from the hotel clerk, all right, but Dankl never returned to her flat after that, and the long and short of it is: I lost track of you both. You didn't meet with her again, did you?"

"No," Zach lied at once—like her or not, he was not willing to tell her about the half-remembered meeting in the Black Forest.

"Well, after that, as I say, she vanished," Imogen went on. "I've been trying to pick up her trail ever since, but I've had no joy of it at all."

Zach was about to say something, about to ask something; but before he could, she held up a finger, and said, "Just . . . ," staving him off so she could finish.

"I did want to mention too that when I was looking for her in Poland at the beginning of last summer, I came upon another suspicious death attributed to animals: a Switzerland-based financier found torn to pieces in the Notecka Forest—in an old abandoned cemetery there that's believed to be haunted. The Polish media kept it quiet. Protecting tourism, I suppose. It got quite a lot of traffic on *Bizarre!* when I wrote about it, but the news never traveled much beyond our sort of audience. The Polish authorities claimed it was a wolf attack. And there still are some wolves in that area. . . ."

"But you think that was Dankl too?"

Imogen's eyebrows arched, her hands parted as if she were opening a hymn book. "She was in the area at approximately the same time. And also. . . ."

Zach waited for her to continue.

"This is rather tenuous," she said, "but the Frenchman, the one who was killed, was a man named Reynard. He worked for an international firm called One World Investments, dedicated, according to their prospectus, to 'progressive strategies for the ethical investor.' Reynard was only a minor player there, apparently, but the company itself was said to have had a hand in several of the currency and market crashes of the last few years. So if you were defending Europe from evil, in other words, Reynard might have made a suitable target."

Zach didn't bother to try his coffee again. He figured it must've gone cold by now. He sat instead with his chair turned aslant so he could lean his elbow on the table, lean his cheek against his fist. He had been listening to the woman all this while and thinking . . . well, he wasn't sure what he was thinking. He wasn't sure what to make of this story at all, or what to make of this Imogen. He did like her. He felt there was something solid and serious and no-nonsense about her. On the other hand, it did seem strange to him—counter-instinctual—that a person of such obvious intelligence should choose the career she'd chosen: reporting on bizarre legends, sort of making fun of them and sort of not. A kook working for a kooky website, as she herself put it. He supposed there was a story behind it. There always was. Still, it gave him doubts, even though his gut impulse was to trust her.

He straightened in his seat now. "So—let me make sure I have this straight, being an American and having no irony and all. You think Gretchen Dankl is some kind of serial killer, basically. A crazy woman who kills people under the delusion that she's a wolf."

"That seems to me a reasonable hypothesis."

"Doesn't all rightly fit together, though, does it?"

"How do you mean?"

"Well, if she's supposed to be defending Western civilization or whatever, you could see why she might take down this Reynard fellow in Poland. But why your fiancé? Seems to've been harmless enough. Why me, for that matter, assuming she was also after me?"

Imogen studied him a long moment. "You're really quite bright, aren't you?"

"For an American? Or a policeman?"

She nearly smiled. "That did sound condescending, didn't it?"

"A mite."

"Well, to answer your question: I don't know whether it 'rightly fits together' or not. I suppose mad people aren't very logical, when it comes down to it."

"Oh, madness has a logic of its own. Pretty much everything has a logic of its own, if you can find it."

"May I ask *you* something?"

Zach tilted a hand toward her, as if to say *Go ahead.*

"Why do you believe me? Bright as you are. I've talked to countless law officers now in countless countries. You're the first to let me get past the word *werewolf* without casting me into the outer darkness. Most of them stopped listening after I told them the name of my website. But you. . . . You've not only listened, you seem to be taking me seriously."

"Cop instinct, I guess," he said. "I can see the sort of person you are."

That was another lie, of course. There was much more to it than that. And Imogen picked up on it. She said, "I'm flattered. But is that all? I don't think it is. I think you know something—something that makes what I'm saying plausible to you."

She's good, Zach thought. *A good reporter.* But all he said out loud was "Why'd you come here? Why'd you come to me?"

Imogen Storm's eyes, Zach noticed, were a very attractive shade of brown, a very pale brown that was almost gold. What drew his attention to them now was the emotion that had come into them for the first time since they'd sat down together. Something had broken through her English reserve, and her eyes were suddenly bright with her sorrow and pain. Zach guessed it was the fact that he believed her, or respected her anyway, that he hadn't cast her into the outer darkness, as she'd put it. She was moved to openness, he thought, because after all this time, all this trouble, she had finally found an ally, or at least a willing ear.

"Bernard was a good man," she told him, her voice still cool and bell-like and steady—defiantly matter-of-fact despite the look in her eyes. "A remarkable man, really, given the challenges he'd faced in life. I loved him very much and I'm not over him. He didn't deserve to die as he did, to be murdered as he was and have it shrugged off, ignored. I find it difficult to let that go. Perhaps I simply can't let *him* go. In any case, you're the last lead I have."

"But do you think Gretchen Dankl is here? Do you think she's come to America?"

"That's my working theory, yes. I don't know why she chose her victims as she did, but I do think she chose them; and if she chose you, and if you somehow managed to escape her. . . ."

She ended with a gesture, and Zach completed her thought: ". . . she might come hunting for me."

"And there's one more thing."

"All right."

"The moon. The full moon. They say there's always an uptick in crime at that time of the month—"

"Most policemen think so," said Zach. "The scientists say it's a superstition—like being able to tell when someone's watching you."

"Well, people with lycanthropy tend to believe in it. Their fits are often associated with full moons—or, to be more precise, those three days a month when the moon is effectively full. Bernard was killed on one of those full-moon nights. So was Reynard. Today is Friday. Sunday will be the first of the three full-moon nights this month. Do you understand what I'm saying, Detective?"

"I do," said Zach.

"I think you should be careful," said Imogen Storm. "I think you should be very careful indeed."

16

LAZARUS

Sunday in church, Zach had a revelation. It was during the sermon and his mind had wandered. In fact, his mind had been wandering all weekend long.

After talking to Imogen Storm, he had had this feeling that everything was somehow better, that every strange and secret thing had been explained away. It was a feeling of relief and release. He thought, ah, these last few weeks with all their weirdness—they had not really been so weird after all. Gretchen Dankl was insane. That was it. She had fits. She thought she was a werewolf. And when Zach had gone to meet her, he had been coming down with this septicemia thing, this fever that caused hallucinations. Her insanity and his delirium had come crashing together in a disastrous confluence, a perfect storm. She had, in fact, attacked him in the woods in a seizure of madness. That part, it turned out, wasn't a dream. She had attacked him and he, in his illness, had seen her transformed, seen her as she believed herself to be. That accounted for all the crazy stuff he half-remembered. And as for the rest? What had happened between them after that? Well, he could only guess. It couldn't have been the way he'd thought it was. He couldn't have killed her. They would have found her body by now, for sure. And she couldn't have wounded him as he'd thought. He would never have healed so quickly. Probably they had struggled and he had escaped and come home—and then collapsed. And that was the story.

And what about his dreams, his visions, the "ghosts," the giant waterbugs? They were all the results of little relapses, little recurrences of his fever. He would have to go see the doctor next week and talk it over with him. But the effect was sure to pass as he continued to heal. The important thing was: he wasn't going nuts and neither was the world. Everything had a reasonable explanation.

That was how he felt after talking to Imogen. That was how he felt through much of Saturday.

But the problem with reasonable explanations of mysterious things is that they almost never hold up over the long run. New doubts creep in. New questions arise—and then the same old questions return as it starts to become clear that nothing has really been explained at all, but only explained away. Mystery is mystery, that's the whole nature of it. The old questions never really die.

If he hadn't killed Gretchen Dankl, then where was she? If the roaches were an illusion, what had bitten his leg? If the ghost of Dankl was a hallucination, why had Grace smelled smoke? And if she really was a ghost, then she really was dead, wasn't she? And so wasn't it possible he had killed her, after all . . . ?

These were the thoughts—the old questions—to which his mind had wandered that Saturday as he raked leaves with his son and chased his squealing daughter around the back yard. At night, he and Grace had hired a babysitter and gone out to dinner with a couple they knew from church, he an ER doctor and she a part-time pediatric nurse. Grace liked to socialize with people who were not "on the job," because she felt it helped Zach forget police work for a while. The four of them ate pasta and drank red wine and laughed about raising kids. They discussed the mess in Europe, the spread of radical Islam, the rise of the new fascists, and the resurgence of the violent left. But all the while, Zach was thinking about Imogen Storm and Gretchen Dankl—and about Angela Bose as well.

He had run a check on Angela's story about her father just that morning, a quick check online, hunting down articles and public records. He wanted to make sure that this Herman Bose of hers was not really an alias for Dominic Abend. But no, there was a Herman Bose, in fact, a Dutch shipping magnate, just as Angela had said. He was an impressive man, according to the news accounts. He had worked his way up from the docks until, a decade ago, at the age of sixty-nine, he had taken over the Amsterdam Line and made himself a billionaire. Rich, powerful, yet respected for his life of probity, he'd been married to the same woman for fifty-two years, the girl next door, whom he'd known since their first day of school together.

So much for Zach's instincts and suspicions about the man's daughter. Everything Angela Bose had told them had turned out to be true. So much for the faint whiff of corruption he thought he smelled around the beautiful Long Island recluse. Zach's illness had affected his perceptions somehow, that's all. Reasonable explanations. . . .

Then the old questions returned. That's what had happened that Sunday in church. That was how his revelation got started.

He hadn't been paying much attention to the service. The liturgy drifted in and out of his mind like music on a car radio.

"Where were you when I laid the foundations of the earth," Mrs. Pennyworth was saying from the lectern in her thin, nasal voice. "Tell me, if you have understanding."

The rest was blah-blah-blah to Zach as he thought about the look in Angela's eyes when she'd examined the photograph of Dominic Abend. She had recognized him. He was sure of it. That wasn't fever or his imagination.

His own gaze drifted around the church. It was a sweet old building, over a hundred years old, dark and solemn with its scarlet carpeting and walnut pews and interior. But the stained-glass windows were the pride of the place: the ascension above the altar, the life of Christ, nativity to resurrection, running along the eastern and western walls. Some old famous someone had done the pictures, Zach didn't know who, but he liked the look of them, especially at this hour in the fall when the sun struck some of them just right and they glowed.

It was that hour now. He was looking at Lazarus on the wall at the end of his row of pews. The Reverend Gray had begun his sermon. "Whoever wishes to become great among you, must blah-blah-blah . . ." he was saying as Zach's eyes wandered over Grace's attentive profile to the stained glass beyond her.

It was just that magic moment—he had noticed it before—when the light from outside filled the Savior's image so that he seemed almost to drift out of the surface of the glass into the air above the aisle, his hand uplifted, his mouth opened on the command: *Come forth*. And Lazarus—this also was a trick of the sun—seemed to be emerging from a darkness that extended backward into space, as if the artist had built the dead man's very tomb into the pane. No wonder the woman—Mary? Martha? One of them, Zach had forgotten which—had fallen to her knees between them with her hands clasped beneath her pale cheeks and her awestruck lips parted.

And Zach was thinking: *My family has been in the Netherlands for four hundred years.* Wasn't that what Angela Bose had said? *My father is named Herman Bose. Von Bose, really, but he dropped the von because* . . . what was it she had said? *He didn't like the aristocratic pretension.* Something like that.

"And if we're honest, don't we all sometimes blah-blah-blah . . . ?" the Reverend Gray was saying.

So if her father was such an aristocrat, Zach wondered, *why was he working on the docks? Working his way up to take over the company. Why hadn't he just inherited the damned company, if he was such an aristo von crat?*

Maybe her family had fallen on hard times. But that was certainly not the impression Angela had been trying to give them. With her ladylike manners and her china decorated with roses. *Pa-pa lives in Amsterdam.* Pa-pa. Who says that in real life anyway?

"It's pride," said the Reverend Gray.

And Zach thought: *It is pride, isn't it?* But so what? So she was a social climber. That wasn't what Zach had smelled on her. That wasn't what he had seen in her youthful, beautiful—and yet somehow strangely withered face. He remembered the rumors that she had partied hard through her teens. Maybe that's what had decayed her, maybe that's where the smell of corruption came from. Still, she was only twenty-seven now, so why . . . ?

Out of the corner of her eye, Grace saw her husband turned her way and glanced up at him, smiling gently. His eyes flashed from the Lazarus scene to her, his wife, with her round cheeks still smooth and rosy. And Grace was in her mid-thirties. He smiled back at her.

Angela Bose was no twenty-seven, he thought. Her father had taken over the company ten years ago when he was sixty-nine, so he was seventy-nine or eighty now. He'd met his wife on their first day of school together, so she was the same age. Which meant she would have had to be fifty-two when she had her daughter. Possible, but not very likely.

So she's older than she claims. What are you gonna do? he asked himself. *Arrest a woman for lying about her age?*

"We do not know the blah-blah-blah," said Reverend Gray. "We do not know the blah-blah-blah or even the blah-blah-blah . . ."

The preacher's voice sank to a murmur in Zach's mind. The church sank into the background of his attention. The pews, the people, the space from roof to floor and wall to wall became flat and dim and insubstantial. Only the image on the window maintained its reality, the figures embedded in the depths of darkness or enriching the dimensions of the glass or ablaze with light and hovering in the air.

You can offer reasonable explanations for mysterious things, but the old questions always return. You can bury the questions, but they won't stay dead. Lazarus, come forth.

Angela Bose was lying.

That was Zach's revelation. Everything about her was a lie. She wasn't as aristocratic as she pretended. She wasn't as young as she pretended. She *had* recognized the photograph of Dominic Abend. And damned if she didn't know about that dagger.

All of sudden, Zach's hunter blood was up. He wished he could get out of his pew, get out of the church, go home, hit the computer, go to work. All at once, he was certain that if he delved only a little deeper into Angela Bose's life, he would find that she was not the woman she pretended to be, and that the man who came to stay with her from time to time was not her father. It was Abend. Zach was on to him. He was sure of it. It was Abend.

Bonnie Childress, who had the best voice in the choir, a yearning mezzo-soprano with more depth of feeling than anyone would have suspected in the giddy Bonnie herself, serenaded their exit from the church with the wistful hymn *Holy Darkness*.

"Holy darkness, blessed night, heaven's answer, hidden from our sight. . . ."

The children, who had returned to the pews from Sunday School after what Grace declared a lovely sermon (was it the part about blah-blah-blah or the part about blah-blah-blah that had touched her? Zach wondered), were clustered around their mother's skirt as they moved up the aisle toward the door, steeling themselves for the dreaded handshake with the rector and eager to get to the much-beloved brownies of coffee hour laid out on the patio beyond. Zach was absent-mindedly patting Tom's hair and distractedly smiling at people whose names he could never remember. He was thinking that now, at last, for the first time, he had a genuine lead he could follow, something that all his cop instincts told him would put him once and forever on the trail of the man who was blanketing the city in an invisible mist of corruption and fear.

They were at the door, out the door, underneath the lintel, poised between the odorless warmth of the church and the grass and asphalt smells swirling through the chilly autumn sunshine. Little Tom was barely able to hold Reverend Gray's hand and dutifully maintain eye contact while his whole body yearned brownie-ward. Little Ann seemed to squeeze herself up inside her bashful blush as the rector bent down to make a fuss over her pretty dress. Grace said, "Such a wonderful sermon, Frank," and Reverend Gray tilted his head at her in response like a girl saying "Aww" over a bunny rabbit. (At the same time, Zach thought he saw the faintest twinkle of lust in the reverend's eyes—for which he didn't blame him one bit. Who wouldn't want Grace if you could get her?) Then Zach shook Gray's hand himself and said some damn thing while thinking, *You're a real nice fellow, padre, but I haven't got the slightest idea what you just said.* Then he turned away to take Grace's elbow. He was about to murmur in her ear that he didn't want to get caught here too long because he had work to do (though good luck trying to pry Grace away from coffee hour before she'd comforted the sorrowful, rejoiced with the rejoicing, gossiped every last bit of gossip, and helped wash every last plate and tray), when his eyes were drawn to a single figure standing motionless at the edge of the departing crowd.

The words died on his lips. Even his pulsing thoughts of Angela Bose and Dominic Abend burst like bubbles. His whole inner world turned heavy and sour.

Because there, on the sidewalk bordering the church lawn, stood Margo Heatherton.

Zach had forgotten how beautiful she was.

17

MARGO

Nothing about her was as it seemed. She was dressed modestly enough in a pink sweater and black skirt, her long blond hair tied back with a ribbon—but she was not modest; glamour came off her like body heat. Likewise, she was standing in an unobtrusive posture, her arms hanging down, her hands clasped together in front of her—but she was not unobtrusive; how could anyone miss her? Everyone else in the crowd was moving toward the curb, fanning out toward their cars, while she alone was still. When, inevitably, his eye was drawn to that stillness, she broke out in a bright, natural smile and gave him a friendly wave—and these, he thought, were also deceptive. There was nothing bright or natural or friendly about her being here, nothing at all.

It wasn't hard for him to disengage from Grace. She was as eager to get to the ladies on the church patio as the children were to get to the brownies there. He only had to release her elbow and she was gone into the coffee-hour crowd. But he didn't kid himself that she wouldn't notice him talking to a beautiful stranger. Of course she would. So he became deceptive too. He put on a false smile and, with his hands in the pockets of his slacks, he forced his body to seem relaxed. He ambled down the front path to where Margo was waiting for him.

"Zach," she said, her voice warm and gracious. "It's *so* good to see you."

She offered her delicate white hand and he took it. He was still smiling. Anyone watching from a distance would have thought they were exchanging pleasantries.

But he said, "Do what you're gonna do, Margo. I won't be blackmailed."

And she, still warm and gracious, answered, "I don't want to blackmail you, darling. But I do need to see you. Talk to you. I think you owe me that much—that much respect, at least, after what we had together."

"Do I?" Still smiling.

"I think you do, yes. Unless you think I'm something—much lower than what I'd like you to think I am. Come see me, Zach. Please. If that's blackmail, it doesn't seem so high a price to pay to protect . . ." she made a movement of one petite hand at the church courtyard, at the clutches of women in red and blue and white and the circles of men in black and gray and the children chasing around their legs. It was a witty gesture, with one sophisticated eyebrow raised. It was meant, Zach knew, to signify the staid, respectable casserole conformity of these funny little church-going creatures—as opposed, he guessed, to the wild, natural passion of what they'd "had together."

He followed her gesture, glanced at the church crowd over his shoulder, smiling at someone he pretended to know. His mind raced over the options and possibilities. He had been planning to confront her anyway, hadn't he? He had only put it off because she had not contacted him for a few days and, in the heat of chasing Abend, he had allowed himself to hope she was going to let it go. But clearly she wasn't, so his resolution had to remain strong. He'd done something wrong. He had to face it. He wasn't going to compound it by letting her terrorize him into lie after lie.

When he looked back at her, she said, "Please, Zach, it really is important to me."

He nodded once. "I'll come."

"Today," she said. Still warm and gracious, except for her unrelenting eyes.

"If I can."

"Good. You know where to find me."

He nodded again. "I do."

"It's so nice to see you, Zach."

"Who was that you were talking to?" Grace's first question as they walked together to the family Ford. Of course. There was no possible universe in which his wife would not have noticed him talking to a beautiful blonde she didn't know.

"That writer I told you about, the one who wanted me to help her with research about some novel. She was visiting the area. Saw me in the church."

"She's pretty."

"She is."

"Did you want to invite her back to the house for lunch?"

He shook his head, making a face. As if to say: he didn't like the woman much and didn't want to spend any more time with her than he had to. That was all Grace needed to know. Satisfied, she let the matter drop.

For Zach, however, the entire tone of the day had changed. A pall of melancholy had settled on it, as if the very air had darkened in the way it does before a storm. He resolved to go to see Margo as soon as he could. He had to. He had to let her have her say and answer her. And then it would be one way or another. It would be over or Margo would expose him to Grace. Better the worst than this not-knowing.

Watching his children chatter over lunch—half-listening to his wife regale him with church gossip—he felt with elemental force how much joy they gave him. They *were* his joy—they and the work he did—just the facts of them. They were what made his life come to life. Which is why the day had turned melancholy for him: he knew that this might be the end of that joy, its last unsullied hours.

He had promised to take the kids to the movies—some animated thing about talking cars or toys or something. He had promised, so he did it. But while he was only too glad to hide his anxieties in the flickering shadows, he was impatient the whole time, wanted to get out of there, to go to Westchester, to get the confrontation with Margo over and done with. By the time the dolls and soldiers and plastic racers had danced through their finale on the screen, it was late afternoon. He couldn't bear any more waiting.

He had already laid the foundation of his excuses to Grace. He had told her about his revelation in the church. He had said he had to go in to the office to work the lead. It was the best sort of lie, the kind with a lot of truth in it. One more lie, he told himself. One last one. Then the truth will out, for joy or sorrow.

"I'll be back in three hours," he told her. An hour to get to Westchester, he figured. An hour with Margo at most. An hour home.

But Grace said, "You'll get lost in your work and be there till midnight. I know you. Take a change of clothes in case you fall asleep on the cot in the locker room. I won't wait up."

When she kissed him at the door, he wove his fingers into her hair and pressed her mouth into his mouth for a long time, even with the kids in the next room. He wished he could make her one flesh with him, like the Bible said. He wished he'd never touched another woman.

He drove the Ford north through the dying afternoon. The sun dropped toward the pastel trees that lined the highway to his left. It shone in through the driver's window, making him squint, the way he did when he was focused on a crime scene. In fact, he was focused on his fantasies, fantasy rehearsals of what he would say to Margo, what she would say, how he would answer. Now and then, quick flashes of other fantasies snuck past his mental defenses. He saw her coming toward him naked. He could almost feel the satin of her flesh on his fingers. He could feel her throat in his hands. He imagined strangling her and disposing of her body so that he never had to deal with her again. But these were only surges of perverse imagination. Mostly, he rehearsed what he would say.

He came off the highway as the daylight started to fade. There was the shopping mall that he remembered from last time, and then the town of 19th-century clapboard houses, and then there was forest with mansions hidden in the trees.

He turned off onto the hard-packed dirt road. It was lined with evergreens and canopied with hardwood branches that blocked out the sky, so that it seemed night had already fallen here. After a mile or so, he turned the Ford into Margo's driveway—wound down the hill into her garden, where orange and yellow flowers were turning colorless with dusk—and approached the stately two-story white clapboard set against the background of the forest preserve.

He parked the red Ford next to her black Mercedes. The house's front door opened as he stepped out onto the gravel of the drive. Margo presented herself in the doorway like a grand hostess welcoming dinner guests. She was dressed in the same skirt and sweater she had worn to church, but the hair ribbon was gone. Her straight silky blond hair spilled free around her porcelain features.

"What can I offer you, darling?" she asked him.

They had come now into the broad main room, an open living room and dining room combined. The furniture was all dark stained wood and floral upholstery, meant to look both rustic and as expensive as it was. There was the sofa on which they'd drunk their wine last time. There was the little corner of wall against which he'd held her while he thrust inside her. There were rows of mullioned windows on two sides, showing the garden to the east and the forest to the south out back. The autumn colors of the leaves were just beginning to grow dim with the coming twilight.

Zach had changed out of his church clothes. He was wearing black jeans and a cowboy shirt and a tan windbreaker. He was looking not at Margo, but at the forest view, brooding on its mysterious depths with his hands jammed in his back pockets. It was a moment before he heard what she'd said.

Then he murmured, "Nothing, thanks."

"A glass of wine?"

Was that mockery in her voice? The glass of wine was what they'd started with the last time. He couldn't tell. It didn't matter. He faced her. "I'm not going to be here long, Margo. I'm going to have my say and go. I don't want you to threaten me anymore."

"Threaten you? Zach, I haven't—"

He cut her off. "The e-mails, the calls, showing up at my church. They're all threats, when you get down to it. You're threatening to tell my wife we had sex if I don't pay attention to you or engage with you in some way."

She started to speak but stammered and fell silent, thrown by his directness, just as she had been in his fantasies driving up.

"I'm not gonna do it," he said. "Any of it. I'm not gonna answer you, talk to you, anything. This is the last time. I don't want you in my life. I don't want you anywhere near me. I'm sorry as hell I had sex with you. It was weak, stupid. I love my wife more than anything and if she finds out about it, it's gonna hurt her. It's gonna *really* hurt her. I don't know if she'll get over it. I don't know if we'll get past it. We might. Or I might lose everything that matters to me. But that's on me. My choices, my actions, my fault. You do what you want."

Margo had now recovered from her first confusion. She stood very still while he spoke, listening politely with her hands clasped in front of her breasts, and the faintest trace of a smile on her lips—like a teacher patiently listening to a prized student's book report. Zach knew, even as he went on talking, that she was regrouping, gathering herself for a response. He didn't care. It didn't matter how she responded. He meant to say what he had to say and go.

"But if you think . . ." he went on. "If you think I'm going to hide and creep and crawl for fear of you—if you think I'm going to turn myself into something small and squirrelly you can chase from corner to corner like a rat you're torturing in a maze, you are living in a dream world, 'cause it's not gonna happen. Tell my wife. Don't tell her. Do your worst or go away. You and I have nothing more to say to each other."

It was that hour of the day when the fall of darkness accelerates so that even during the moments Zach was speaking, the air in the room had dimmed, and the details—of the furniture and appointments, of the people's figures and faces—had lost some of their clarity. Still, Zach saw Margo tilt her head forward in a majestic nod. And, "Well!" she said. "That's quite a speech."

Her heels clapped on the wood floor as she moved to the wall. She pressed a switch and brought the top light on so they could see each other better.

"Manly, direct, full of bluff integrity," she continued. "It's all bullshit, of course, but then so much polite conversation is."

"It's not bullshit, Margo. I mean it."

155

"Oh, I know you do, darling. I didn't mean to suggest you didn't. All I meant was: it's none of it true, strictly speaking." He started to protest, but it was her turn to cut him off. "Oh, I believe you. Don't get me wrong. I believe you're fully prepared to toss me out of your life like a cigarette out of a car window." Her heels clapped again—then stopped clapping—as she came toward him, stepping onto the braid rug. She stood close enough for him to smell her perfume and her money, her self-certainty and her barely hidden rage. "It's the part about you being sorry about what happened, that's what I don't buy. The part about your family being what matters most to you. About how much you love your wife. Those are things a person says, of course. What an awful bastard you'd be if you didn't say them. Still, I expected a little bit more depth and insight from you. I mean, the way you tell this little story—it doesn't even make sense when you think about it, does it?"

In his mind-rehearsals, Zach had walked out at about this point. In some of his fantasies, she'd agreed to leave him be. In some she was in tears. In some she screamed her threats and curses at his back as he walked to the door. But in any case, in his fantasies, he figured: since nothing she could say was going to change his own actions, there wasn't much point in hanging around to listen.

In real life, however—now, standing here—he found that he didn't walk out, somehow. He just didn't.

And Margo went on. "Let me put forward an alternate theory. Before you stride out heroically to face the consequences. Let me at least explain how I see it, all right? That's why I've been calling you. Because I've wanted to say this. I thought you should hear it before you just decided you could *fuck* me once and forget all about it."

Anger flashed in her eyes as she spoke the obscenity. Zach realized that, for all her airs, she was beginning to lose control and he really had better get out of there. But he didn't get out. He just didn't. He said: "All right. Say your piece."

Margo gave another of those majestic nods. She paced away from him a step or two and faced him from a little distance. Now she was standing by a side table decked with crystal candlesticks and an empty fruit bowl. The twilit garden was at her back and so was the little stretch of wall against which Zach had had her. Maybe she'd posed herself purposely so he'd be looking at the place, remembering. He didn't know.

"I will speak my piece," she said in that rich, warm voice. "If just for one second, you will lay aside your pieties and platitudes. Yes? Maybe? For just one second? If just for one second, you will see the thing clearly, all right? You say your family's the most important thing? You say you love your wife? And you know—you *know* she's such a small-minded little church mouse that she'll throw away everything you have together if you so much as indulge in a meaningless fling. And yet, you go ahead and have that fling? Knowing the consequences? What sense does that make, Zach? Would a man throw away what he truly loves for nothing? For something meaningless? What sense—what sense is there in that? Who could ever believe it but the most self-deceived hypocrite?"

This time the anger not only flashed in her eyes, it made her mouth spasm in a twisting sneer. He could see that the rage was like a red force rising inside her, taking her over, possessing her. Once again, Zach thought he should leave. And he didn't.

"Of course it wasn't meaningless!" Margo said ferociously now. "Of course it wasn't nothing! It was you finally being you, Zach. Admit it. It was the real stuff of your life. It was you in your true nature—not in the guise of some upright western lawman from a TV show, and certainly not as some complacent *paterfamilias* enduring dinner with your squealing kids and your simpering wife—or in that godawful church with its stuffy gray-haired zombies passing around coffee cake and chitchat. God, how can you even stand to pretend that's what you're like? How can you *stand* to go back to all that after what we had?"

"What we had?" In his pent-up frustration with her, the words burst from Zach before he could stop them. "What we *had*, Margo? Christ, I banged you against a wall for five minutes!"

She swept up one of the candlesticks and casually hurled it at him. "They were the only honest five minutes of your life!"

The moment of violence was so natural, so much a part of the flow of her argument, that Zach hardly realized it was happening and had no time to duck. The candlestick thumped painfully against his collarbone and dropped to the rug with a thud. Stunned, he watched it roll under an armchair, out of sight.

"You didn't throw away what you love for something meaningless," Margo snarled at him. "You threw away something meaningless for what you really love."

He raised his eyes to her with wonder. "You?" he said, in genuine amazement.

"Me. Yes, of course, me."

"Do you really believe that?"

"It makes no sense otherwise."

"But don't you see how crazy that is?"

She picked up the other candlestick. This time, he was ready and raised his arm in self-defense. She brandished the crystal cylinder a moment. It sparkled in the light. Then her eyes blurred with tears and she slowly lowered the stick back to the table with a trembling hand.

"You say you threw away what you love in exchange for five minutes of meaningless pleasure. I say you cast off a lifetime of hypocrisy for five minutes of real life as you truly are. Which version makes more sense to you?" she said.

She straightened. She put her hands together before her skirt as she had outside the church that morning. She composed herself. And when he didn't answer her, she went on with restored dignity, "Well, then, have it your way. But no, do not think for a minute I'm going to allow you to keep all this theoretical. To be noble in theory. To do the right thing in theory. No. If you're going to throw away a woman as valuable as myself, if you're going to throw me over for Saturday cartoons and coffee cake, then, so help me, I'm going to make you live out the logic of your lies. I'm going to make every kind of trouble for you, Zach. With your wife. With your children. With your employers. With the news media who made you a hero. Go ahead. Tell them I seduced you. I'll tell them you took me. I'll tell them you wanted me so much, you wouldn't listen when I said no. I'll set my lies against yours, and see which ones make sense to the rest of the world. I have money and powerful friends, and I promise you I will lay waste to your *kabuki* marriage and all the rest of it. I'm doing you a favor, Zach. Really. I care about you too much to let you throw your only life away on all that . . . fraudulent sanctity."

When she finished speaking, the room was silent, except for a clock ticking somewhere. Neither of them moved, but instead they stood regarding each other steadily, she with haughty defiance, he with his broken heart showing in the slump of his shoulders and his weary frown. He didn't know how much trouble she could really make for him, but he didn't kid himself: it would be enough. If she only told Grace—if only the children found out—it would be enough.

He drew breath, and his forlorn gaze shifted to the windows. Dusk had shaded to the edge of night outside. The trees beyond the garden were turning black against the dark blue sky. A dazzling burst of silver was just now appearing on the horizon. It caught Zach's eye and he gazed at it, thinking: *She saw me coming from a mile away. She saw that picture in the paper and she wrote this script and played it out. She saw something she couldn't have and she set out to ruin it—and I let her do it.*

He went on gazing past her out the window. The silver dazzle behind the trees resolved itself into a silver arc. The silver arc bloomed into a magnificent circle of white and silver light. The silver circle rose like the music of an overture into the twilight sky.

Musing distantly, Zach realized that, with all the troubles on his mind, he had forgotten Imogen Storm's warning that this would be the first night of the full moon.

PART III

A STRUGGLE WITH TRUTH AND LIES

18

MONSTER

He woke up half naked and covered in blood. He didn't know where he was. He couldn't imagine what had happened. The transition was so sudden that, for a moment, he thought he must be in his bed at home. For one blessed moment of sweet relief, he thought his confrontation with Margo must have been a dream.

Then the smells of the woods overwhelmed him. The smells of the dead leaves and the dirt, of the spoor and tree-life and water and fish and scrabbling frightened fur-creatures in the underbrush—their various odors swept into his nostrils on an inhalation and overpowered his senses like sunlight blinds the eyes. He felt twigs and stones pressing into his flesh. He sat up fast. He found that he had been stretched out on the forest floor.

Shocked, he looked around him. He was at the bottom of a gorge, on the narrow muddy strand of a lake, forest rising around him on three sides, the expanse of water at his back. The full moon had breached the meridian and was now shining over the water. It cast a splash of light into the middle of it, threw a sparkling line across the surface ripples and laid a soft blue-gray glow down over everything.

He gaped at the scene. Then he looked down at his nakedness, his clothes hanging off him in tatters, his stained hands. He understood the smell before he saw it clearly: blood!

He scrambled to his feet, breathing hard. He didn't dare to think, but his mind was black with foreboding.

"Oh, God." His first words. His voice hoarse and guttural. It made him aware of the noise all around, the steady cricket call and the frogs like ancient car horns and the whispering undulations of the lake water and small paw-steps skittering over the leaves.

What had happened? What could have happened? His memory had never been so blank . . . or, wait, yes, once. On the operating table, when he'd had his appendix out. That's what came back to him. They'd put the anesthesia mask on him, and the next instant he was in the recovery room. It was a blackout so complete, it made him doubt the immortality of the soul. This was just like that. There was that thorough a blackness between Margo's last words and this. But at the same time, even though he remembered nothing, thoughts were rushing in from the edges of his mind to the center of it, unthinkable thoughts about Gretchen Dankl and Peter Stumpf and the Black Forest and Dominic Abend and those waterbugs. . . . He was thinking about all that—and only the fact that it was all so unbelievable kept him from putting things together and fully realizing the truth.

What time was it? His watch was gone. He checked the moon. Had to be midnight or not long after. Grace! And, Christ: Margo. He had to get out of here. He had no idea where he was, how far he'd traveled. But the road was at the brink of the gorge and he was at the bottom of the gorge—so just head up the hill. That would lead him back to the road eventually.

He took a step and grimaced. Of course—he was barefoot. The twigs and rocks bit into his soles, the mud rose uncomfortably between his toes. It didn't matter. He had to get out of here. *Had* to. He edged along the narrow strip of shore until he spotted a trailhead in the blue moonlight. Then he headed up into the woods.

It was a half-hour climb. Not easy. Beneath the autumn trees, the moonlight reached him only intermittently and there were long stretches of deep shadow. It was difficult to keep to the trail and, whenever he strayed from it, unseen branches scratched at his face and arms. Sticks jabbed into his feet. Sudden slithering movements in the duff made him pull up short, alert, listening. The cold began to seep into his skin and make him shiver. He had to fight through tangles of thick vines and roots to make his way back to the path again. Then he plodded on—up—out of the gorge—through the moonlight and darkness. Thinking: What happened? What the hell happened? Black-hearted with foreboding all the while, because deep down he understood. He finally understood, but he couldn't bring himself to face it. He couldn't see what he could not bear to know.

Finally—there—up ahead: a glow and then a yellow light. A house window through the branches. The ground began to level out. The sky appeared and even though the moon was slipping down behind the forest, the trail became brighter.

Panting from the climb, he edged toward the tree line until he saw the house clearly in the glowing midnight. It was Margo's place. He recognized its shape against the stars. A few more steps and he could make out her living room through the lighted window. He stopped at the brink of the forest, holding a branch to keep himself steady. He stared at the place.

He was afraid of what he would find there. He had never felt so afraid.

Slowly, he moved onto the lawn. The grass was soft and cool beneath his feet, easier to walk on. He stumbled toward the house, a man in a daze, carrying his misgivings like a weight against his belly. As he came around the side of the building, he saw something sparkling at the edge of the driveway, where the grass met the gravel. Shattered glass from the window there, the very window he'd been looking through when the moon came up. It must have burst outward violently.

Please God . . . he thought. *Please God. . . .*

He walked around the glass by sticking to the thin strip of lawn at the edge of the garden. He glanced through the busted window as he passed it—but he only looked in briefly, and all he saw was the living room, all he noticed out of place was an overturned wing chair.

He walked over the gravel drive. The gravel stung but he barely felt it, barely felt anything now. He sleepwalked to the front door and tried the knob. The door was unlocked and swung open. He stepped in after it. *Please God. . . .* He wanted to turn back. He wanted to climb into his car, naked as he was, and drive away and keep driving. But helplessly he went on, passing through the foyer to the living-room archway.

Aside from that overturned wing chair, the room seemed strangely undisturbed. From where he was, beneath the arch, he could see the crystal candlestick—the one Margo had thrown at him—lying under the armchair. As he came forward, he saw that the other candlestick had also fallen and lay chipped on the wooden floor at the base of the table on which it had stood. He dared to hope that he wasn't going to find what he knew he would find, but that hope died when he came to the edge of the sofa and saw his clothing on the floor.

The rags of his jeans and his jacket and shirt, the scraps of what had been his sneakers, his wallet, his cell phone, some spare change—it all lay in a weirdly neat circle, half on the braid rug, half on the wooden floor, a hollow at the center. It was, he thought, as if he had exploded, sending his clothes and pocket-stuff in one burst around the spot in which he'd stood.

He slowly turned his head to look at the place where Margo had been standing when his memories ended—there, by the window, the one that was broken. No sign of her. His gut was clenched so tight, he couldn't even release the prayer at the center of it.

Please God. . . .

He took one more step and brought his gaze around to the opposite wall. That's when he found her.

Margo had tried to escape down the hallway to the guest bedroom. There she still was, what was left of her, which wasn't much. She was now little more than a red smear from one end of the blue-walled corridor to the other. She was raw meat and splayed viscera in gory piles at stations along the way. She was bones, some of them chillingly white and clean. Even her face, Zach saw, had been ripped to tatters. Only an eyeless patch of her features still adorned her shattered skull. A silky hank of yellow hair hung twisted down the side, the end plastered to the bloody corner of what was left of her mouth.

But it wasn't the carnage that made his gorge rise. He'd seen plenty of carnage. It was the full moral understanding of what had happened, of who he was now, what he was now—that's what filled him with sudden, staggering nausea. He—Zach Adams—had done this thing. To Margo, who had been vivid and beautiful not seven hours ago, who had been angry and calculating and self-assured and in emotional pain, whose body and manner—not very long ago at all— had been alluring enough to make him draw her warm flesh against him and press his body inside hers in at least a semblance of passion and affection. He—federal Agent Zach Adams—had transformed that human being with all her attractions and flaws and feelings and points of view into these smears of blood, these empty piles of bone and flesh, this dead ruin haunted by the thought of her. That—that understanding—not the gore itself—was what made him stagger across the hall to the bathroom door. That's what made him drop to his knees on the elegant parquet flooring in front of the toilet. And when he saw what he vomited into the bowl, the horror was complete, the realization was sealed, the new nightmare of his existence enveloped him wholly, the old reality gone forever.

Gone forever. When he was finished, he stood up slowly. He looked around him, and everything was different. He was different, and that changed everything else. He had passed from his fears and his desperate prayers into full knowledge—the full knowledge that he was not the man he had been seven hours ago. He was not a man at all anymore.

He was a monster.

19

THE DEAD MAN IN
THE BACK SEAT

Zach had killed twice before in his life. Once, as a young patrolman in Houston, he had exchanged gunfire with a rapist punk who had been terrorizing the Trey. Everyone in the neighborhood saw the shootout and no one was sorry when the kid went down. Then, of course, there was Ray Mima, the crazed kidnapper of five-year-old Emily Watson.

When you kill someone, Zach had found, he becomes part of you. Ever after, his soul runs in your veins. The rapist punk—Trevor Standard, his name was—and Ray Mima—they never left him. In the flesh, he had encountered each of them for mere frozen seconds of live-or-die danger: good guy—bad guy—bang, bang, bang. But afterward, when they lived inside him, he came to know them in their full humanity. Their sorrow and pain, their yearning and love, their wickedness and cruelty and their thwarted desire for the life he had taken away from them—all these stared out at the world through his eyes. They deepened his sense of pity, his sense of connection to his fellow travelers from the universal cradle to the universal grave.

With Margo, it was different. It was murder, first of all—at least, he felt it was. And whereas Standard and Mima, whom he'd killed in self-defense, had more or less dissolved into him, melded with him, their sin and suffering and desire becoming part and parcel of his own, Margo remained whole unto herself, a thing apart. She stood like a ghost inside him, a motionless figure, staring at him, staring at his spirit from within. Her hollow and accusing gaze was unrelenting. Unbearable. He knew he was not going to be able to live with what he had done to her.

An hour after he found her remains spread over the hallway, he stepped out of her house into the drive, leaving the front door open behind him. It was past two A.M. now. He was wearing nothing but a bath towel of Margo's he had wrapped around his middle. He was carrying the tatters of his clothes in one of her garbage bags. He was carrying his car keys and his cell phone and his wallet and his spare change in his other hand.

He moved to the Ford. He used the button on his keychain to pop open the trunk. *Take a change of clothes*, Grace had said to him when he'd left the house yesterday evening—and there it was in his gym bag. *Is that woman the perfect wife, or what?* He made the joke to himself humorlessly. Unsmiling, he proceeded to climb into fresh underwear, his suit pants, and a clean white shirt. Margo, the inner ghost of Margo, stared at him, stared into him, the whole time.

He had cleaned the death scene and the surrounding grounds. He had retraced his footsteps and removed as many signs of his presence as he could find, including the muddy footprints on the floor and on the front step and in the driveway gravel. It wasn't a perfect job, nowhere near it, he knew that. But he also knew it didn't have to be. Margo had not been killed by a man. Only an animal could have torn her to pieces that way—anyone could see that, and the forensics would confirm it. Even if the police found out he had been here, he doubted they would suspect him of anything. They might not even bother to track him down.

And even if they did find him, even if they did suspect him, it didn't matter, he didn't care. As long as he could hold them off just a couple of days, it would be all right. A couple of days was all he wanted—it was all he needed to try to do what he meant to do. It was all he was going to be able to stand, in any case.

He finished dressing, closed the car trunk, took one last look around at the scene, then got into his car. The headlights came on with the engine. He backed the car up, swinging it around. Then he faced front—and saw the shadow of a man in the headlight beams.

Zach gasped, and braked and stared through the windshield. The man was gone, just like that. Zach put the car in PARK. Pushed the door open. Stood up with one foot out of the car on the gravel and peered into the early-morning darkness. No one was there.

His heart beating hard, Zach lowered himself unsteadily behind the wheel again and shut the door.

He drove back up to the dirt road and motored under the canopied branches toward town and the highway. About a half mile on, he saw the shadowy man again. He was standing just within the trees now. A heavy-set man dressed in black, bald with a fringe of gray hair and a sharp gray goatee. His eyes followed Zach eerily as Zach drove by him.

Zach's heart sped up again at the sight of him, but his mind remained clear and calm. It was a false calm, he knew that. It was the calm of shock. He had suppressed his intolerable feeling of guilt at killing Margo, and as a result he couldn't feel anything. Still, whatever caused it, his thoughts were cool and crystalline and bright, like diamonds in the black setting of a jewelry box.

He thought: *History is in my blood, and the sins of history. I'm one of them now.*

He reached the end of the dirt road, paused on the brink of the two-lane. He checked to the left and right. The way was clear. He was about to step on the gas when his nostrils filled with the smell of rank and awful death. He looked up into his rearview mirror and saw the man sitting in his back seat, gazing at him.

It was a jolt. He was startled. But he wasn't surprised.

I'm one of them.

He said nothing. He started driving again, past the mansions in the forest toward the center of town. He was sick with the smell of the corpse behind him.

"We all want to die at first," said the dead man in the back seat. He was speaking a foreign language. German, probably. Sounded like it. But somehow Zach understood him. The words weren't translated exactly, and yet his brain comprehended their meaning instantly, as they were spoken. It was more like seeing than hearing.

Zach buzzed one of the back-seat windows down halfway. The smell of rotted flesh was just too much. He cracked his own window open a little and the cold night air washed in, refreshing him. He looked out the windshield at the two-lane in the headlights, but he knew the man was still sitting behind him.

Raising his voice above the sound of the rushing wind at the windows, he said, "Look, I know what y'all want me to do. And I'll try, I will. But I can't live with this, not for long. I'm sorry. I just can't."

"It is dreadful, isn't it?" said the dead man. "I have killed many men. Women too. With my sword. With ropes and hot pincers. Sometimes I crushed them to pieces with a wagon wheel. They were deemed criminals and I was an executioner. This was the law in those days. And everyone I killed, I carried with me afterward. They made me wiser somehow, in a dark, sad way."

"I know," said Zach. "I've killed men too. But this is different."

"Yes," answered the man simply. "The innocents. After the curse first began . . . I remember: it was intolerable."

"That's right," said Zach. "That's the word. Intolerable."

"And yet," said the man with a sigh. "And yet, you must tolerate it. For as long as you can. You must. The rules of what is real have changed for you, but the rules of good and evil are everlasting. You are one of us now. You are the werewolf. But you are still the lawman too, as was I. That is why Dankl chose you. And you must do what it is given you to do."

The Ford was moving through the town center now, back past the stately Civil War-era clapboard houses. All of them dark, quiet. Everyone sleeping.

"But you already know all this," said the corpse in the back seat. "This is why you cleaned the house, yes?"

"I guess. But that won't hold them off for long. Maybe a day or two. We have science these days. There are always traces. They can always find them. They'll come for me soon enough."

Zach glanced up into the rearview just as the Ford passed the darkened shopping mall and moved beneath the town's only street lamp. He had a moment's clear view of the executioner's face. Horrible. His flesh was somehow whole and rotting at the same time, a shifting kaleidoscopic image of vitality and decay, much more terrible together than either one or the other would have been by itself.

The executioner gave a heavy Germanic shrug. "Even science sees only what men see, and men see only what they believe. Science makes their vision even more narrow, in fact, like a bright torch in the night. Everything it doesn't illuminate sinks into even deeper darkness, yes? All that mystery you become blind to—my Jesus, but it's vast! This too you know now, eh? About the mystery."

Zach turned the car onto the highway, bringing it smoothly up to speed. The air washed in through the open windows in a noisy rush. The smell of the executioner's decay grew even thinner, for which Zach was grateful.

He glanced at the dashboard clock. Nearly two-thirty now. The road before him was all but empty. With clear driving, he'd be home in an hour at the most. Then there would be all Grace's questions to deal with. Why hadn't he answered her text messages last night? Why was he all scratched up? Where were the clothes he'd worn? There'd be all those clumsy, implausible lies he'd have to come up with, and God, it hurt to lie to her, as trusting as she was. . . .

"It doesn't matter," he said aloud. "Whether they find me or not. I can't live like this. With the guilt, with the lies. I can't. I won't. I understand what you want. Only the wolf can defeat Abend, right? Is that the deal? Well, there are two more nights of the full moon and I'll do my best. But if I can't find Abend in that time, I won't live as a murderer. I won't live as—"

"No, no, no," said the man in the back seat. His voice seemed farther away under the noise of the air from the windows, and yet Zach realized it was as close as his own thoughts. "You do not understand. Abend is only a part of it. There have been many Abends. I myself have killed a few."

"But Professor Dankl said—"

"Yes, yes, I know. That is what she told herself at the end. Many have told themselves something like it at the end. But she knew better. We all know better. The Abends of the world—they come and go. It is the baselard you must confront!"

"The dagger? What about it?"

"It is the baselard," the executioner murmured again, and then fell silent.

Zach glanced up into the rearview and saw that the dead man was gone.

He looked ahead, frowning grimly through the windshield at the open road. The blankness inside him was giving way to bitterness. *That is why Dankl chose you.* Yes, he could see it now. Now that his denial was gone, now that he knew it had all been real and no dream, he remembered his last encounter with Gretchen Dankl clearly. He remembered that moment when he had fallen underneath the raging beast she had become. He remembered how the great wolf had hesitated then, and how, in that moment of her hesitation, he had gotten away from her and grabbed the gun—the gun she had given him herself. He understood now. She had meant for him to kill her. Worn out by her failed quest and in despair, Dankl had been looking for a candidate to take her place. She had gone after Bernard Albright first, Imogen Storm's fiancé. She had tried to pass the curse on to him; but either he had failed to destroy her or had chosen not to and, in the grip of the wolf's bloodlust, she had slaughtered him instead. Then she had heard that Zach was on Abend's trail, and she had chosen him next. She had passed on the executioner's curse and freed herself by his hand—suicide by cop. And now look what she had turned him into! Look what he had done to Margo! It was so unfair. It was just as the executioner had said: intolerable.

Intolerable, yes. Zach could not live with this. He wanted to die—right now, right this minute. He wanted to floor the gas and drive the speeding car into a tree or a wall. Why not? He deserved it. Only the thought of Abend stopped him. The thought of what Abend had done to Europe. Of what he was doing now to the city. Of what he would do to the country if he was not stopped. The executioner was right. Whatever else Zach had become, he was still a lawman. . . .

Two nights, he thought. *Two more nights of the full moon. I will try to find him; but after that, either way, I will end this.*

He drove on through the darkness.

The rest of that awful morning, luck was weirdly with him—the luck of the devil, he thought bitterly. The devil's blessing on his own. For instance: he tossed the garbage bag full of torn clothes in a dumpster about a mile from his house, and the sanitation truck came to collect it even as he drove away. As he neared home, he spotted not one car or pedestrian on the streets surrounding his. All his neighbors' windows were dark. He showered and went to bed without rousing anything more than a sleeping murmur from Grace. The luck of the devil.

Tired as he was, he lay awake a long time. The ghost of Margo stared at him from within, her ruined face, the eyeless scrap of flesh on her stripped skull, the hank of hair plastered to all that was left of her mouth. Unbearable. All the while, he was painfully aware of the scent of Grace beside him, that mysterious atmosphere she gave off. The way he felt now, her presence struck him like the memory of a long-lost country, so far away that he knew he'd never touch its shores again. It was an agony to be so close to her and feel so far. Unbearable. Again and again, as the slow night hours passed, he resolved to die, to destroy himself whether he tracked down Abend and his baselard or not.

When the alarm went off, his devilish luck continued. Grace was in a rush because Tom's kindergarten class was going on a field trip and she had to get him to school early.

"You must have really been wrapped up in your work. You didn't even answer my messages!" she said with good humor as she hurried into the bathroom.

She was downstairs before he got out of bed himself. And when he came down for breakfast, she was darting around so much, she didn't even notice the scratches and bruises on him: they were mostly covered by his clothes now anyway.

When she and the kids were gone, he used the family computer in the kitchen nook to check for news. He didn't want to search for Margo's name or visit the police pages or do anything that might leave any kind of suspicious trail at all, so he simply checked the standard news sites. There was nothing there. Either they hadn't found the body yet or hadn't publicized it. But then, it was still early.

He listened to all-news radio as he drove the Ford into Manhattan. Nothing about Margo there either. Hard to tell what that meant. The riots in London and Amsterdam and the widespread persecution of Jewish people in France had grown so dramatic, they were now dominating the reports, sweeping local stories aside. He could have tuned in to Westchester police bands; but again he didn't want to do anything suspicious, not for the next two days at least.

As he pulled up outside the one-six, the radio anchorwoman handed the broadcast over to the sports reporter. So that was it for now, no more news. Zach snapped the radio off and killed the engine. He fetched his messenger bag out of the trunk and went into the precinct.

He wasn't planning to stay long. He wanted to find out if he had missed any weekend developments in the case; then he was going to head out to Long Island to see Angela Bose again, to try to browbeat the truth out of her. That had to be his focus now; all his focus: finding Abend. He wasn't sure what the executioner had meant about "confronting the baselard," but he thought he was close to Abend now—very close—and he knew he didn't have much time.

As he was riding up in the elevator, he was trying to think about Goulart—what he was going to tell Goulart—but he was distracted by the uniforms standing on either side of him. He had that criminal sense that his guilt was obvious to them, that Margo's blood was practically dripping from his fingertips for all to see. He wished to God that he had no conscience. His conscience was killing him.

It was with that heavy sense of guilt and exposure that he stepped into the Extraordinary Crimes squad room—and stopped just within the threshold, catching his breath. He stared across the long room and realized that his devilish luck had at last run out.

Goulart was propped on the edge of his gunmetal desk, one hand draped over one knee, his foot casually swinging, his other hand in motion. Even from where Zach was standing, he could see that his partner was flirting with the pretty girl who was seated in the desk chair, looking up at him.

Zach could see the girl's face in profile.

Damn it, he thought.

It was Imogen Storm.

20

SUSPICION

I mogen stood up as Zach came toward her. He saw the flush of excitement on her elfin features. Her brown eyes were bright. He thought: She knows.

Goulart was standing off his desk. "I guess you two've already met."

"Agent Adams," said Imogen eagerly, offering him her delicate hand. Even with her clipped British accent, he could hear the thrill and tension in her voice. "I'm sorry to bother you here, but there's been a killing in Westchester."

"I got calls in to Mt. Kisco and the staties," said Goulart, pointing a thumb at the desk phone. "I'll try those rubes again."

This last was directed toward Imogen with something like a gallant wink—at which she nodded in girlish gratitude. This close, Zach could actually smell the attraction between them.

"I don't know much," she said, turning back to Zach. "It was a woman. In her own home in a town called Bedford, apparently. The police are saying it might have been a bear. But I thought: given that there was a full moon last night, it might well be our friend Dankl."

"I didn't hear anything about this on the news," Zach murmured, stalling for time to think as he set his bag down on his desk. He had packed a change of clothes. There would be another full moon tonight.

"I have a program on my phone that scans police reports," Imogen told him. "I have it set to alert me to anything involving animal attacks on human beings."

"Handy," he said. He looked at her with as much cool irony as he could muster. His throat felt constricted. His mind felt thick. And his hands felt bloody. He did not know how he was going to get through this conversation, let alone the next two days, without giving himself away.

"It's a powerful coincidence, at the very least," said Imogen. "You have to grant me that. That's why I hurried right over. I thought you might. . . ."

Zach did not hear the rest of the sentence. His eyes had gone past her to where Goulart stood with the phone lifted to his ear. Goulart's lips had just parted. His eyes had widened. He was turning, as he listened, to gape at Zach. Zach understood: the Westchester boys had given him the name of the victim. He knew it was Margo.

Zach tore his gaze away from his partner and turned it back to Imogen. Goulart would guess the truth, or something like it, there was no help for that, but Zach didn't want him to read it on his face. Not yet, anyway.

Imogen was waiting for his reply—to something. He had no idea what she'd just said.

"So you think it was Professor Dankl," he said. And added drily: "In wolf mode."

"I think it's at least a possibility worth considering. Don't you?"

Goulart had set the phone down now. He was stepping over to them. Still staring at Zach.

"Has Miss Storm told you about her magazine?" Zach asked him, again with as casual and droll a tone as he could manage. "What is it? *Absurd?*"

"*Bizarre.*"

"*Bizarre,* right. Has she explained her theory? The whole lycan-thropy angle."

"Yes," said Goulart, speaking slowly, as if in a dream, distantly, as if from many miles within himself. "Yes. Some of it. Listen, I just spoke to the staties."

"What'd you get?" said Zach. He was mentally preparing his reac-tion. Surprise. Restrained concern. Not grief; he hadn't really known Margo all that well according to the lies he'd been telling. He'd never been much of an actor and he wasn't sure how convincing he could be, but he had to try.

"The vic was a woman named Margo Heatherton," said Goulart in that same slow, distant way. His eyes never left Zach's face.

In the event, Zach's performance was flawless. Mouth opening just enough. Head drawing back ever so slightly in surprise. "Margo . . . ?" He thought again that the devil must be working with him.

"You knew her?" asked Imogen breathlessly.

Zach and Goulart were now staring at each other. Zach was pre-tending to try to make sense of all this and Goulart was trying to make sense of Zach's pretense. They exchanged small, secret gestures between them. Zach narrowed his eyes—*What the hell?* Goulart lifted his shoulder—*Don't ask me.*

"But don't you see?" Imogen went on. "This only confirms it. It must've been Dankl. It must've been. She's followed you here."

Zach ignored her. "What are they saying?" he asked Goulart.

It was a moment before Goulart could break out of his own thoughts. "They don't know much. She was in her house. Definitely some kind of animal attack, they say. They're figuring a bear or wild dogs. Nothing else up there that could do that. They say she might have heard a noise and opened the door. . . ."

"Really? And it just came into the house?"

Goulart nodded vaguely. Then, pointedly, he said: "They say someone else might've been with her at the time. At the time or just before. They're not sure. They're searching the woods in case he or she got dragged off or something. Right now, it's all pretty much of a whodunnit."

"But don't you see . . . ?" Imogen began again.

Zach acted as if he'd just remembered she was there. This whole acting dodge was pretty easy, it turned out. Amazing that they actually paid people to do it. "Miss Storm," he said. "I really doubt this has anything to do with your fiancé's death."

"But it does! Of course it does," she said. All her British restraint was gone, and her urgency made her seem very young somehow. She appealed to Goulart. "What was this Margo Heatherton's profession, did they say?"

Goulart shrugged. "She was a writer, or wanted to be. She didn't have to work, apparently. She was the daughter of some muck-a-muck in White Plains."

"Jack Heatherton," said Zach. "He's the chairman of a bank up there."

"Well . . ." said Imogen, at a momentary loss. "I'm sure Dankl saw some connection between him and Abend or him and . . . I don't know what exactly. But that's just it: she's utterly mad. Think of her victim in Poland. The connection might be tenuous, but. . . ." Her voice trailed off.

"The locals are pretty sure this was an animal," said Goulart. He was starting to come out of his daze a little bit. "A real animal. Not a person pretending to be one. There's claw scratches in the wood floor. Traces of fur. Forensics is looking at it, but they're pretty sure that a human being, not even a crazy one in some kind of fit, could've—" He stopped himself with a glance at Zach. "I mean, it was a pretty ugly business."

Imogen started to protest, but Zach cut her off.

"Miss Storm, I think we understand your theory. We'll definitely keep it in mind. For now, there's not much we can do but let the locals get on with their jobs. If there seems to be any connection between this and the death of your fiancé, we'll be in touch."

At that, Imogen Storm's pixie face went stony with hurt and derision. Every expression shut down except the angry flash of her eyes. It actually pained Zach to see it. He did like her. He hated to shut her out. But what other choice did he have? It wasn't as if he could tell her the truth.

"'We'll get in touch,'" she echoed him thickly. "I think I've heard that from every policeman in every country on two continents."

Goulart stepped forward. Took her elbow in his hand. "But we mean it," he said, drawing her away toward the door. "I mean it, anyway. I'll call you later today. I promise. With whatever we have. I think what you're saying . . ." the rest of this was lost to Zach as the two moved out of earshot.

Zach had a few moments to prepare for what he knew was coming next. Goulart and Imogen had paused just beyond the cop-shop threshold. They were close together, face to face, girl-shape to guy-shape, Goulart's hand moving between them as he reassured her, as he renewed his flirtation even in her distress.

What Zach was thinking meanwhile was: he had to get out of here. Had to get on the road. Had, most of all, to get away from Goulart.

Up until now, up until the horror of last night, Zach had been half-convinced that he was . . . he didn't know what. Insane. Hallucinatory with fever. Something. *Men see only what they believe.* That's what the dead executioner had told him. Up until now, Zach could not believe what was happening to him, so he couldn't see it. And the fact that he doubted his own senses made him doubt everything else: his instincts, his observations, his deductions, everything.

But as it turned out, his instincts and observations and deductions had all been exactly accurate, exactly true. He was beginning to rely on them again.

And his instinct was that Goulart could not be trusted.

He hadn't had time to reason it out. He hadn't been able to think clearly at all after last night's catastrophe. But he was suspicious enough to feel that, if he really was on Abend's trail, he had to go after the gangster alone. Not only was that his best option in terms of the investigation, but it was his safest too: he only had another nine hours or so before the full moon rose again. He couldn't have Goulart around for that—he couldn't have anyone around but Abend himself.

Goulart shook hands with Imogen, and only released her hand reluctantly. She headed for the elevators. He watched her go. Then she was gone and, a moment later, the New Yorker was marching back Zach's way, grim, determined, twitching his head toward the small interview room in the back of the shop: *In here.*

Zach followed him.

"What the flaming fuck, Cowboy?"

Zach was still closing the interview room door. Goulart was ripping the plug of the video camera out of the wall. Done, he strutted back

Zach's way, throwing his hands wide in a belligerent gesture that said *What the flaming fuck?*

"What?" Zach asked.

"'*What!*'" said Goulart. "We gonna talk about this or not?"

"About what?"

"'About what!' Margo Heatherton!"

"What about her?"

"What . . . ? She's dead, that's what! You were banging her. She was blackmailing you. Now she's dead."

"Blackmail? I wasn't banging her! I told you!"

"Oh, for . . . Oh . . . co . . . for . . ." Goulart spluttered with disbelief.

Zach had to remind himself that, if he was right about his partner, then he, Zach, wasn't the only one acting here. If Goulart was in with Abend somehow—and Abend was what Dankl said he was—Goulart might know more about even this than he let on. He might know all kinds of things. There was no way of telling.

"Were you the other person who was there last night?" Goulart asked him. "Was that you, or not?"

"No! Of course not."

"Oh, yeah. Oh, right. Where were you last night, then? Huh?"

"I was home. Jesus, Goulart. What the hell?"

"And you're gonna stand there with your face on display telling me you weren't banging her? That's your story and you're sticking to it?"

"I knew her. I told you. She asked for help researching a book."

"Right. And then she texted you and called you and called *me* when she couldn't reach you which, hey, is what anyone researching a book would do. *If you were also banging her!*"

"Keep your voice down. Christ."

"I'm your partner, Cowboy. If you were there, if you're in this, I'm all you've got. You gotta let me help you."

"Don't talk to me like I'm some knucklehead in crossbar. I didn't bang her."

Goulart stuck his chin at him, hands on his hips. "And you know what?" he said: "I would believe that—if you weren't so obviously lying."

Zach tried to laugh this off. He did his best imitation of an oh-I-give-up head shake as he lowered his butt onto the room's long table.

"What?" said Goulart. "You don't trust me?"

"I trust you," Zach lied. "What's that got to do with it?"

"You don't think I'd stand up for you? My partner? Listen, I don't know how they do things down in Asswipe, Texas, but where I come from? Your partner: you find him standing over his dead girlfriend with a smoking gun, you come up with an alternative theory. Know what I'm saying?"

"I get that."

"Yeah, you get that," said Goulart bitterly. "You, who went after Abend on your own because bitch-twat upstairs told you I was on the take."

Zach could see this was threatening to turn into one of those all-over-the-place arguments that business partners and married couples have: you did this; you always do that; oh, I'm not the one who twenty years ago said such and such. Everyone more sinned against than sinning and no way out of it until they'd yelled their voices raw. He didn't have time for it. He had to get out of here. He had to get out to Long Island.

"All right," he said. "I confess. I went up to Westchester with my pet bear in the trunk of the Ford and when Margo said 'What's knocking around back there, big boy?' I popped the latch and sprang it on her."

"Ha ha ha," said Goulart, hot-eyed, pointing at him. "You were banging her. She was blackmailing you. You were there last night. Now she's dead. They may be hicks up there in the woods, but how long before they come looking for you?"

Zach stood up. "Good point. I may not have much time, so I better get back to work."

Suddenly, Goulart changed his tone. He stepped close. His voice went low and earnest and confidential. "Cowboy. I'm the one here who may not have much time. Remember? I mean, you know this."

In spite of everything, Zach was concerned for the guy. "You've heard something from the docs? Something new?"

"I will. Today. Maybe tomorrow. But we both know what's coming."

"No. . . ."

"Come on. These doctors. They lead you on. They have all these comfort phrases. 'Let's not get ahead of ourselves.' 'We'll know more when the tests come back.' 'We still have some treatment options.'

Stuff to help you sleep at night. Which is a laugh. I don't sleep at all anymore. You know what I do? I stare into the darkness and think 'Soon it'll all be like this—dark like this—and never changing.' Not that I'm scared exactly, it's just. . . ."

Zach couldn't help it; he felt for his partner. "I understand," he said.

"It's crazy, right?" said Goulart. "'Cause if I'm not here, I won't even know how dark it is, so why worry? But that's my point, that's the point I'm trying to make. Last week, you asked me what I believe. And I been thinking about that. And I realized: I do believe in something. I believe in the bad stuff. You know? I mean, look around you, Cowboy. We got proof of the bad stuff coming out of our ears. Guys strangling their wives 'cause they brought home the wrong breakfast cereal. Women selling their two-year-old daughters for a high that lasts thirty seconds. I don't have to tell you."

"No."

"But what's good? Where's any good anywhere? You tell me. Guys like us? Are we good? No, we just take out the human garbage, that's all. Doctors, nurses, charity workers, firemen—the same thing. They're just reacting to the bad stuff—cancer and poverty and fires—all of them." Goulart moved even closer. Zach thought he could smell the man's disease on his breath, but that may've been a fantasy. He could definitely smell his cologne and his desperation. "But name me one good thing. One good thing that's not a reaction to something awful. It's the bad stuff that always comes first. The bad stuff is the only thing that's real. So since you asked, that's what I believe in from now on. The bad stuff. It's not about God and the devil. God is the devil. The devil is God."

Zach didn't have the slightest idea how to answer any of this—hell, this argument had now gone way more global than he'd even bargained for. He could only look down at his partner—who was also, in spite of all his doubts, his friend, maybe his best friend—and ask him: "So, like . . . what are you saying here, Broadway?"

Goulart gave one of his silent laughs. "I know, I know, I'm rambling, but . . . I'm trying to tell you: if it is like that, if this is all just one big sliding pond into hell, then what is there, you know? What've you got to live for? You got your dick. Right? You got your dick going in and out of a snatch like velvet. A glass of whiskey maybe. A ball game. A friend. Life—that's all you got. A minute, an hour, a day, as much as you can get before the Big Terrible begins." He rapped the back of his hand against Zach's chest. "Right? Am I right? What's the point of anything else? That's what I'm saying. Friends. Partners. You and me. We should be watching out for each other, Cowboy. You for me, me for you. What else is there? I'm not perfect. I never said I was. And you with Margo? Hey, who am I to judge? That's just the point. It doesn't matter. You're my partner. I never knew her. Like you with what's-her-name. Bitch Goddess Hartwell upstairs, whatever. What is she to you? I'm your partner. I'm your partner. Right? Am I making sense here? Am I making any sense?"

"You are," said Zach slowly. And he was. After the events of last night, Zach understood him perfectly. If we're all just damned or dead men, why not drink the wine of life and live? Goulart could cover for him. He could cover for Goulart. They might just get away with it. Who could say? He wished it could be like that for him. He wished he couldn't feel her—Margo—inside him. Watching him. Staring, hollow-eyed, at his soul. He wished he could let Goulart take Abend's dirty dollar and turn a blind eye. Then maybe he could play this little game of life with his partner. But no, there Margo was. And there was Abend, who needed killing. And in truth, he couldn't imagine it any other way, Goulart's way. He had known men, seen men, plenty of men, without a conscience. You would think they would do nothing but laugh, but no. Maybe on the outside they laughed; but inside? They twisted like snakes in a vise, all of them. The vise of the moral world, Zach thought. *The rules of good and evil are everlasting.* He could not make himself forget that.

"Listen, partner," Zach said. He had to end this. He laid his hand on the fine French serge on Goulart's shoulder. "I got a CI to see on this Paz case, maybe a link to Abend. I gotta go and meet with him. You call me right away if you hear anything from your doctor."

He could've slapped the guy and gotten a similar reaction. Goulart's head jerked back and his mouth opened and he spread his hands again: *What the fuck? What the flaming fuck?*

"That's it? You're gonna walk out on me?"

"I gotta do this, man. Come on!"

"All that garbage on Margo."

"It's not garbage."

"You know it is. And then you're heading out alone again on Abend? Because of that bitch upstairs? What she said?"

"It's a CI. I can't bring you. It'd spook him."

Goulart's lips tightened and his hands jerked out again, and he said "So that's where we are."

"For Christ's sake, Goulart. You're getting it all wrong."

But he wasn't, and they both knew it.

Zach drifted toward the door and Goulart went on standing there, just as he was, arms lifted, lips tight. Zach felt bad about it but hey, last night, he'd ripped his mistress's head off, so there was a lot to feel bad about: it was all a matter of priorities at this point.

"Seriously, call me if you hear anything," he said again.

And he left Goulart standing there. Headed out to pick up the Crown Vic. Headed out to the Guyland.

21

CARNAGE

A ll through the long drive, Zach was haunted.

He was haunted by the radio news, for one thing. Even with the violence in Europe—even with Islamists rioting in Amsterdam, neo-Nazis battling neo-Communists in Berlin and London, the burning of a synagogue in Paris with fourteen people dying while the *flics* looked on—even with all that, the stations couldn't pass over a good heiress-killed-by-a-bear story. Hell, they led with it, as if they thought it was the only part of the broadcast their audience would give a damn about. During the two-hour journey out to Sea View, Zach heard Jack Heatherton give a tearful press conference: "No expense will be spared in finding out the truth about my daughter's death." He heard experts discussing the anomalous aggression of bears in autumn (experts always had an explanation after the

186

fact for something they would have deemed impossible before it). He heard the local police chief put out a call for anyone with information to come forward: "If you were present at the time of Miss Heatherton's death, you are not a suspect. We know this was an animal attack. We just want to talk to you." All of this haunted him as he drove.

And he was haunted by Grace. By thoughts of Grace, by thoughts of what Grace might discover. She didn't follow the news all that much, but a story like this . . . ? A woman killed in her own home by an animal? How could she miss it? Images of his wife kept popping into his mind. The moment when she would see Margo's face on television or online. The moment when she would recognize that this was the very woman Zach had spoken to outside their church. . . . All the questions she would ask him. All the lies he would have to tell her. . . . This haunted him too.

And he was haunted by ghosts. The actual presence of the dead. Margo, continuously. Those inescapable hollow eyes inside him. Look what you did to me, Zach. *Look at my face. I was so beautiful. Look what you did.* . . . That was bad enough; but then, from time to time, there were the others. Standing by the side of the road, watching him pass. It was truly unnerving.

Right outside Great Neck, not far into his trip, he spotted Gretchen Dankl smoking a cigarette beside the hedge that lined a golf course. It made his heart leap in his chest when he recognized her. He swiveled his head to look back at her, but she was already gone—and when he looked forward again, he had to brake hard to keep from plowing into the pickup just ahead of him.

That was only the beginning. Out in the autumn scrublands midway, he was startled by the sight of a man framed against a highway sound barrier. The man was wearing clothes from an age gone by: a gaudy blue coat with what looked like gold and silver embroidery. He watched the Crown Vic with an unwavering stare and a mournful countenance. Zach had no idea who he was, but he knew he had been dead a long time.

A bit farther on, where the Island became flat farmlands pocked with enclaves of small houses, there was another man he'd never seen before, this one standing shin-deep in the brush. He was wearing an old-fashioned black three-piece suit with a long coat, like a character in one of those British historical dramas Grace liked to watch on TV. It was the costume that made Zach turn to look at him; and when their eyes met, he realized that this was another one, another specter.

As badly as these apparitions rattled him, he understood somehow why they were there. A whole cursed history was in his bloodstream now, the guilt of sins he hadn't committed, the memories of people he had never met and of events that had taken place before he was born. These roadside shadows were but intimations of what he didn't want to know he knew. And there'd be more of them, he suspected. Phantoms, visions, nightmares, each more substantial and tormenting than the last.

Even as he was considering this—and even as the radio newsman was yammering at the edge of his consciousness—he got a whiff of earthworms and rotting meat. He looked into his rearview, terrified that he might see the executioner sitting in the back seat again—and he did! There he was. Zach nearly swerved into the next lane. By the time he got the car back under his control, the ghost was gone and the smell was dissipating. But Zach had to get off the highway for a few minutes to calm himself.

He parked in a little neighborhood near the service road. He sat behind the wheel with his eyes shut, his fingers pinching the bridge of his nose. He told himself that this would pass. He'd track Abend down. He'd "confront" the dagger, whatever that meant. After that, he'd be free to turn himself in or die or . . . do something to make this stop. Meanwhile, though—Jesus! The guilt and horror were like thrashing, ravenous animals in him. Guilt and horror—and grief too. Because he'd lost something precious, something he'd barely known he had: he'd lost his sense of himself as a good person. Even death wouldn't restore that. Nothing would.

Before he got back on the road, he raised his eyes and looked around. Out the windshield, down the sidewalk. Out the window, at the windows of the houses nearby. In the rearview mirror, expecting to see a dead man's eyes staring back at him. There was no one there, no one anywhere. All the ghosts were gone, for the moment. But they'd be back. This was what it was going to be like from now on.

He put the car in gear and pulled away from the curb and got back on the highway.

Another forty-five minutes of haunted driving and he was near Westhampton Beach again. He made his way to the winding ocean-front road that led to Angela Bose's driveway. A screen of trees was planted along the road's shoulder. Zach caught only glimpses of Sea View through the branches. All the same, by the time he reached the estate's brick entrance, he knew that something was wrong.

He slowed the Crown Vic. He came down the cypress-lined driveway at a crawl. He was on alert, his eyes scanning the area for anyone—anything—in motion. But that was just it. That was what bothered him. Nothing was in motion. Nothing human, anyway. A heavy, pewter-colored sky hung stagnant over the fountain out front. The flowers around the fountain stirred in the breeze, but the fountain itself wasn't flowing. The lawn moved in the wind too, and the branches of the black oaks rattled. But the windows of the house behind the branches—they were dark on all three stories. The silver-blue Bentley was nowhere in sight. And as Zach drove closer, he saw that the front door was standing ajar.

The Crown Vic made a lot of noise rolling over the gravel, so when Zach stopped, it seemed very quiet inside the car for a moment. Then he stepped out and there was the wind noise and the noise from the ocean and the seawater tang of the ocean carried by the wind. But underneath all that, there was a deeper silence and a sense of empti-ness and the faintest trace of that smell he remembered from his first visit: the smell of blood.

He walked cautiously toward the door, his feet crunching on the gravel. His eyes kept scanning the area. Nothing was moving but the waves on the water behind the house, and the seabirds sailing past in the overcast sky.

"Hello? Anyone home?" he called in through the open door. He got the answer he expected—no answer. He pushed the door in and stepped over the threshold.

Inside, everything was still. He closed the door to shut out the noise of wind and sea, then stood on the brink of the foyer and listened. Nothing. He noticed a light patina of sand lying on the parquet. The door must have been open for days. No lights on anywhere. Shadows draped the corridor that led toward the back room. Shadows folded over the switchback stairs. His first thought was to head up to the second story. Check the bedroom. The bath. But no. There was nothing up there. No one. He could feel it. Smell it.

There was something, though. Something. Someone. Somewhere. Down the hall. In the shadows. Close.

It was at this point that he drew his weapon.

Gun held low with both hands, he edged over the parquet and the Persian rugs and into the back room with its picture-window view of the beach: pewter sky over a muddy green ocean, the water seizing, rising, tumbling, white-capped, foam-splayed, violent. He edged past the window, down another hall, a darker hall, with a doorway of gray light at the end. Angela Bose must have abandoned this place right after Goulart and he had questioned her. She had run for it, basically. But why? Because she looked at him, at Zach, and saw that he knew she was lying? No. She was a wealthy woman with access to the kind of lawyers who could easily protect her from the likes of him. Plus she was prideful and—his guess—she would have thought she could run rings around him with her lies, whether he believed them or not. And she was probably right about that too.

He edged through the shadows toward that gray door up ahead. It was the kitchen door, he could see now. He could see the cabinets and counters in the gray daylight, the granite table centered on the darker parquet. And now he caught an even stronger whiff of . . . what? He drew a long breath in through his nostrils. Death. Blood. Yes, and something else. Something alive. Something tense, waiting for him. All across the surface of his flesh, he felt now that he was not alone.

He stepped into the kitchen. Surveyed the still and silent room. There was another open doorway across from him. Through it, he saw a back hall and another door and he thought: *There.* He crossed the kitchen quickly and went through the hall to the second door.

He unwrapped his left hand from the pistol grip and used it to pull the door all the way open.

Cellar stairs, down into deeper darkness.

"Shit," he whispered.

There was a light switch, at least. Did it work? He flicked it up and—yes—a pale yellow glow spread over the bottom of the staircase. He started down the steps crabwise, both hands on the gun again. He felt now as if his skin had flipped and his nerves were on the outside—he was that sure that he was walking into trouble.

He stepped off the bottom stair. Stepped down onto the tiled floor of the basement. He caught that smell again, that smell that he had smelled the last time he'd been here. That atmosphere so engorged with blood, it was like being inside a tick on a dog. Before, he had thought the smell was coming off Angela Bose herself. But here it was again. Did that mean he was about to find her? Find her body? He was about to find something, that was for sure.

To the right was a stone archway into a corridor. He stepped to the left instead, into an open room. There was an elegant wooden bar with cushioned stools. Bottles of wine in wall racks, bottles of whiskey on glass shelves. A television embedded in the wall. He swept his gun barrel over the corners and hidden places and the space behind the bar. No one there. Nothing. He moved back to the corridor.

It was built to appear ancient. Flagstone archways with shady niches. Colored fiascoes on old wooden tables along the stone wall. Too many nooks and crannies to check out completely. Someone could easily have been watching him as he passed.

The heavy door at the end of the hall was decorated with an elaborate monogram B: the airtight door to a wine cellar.

There, Zach thought again.

He kept the gun moving as he stepped slowly toward the door. The smell of blood was so thick now, it overwhelmed that other smell, that living, waiting smell. But he had not forgotten it. His nerve ends felt that living presence, somewhere, somewhere close.

He reached the door. He pressed down the handle. There was a heavy suction sound as the seals around the edges came away from the frame. The lights within the room beyond flickered on automatically. The smell of death came rolling out like fog. It covered him.

The body was on the heavy oaken table in the center of the room. Its hands and bare feet were manacled to chains which were, in turn, secured to the table's heavy legs. Oaken wine racks surrounded it, rack after rack, bookshelf wide, floor-to-ceiling tall.

It was a man's body, red-haired, red-bearded, maybe forty, in jeans and a woolen shirt. Homeless, Zach guessed, from the lesions on his face and from his swollen feet and fungus-blackened toenails.

His head was turned to the side. He was open-mouthed and staring as if in pained surprise. His torso was drenched in blood. The killing wound was a gash in the dead center of his chest. The blood had splashed down and stained the table on either side of him. He hadn't been dead very long.

Zach came forward behind his gun. He could feel everything growing brighter, every detail becoming more sharp. His hyper-focus, Goulart called it; but this, he realized now, was more than that. This was hunter focus. Wolf focus. Every edge and splinter and thread around him glimmering with presence. His mind was working faster too, arranging sights and smells and deductions in various permutations, like sliding pieces of a puzzle picture into different slots to test where they fit.

He was thinking: No chairs around the table. Old stains down the table's side. Old smells like these smells suffusing the wood of the walls and the racks. . . .

This wasn't the first killing that had happened in this place. This was a murder room, a place set aside for the purpose. And more than that . . .

. . . *the mixture of werewolf's blood with holy water on the blade . . . transforming the blood of human sacrifice into a panacea, curing every disease, and retarding the aging process . . .*

Zach's eyes flicked over the wine racks—all the racks all around him.

"Oh Lord," he whispered, because he already knew.

He stepped to the nearest rack. He reached for it with his left hand, still holding the gun with his right because something else was here, something alive and dangerous nearby. Still keeping an eye on the room and the dead man, he felt along the edges of the rack. Tried various ways of pulling it and pressing it. Then he heard a click and felt it give.

The rack swung outward. The bodies were hanging behind it. Three of them, each in a transparent plastic bag, each hooked to a metal rod like a suit of clothes. Inside each bag, a gaping mouth showed black, eyes stared obscurely, blood smeared the plastic, gore pooled around the corpse's feet.

Eyeing the room, holding the gun, breathing hard now, Zach moved to the next rack. Pressed it. Three more bodies hung behind.

"Good Jesus."

Four were behind the next rack. Zach kept moving around the room. Pressing the racks so that they swung out, revealing the bags, the bodies. The corpses dangled and stared through the plastic. They were men and women both. They were white and colored. Some looked to Zach like teenagers, most were middle-aged, some were old. No, not a serial killer, Zach thought. This was human sacrifice. The work of Dominic Abend—and of Stumpf's baselard.

When he had done the full circuit of the room, all the racks were open; the dead surrounded him, hanging from every wall. All those mouths open as if gasping for air inside the plastic. All those wide eyes staring as if begging for release. All that flesh and pooled viscera and smeared blood. An overwhelming array of slaughter.

Staggered by the sight, Zach slowly lowered his gun and gaped. He stood near the foot of the corpse on the center table. He checked the door that was still open on the empty corridor, then turned to the body beside it, then turned to the next body and the next, from one chamber of hanging corpses to the next and next, coming around in a complete circle until he faced the door again.

There was a living man standing in the doorway now. Zach recognized the stooped, monkish figure in his robe-like overcoat, his long greasy hair, his rat-like features: one of the gunmen who had fired on him in the Long Island City hallway. In a frantic flash, Zach thought of the Dezzy .50-cal that had nearly blown his head off. He saw the gun in the monk-man's hand. He tried to bring his own weapon to bear. Too late.

The monk fired and hit Zach dead center. Zach sank to the floor and kept sinking into a pool of tarry blackness.

22

THE BEACH HOUSE

There was a fire on the southern horizon. Enormous cylinders of orange flame rolled and roared across the twilit sky. Cottages and barns were crumbling in on themselves, the wood splintering loudly, the sparks exploding upward. There were screams amidst the other noises—ragged women's screams; the high screams of children— the screams dying as the people died.

Zach could see and hear it all from where he was, half a mile or so to the north. He continued trudging up the hillside, making his way toward the peak behind which the sun had set. A man stood waiting for him up there on the ridge, a man turning to shadow as the dusk deepened.

Zach knew this was all a dream, but it was also not a dream, not *just* a dream. It was also real somehow. The smell of the sere winter grass was real and the crunch of it under his shoes. The smell of smoke from far off when the wind shifted, and the bright angry life of the fire and the pitiful screaming and the pitiful way the screams ended—these were all real. Each dying woman and each dying child, Zach knew, was just as real as he was. Each was an entire inner world of tenderness and anxiety and yearning. And each was being slaughtered like a beast, cut down by the cold edge of a sword or cooked alive inside one of the burning structures, a point of view extinguished in agony, then gone. More than a dream. This was history.

Zach crested the hill. He reached the waiting man. He could make him out through the thickening nighttime: a man wearing black with a frilly white collar. Zach recognized the bald head, the long face, the sharp gray goatee of the executioner.

"Am I dead?" Zach murmured to him. He remembered the rat-faced monk who had shot him in the wine cellar.

"No," the executioner said. He gestured down the other side of the hill with his open hand. "*They* are dead."

Zach looked and saw a vast field of winter trees with hanged men dangling from their branches. The black dead figures—the trees and the suspended bodies—were starting to blend with the gathering darkness.

Zach stood appalled: all those strangled inner worlds—their longings and their speculations, their love for their mothers and the way cherries tasted on their tongues—flung into the pit of nothingness like so many handfuls of sand tossed down a well. All those lives.

He shook his head, heartsick. "I have my own soul and my own sins," he said. "I can't mourn for everyone."

The vision—the village in flames, the orchard of hanging corpses—threatened to engulf him. He was drowning in the horror of it. He had to get out, but he couldn't. He was unconscious, he realized. He had been drugged—that was the problem. He fought to wake up. He struggled toward the surface of reality. Whatever waited for him there, he thought it had to be better than this.

But he was wrong about that.

He broke, gasping, into the light of the present. Chained to a metal cot. Lying on a bare mattress. Face and hair sticky with his own vomit. Thighs burning from his own urine. He was wearing nothing but his sodden jockeys. He was cold. He was sick as hell.

He groaned, tried to curl up. Chains rattled. His wrists and ankles were manacled. There were burns on his sternum. His neck ached. That weird little monkish rat had shot him with a stun gun, not the .50-cal, then plunged a syringe into his neck as he lay helpless. Shocked him first, then drugged him.

Where was he? How long had he been here? He twisted his head, trying to see. He was in a small bare room, white walls, wood floors. One door—closed. Heavy curtains on the one window. A skylight showed a square of high leaden sky, no trace of sun. It was much darker than before. Looked like a storm coming. It was chilly too. The chill had eaten into him. He remembered that the monkish, rat-faced killer had come in here at least once, maybe twice or even more—come in and casually jabbed another syringe into his neck, keeping him down.

He'd been here quite a while, in other words.

He was nauseous and uncomfortable in his own filth. His head was swimming in the smells of piss and puke. His eyes sank closed and he spun down woozily into the dusk vision again: the burning village, the screaming women and children, the orchard of hanging men. He could smell the grass and the smoke. His eyes flashed open as he fought back to the surface. The room reeled around him.

Blinking hard, he made his mind work, his cop mind. He tried to put the pieces together. The monk must've hidden in one of the crannies in the wine-cellar corridor. Did he and Zach just happen to be there at Sea View at the same time by coincidence? Not likely. Had the monk been waiting for him? Maybe. Maybe he'd been tipped off by Goulart. Or maybe he'd been waiting for someone else, and Zach was just the one who happened to show up.

And now . . . well, now it was going to be bad. Death was the best-case scenario. The worst? He remembered Johnny Grimhouse, flayed and mutilated with the giant waterbugs feeding on him.

Not much chance of getting out of here, but he had to try.

He twisted to get a better look at his chained hands. . . .

That was as far as he got. The door opened. The monk came in. This was Zach's first clear look at him. What had seemed like a robe before was, he saw now, just a heavy black overcoat, weirdly tented under the man's stooped shoulders. The stringy, greasy hair framed a preternaturally thin face, sharp nose, reddish eyes. Zach looked into those eyes and saw the sadism of slaves and true believers. Clearly, this was Abend's acolyte down to his soul. Zach's heart sank. A man like this—he would just love to lay the hurt on the infidel, to take revenge on the heathen for being free of the chains of devotion he himself was bound by. Zach just had time to think this—then he saw the stun gun in the bastard's hand and thought, *No, don't!* and then the monk shot him again.

The other gunman, the goateed Satan lookalike, was right behind the monk. The two men went to work around Zach's twitching body. They loosed his chains from the cot frame. Then, the monk at his shoulders and the devil at his heels, they carried him through the door as he spasmed and choked on his own drool. Clouds swam over Zach's mind as the monk and Satan hauled him into a broad empty room. Vaguely he made out white walls and a huge picture window with a view of ocean heaving beneath the ominous and stormy sky. Muttering instructions to each other in chittering insectile voices, the thugs hoisted Zach upright. They chained his wrists to an iron chinning bar that was wedged into the top of an open doorway. They chained his ankles to a bar wedged into the doorway's bottom. Zach stood there slack-kneed, head hanging, blinking stupidly at the view of the sea.

Then something seemed to strike him from within himself: a living bolt of blackness. A crash of desolation, a flashing shock of death beyond despair. He remembered this feeling—he remembered the terror of it—from the hallway in Long Island City.

He knew that Dominic Abend was coming.

Now, sure enough, he heard the approach of slow footsteps. Hard boot heels on wood. Zach shook himself like a dog throwing off water, stiffened his legs under himself, trying to get his body more or less upright, trying to get his brain clear, trying to prepare himself for the meeting.

He was not prepared. He could not have been.

Dominic Abend was no longer the man from the photograph of Times Square on New Year's eve. He was not even the man who had summoned the giant roaches in the hallway in Long Island City. Something awful had happened to him since then. Zach recognized the large powerful body in the long black coat, recognized the shaved head, the bulbous nose and thin lips. But his flesh. . . . The flesh of his cheeks was darkening and wrinkling in patches. It was drawing tight so that the man's eyes bulged bizarrely and his teeth, no matter what his expression, were bared. An unmistakable smell of rot was coming off him. He was decaying, Zach realized. He was moldering even where he stood.

Zach's gaze dropped to the sword Abend was holding down by his side, the naked blade pressed against his pants leg. A fearful sight. Zach had to fight off the awareness of his own nakedness and vulnerability. But he had seen the body of Johnny Grimhouse. He knew what was coming.

With effort, Zach lifted his heavy head and met the killer's eyes. Looking at the photographs, he had always imagined that those eyes would be knowing and cruel. But bulging the way they were, with the skin around them black and sunken, they just seemed weirdly bright and full of a wild preternatural terror.

Abend came to stand in front of Zach. Zach could hear the phlegmy breath of the monk standing to the right of him, the doggish pant of Satan to his left, both of them eager with anticipation of what was coming.

Abend looked the chained cop over casually, without much interest. Zach swallowed hard. He was afraid.

"You are the lawman, yes?" Abend said briskly—he had a thin voice with a German accent. "You are the one they call the Cowboy. Adams."

Zach nodded. "I am."

"Extraordinary Crimes, they call your people, correct? Task Force Zero?"

"Yes."

"And I am Dominic Abend, the one you are all looking for."

"I know."

"Congratulations, then. You have found me. Hm?"

"Yes."

Abend smiled a little at the irony. "You went to Germany, did you not? To talk to the Dankl woman."

A thought occurred to Zach, and he spoke it. "Did Goulart tell you that?"

Abend seemed to appreciate the question. He nodded at it. He said "Hm!"

Then he sliced Zach's chest open.

It was a move so swift, Zach barely saw it—barely even felt it until it was done. Without warning, Abend brought the sword across himself and whipped it backhand over Zach's breasts. The blade dug deep and ripped a gash from one side of Zach to the other. Zach's head flew back and he screamed in agony. As he sank forward in his chains, a thick line of blood bubbled out of the wound and spilled down over his abdomen.

"I will ask the questions, yes?" said Abend quietly. "You went to Germany and talked to the Dankl woman, is this correct?"

Zach shuddered and sucked in air through his teeth, fighting down his sobs of pain. His head hanging, he coughed wetly, stupidly watching the blood run over him. The violation of his flesh had hollowed out his spirit on the instant. He felt as if liquid fire had been splashed over his torso, wounding him so deep he'd never heal. Terrified that Abend would cut him again—and he knew he would cut him again—he tried to answer the question before the killer grew angry. He only just managed to gather enough strength to nod and gasp, "Yes. Yes."

"And so you know about the baselard, in other words," Abend went on at once.

"I do," Zach groaned. "I know about it."

"But of course, you don't know where it is, do you? No, or you wouldn't have been out here at Sea View. You talked to Angela, realized she was lying, came back to talk her again, so on and so forth, yes?"

"That's right," said Zach. And as his mind began to grind back into action, he realized: this man was smart—really smart—dangerously smart. And how much did he know? About Dankl. About Margo. About him, and the old curse. . . .

Abend paced away from in front of him. Zach was too weak and foggy to watch him go. He lifted his chin from his chest and saw the window across from him. The storm must have been coming fast. The clouds had grown nearly black now. The surf was high, a vexed beast that rose up roaring toward the sky and hurled itself in seeming rage upon the dull sand.

Zach's head rolled. There was the monk beside him, greasy and unshaven, grinning with his red eyes bright and vicious and submissive. And there, on the other side of him, was the lean, grinning, goateed Satan whose expression was duller and more inward, as if no outward brutality could give him as much hellish pleasure as what he saw in his own mind.

Abend paced back in front of Zach again. The bulging eyes and slowly mummifying features tilted as he studied the blood-soaked investigator with that same musing disinterest.

"Did she follow you here—Dankl? Is she in the United States?"

Zach shook his head. "I don't know."

In what seemed a sort of arbitrary experiment, Abend lifted the sword again, jammed the point into the gash in Zach's chest and twisted it back and forth.

Zach thrashed in his rattling chains, shrieking mindlessly: "I don't know!" After a moment, Abend lowered the sword. Zach slumped in his manacles, bleeding.

"Skin for skin," said Abend softly. "Do you know this saying?" When Zach slumped there silently, too weak to answer, Abend put the sword point under his chin and pushed so that Zach had to raise his head. "Hm?" he said. "Skin for skin? You know this?"

Zach began to shake his head no, but then remembered. "It's in the Bible somewhere. In the book of Job."

"Very good. Very good." Abend took the sword away and Zach's head fell forward. "Do you know what it means? It means a man will give anything to save himself, his own skin. He will give anything to make pain stop, anything."

Abend studied the blade of his sword. Zach's blood ran along the shiny steel and dripped off it, falling to the floor. Abend seemed mildly amused by the sight, a break from his general boredom.

Zach couldn't look at it. It sickened him. He looked past Abend instead, to the window again. It was even darker out there now—much darker, in fact. The far waters were sinking into the obscurity of the cloud-covered horizon, gray blending with gray and the whole scene beginning to turn a thick blue-black. Zach licked his lips. Some small, fine something—wonder or maybe hope—ignited in him: a tiny particle of light in the blackness of his tortured spirit. *Wait*, he thought, *that's not a storm coming, is it? That's nightfall!* Could that be right? Could it be nightfall? Already? Had so much time gone by while he was drugged?

"I would rather corrupt you than kill you, you know," Abend said thoughtfully. "You don't have any information I need. There is nothing to torture out of you. Dead, you are only a headline. Which means publicity from the media—until my media can distract them. Pressure on officials—until my officials can form a committee or call for a study. Policemen manfully swearing to catch me—until my lawyers baffle them into impotence. All not very helpful—or very interesting, really—commonplace, in fact. Just a great waste of time for everyone. But if you were to work with me, become one of my people, I could find uses for you, I'm sure. Skin for skin, yes? Then I do not have to hurt you anymore or kill you—as long as you remain loyal. To the public, you will be the hero who escaped my clutches. You will sleep at home tonight with your wife and children instead of dying here in bloody bits and pieces. You would like that, wouldn't you? To sleep at home with your wife in your arms."

Zach's head had fallen forward again, nausea and pain and weakness overcoming him. But he knew he had to answer Abend or suffer more, so he lifted his head. He saw the decay creeping under the gangster's skin like maggots. He met the gangster's bulging eyes.

And instantly Abend saw into him, into the heart of him. He saw what he was. And he chuckled. "Never mind. I understand. You are incorruptible. Yes?" But as his chuckling faded, a small hint of intense feeling—a brief contraction of the lips—momentarily darkened his expression. In a musing tone, he said, "Why, though? Hm? Why are you incorruptible? Do you know what I will do? I will let *them* torture you, these two." With apparent nonchalance, he waggled his free hand at Satan and the monk. "I don't need anything from you and haven't the time or interest to do it myself, but they. . . . They are madmen and will do it for the pure pleasure. And so you will know it is useless—your incorruptibility—useless and troublesome—and then you will be dead. And do you know why I will do that to you? Hm? I will do it because it offends me. For you to think there is a reason to resist me. For you to think that you are better than I am in some way. This offends me. It does."

For a moment, Abend seemed ready to leave it at that and walk away. He lifted his chin to the monk as if instructing him to begin Zach's slow annihilation. His body leaned toward the exit. But he hesitated.

"Do you know what I have seen?" he said—more forcefully than before, with more emotion. Somehow Zach seemed to have reached him, angered him, without even meaning to. Zach glanced from him to the window. He was sure now. That was no storm out there. That was night, full night, past dusk already, full darkness. Let Abend keep talking, then. . . .

"Hm?" Abend said. "Do you know what I have seen? I have seen the doctors of the Third Reich dissect children—living children—little children mild as Christ. And do you know what else I saw? When it was over, what I saw? They died. Both. The doctor and the child. They both died, and there was no difference—only one died sooner than the other and in more pain. No difference between what happened to one and what happened to the other in the end—none. And so why? Hm? Why are you incorruptible? You will suffer and then die when you could have gone on living—and so: why?"

Zach stared at his tormenter, his body slack in his chains, his mouth hanging open, his spilled blood soaking his jockey shorts and dripping *pat pat pat* upon the wooden floor.

"ANSWER ME!" Abend shouted suddenly, his rotting face twisting in its rage. He raised his sword across himself and slashed it downward slantwise so that the new gash on Zach's chest tore across the first. And as Zach howled out his agony, Abend shouted in his face, "ANSWER ME WHY!"

His chains rattling, Zach fell forward, hanging limply from the bars. Through misted vision, he saw his blood spattering the floor between his bare feet and Abend's black boots.

"Because . . ." he tried his best to appease the German with an answer, but his throat was too dry.

"Hm? What? What?" said Abend.

"Because," Zach croaked. "I can't believe that. That there's no difference."

"Hm? No . . . ? Oh. . . ."

"Between what happens to the Nazi and what happens to the child."

"Oh-ho." Abend laughed, and a piece of gray flesh fell from the corner of one eye socket. "Can't. Can't believe." He straightened his shoulders beneath his dark overcoat, smiling thinly. "Well. You should, you know." He laughed again. "Oh yes. You should. You will, by the time these two are through with you." Again, he made as if to leave. Again, he stayed. "You are afraid of hell, then? That's what you are saying."

Zach shook his hanging head.

"Hm?"

"No," said Zach. "It's not that."

"Well, I will show you hell." Abend checked his watch. He seemed annoyed by something. The lateness of the hour? The fact he couldn't stay? "I will show you hell," he repeated.

Then again, he made that gesture to the monk—that motion of his chin. "Make it unbearable for him," he said. "Make it last forever." And to Zach he added, *"Auf wiedersehen,* Cowboy." Then he moved away, muttering "Incorruptible!"

Zach heard the rapping of his boots fading away. With an effort, he managed to raise his head. He saw the monk and Satan shift around to stand in front of him. The rat-faced monk bared his rotten teeth in a rat-faced grin. He obviously relished what was coming. The long countenance of the devil beside him simply looked mournful: the expression of an aging debauchee who knew full well that the pleasures of this life could never match his fantasies.

The monk opened his coat with slow melodrama to show the hilt of the combat knife sheathed on his belt.

Zach, his bloody flesh ablaze with pain, not certain how much more of this he could stand, silently recited an Our Father in his mind and forced himself to look away from the weapon, forced himself to look instead between the two thugs' faces to the picture window.

Nothing on the glass now but blackness, not even the sea: only blackness and the reflections of the three men there in the lighted room, the torturers' backs and Zach's crucified nakedness; only blackness . . . and now, at the center of the pane, a shapeless patch of illuminated cloud, a brightening silver-gray radiance at the border of sea and sky.

Moonrise.

23

THE USES OF LYCANTHROPY

The grinning monk drew his knife from its sheath. He brandished it sadistically, holding it up in front of Zach's eyes, turning it slowly to display first its razor-wicked edge and then its vicious serrations.

As if in response, Zach gave a long groan. He straightened abruptly in his chains. He seemed to stick his chest out at his tormenter, as if in defiance.

And then, impossibly, the crossed gashes on his torso began to knit themselves together.

There was a horribly wet sucking sound. The raw meat exposed on Zach's breasts folded in on itself, the gory scarlet of it disappearing.

The parted edges of flesh met and with a sort of leathery bubbling noise—and a busy particulate scrabbling as if a mass of tiny beetles were working just beneath the skin—they began to weave into one solid and unscarred whole. The spilled blood remained, staining Zach's abdomen and dripping from his shorts, but the body beneath the blood healed completely in the course of seconds.

The monk and Satan stood aghast. They had seen some squirrelly supernatural shit during their tenure with Abend, but not this, nothing like this. This made the monk's grin fade and Satan's studied *Weltschmerz* resolve itself into a wholly unaffected expression of gaping stupefaction. It was a definite *uh-oh* moment for two enterprising young henchmen in the very heyday of their careers.

As for Zach, he could only look down—stare down at himself dumbfounded—and watch his injuries vanish, unable to comprehend what he was seeing, his mind gone blank. At first, he felt his transformation as little more than a tickling itch all through him. But as the wounds healed, the deep pain and even deeper sickness that had pervaded him suddenly rose to the surface and molted off, and they were replaced by a heady sense of strength and well-being. He drew a deep, restorative breath. There followed one last moment of full awareness, one single second in which his understanding overcame his disbelief, when he realized what was about to happen.

Then the change went off inside him like a bomb. Truly, it was as if another self inside himself exploded, expanded and filled him, and obliterated who he had been in the blast. There was new pain—writhing, groaning, straining agony as his body was violently wrenched out of shape by a force like an internal tornado. His flesh erupted enormously. His bones expanded in a shattering rush. The wild stiff bristling fur stabbed out through his mutating skin. The pain—but also and at the same time an indescribably elemental upsurge of pleasure—made him twist and cry out and stiffen. The agony of it and the thrill became indistinguishable to him, a single sensation beyond either, more than both.

It was that pain, that pleasure, that larger sensation without a name, that threatened to eradicate him. He could feel his very soul nearly blown to smoke by the beast he was becoming. His consciousness was on the verge of being extinguished by the force of Great Nature that was taking him over from within. This, he understood even now, was why he hadn't remembered what had happened that night with Margo. He had been gone. He had been consumed in the metamorphosis. He had become the wolf.

He could not let that happen again. He could not lose control of himself so utterly. He had to fight it. Unbelievably powerful as the force of transformation was, he had to remain who he was in the midst of its whirlwind. Somehow, he had to keep his mind alive inside the burgeoning monster.

Impossible to say in words how difficult this was, what an act of will it required to fight the force of the event. He was becoming so powerful so quickly, so large in such a little instant, that the very experience of it was enough to destroy his saner self. His substance was morphing into incarnate power, his chest blossoming, doubling, tripling, quadrupling its size and strength. The spikes of fur impaled him from within and burst out into the open with a power of their own. His arms and legs grew so massive in so short a time that the manacles on his wrists and ankles broke at hinge and lock and flew away in pieces. He was free—and the blazing sirocco of wild animal passion blew up out of him in an uncontrollable roar that became an uncontrollable and raging howl. And through all this, he had to fight to retain some portion of that Zach who had looked in the mirror that morning and tied his tie. He was becoming a monster, but battling with all the force of his conscience to hold on to the inner man.

So he changed, but he was still there. He saw what was happening as if peering out from within a creature wholly beyond himself, wholly out of his control.

The monk and Satan, meanwhile, staggered back in open-mouthed shock. Satan screamed. The monk let the combat knife slip from his slack fingers. It spun down through the air and bounced on the wooden floor and lay there still. The two killers ran. Satan, his eyes like suns, shot away as if fired from a pistol. But the monk in his incredulity staggered back another step and stumbled when he tried to turn. He had to claw the air to get his balance back. He let out a girlish shriek of pure terror as he fought to get his feet under him. Then he motored from a slow, clumsy start into a full escape.

All this occurred while Zach was still transforming, while the beast was still bursting through his human boundaries as he writhed and screamed and howled.

Then the transformation was complete and Zach went after his tormenters.

He was a cop and had felt the thrill of the chase before, had forgotten himself and every danger and even all common sense in the excitement of running down some alleyway after a hightailing punk. But that was nothing compared to this. When he saw these two hapless schmucks scrambling for the doors, he felt as if some potion concocted of energy, hunger, and joy had come bubbling and snapping and sparking out of his heart to flood through him and commandeer his being. Suddenly, he was chase; he was capture; he was devour: these were all his life and purpose, and they compelled him. His small remnant of Zach-self could only look out helplessly through the wolf's immense yellow eyes as he gave a roar of the purest bloodlust and took off after the running thugs.

All his senses sharpened. He felt a complete instinctual command of distance and terrain. He was at the door of the room with a single leap. The scent of his prey infused him with fresh desire and drew him to its source as would a female in heat. There was the front door down the hallway and the smell of asphalt, sea, and sand beyond and, just darting out of sight around the edge of the jamb was oh, oh, oh, the hot, red blood-being of the running monk.

Zach—or the beast that carried him inside it—the wolf he had become—raced after the monk with a wholeness of intent so complete that its very completeness made him let out another roar. Exuberant purpose so pure that no merely human endeavor could have inspired it seemed to propel his enormous form out of the house and into the open.

He skidded over a patch of gravel, then got his huge claws dug into the verge of grass. He steadied and, in one glance of electrified intensity, saw the whole scene.

Across the little hill of lawn, Satan had reached the driveway and tumbled into his car, a sleek, silver-blue Camaro. He must have started it by remote control because its engine was already running, its headlights already on, and he, behind the wheel and hysterical with panic, was trying to shift it into gear with one hand and pull the door shut at the same time with the other.

The monk, meanwhile, was scrambling and stumbling toward the car across the grass, shrieking "Wait-wait-wait!" in a voice so high-pitched it no longer sounded even like a little girl's but was more like crow-call or the irritating creak of some unoiled machine.

Zach was appalled by his own sense of hilarity at this. The wolf's hunter-joy filled him, transformed him. He relished what he was about to do even as the feeling made him disgusted with himself.

After that, whatever he felt didn't really matter anymore, not even to him. There was only the pure motion-thrill of racing over the grass, the heat of blood in his nostrils, and the welling desire for running meat that made him slaver so that the drool flew out over his bared fangs.

He flew through the air, free as free, and pounced on the monk in the middle of yet another corvine cry. The monk's "Wait-wait-wait!" was truncated to "Wait-wait-wuh . . ." as the weight of the monster-Zach landed on him and bore him heavily to the earth. The monk began another syllable of some sort, but Zach's great jaws clamped shut on his throat and savaged it into a guttering glut of blood. So very good. The monk's body jacked and shivered as if he were being electrocuted, but this was nothing in the wolf's powerful grasp. Zach savored the monk's blood and ripped a hunk of delicious meat out of him and disemboweled him with his claws as well—and all before the poor son of a bitch could rightly die.

The monk was such a pleasure in his gullet that Zach would've gladly stayed where he was and eaten every succulent morsel of him. But even as he settled in—with his prey's last spasms radiating through his own flesh and intensifying his pleasure—he heard the sleek growl of Satan's sporty ride and looked up, dripping gore, to see the silver-blue Camaro reverse down the beach house driveway.

At this point, the cop and the wolf became bizarrely one. The beast, having hunted, would probably have stayed and eaten; but at the sight of the bright racing object with more red flesh-and-blood inside, he felt torn between hunger and the atavistic desire to give chase. And Zach, the man, the federal agent who wanted to bring down the escaping felon, felt the wolf's uprising urge to hunt and thought into his beast-self, *Yes! Go!* and that decided the matter.

He was off again. Springing across the grass, with monk-stuff still dripping from his jaws. His enormous paws hit the asphalt just as the

Camaro backed to the end of the driveway. The goateed killer behind the wheel looked up to see the monster in his headlights—and Zach caught a glimpse of Satan's face in that moment of his wildest terror. Once again, he was appalled at the uproarious vitality that filled him at the thought of running the evil idiot down and ripping him to pieces.

The Camaro's tires screeched as it swung around onto the narrow road. It stopped hard as Satan braked to throw it from reverse into drive. Instinct flaming, the werewolf left the asphalt and raced slant-wise across the lawn, not at where the sports car was, but at where it was headed: down the road.

There was a windbreak hedge along the border of the beach-house property. The Camaro shot forward and disappeared behind it, only the glow of its headlights visible through the shrubs. Zach was bounding on all enormous fours across the lawn at the hedgerow, his angle meant to intersect the Camaro's path. He reached the windbreak and leapt, flying right over it.

Even from inside the car, even over the noise of the motor, Zach heard Satan scream as he landed on the Camaro's roof. The weight of the massive supernatural creature threw the car into a zigzagging skid. It spun sideways hard, throwing Zach off it. The great wolf body tumbled through the air, hit the soft shoulder of the road, and rolled. He rose up, howling and brandishing what were still as much human arms as forelegs, the deadly claws extended.

The Camaro was turned across the pavement, frozen there for a moment, its headlights shining into Zach's hyper-sensitive eyes. A second later, the car started to straighten. At the same instant, Zach sprang toward it and ripped the driver's door open.

Even he was surprised at the power coursing through him. His wolf-self had acted on impulse, swiping a massive paw at the silver object as it tried to escape. But Zach the man had known to go for the edge of the door frame. He snagged it with his claws and tore with all his might. How easy it was! There was a loud crunch and scream of rending metal, and not only did the door's latch burst asunder but the door came flying open so hard that the force of it bent the hinge so that when the door bounced back it could not properly close.

This, not surprisingly, made Satan scream again—nothing intel-ligible, just a babbling yell of fear as he hit the gas. But even as the car was lurching forward, Zach was on it, hurling the broken door open with one paw and reaching in for the driver with the other.

Smothered in muscle and fur and pierced by dagger-like claws, Satan was yanked from behind the wheel and hurled through the darkness, his head and feet changing places as he flew. The Camaro shot forward a yard or so without him, then settled quickly to a slow, dawdling, aimless roll until it reached the edge of the road, dropped onto the shoulder, and came to a halt.

By then, Satan had hit the dirt, an impact hard enough to daze him. Still, powered by fear, he scrambled mindlessly to his feet. The wolf's triumphant howl seemed to come from everywhere so that he turned in confusion—until he saw the thing charging after him.

He didn't run. There was no point. Bounding toward him, Zach saw the goateed gunman throw his hands up in front of his face uselessly, babbling and shrieking—also uselessly.

Another moment and the prey's legs gave out under him and he sank to his knees.

As the werewolf flew at him through the air, Satan wept.

24

A LOVERS' CAMPFIRE ON THE BEACH

The werewolf ran. Full of blood and flesh and moonlight, he felt the life of ages in him and the ancient joy of life. These powered him over field and forest in a mindless ecstasy of muscle and motion. The man within was overwhelmed by the force of it. He could only ride along, a more or less helpless point of view.

Over a fence, and through high grasses. Out to the beach and the wonderfully open sand. The sky was wide here and the earth was far and the moon had broken through the clouds and shone on him and made him mighty. The sound of the surf was the echo of his heartbeat. His breath was one with the boundless salt-scent of the sea. Nothing in God's great heaven for men could match this. Running, he was the will of animal life which never dies.

The meals he had made of his torturers were with him, in him, not as a memory exactly, but as a general sense of well-fed well-being. The moment when he took them down and the moment when their heat-of-life became his heat were with him too, not as cherished mind-pictures but as fulfilled sensations still present in his moving body. If man-Zach retained any sense of disgust at these savage doings, it was less than a still-small voice in the beast. It was merely an observational glitch as good as silence. He didn't care anymore, in other words. He simply ran.

After a while, he didn't know how long, the postprandial exuberance went out of him and he slowed to a walk, his head hanging. He stopped and looked around him. The moon was nestled in the arc of the sky-dome now, the clouds drifting over its face like veils in a dance. Its light made the white dunes gleam. Zach looked up over them and saw high grass and sensed fresh water. He trudged up the sand and found a number of shimmering puddle-pools and drank gratefully.

He edged on, deeper into the grass. He found a dry spot and settled down to rest himself. He lay his head on his fur-soft arms and slept—or napped, at least, always with a sense of what was around him. His snoozing mind took stock of potential dangers in the same way his skin registered the flies that landed in his fur.

So, a little later, he became aware of presences nearby. Voices. People. Down by the beach.

He opened his eyes. Sleep had interknit the man and beast more completely. He could think, but his thoughts were a wolf's thoughts. *What is happening here?* he wondered. *Is it threatening to me? Or is it food?* He lifted his head and listened and breathed. He heard a sound he knew was laughter. He smelled a smell he recognized as blood. People near, but not so near as to be a hazard. Zach licked his chops, considering whether he was hungry again—and he was, in fact, not for food so much, but simply for the hunt-and-kill and the pleasure of it.

He stood up slowly and stretched his back. He prowled cunningly through the grass so that it barely rustled. He reached the edge of the plant-cover atop the dunes above the beach. He looked down and saw the humans and the flame.

There were two of them, one male, one female, young and healthy but small, small enough to take easily. The boy first, he thought—in his jeans and sweatshirt, his hood pulled up against the night cold. Scrawny, but he would be the stronger and faster one. Then the girl, yellow-haired and slender in her jeans and sweater and wool cap. Slower and weaker, she would have no chance to get away. She was deliciously fertile-smelling too, Zach noticed: to bite into her would be to devour generations. He would feed on them both at leisure, then lope off to find a place to rest until morning.

He watched them from within the grass. The bloodlust rose like Saturday passion in him, a warm, slow, comfortable rise. The clouds had scattered. There were wind-blown shreds at the horizon, and lofty residual patches up high, but the moon was bright and silver-clear near the meridian. The whitecaps flashed in its light as the waves lifted to it, and when they slapped face-down upon the sand, their froth was fairly glowing.

Zach moved stealthily along the edge of the grass, until he was directly above the lovers. It was the break in the weather that had brought them here, he understood. They were in their teens and hot to be romantic with each other. They had been planning this and waiting for the night to clear. They had brought some logs and gathered dead seaweed and some driftwood and built a fire. The orange flames were high and snapped in the wind. Pungent smoke trailed black across the deep blue sky.

But Zach's soul was filled with the boy's deodorant and the girl's perfume, a savor on their underlying skin. The flames worried him only a little. He could take the couple safely, he was sure of it. And he wanted them. He wanted his jaw on their throats so very much.

He watched. The boy, returning from a search of the sand, threw another plank of driftwood on the fire. The girl sprinkled seaweed on it as if salting a meal. She danced around, waggling her bottom at the boy. He dropped down onto the sand and lay back and beckoned to her. She came. Dropped on top of him. They rolled together, embracing, and kissed, the firelight turning them to silhouettes.

All this—the action and lust and raw youth of it—made the hunger mushroom in Zach's being until it filled him, irresistible. He was ready now. He settled back on his massively powerful haunches, preparing to spring.

But all this time—all this time he had been watching—the voice of man-conscience had been struggling to wake itself from the dream of the wolf's desire. All this time, the silence of Zach's human point of view was fighting to rise to at least a still, small voice again. He wanted those children—wanted to devour them—oh, he did—*he* did—there was no division at all anymore between him and the wolf he was. But by the same token, the wolf was troubled by some human sense that these were not merely two hunks of living meat but each an interior universe—attachments and sensations and the ability to love—that he had no business—no right—to annihilate in the service of his hunger.

Still—still—the urge to pounce was nearly overpowering in him. He was like a mechanism that was coiled beyond its limit and had to spring. He was drooling with readiness, heaving with readiness. Now—he wanted them now.

The boy and girl were rolling on the sand in each other's arms, laughing and kissing. Now they were sitting up. He was drawing her to him. She was resting her head on his shoulder and he had his arm around her. They were dreamily watching the flames. They would have no chance to get away from him. Now. He wanted them now.

Zach felt all that power, all that lust, all that force, that impetus to leap—and had nothing—nothing—to stop it, nothing to hold it back, but that little whisper, like a string on a rocket, that sense he had of what they were, of what he was—man, adult, police, sworn to protect them, to make the world safe for them to kiss in—but oh, the wanting, the taste of their hot life-liquid—he could already feel it in his throat. . . .

The massive, uncanny were-beast gave a shake of his great head and snorted, trying to dislodge the troublesome voice that held him there against his nature.

The girl straightened where she sat. "Did you hear something?" she murmured.

The boy listened.

Zach looked on, thinking he had to take them now—now, or they would leave and he would lose them. But still he hesitated. He had a son. He had a daughter. They would one day go to the beach with lovers of their own. . . .

"No," the boy said. "I don't hear anything."

"Sounded like an animal or something. Up there in the grass."

"Maybe a dog. Nothing else would be out here. I wouldn't worry about it."

They relaxed. She settled her head back down on his shoulder.

Zach pounced on top of them in his mind, in his yearning, but his conscience held his body back another second and another. He was thinking: *Do not!* He was pleading with himself: *Do not!* But he wanted them, wanted them the way he had wanted Margo when his hand first touched her naked waist. More.

He hesitated there yet one more second, struggling with himself.

Then the moon crossed the meridian and the curse released its grip on him.

It was a feeling like falling. Less painful than the original transformation, but less pleasurable too. Less violent and less orgasmic both. Just a long drop—as if from black empty space down to the living, blue-green earth—out of the simple immensity of lupine power and instinct into the complex, small morass of his fragile and human being. He whined like a wounded dog and staggered back helplessly into the grass.

"There really is something back there, Brad," the girl said. "I heard it moving."

"Yeah, I heard it too that time. Just sounded like a dog or something. What else is it gonna be out here?"

"Well, should you check on it? It might be hurt or something!"

"Really? You want me to go walking through the high grass looking for, like, a wild dog?"

"Well . . . no . . . I guess that's not a very good idea."

"It's not gonna bother us. Listen, it's moving away."

Zach was. Feeling the falling change begin, he was dragging himself as far as he could as quickly as he could, deeper and deeper into the grass, farther and farther from beach and fire, boy and girl, until the change overtook him fully and he collapsed by one of the freshwater pools. He lay there, writhing in the dirt and reeds, his immense limbs and torso shriveling, his miraculous strength draining out of him, his fur retracting into the skin to reveal his puny nakedness. His wolf-form curled and shrank into his man-body like paper charring to ash. Finally, metamorphosis complete, he settled onto his back, limp with exhaustion.

He lay there motionless, weak and spent, staring up through the grass-stalks at the moon. He could hear the slap of the waves, and the snap of the lovers' campfire, and the hiss and sizzle of the retreating surf. And he could hear the lovers themselves, the girl and the boy, reassuring each other there was nothing bad out there in the darkness, nothing they had to fear. She giggled and he murmured and Zach could tell that they were kissing again.

He shuddered and began to cry. He rocked himself back and forth, the tears streaming down his temples, dampening his hair. So close. That had been so awfully close. He had nearly killed those children. Another moment or two and he would have. He bit back sobs. He stared up at the blurring moon. He thought thank you, thank you, thank you to the God of his creation, who had spared him this one horror at least—thank you, thank you to the God who had taken from his blood-drenched lips the bitter cup of at least this horror.

PART IV

A VISION OF
HELL AND HEAVEN

25

SUPER COP IN HOUSE OF HORRORS

The werewolf called his wife. It was after two A.M. now. Her voice was small and childlike with sleep, so he could tell that he had wakened her. He could also tell, by how quickly she had answered the phone, that she had dozed off in a chair or on the living-room sofa, waiting for his call.

"Zach?"

"Yeah, it's me, baby, I'm okay."

"What happened, baby? Are you okay?"

"I'm okay, yeah."

"Everyone was so worried. No one knew where you were. Even Martin didn't know."

"I had some trouble with the bad guys, but it's all right now."

"Are you hurt? Did they hurt you?"

"They did not. I am okay. I'll be home in a few hours. Go to bed."

"They were all out looking for you. I was afraid."

"It's all right now, sweetheart. Go to bed. I'm okay."

He slipped the phone into his jacket pocket. He bowed his head, pinched the bridge of his nose with his fingers, and closed his eyes, weary to the bone. The red and blue lights played over him where he stood.

He was at Sea View again. He'd retreated to a corner den for privacy. The cops were everywhere out there, inside the house on every floor, down on the beach, and out in the driveway, where their figures were lit by the red and blue flashing lights of their cars—the same lights that came through the den window and flickered on him. The coroner was already in the wine cellar. The meat wagons were pulling up outside to collect the bodies.

It had all happened that quickly—very quickly, when he considered where he'd been and what he'd been up to when the moon crested.

Cleaning up the aftermath of his wolf escapades had been even easier this time than the last. The devil was on his side again, he thought. The devil was with his own.

After finding himself human in the tall grass, he had made his way naked along the dunes back to Abend's secluded beach house. It wasn't far. He was there in under twenty minutes.

Still naked, he had gotten rid of the corpses: he had dragged the bloody remains of Satan and the monk deep into the surf, trusting to the sharks to dispose of them. He had driven the wrecked Camaro back into the driveway. He found his own Crown Vic behind the closed door of the garage.

His clothes were inside the house: his phone, his wallet, his change, everything was lying atop his neatly folded suit on the floor in a small empty room near the room where he'd been shackled to the cot. He found his shredded, blood-soaked undershorts on the floor in the living room. He took the rags with him to toss out later and quickly cleaned his blood off the floor.

As it had been with Margo's house, so here: he wasn't worried about forensics. Abend had chosen this place for its isolation. The cops might never find it. If they did—well, he had an excuse for having been here: the bad guys had brought him here after they'd kidnapped him. If anything, the story of his travails in the clutches of the evildoers would help explain the bruises and scratches he'd gotten in the woods after his wolf-self had murdered Margo. As for the monk and Satan, if their remains happened to wash up onshore, so be it. He didn't know how they had gotten themselves killed. Maybe Abend had punished them for letting him get away. Anyone's guess was as good as his. *If* they washed up. Which they probably wouldn't. Probably the sharks would get them. The devil helps his own.

And as before, he didn't have to get away with it forever. Just one more day. Just one more chance at Abend and the dagger. After that, win or lose, it wouldn't matter. After that, win or lose, he couldn't go on living with himself anyway.

When he was done with the cleanup, he got in his car and made his way back to Sea View. He didn't turn his phone back on until he reached the place. Once there, he called the local law, then Rebecca Abraham-Hartwell, and finally Grace. He told them the story pretty much the way it had happened. He had been suspicious of Angela Bose. He had returned to question her. He had found her house deserted and unlocked. Fearing that Bose was in danger, he had searched the place and discovered the bodies. Then the bad guys had captured him.

On what had happened after that, he was unclear. He had been drugged and held for hours, unconscious most of the time. He had a vague memory of being questioned by Abend, but ultimately the gangster had left him to the tender mercies of his two thugs. Zach had managed to escape them somehow and to drive back to Sea View. But he'd still been under the influence of the drugs, and he couldn't remember where he'd been or how he'd gotten back.

He conveniently left out the whole turning-into-a-wolf-and-eating-people business. Too difficult to explain.

There were more cars outside the mansion now, more flashing lights, more cops. Zach came out of the den and wove his way through the milling crowd of uniforms and detectives. He found the homicide guy in charge, a balding, beefy working stiff with the unlikely name of Stinger Blaine. Taller than Zach and much bigger around, he was in a rumpled gray-blue leisure suit—looked like he'd dropped it at the foot of his bed before collapsing for the evening. A taste of beer was on his breath, but he seemed sober enough. His cop-suspicious eyes were alert, at any rate.

"What a mess," he said, shaking his head, resting from the general melee with his hands on his wide hips.

"How many are there, does it turn out?" said Zach.

"Seven-fucking-teen of them, can you believe it? The last one, the M.E. says, within the last forty-eight hours."

"Yeah, the one on the table. He looked pretty fresh."

"One of them in the closets I recognized. Pross. Questioned her a year or so ago after one of the local girls helped her john speedball himself to death. Fucking Guyland, man. You city boys have no idea."

"Was she homeless, the pross?"

"Off and on, yeah, why?"

"I'll bet they all were," said Zach. "Bose supported homeless shelters all across the island."

"You're thinking she gave some of her clientele a lift home from time to time."

"Brought them back to Abend, yeah."

"I thought this Abend guy was gangsta. Organized crime and such. What was this—his hobby?"

Zach gave a snort and nodded vaguely. He didn't want to mention the dagger or human sacrifice or the whole centuries-old-evil angle, though he was pretty sure that's what this was about. In fact, he was pretty sure that if he could get some time alone to think it through, he could figure out the whole case now. He had a sense that he was closer to Abend than ever, closer than anyone had been since he'd escaped the gulags and recovered the baselard. That was the thing that was keeping him going, despite all the horror: he was so close.

Driving home, he tried to focus on the facts he knew. If nothing else, the exercise was a refuge from the chaos in his mind. When he wasn't thinking cop-thoughts, he had to fight off the wolf-flashbacks of the night: the monk's throat in his mouth—running on the beach with the weird eternal animal life-force in him—the urge to kill like lust coursing all through his body as he crouched poised above the teenage lovers, his muscles tensed to spring. Memories no human mind should hold. Sensations no man ought to know.

The intermittent highway street lamps glared in his face through the windshield. The interplay of dark and light was soporific and God, he was already tired to his bones. But the flashbacks—ripping open the monk's belly like tearing a canvas sack—pausing to savor the weeping terror of Satan before he struck—these jolted him awake whenever his head bowed toward the wheel. Then, alert for a while, he focused his mind on the case to hold the flashbacks at bay. Dark and light. Thoughts and flashbacks. A hypnotic checkerboard pattern within and without him.

"The dagger was never stolen," he murmured aloud. "It was never missing at all."

The headlights of an oncoming semi blinded him. When the truck passed with a rumble and whoosh, he had to squint through the glass to make out the black highway. Then, suddenly, his own high beams picked out a woman standing right in front of him.

There was no time to brake. He drove right into her. He gasped—but there was no impact: the fender passed straight through her. The next moment, Zach smelled cigarette smoke and the sour aroma of meat going rotten. He turned to see Gretchen Dankl smoking sullenly in the seat beside him.

"She had it," he said to her groggily. "Angela Bose had the dagger all along."

"There is always a woman," said Dankl, lifting the cigarette to her lips in those long witchy fingers, the smoke swirling around that anxious-monkey face of hers. "But it never lasts." Then she dissolved into shadow, leaving only those faintly sickening scents to stale the air of the car.

Only after she was gone did Zach think of all the questions he wanted to ask her. He remembered Abend's blade ripping him open— the agony—the sense of mortal violation—and the wounds miraculously healing as the full moon rose. Was it like that now? Was he indestructible? Could only a person of faith with a silver bullet end him—as he wanted to be ended—as he had ended Dankl herself?

And was that the power that had entered the baselard when the executioner had cut Peter Stumpf's hand off, when the demonic blood and holy water had mingled on the blade? The power of life? The power of rejuvenation? Or was there more to it than that?

He sensed that the rules of this new game were more complex and dangerous than he yet knew, but still he felt his way forward, figuring out what he could.

Dominic Abend had been alive for a long time. Zach thought back to the photograph Dankl had shown him: a man in his thirties in a Nazi uniform. And he remembered his own naïve reaction: *Why, he'd be well over a hundred years old by now!* That was just it: he *was.* Something—the power of the dagger—had extended his life.

Here, a street lamp shone in on him sharply, and he flashed back to Abend's strangely bulging eyes, his sunken cheeks and sockets, the shifting in his skin like maggots. . . .

He was rotting. Abend. He was dying. He had lost the dagger and was decaying. That was why he was so desperate, so crazily violent, so willing to break his own rules and show himself in his quest to get the dagger back.

Zach shook his head quickly, fighting off sleep. This was falling into place now, all falling into place as he had hoped it would. Seventeen dead in the Sea View wine cellar. Angela Bose had been there for a year and a half. One sacrifice a month. At the full moon when the wolf's blood in the blade became active. The magic of the dagger supercharged the blood of those it slaughtered. The blood of the sacrifice reinvigorated the blood of the living. . . .

"Am I getting this right?" Zach murmured. Because it all sounded so much like madness—but here he flashed back to the change that had exploded through him as he hung chained to the bars in the beachhouse doorway. What could seem like madness after that? What could "madness" even mean?

There was a faint fizzle of static from the radio. Zach cursed. His lips twitched as he tried to sneer the machine into silence. Because he hadn't turned the damned thing on, for Christ's sake. It ought not to be making a sound.

He went on thinking, working it through. There was always a woman, but it never lasted. Angela Bose had sensed that her time with Abend was ending. How long had they been together? A year and a half? A decade? Two? Twenty years of never aging. But Abend was tired of her. Soon he would get rid of her and find another companion, and she would be left to grow suddenly old and die.

Then came the Guyland heists. Maybe it had just been a coincidence that the Grimhouse brothers had hit Sea View. Maybe she had heard about the heists and enlisted them. Or maybe the whole burglary spree had been her plan from the beginning. Zach favored the coincidence theory: if the Grimhouse brothers had known Bose was involved, they would have given her up when Abend tortured them.

So Sea View was hit in the heists, and Bose seized the moment to claim that the dagger had been stolen—when in fact it was probably so well hidden, the Grimhouse boys could never have found it. Abend trusted her. He believed her. He was in a panic. He knew he had to get the dagger back before the full moon faded or the years would catch up with him all at once. He went on a rampage, tracing the goods to the man who had fenced them—Paz—torturing Paz for the names of the Grimhouse brothers—torturing the brothers then. . . . And finally, when he could get nothing out of them, he realized the truth, that he had been betrayed by his lover. Bose—too afraid of Abend to steal the dagger outright—had seized upon the heist to pretend it had been stolen so she could keep it for herself, live on as Abend decayed and died. It was she—and she alone—who had sacrificed the homeless man Zach had found on the table. Then she had run for it, taking the dagger with her. If she could stay out of Abend's reach for one more day and night, he would die, and the dagger would be hers.

"Stop," said Zach aloud to the radio.

Because there was more static now, louder though still barely audible beneath the wind and engine noise. He wanted it to go away. He was sick and tired of hearing from the dead.

But they insisted. The radio flared, a loud white sough. He heard the soft voices buried within the hiss, like the cries of a civilization that had been swallowed by a snake. He heard the snicker of fire. Women's pitiable screams. Children weeping for their mothers. Men gagging out their lives at the ends of ropes. He recognized all of it. It was the soundtrack of the vision he had had while under the influence of Abend's drug. He hit the radio's OFF button angrily, but the static didn't even waver, and neither did the noises within the hiss: entire dying generations calling out to him over the airwaves.

"I have my own soul and my own sins," he snapped at them.

But history flowed through him like animal life had flowed through the wolf. And amidst the static and the violent cries, he realized there were other voices. The dead trying to reach him, trying to tell him something, something he'd missed. In spite of himself, Zach listened. The radio sputtered and hissed. The voices whispered. Something about life. Something about fear. Something he'd missed.

The radio went silent.

Zach thought, *He who would save his life at any cost must first become the servant of fear.*

It was not his thought. It had come to him . . . through the radio? From somewhere, anyway. He had no idea what it meant.

All he did know was that there was one more night of the full moon left, one more night for Abend to find the dagger before decay overcame him. That meant Abend had to find Angela Bose before the moon reached its meridian this evening.

And that meant Zach somehow had to find her first.

Police everywhere would be on the lookout for that silver-blue Bentley of hers—how difficult could it be to spot? But Abend's lines of influence ran deep into the police and government at every level. If someone saw Bose's car, would the law learn about it before Abend did? The answer was by no means certain.

The long and dreamlike drive took him home again. After four A.M. now as he stepped out of the Crown Vic. Hardly worth going to bed, but he had to. He had to sleep.

The moment he came into the darkened bedroom, his wife rolled onto her back and put her white arms out to him. He kicked off his shoes and crawled across the mattress to her. He laid his head on her breast while she held him. He drew in that aroma she had, the scent of that other world inside her, that world he yearned for, a country on a far horizon, a homeland he was journeying away from, like the old emigrants on the sailing ships of yore.

"I was so worried," she whispered in his ear and kissed him.

"I'm okay."

"You can't die, you know. You're not allowed. We need you in this house. You're our guy."

It made his heart ache, because he was not okay, and he would have to die when this was over. There was no other way out that he could see. He had murdered Margo and he would have to die for it, and the best he could hope for was that Grace and his children would never find out what he had done, what he had become.

He held his wife and told her that he loved her, but that didn't say half of what he felt. He didn't have the words for what she was to him. There was nothing on earth to compare it to.

"Y'all smell bad," she teased him, tweaking his ear with her fingers.

"I'll shower."

"Brush your teeth too."

He flashed back on the monk writhing in his jaws, the hot blood coursing down his throat. He pressed his wife's soft, warm body against his own. He pressed his face into her silky neck-skin, and smelled the blood coursing through her jugular.

"I will," he said.

He pushed up off her, giving her one more lingering kiss as he drew away, hesitating then to look down at her, the sweet, faithful face in its tumbling curls, only just visible in the darkness.

She stroked his cheek. "I know God says we're not supposed to hate them." Her soft Texas twang was audible even when she whispered. "Or answer evil with evil. But the things they do. . . ."

"I know it."

"I can hardly listen to the news. I think about y'all out there trying to stop them."

"I know."

"And when they try to hurt my sweetheart. . . ."

"Ssh. Don't say that. They can't hurt me, baby."

"I can't help thinking if they'd just stop—all the killing and stealing and hurting people—everyone'd be fine."

"It's a fallen world."

"I know it."

He smiled down at her in the dark, but the terrors of the night came back to him again. He remembered himself crouched above those two kids on the beach. Him—Zach—thinking how fine it'd be to devour them, how good they'd taste. He knew he had been only moments away from losing control of himself and tearing into them both . . . which made him remember the hunks of Satan's flesh in his gullet. . . . A fallen world? All he wanted just then was to put his head back on his wife's breast like it was his mama's and listen to her talk the Bible talk that, sometimes, at times like this, he couldn't even understand anymore.

He showered and brushed his teeth, fighting off memories all the while. He bent to spit toothpaste into the sink—and just as he straightened, he caught the face of a dead man in the mirror behind him—that dandy he'd seen by the side of the Long Island Expressway, the one in the blue-and-silver coat. He was standing right behind his shoulder now, staring at him somberly.

"Holy . . . !" Zach said aloud, startled.

The dandy had already vanished, but Zach's heart was beating so hard, he thought he'd never get to sleep.

But he did. He slept for two hours, his head on Grace, her arms around him. Incredible peace. Even when the alarm woke him, he could feel how good it had been.

The children were at the kitchen table spooning milk and cereal into their mouths and Grace was pouring coffee for him when he turned on the family computer and saw the headline on the news site: "Super Cop in House of Horrors." The story of the bodies in Angela Bose's wine cellar had blasted Margo Heatherton's picture off the site, at least. There were fresh riots in London too, so maybe with a little more devilish luck, Grace would never find out about Margo's death at all, never match her face to the woman Zach had spoken to outside the church.

"That's you, Daddy!" said little Tom, pointing to the monitor.

The site had used the old picture from the Oklahoma farmhouse, the one that showed Zach holstering his weapon after he'd gunned down Ray Mima, Goulart behind him, the rescued child in his arms. Tom had a copy of that picture taped up on his wall. He was proud of his Dad.

"Super Cop," the child said. He was only just learning to read, but he knew those words from his comic books. "Are you the Super Cop, Daddy?"

"That's just silly talk," he said.

"We're gonna have to get Daddy a uniform with a big S on it," said Grace, looking over her shoulder from the coffee maker on the counter.

"I think my S looks big enough in my jeans," said Zach.

Grace rolled her eyes. A moment later, Tom got the joke and snorted milk into his hands. "My S looks big enough in my jeans!"

"Oh, now look!" Grace scolded her husband, but she could hardly keep from laughing herself.

Zach ruffled the boy's soft hair as he stood over him drinking his coffee. He winked affectionately at his daughter, who was giggling because Tom was.

They could never know, he thought, heavy-hearted. He had to die when this was over, and they could never know what he had become.

Grace went to the stove now to cook him some eggs, her voice trailing back to him as she moved: "Did you hear about that poor woman got killed by a bear in her own home up in Westchester? Sandy was telling me about it. . . ."

Before Zach could begin to rattle off the complex mix of half-truths and lies he had prepared for this moment, the phone in his pocket buzzed.

"I guess I know who *that* is," Grace said, clattering a frying pan onto the stove top. And as Zach lifted the phone to his ear, she sang out, "Morning, Rebecca!"

"You better get in here," said Rebecca Abraham-Hartwell.

Not her usual self-conscious I'm-all-business tone. Something more than that. Something that made Zach draw in an unsteady breath.

"What's going on?"

"I've got a couple of detectives here from Westchester," said Rebecca Abraham-Hartwell tensely. "They want to talk to you about Margo Heatherton."

26

ROTH AND WASHINGTON

The detectives—Inspectors, they were called—were named Danny Roth and Alonzo Washington. Except for the fact that one was white and one black, they looked pretty much alike. Both were enormous: six-foot-something top-to-toe, huge shoulders, huge chests, huge bellies. Both had close-cropped salt-and-pepper hair, baggy eyes, saggy features, mournful and grave. The white guy's big nose went out and down, the black guy's big nose went splat across his face. Other than that: cop twins.

They met with Zach in Rebecca Abraham-Hartwell's office. Zach sat on the sofa, his arm across the back of it as if he were relaxed. Roth—the white guy—perched on the very edge of Rebecca's armchair, as if the broad seat were too tiny for his bulk to squeeze into. The black guy—Washington—sat on the sofa as far from Zach as he could, even drawing his big frame back a little as if to increase the distance.

Rebecca sat behind her desk, her legs in their navy slacks crossed at the knee, her long chin pinched between thumb and finger-knuckle as she looked on with great seriousness. The TV on the wall was turned off: that's how serious she was.

Outside the window, a sky-load of dark gray clouds hulked ominously behind the wedge-topped skyscraper.

"You understand, you're not a suspect or anything," said Washington. He was one of those outsized men who had to breathe hard when he spoke. His tone suggested that they were all reasonable people here, all here to be reasonable. "We know this was a wild animal attack."

"We're just trying to ascertain what exactly happened," said Roth, who was also one of those heavy-breathing fat guys and also tried to sound reasonable. "So we can make sure there's no ongoing danger to the community."

"We don't get a whole lot of bear or wolf or wildcat attacks," Washington explained with a hint of a smile.

"We don't get *any*," Roth explained, likewise smiling. "Whatever it was."

"Uh-huh," said Zach dubiously—because he knew what interrogating cops were like and he didn't trust them. Lulling you with their smiles and reason before they brought the hard hammer down. Why couldn't they just leave him alone and let him get on with the work of catching Dominic Abend?

The thought struck even him as irrational. He was doing that thing perps do—that thing they do in their minds where they convince themselves they're innocent even though they're guilty as hell, where they begin to feel put-upon and hard-done-by. *Why are these mean people persecuting me?* He was sitting there with his fake-relaxed arm on the sofa back, fish-eyeing his fellow lawmen and feeling basically pissed off that they were wasting his morning—and yet, all the while, he had, in fact, ripped poor Margo to pieces.

"So what's this got to do with me?" he said.

Roth made a two-handed gesture at him as if he were laying his cards face up on the table. As if. "You knew her, right?"

"I met her."

"And you didn't mention this?" Rebecca Abraham-Hartwell cut in suddenly—again setting off in Zach some vague sense that he was being unfairly hounded by the powers that be.

"I didn't hide it. Goulart knew—my partner," Zach explained to the inspectors. "It just didn't seem relevant to anything. I met her a couple of times, helped her with research on a book. And yeah, then. . . ." He had already guessed they knew more than this, or they wouldn't be here. He knew he had to tell them something: but how much? How many suspects, he wondered, had asked themselves the same question when he was pressing himself into their sweating faces in the interview room?

"Then?" said Washington.

"Well, she developed some sort of thing for me, I guess. Some sort of fascination. Calling me all the time. Texting me."

"Well, you're a handsome guy," said Roth.

"Well, thanks kindly," said Zach. "But like I told Margo, I'm already spoken for."

"You didn't give her any reason for this fascination," said Washington. "Other than your good looks, I mean. I mean, there was nothing between you two."

Zach snorted as if the idea were absurd. And yes, he did feel a beaded line of sweat arise just beneath his hairline. "In her imagination, maybe, but not in real life, no."

Washington gave a soft grunt—doing that cop thing, Zach knew, pretending to be confused, in all innocence, about the puzzling discrepancy between the perp's story and the facts. So here it came.

"Thing is—reason we're here—Miss Heatherton kept a journal. On her computer. Thoughts and events, that sort of thing."

"She had her eye on you for a long time, it seems like," said Roth, his breath laboring.

"Seems she fell for you when she saw that picture of you that was in all the news stories a few years back," said Washington. "You walking out of that farmhouse after you shot Ray Mima."

"I know the picture," said Zach.

"Holstering your six-shooter, all cowboy style."

"I know."

"I liked that myself," said Washington heavily.

"So did she," said Roth. "She wrote in her journal that you were just the kind of man she wanted."

"She devised what you might call a . . . a campaign," said Washington.

"To seduce you," said Roth. "It was very well worked out." With this, the big man—who was perched precariously so near the edge of Rebecca's armchair that Zach thought the movement might unbalance him and make him slip to the floor—reached into his jacket pocket and drew out the phone he kept his notes on. "This is her journal entry for September the 17th." He read off the screen: "'Success at last! I've never known such passion! We were both swept away by it! We couldn't even make it to the bedroom! He's mine now, finally!'"

Rebecca Abraham-Hartwell's hand slid from her chin up to cover her eyes. "For Christ's sake, Zach."

"It never happened, Rebecca," Zach protested—and he genuinely felt offended that she would believe such a thing about him—even though, of course, it was true! He continued, as if admitting a painful fact: "I went up there one night. Must've been right around then. Around mid-September. She said there was going to be a reading of this book I'd helped her with—"

"You tell your wife about this?" said Roth in an insinuating tone.

Zach ignored him, shrugged it off. "When I got there, the reading was canceled and she said she needed a lift home. She made it clear she was available. I didn't take her up on it. That's all that happened."

Roth and Washington went through their routine. They looked at each other with smirking incredulity. They looked at him with smirking incredulity.

"Awful pretty woman," said Roth.

"But you just turned her down," said Washington.

Zach spread his hands, the image of innocence. "That's what happened, fellahs."

Washington nodded. Roth nodded, slipping his phone back into his pocket.

"So you weren't there the night she died, were you?" Washington asked.

"Someone was," said Roth. "But that wasn't you?"

"Of course not," Zach said. "I would have reported that."

"Sure, you would," said Roth.

"Of course you would," said Washington. "Because there was nothing between you two."

"So it's not like you had a motive to kill her or anything," said Roth.

"I thought y'all said a wild animal did that," said Zach. At this point, the sweat beneath his hairline was cold and his whole face felt clammy.

Washington addressed Roth—more cop stuff—as if they were working out their line of reasoning as they spoke. "Of course, some crazy broad with a rich fantasy life can cause a lot of trouble for a man. Especially a family man. Texting him. Calling him all the time. Claiming they'd had sexual relations."

"Some hot babe like Margo showed up at my house, told my wife we did the deed? Wife'd believe her, no question."

"Who wouldn't?" said Washington, rounding on Zach again. "Good-looking girl like that."

"Anyone would believe her," said Roth. "What red-blooded man would turn her down?"

"Gotta make you crazy," said Washington. "Being falsely accused like that, and no one taking your side. Be enough to make a man lose his temper."

Zach looked from one to the other of them, and to Rebecca, who stared at him dolefully now. She had already convicted him—and he could practically see the gears turning behind her eyes as she worked out the political implications of his downfall. With him gone, she might have more power, no universally respected lawman to stand against her. Maybe she could even get rid of Goulart. . . .

"I didn't sleep with her," Zach said. "And I wasn't there the night she died." He felt simultaneously convinced of these bald-faced lies as he spoke them, and satisfied at how believable they sounded coming from a man known to be as honest as himself. It was a kind of perp madness that disturbed his heart even as it unstoppably took over his mind.

Now it was Washington's turn to bring out his phone. The gesture made Zach feel claustrophobic. How many poor criminal bastards had felt this suffocating sensation as Zach confronted them with a fresh piece of damning evidence? Wondering: What now? What more did they have?

As Washington thumbed through the phone files, searching for what he wanted, Roth said, "We have a lot of hunters in our area. Ever since they heard there might be a bear or mountain lion on the loose, they've been roaming around the woods with their rifles and crossbows and whatnot, wearing their night-vision goggles and so on, and looking to be the hero who brings the mad creature down. Apparently they found a lot of evidence that some large creature had been through there. Bear probably."

"Well, there you go," said Zach.

"Of course, they destroyed the trail, tromping all over it like that."

"Figures."

"All lots of fun until someone gets an arrow in his eye."

Here Washington took up the story, handing his phone to Zach to show him the photo on it. "One of these hunters took this picture last night near Miss Heatherton's house. You recognize that woman?"

Zach was expecting some green-night-lens mess of an image with a blurred figure on it but, dang, this shot was clear as day. And he surely did recognize the woman—a woman sneaking around Margo's tree line on the night after she was slaughtered, the same night Zach was being tortured in Abend's beach house. And just as surely as he knew her, he damn well wasn't going to tell Roth and Washington that he did. Because who she was wasn't half the shock of it. It was what she was doing that hit Zach so hard, that told him so much that he could never explain to these two. That is, she was carrying a gun, a .38 revolver, holstered at her slim hip, visible—and reachable—in the gap between the two panels of her unbelted purple woolen sweater-coat-thing.

"Amazing what they can do with those night lenses nowadays," said Roth, who must have spotted the surprise and recognition in Zach's eyes.

Zach handed the phone back to Washington. "Not all that clear. Hard to make out her face. Don't *think* I know her, anyway."

And with that, he stood up. He ran his hand up over his hair—vigilant enough to use his left hand so that, if the inspectors shook his right, they wouldn't feel the sweat on it. He was already getting good at this lying, murderous perp stuff. Didn't take long.

Rebecca Abraham-Hartwell lifted her long face—like a horse who's heard a noise in the nearby brush, Zach thought. "Where the hell do you think you're going?"

"Rebecca, y'all may not have noticed, but I am hot on the heels of the man who gives this Task Force its reason for being," Zach drawled—his stubborn drawl. "This woman was a minor pain in the neck to me. I didn't sleep with her. I wasn't there when the bear or whatever it was killed her. I can't spend any more of my morning like this. I really can't." He nodded at Roth and Washington. "Gentlemen, I'm sorry. But I've got to go to work."

Both inspectors stood up.

"We still have some questions," said Washington.

"Send me an e-mail," said Zach. "I'll answer when I have time."

"Sit down," said Rebecca Abraham-Hartwell.

But he did not. Would not. He walked to the door.

"We may have to talk to your wife," Roth threatened him.

He didn't look back. He pulled the door open.

"Zach," Rebecca called after him angrily.

He was already in the hall. He slammed the door behind him and kept walking. Off to find the woman in the picture. The woman with the gun.

Imogen Storm.

27

THE TROUBLE
WITH IRONY

The autumn gloom gathered as the morning wore on. There were rumblings of thunder audible above the rumbling trucks on Tenth Avenue. Zach parked the Crown Vic across from a dreary white brick building—apartments over a liquor store—the address Imogen Storm had scribbled on her *Bizarre!* business card.

He moved to the glass door, which was set in an alcove a step off the sidewalk. He pressed the button over her apartment number. He waited. His nerves were humming like electric wires. He could feel the truth closing in on him like the stone walls of a trap that would smash him flat. The space he could move in was getting smaller and smaller. And every likely outcome was unthinkable. If Abend got that dagger back . . . if Abend found Angela Bose before he did . . . or if Angela Bose got away with the dagger herself . . . or even if he somehow put an end to them and then blew his own brains out with a silver bullet. . . . He could picture his son's face when Mommy explained that Daddy wasn't coming home anymore. His little daughter's face. It was all unthinkable.

Imogen's clipped British tones came over the intercom. "Forget something?"

Despite everything going through his mind, Zach smiled a little, one corner of his mouth lifting. His intuition was firing like a fine machine. Maybe it was a wolf thing. He understood all.

"It's Zach Adams," he said.

There was a momentary silence—an embarrassed silence, Zach imagined. Then the entry buzzer sounded. Zach pulled the door open and stepped into the dark foyer. The door hadn't even swung shut behind him before his intuition was confirmed. Even there in the lobby, his heightened wolf senses caught the smell of the familiar cologne—and the disease and the desperation—of Martin "Broadway Joe" Goulart.

Imogen was dressed to stay home. Jeans buttoned around her *Stay Calm and Carry On* nightshirt, no bra. She'd put on some lip gloss in a hurry, and some scent. She was hopping on one foot, pulling on her second flat as she opened the door to her apartment.

"Sorry to disturb you, Miss Storm," he said.

"Not at all. Come on in. *I'm* sorry the place is such a mess. I wasn't expecting company."

It was a small studio, the floor space nearly overtaken by the unmade sofa-bed. One wall was made of brick, and there were pastel landscapes on the other walls. Not her sort of paintings, Zach knew. There was a narrow corner shelf with knick-knacks, and Zach knew those weren't hers either: unicorns and crystal wizards and God knew what other sentimental crap. The kitchenette was a narrow sliver behind a metal counter. Dirty dishes in the sink.

A small flat-screen device sat on top of a small bureau. It was playing the news. Sometime between when Zach had left home and now, the rioters had set the Palace of Westminster, the home of the British Parliament, on fire.

"I don't so much mind the animals who did it," said Imogen Storm. She was standing by his elbow as he watched the flames, hugging herself as if she were cold. "It's the bloody fools cheering for them. What do they think will follow? Peace and freedom?" Her cheeks were pale, her eyes haunted.

Zach, meanwhile, found himself calculating the effect on the news cycle. He knew it was only the telegenic flames that kept the programmers interested in the burning building for now. As soon as the Parliament building was charred black or completely in ashes, they'd go back to the Super Cop in the wine cellar full of bodies—and from there, how long would it be until they got the word that Westchester was questioning Super Cop about the dead bear lady? The fire thirty-five hundred miles away had given him a little time to act without the press corps dogging him, but it wouldn't be long.

He and Imogen both watched silently a moment, their thoughts their own. The voice of the TV reporter was the only voice in the room.

Then Imogen stepped forward and switched off the device. "I can't watch any more. Let me make some space for us."

Zach helped her fold the bed back into the sofa. Imogen's scent had masked it on her own body, but the smell of Goulart was almost over-rich on the blankets. The smell of sex was growing stale on the sheets. His partner had worked fast, Zach thought. But then there had been a connection between these two from the get-go, plus he could guess Imogen's weakness, and Goulart would have been able to guess it too.

"It's one of those online exchange flats," Imogen said by way of excuse as she picked the sofa cushions off the floor and tossed them over the folded mattress. "It serves my turn, but there's not a lot of breathing room."

By the time she was finished, Zach, pivoting back and forth on his heels, focusing in that way he sometimes did, had spotted the small canvas bag buried under laundry on the floor of her half-opened closet.

"Coffee?" said Imogen. "It's already on."

"Thanks."

She was on the other side of the kitchenette counter, her back to him as she filled his mug. When she turned to put the mug down in front of him, he slipped the canvas bag onto the counter beside it.

"I'm guessing if I opened that, I'd find an illegal firearm," he said.

"Milk and sugar?"

"A little, thanks."

She was as Brit-cool as he would have expected. He sank himself onto one of the counter stools while she rooted in the refrigerator for the milk carton. Her nose buried in the bright box, she said, "Aren't there some sort of rules about searching a person's domicile in this country, or have we abandoned all those niceties now that we're burning Parliaments and all?"

"Some hunter took a picture of you at Margo Heatherton's house last night. The gun was visible in the shot. That might make probable cause, but it doesn't matter much. The gun isn't why I'm here."

She set the milk before him as the fridge swung shut. She leaned her elbows on the counter and met his gaze. Cool as he'd expected, but more intense, more ferocious than he'd realized up till now. Those brown eyes of hers—so pale, they were nearly golden—fairly gleamed with her determination. Her thin lips with their hurried purple gloss were pressed together tightly. Well, her fiancé was one of the victims of this whole business. Not to mention her country. Zach still couldn't help liking her. He poured a dollop of milk into his coffee.

"Why *are* you here, then?"

"I'd like to know what you were doing up at Margo's house last night."

"I think whoever killed her killed Bernard," she said, as if this was obvious. "So I went up to do a little investigating of my own, having got no joy from—" she tipped a hand at him "—the local constabulary. I'm a reporter, remember. What did you think I was going to do? Say 'Thank you ever so much for your time, Agent Adams,' and quietly go home?"

Zach raised his mug to his lips and sipped the steam off the surface. He'd had enough coffee this morning and didn't really want any more. His eyes shifted toward the bag. "If I opened that and took the gun out. . . ."

"As I say, there are rules. . . ."

"And if I emptied the gun onto the counter. . . ."

Imogen stopped talking. Her expression went serious. She had only now caught up to him, only now begun to see where he was heading.

"I'm guessing I would find it loaded with silver bullets."

She drew a sharp breath through her nose—that was her only response.

"You went up there at night, the second night of the full moon," Zach said. "You weren't investigating, Miss Storm. You were hunting. You've been hunting all this time. You wouldn't have been doing that if you were only after Gretchen Dankl. You'd have left her to the police. But the police don't have the right weapons, do they?"

"You *are* a good detective," said Imogen—and her lips pressed together. To make the *M* sound, Zach thought, his instincts humming. To say *Martin told me you were.* But she stopped herself.

"Call me a dumb old American," Zach said, "but the trouble with irony is that you never really have to commit yourself, do you? Your *Bizarre!* website—y'all might be making fun of things or you might not. You play it both ways. But you never have to take a stand. You never have to tell people what you believe and what you don't."

"It's called 'Negative Capability—'"

"It's called 'yellow' where I come from." He set his mug down and flicked a finger toward the canvas bag. "All that psychological lycanthropy stuff. . . . Why didn't you tell me you were after a genuine werewolf?"

She pushed off the counter, standing straight across from him. "And what would you have said to that, Agent? 'Ah, good, let me get my silver bullets. Plus a cross and garlic in case we run into any vampires.' You'd have treated me like a crank and sent me away. You nearly did as much as it was."

"But that's the truth, isn't it? Irony aside. You believe you're after a werewolf."

"I identified Bernard's body," said Imogen Storm. "The police were right. No human being could've done that. No animal that lives in Britain could have either."

"And so your plan is to hunt Dankl down and shoot her."

"To hunt down the creature who killed Bernard, yes."

"And the whole Dominic Abend side of it. . . ."

This was the first time she broke eye contact with him, looking at the floor almost as if she were ashamed. "Not my department," she said tersely.

"Even though Dankl said he was evil. That she was trying to stop him before his corruption destroyed everything she loved."

"Well . . . that's her excuse for being what she is, isn't it? 'Tore a man to pieces? Ah, well, so sorry, too bad. But heigh-ho, it's all in the service of fighting evil.' It won't wash."

He kept silent until she glanced up at him again. "Except you do believe her, don't you? I saw it when you were watching Parliament burn. Everything that's happening over there, it all leads back to him and that dagger somehow. That's what she was trying to tell your fiancé."

She leaned forward, her expression ferocious, her hand splayed on the countertop as if she'd slapped it down. "I don't care. I loved Bernard. She killed him. She has to be stopped."

Zach nodded slowly. "And no one will help you."

"No one will believe me," she said bitterly. "Who would?"

"Only Broadway," said Zach. "Only Goulart. He believes you, doesn't he?"

She drew up, as if offended. Regarded him with stern, haughty eyes and pinkening cheeks—a girlish change in her pixie features that made Zach feel protective toward her.

"That's right," she said. "Martin believes me."

She said it with pride and fierce certainty, but Zach could hear that she felt defensive, that she wasn't certain at all. Because that was her weakness: her need to find someone to believe her, a man, preferably, preferably a man with a gun and a badge. That was her weakness, and she knew it. Sure, she did. She was a smart girl. Loyal, brave, determined, and very smart. She knew herself well enough to know where her vulnerabilities lay. After the heat and comfort of having Goulart in her fold-out bed with her, in the calm that followed, it would have occurred to her that she might have been played. Pretending to believe her, pretending to take her seriously, was the sort of thing a man *would* do if he was on the make. A good instinctual detective like Goulart— he would know that that was the fastest way into her.

"So you called him—Goulart—after you went to Margo's house," said Zach.

Imogen was embarrassed and angry now. She strode from behind the counter. "This is none of your business." She stationed herself at the front door, arms crossed beneath her breasts. Poised to throw him out. But she didn't throw him out. "You're lucky he does believe

242

me, you know," she said. "If he didn't. . . ." She stopped herself before she'd finished.

If he didn't believe a werewolf had killed Margo, he would suspect it was you. That's what she had been about to say. But Zach let the words trail off to nothing. He didn't want her to think about it too much. As things stood now, Imogen was so intent on finding Dankl, had been hunting Dankl so ferociously and for so long, that what seemed so obvious to Zach hadn't even occurred to her yet: that Dankl was gone; that she, Imogen, was hunting someone else now; she was hunting him.

He stood up from the stool and came to her. "Did you find something? At Margo's? Is that why you called Goulart? What did you find?"

"Don't patronize me. I know you think I'm a nutter."

"Did Goulart tell you to keep it secret from me?"

"He just told me not to waste my breath on you, that's all."

"What did you find, Imogen?"

Arms still crossed defiantly, she frowned and said "What are you, looking for a good laugh? Is that it?"

Zach grimaced. It was the first time she'd sounded as young as she was, as fearful and alone as she obviously was. "Come on," he said. "What did you find?"

A moment more, then she confessed it: "I found Abend."

Zach tried not to let her see him react. "Abend was there? Last night? At Margo's place?"

"I'm almost sure of it."

"You didn't see him, then?"

"He was in the house. It was dark in there. But I'm almost certain I caught a glimpse of him through the window, and also I. . . ."

"You what? What else?"

Again, she was defiant. Frowning, silent a long moment, before she hurled it at him like a challenge. "I felt him. I felt the . . . the presence of evil." When he did not laugh at her, she was bold enough to add, "It's not the first time I've felt it, either."

He still didn't laugh at her, or roll his eyes, or make any of the stonily sardonic expressions she'd seen on the faces of policemen across the continent of Europe and here. And she, weary of standing up to him, uncertain of Goulart, desperate to be believed, finally dropped her crossed arms and her defiance and moved with slumped resignation into the central part of the room. She sank down onto the sofa. She was facing away from him. She wanted it that way.

"I've been following Gretchen Dankl for over a year now. During that time, I've crossed paths with Abend twice. Once in Vienna, outside the opera house. Once on a back street in Prague. Both times, it was just for a moment. We passed each other. I wasn't even sure who he was. But both times, I felt . . . something. A shock of darkness. A terrible emptiness. As if I were walking along and suddenly found myself on the edge of a pit, staring down into a black abyss."

"Yes," Zach murmured. He had, of course, felt it too, once in that hallway in Long Island City, and once in the beach house.

"After that first time, I realized, I always felt him near when I got close to Dankl. That part of what she says is true, at least. She is hunting him. Him and his dagger. She does believe. . . . Well, it was all in Bernard's notes. She believes the dagger is a kind of doorway. It's a passage into life for something that can't live otherwise. A force that can't become real without a human will to embody it."

"That was in Bernard's notes? I thought the baselard was just supposed to give Abend eternal youth or something."

That is what she told herself at the end. The words of the ghostly executioner came back to him. *Many have told themselves something like it at the end. But she knew better. We all know better.*

"No, it's more complicated than that," said Imogen Storm. "Youth—health—that's the reward he gets. That's the bait, as it were. For using the dagger. But, in fact, it's the dagger that's using *him!* I mean, think about it. Abend is nothing but a . . . a low-level Nazi thug, after all. He could never have corrupted our politicians and our police and our bureaucrats if there weren't some other force that had rendered them all ripe for the taking. Everything that's happening now back home . . ." she nodded her head at the flat-screen on the bureau, conjuring the burning building no longer visible on the black surface, ". . . Abend didn't do that alone. He couldn't have. But when he uses the dagger, it releases the force that does."

Zach stayed where he was, behind her, letting her gaze away from him into the room. "So what you're saying: after following Professor Dankl all this time, you've come to believe her. You believe that what she told your fiancé was true."

Her voice was hollow. "Yes. More or less."

"And that she really was . . . *is* trying to stop this. To stop Abend. To find the dagger. And that somehow, for some reason, she can only do those things in the form of the wolf."

"That's right."

"But you still want to kill her. You want to kill her anyway."

She turned her head to look at him over her shoulder, miserable. He saw what Goulart must have seen, what she hid behind the clipped accent, the intelligence, and the irony: her solitude and her uncertainty. She had started out on a mission of revenge, but now. . . .

"It's all got very . . . confusing," she said.

"Things do that sometimes."

"Bloody hard to know who the good guys are, isn't it?"

"It is," said Zach. "I'm not even sure that's how it works, exactly. With good guys and bad guys, I mean. It's more like—messed-up guys, some fighting for the good, some for the bad, and the rest just wandering around bumping into the furniture."

She faced forward, shoulders sagging, head down. "Yes. Something like that."

Zach was about to speak again—all sorts of mysteries and questions and possibilities were occurring to him. But just then, the phone in his pocket buzzed. He fished it out. It was Goulart calling.

"Hey," Zach said.

"Connecticut State cops have got a hit on Angela Bose's car," said Goulart.

His breath caught. He had to work to keep his voice steady.

"I'll pick you up in a couple of minutes," he said.

28

THE THING
IN THE RAIN

Mysteries, questions, and possibilities.

Zach maneuvered the Crown Vic back across town toward the one-six. The rush hour was over, but traffic never dissipated in Manhattan anymore these days. Every street was as crowded as a sugar-coated anthill, all day long. Zach slapped the Kojak light onto the roof and maneuvered between cabs and delivery trucks, letting off an occasional siren blast when he slipped into the oncoming lane.

And all the while, his mind was preoccupied with mysteries, questions, and possibilities.

What had Abend been after at Margo's place? He must've raced there after leaving Zach in the beach house with his torturers. The gangster whose influence was spreading like black poison through the city's bloodstream was himself at his weakest and most desperate now. Tricked and betrayed by his woman. She on the run and he with only one night left to find that dagger. He must have figured: the wolf follows the baselard, so he would follow the wolf. At that point, like Imogen, he still hadn't realized that Gretchen Dankl was dead, that she had been replaced by another.

He must know now, though. With the monk and Satan gone, and Zach in the news. With Goulart telling him that Zach knew Margo. He would have done what Imogen, in her obsession, had failed to do: put the story together. He would know that the curse had been passed from Dankl to Zach.

What about Goulart, then? Did he know? Did he care? Or was he just taking Abend's money in exchange for inside info on the task force?

And what was he playing at with Imogen? Why was he humoring her, teasing her along? Was he just trying to get into her pants? Was he trying to keep her distracted so she didn't get too close to the truth? Or was he maybe trying to make sure she wouldn't trust *him*—Zach— wouldn't help him get to Abend before the dagger was found and the gangster was once again secure in his power.

Mysteries, questions, and possibilities. Zach could only guess at the answers. Only one thing seemed sure to him: this—this day, this night—was his last chance to get his hands on Abend. If the gangster got to the dagger first, he would disappear again, becoming the unknowable but pervasive influence he had been in Europe.

And right now, Abend was way ahead of him. If Goulart knew that Bose's car had been discovered, then it was pretty certain Abend knew as well. If Abend knew, there was little chance Zach would reach Angela Bose (and the dagger, assuming she had it) before he did.

The moment the Crown Vic slid to the curb in front of the precinct, Goulart—wearing another of his fine gray pinstripes—was out the building's front door and hurrying toward him. He slipped into the passenger seat, smoothing back his hair with a pass of his palm. Zach hit the gas and they headed for the highway, out of the city.

"They have her?" Zach asked. "They find Bose?"

Goulart shook his head. "They were canvassing motels and one of the clerks had checked her in, up by Sharon on the border. By the time the staties got there, she was already gone. They say she can't be far. She only had an hour start. Silver-blue Bentley's gonna be tough to miss, up in farm country."

Zach cursed. The Bentley would be tough for Abend to miss as well—and whatever leads the police had, Abend would have them too.

Gray-green storm clouds roiled above the slate-drab river as they rolled up the highway. The two detectives traveled in silence, seething silence, the truth hulking between them like a great dumb beast. After that last argument they'd had in the interview room, what secrets were left between them? Not many. The way Zach understood it, Goulart had all but come right out and pleaded with him: Don't tell anyone I've sold my soul to Abend, and I won't tell anyone you killed Margo Heatherton. And that was back then, all the way yesterday, before Abend realized Zach was the wolf, before Goulart could have understood it or believed it, if in fact he knew it or could believe it even now.

But today? What secrets were left? Goulart, bitter and cynical in the face of a fatal illness, had gone on a gangster's payroll. And Zach, in the grip of a nightmare he couldn't begin to comprehend, had, one way or another, ripped a woman to shreds. Zach knew what Goulart had done. Goulart knew what Zach had done. Each knew the other knew. They drove in silence, knowing.

It wasn't until the gray towers of Manhattan had dropped away behind them—not until the gray plains of the Bronx had melted into grassland—not until the autumn trees of the downstate counties were crowding the edge of the highway, their last pastel leaves gone dull beneath the louring clouds, their branches quivering in the gusts from the coming storm—not until then that either man spoke a word.

Then Zach said, "Funny, isn't it? You and me."

And Goulart, looking out the window, drawled sardonically. "Funny, yeah."

"You New York, me Texas, all that."

"Yeah."

"Strange combo."

"Broadway Joe and Cowboy."

"It made good copy for the journos."

"We did good work too," said Goulart.

They drove in silence again. After a while, the first droplets of rain patted the windshield.

"I gotta bring him down, Martin," Zach said.

"Hell, I know it."

"Nothing else makes any sense to me."

"That's why you're the Cowboy, Cowboy."

"It ain't right what he does. Buying and selling people. Making their lives go where he wants instead of where they want. Shutting them down when they stand against him. Killing 'em when he can't get his way. It ain't right."

Goulart gave him a glance of surprise. "But everyone does that. Everyone who can. The rest just haven't had the chance."

Zach turned his eyes from the road only long enough to return the glance. "Even if we all did it—even if we all thought it was right—it still wouldn't be. I gotta stop him."

The rain grew steady—not heavy yet, just steady. Zach clicked the wipers on. They set up a rhythmic beat. There was a long, low roll of thunder from off in the northern distance somewhere.

"He'll kill you," Goulart said. "Just by the way, in case you're interested. You don't know what he is. You haven't got a chance against him. He'll kill you. And for what? He already owns half the force, half the city. All the pols—they were always his at heart, just waiting for him. He's already moving into Boston and Philly. D.C. It's a done deal, brother. There's no point. And even if there was, there wouldn't be. That's the part I've been trying to tell you. That's what I've learned these last couple of weeks. You just die in the end, so what the hell? Go for the gusto, right? Take what you can get and run."

There was no profit in having this argument again, so Zach didn't answer him. It was, as Imogen had said, very complicated. Bloody hard to know who the good guys were.

After that, they listened to the radio. Overseas, the riots had spread to the north of England, Germany was shut down by strikes and demonstrations, the news out of France was being censored but Jewish refugees were turning up here and there with horror stories. All this the newsmen covered in about ninety seconds, then they were back on the Super Cop in the house of horrors, followed immediately by unconfirmed reports that the Westchester police were searching for an unnamed man who might have been present when heiress Margo Heatherton was killed by a wild animal. . . .

Goulart sent Zach a meaningful glance: how long before those two stories became one story, the Super Cop and the dead heiress? Zach didn't even bother to meaningfully look back at him. There was no profit in having this argument again.

By the time they left the Interstate, the rain was coming down in sheets. Dramatic jagged lances of lightning stabbed the earth and sent static through the radio. The Crown Vic skimmed the New York-Connecticut border on a winding two-lane. The falling leaves swirled and whipped past the windows on the wind. The naked branches of the roadside trees bowed and waved at them, making Zach think back on Gretchen Dankl's witchy fingers. He thought he caught glimpses of her in his peripheral vision, watching him drive past from within the woods. The thunderclaps now were sudden, short and loud.

Goulart's phone rang. He drew it out and listened. "We're ten away," he said. He killed the connection and said to Zach, "They found the Bentley."

"But not Bose."

Goulart didn't answer. He didn't have to. Zach felt as if he were carrying an anvil in his gut.

The Bentley was in a ditch on a forest road, one tire flat, its fender mashed against a tree. The passenger window was shattered. There was glass all over the seat. There were three patrol cars pulled to the shoulder, one in front of the Bentley, two in back. Lots of staties in gray cowboy hats and fluorescent green raincoats milled on the pavement. Sizzling red flares warned traffic off the road, but there was no traffic.

"Looks like she blew a tire and lost control," said a Captain Mansfield. The rain ran down his green sleeves. It darkened his hat. He was a solid block of a guy, athletic, plodding—not stupid, but talking nonsense all the same.

Goulart—his sleek suit now hidden under his official Extraordinary Crimes rain jacket, his slick hair under a task force baseball hat—was nodding at the guy as if he weren't spouting total crap. Zach, in an identical jacket with the plastic hood pulled up, was bending down to look through the Bentley's passenger window. The rain drummed on the back of his head, making it hard to hear the surrounding conversations.

"Then where is she?" he said now, straightening up, looking back at the captain. "If she blew a tire and ran into a tree. Where'd she go?"

The captain shrugged his big shoulders. "Car was here a while before we found it. She could have run for it or flagged someone down. We're checking doctors and hospitals. She's a fugitive, after all, right? She could be anywhere."

Zach pointed to a scratch in the Bentley's silver-blue paint, a dent and a gash back near the right rear tire.

"Looks to me like someone ran her off," he said. "Ran her off the road, broke through the window and took her."

Zach thought Captain Mansfield gave Goulart some sort of look then, but he didn't know how to interpret it. Could've meant: *Your partner here is a pain in the ass.* Or it could've meant something more like: *As fellow servants of the powers of darkness, we must conspire to confuse and destroy this infidel.* At this point, no suspicion was too crazy or too paranoid.

Zach moved away from the Bentley, moved toward the center of the road where the red flares were burning. He looked off into the distance in one direction, then into the distance in the other. Nothing much either way. Forest. Road. Lightning flickered in the green sky. Thunder rolled.

"Don't suppose there are any traffic cams near here," Zach called to the captain through the drumming rain.

The captain shook his head. "Nothing at all between the highway and Main Street over by the bank in town."

Zach moved back to the shoulder of the road, to the rear of the Bentley, to the edge of the woods. Beyond the pavement, the ground rose, a smooth incline into the forest. He looked up the hill into the trees, his senses alert. The rain fell hard and loud on the forest floor. It rattled in the skeletal branches. The branches swayed and creaked in the wind. Their tangled lacework grew denser and denser the farther back they went, darker and darker the closer they came to the sky. Zach sniffed the air, but the downpour had washed away every living scent.

They were gone. Bose. Abend. The dagger. Gone. The rain pattered hard on Zach's plastic hood as he realized the full extent of the catastrophe. Abend had what he wanted. He would now go back into hiding to complete his criminal work unseen. Which left Zach to do . . . what then, exactly? To live on in a monthly cycle of murderous brutality? Live with more and more blood on his hands as the useless chase continued? Pass the curse on when his own crimes became too many and too horrible to bear? He couldn't live like that—couldn't live as all the wolves before him had lived. Maybe it was weakness on his part, but he couldn't. He wouldn't.

He peered up into the woods, deeper and deeper into the inter-weaving patterns of vines and branches, deeper into the shadows of forest obscurity and the fog of the sheeting rain.

Suddenly, there was a sizzling snap of forked lightning on the shrouded hilltop. At the same instant, Zach gasped as he was hit by a wave of inner darkness, that nasty shock he had experienced twice before. It was such a strange, bleak, internal—such an *emotional* experience that he hadn't thought of it as being real until now. Now, since Imogen had mentioned it to him, he understood that it always accompanied the presence of Dominic Abend, as if Abend's presence contained a greater presence than himself.

The darkness—and the sense of hopelessness and terror that came with it—struck him and washed over him and was gone and then the thunder rolled. But in its wake, Zach lost all thought of everything and everyone around him. The police—Goulart—the wrecked Bentley—they all fell into the background of his consciousness. Dwindling figures, diminishing voices, gone. He was alone in his own mind.

And he thought: *There's something here.*

He left the road. He began to climb the hill.

"Zach!" Goulart called after him.

Zach hardly heard him. He didn't look back. He went up the hill, deeper into the woods, his shoes squelching in the soaking duff.

"Zach! Where the hell you going?"

Zach marched on to the crest of the rise, and there stood still and looked around him. Forest thickened in every direction, the pastel green of autumn conifers showing here and there amid the brown and empty hardwood. The rain slanted down steadily, and the falling leaves swirled once or twice in the wind and then plummeted to earth.

A little breathless from the climb, he scanned the scene. His whole self was attentive now, his flesh, his soul. It was that hyper-focus Goulart sometimes talked about, but more than that too. It was as if that shock of darkness he'd felt inside him had connected him to his surroundings somehow, as if it and he had blended with the storm, had become one with the rain and the gloom. Every other thought he had, every worry and consideration, fell away. There was just the forest. Just the green-black sky. Just the white noise of the downpour. And they—and he himself—were all part of the darkness.

Something here.

He went on moving his gaze across the vista in a slow arc. How strangely colorless this place was! How drained of even the dying life of autumn! The rain washed over everything like a kind of acid, eating away its clarity. The lightning too—it struck again now: it burned the vista to an x-ray, all white bones and black backgrounds. What was he sensing? What was he looking for? Where was it?

There! Something! A movement . . . ! What the hell?

Zach stared into the streaming curtain of rain—and the rain began to shift and change. It was as if the water were bending around some presence otherwise unseen. A shape appeared within the downpour, huge and hulking and metamorphic, humanlike one moment, bestial the next, the next a mere shifting presence inhabiting the core of the atmosphere as if it were the very spirit of the storm.

Zach saw it and, at the same time, he felt it inside him: a cancer of oncoming darkness linking him to the cancer spreading through all the world.

Astonished, he thought: *Who are you?*

The thing in the rain shifted and grew and moved. It answered inside his head, but not like a thought, like a voice, as real, as present as the spoken word, more real, more present, a bizarrely overwhelming whisper, filling him with a meaningless susurrus of words that seemed to have neither beginning nor end.

I AM NOT I AM THAT I AM NOT I AM NOT I

The heart went out of Zach on the instant—all his courage: it just dropped out of him like water from a broken sack. He suddenly understood—not in language, but viscerally and completely—the full meaning of the curse that had fallen on him. He suddenly understood that Gretchen Dankl and the executioner had not told him the whole truth, had not been able to face the whole truth themselves. He understood why they, why every wolf who had come before him, had failed, why none had reclaimed the dagger and ended the evil business, why each had merely passed the nightmare along to the next, mollifying himself with the idea that the hunt for the baselard would continue without him. . . .

It was the fear . . . the paralyzing fear . . . of this . . . of this. . . .

He stood mesmerized, staring. And all the while, the thing in the rain came toward him, burgeoning and blooming into an atmospheric immensity and shrinking back into a beast and then a human form but always coming closer, closer so that Zach lost all sense of anything else around him, the forest, the thunder, the lightning, the fact of the world itself—all gone as the murmuring thing came closer and closer until, without warning, he was seized by the arm. . . .

He shouted in terror and turned.

It was Goulart—standing beside him, eyes like lanterns, good and scared.

"You all right, Cowboy?"

"What? What?"

"What're you doing? I saw you come up here. What're you doing? You see something? You all right?"

Zach blinked. His own eyes, he knew, were as wide and terrified as Goulart's. He turned them, this way, that. There was nothing— nothing unusual. No shape inside the rain. It had just been a remnant, a memory, a scent—a trace not of Abend, but of the dagger itself. Now it was gone and there was only the forest everywhere, the stolid trees bowing and rattling in the wind. Only the downpour, setting up a steady hiss on the fallen leaves.

Breathing hard, he looked down the hill. The sizzling red light of the flares on the pavement—the aggressively prosaic patrol cars, the smashed Bentley—brought him back and anchored him to what had to be reality. The thunder rolled.

"He killed her here," Zach said. His voice sounded distant even to himself.

"What?" said Goulart. "What do you mean?"

"He's gone, but this is where he killed her." Zach kept turning, kept looking through the rain, through the trees. "Somewhere," he said.

Now Goulart was looking around him too. But Zach spotted it first. He called down to the staties.

"Up here!"

Only part of her hand was sticking out from the leaf cover. The top joints of three fingers, that's all, as if she were trying to dig free. They never would have spotted it in this storm. It might have gone unnoticed for days.

Captain Mansfield and one of his troopers came stomping and crunching and squelching up the hill. Mansfield knelt in the muddy duff and brushed enough of the leaves away to expose Angela Bose's gaping eyes, her slashed throat.

"God!" said Goulart. "Look at her!"

"I thought she was in her twenties," Mansfield said, kneeling there, turning his head away to look at them, to look away from the horror.

The blue eyes gaped out of a face like a skull, the dry, leathery skin shriveled almost to the bone. The mouth was wide, black, toothless, an old, an ancient woman's mouth. A beetle crawled out of it to scramble down the desiccated chin.

"God!" said Goulart again.

Zach stared through the rain at what had been Angela Bose. He remembered the smell of blood that had come off her, and he thought: that was all she had been in the end, a withered sack made lifelike by the blood. Nothing left of her for Abend to use for himself. . . .

A thought began to form in his mind.

But then the phone in his pocket buzzed. He blinked again at Goulart. Goulart gazed at him. They seemed to understand each other entirely, but neither could have said just then what it was he understood.

The phone in Zach's pocket buzzed again. Goulart nodded toward the low hum of it. Zach fished it out of his pocket, cupping one hand over it to shield it from the rain. It was his wife calling.

"Grace?"

"Zach?" she said. "You have to come home. You have to come home right now."

She was weeping.

29

HOME

I t was late by the time he reached her, nearly four o'clock—after three-plus hours of travel through the storm-hampered traffic. Even so, the signs of ransack were still visible here and there: shards in the living-room carpet from a broken china urn Grace had loved, stuffing from a torn sofa cushion, disarray on the bookshelves, a slanted photograph on the wall. Even the champion housewife Grace had not been able to fix all of it in mere hours.

She had not been able to stop crying either. She was still in tears. Sitting at the dining-room table. Contemplating a scratch the bastards had made in the glass on one of her mama's picture frames, turning it this way and that in the light, measuring it with her fingernail to see if she might be able to buff it away. There was a Bible on the table by her elbow—and a woman's devotional—both of them—so Zach knew she'd been hungry for comfort. But that wasn't the worst of it. The worst of it was that she didn't run to him when he came in, didn't bury her face in his chest, sob into his lapels the way she had when the plumber was so rude to her that one time.

Instead, she only turned to him after he'd been standing there a while. It was poignant to him—it was heartbreaking—that her face was still pretty, still sweet-looking, even as haggard as it was, even so ravaged by tears.

"I sent the kids to Molly's," she told him. "So I could . . ." she gestured to the living room ". . . clean up."

He echoed her gesture with a helpless gesture of his own. "I'm so sorry, baby. I told them. . . ."

He had told them a lot of things as he'd driven back this way, growling tensely over the phone first at Washington, then at Roth, then at Washington again. The Westchester inspectors had answered the rising heat of his tone with the immovable drollery of cops armed with a legal search warrant, which is what they were. Zach, who almost never raised his voice in anger, did not raise his voice now either but finally said to Washington, "So help me, there is going to come a time when you and I will discuss this personally, Inspector."

"Is that a threat, Agent?" Washington said, amused.

And Zach thought, *It's a full moon tonight and I can't find Abend, but I can find you, you son of a bitch!*

But he hung up without answering aloud.

Goulart, who was behind the wheel for the first part of the journey before Zach dropped him off in Manhattan, listened in, shaking his head. Now and then, he murmured a curt single-syllable profanity, his description of the Westchester cop twins. It was meant to be a show of support for his partner, but Zach couldn't help but feel there was a hidden message too: *You could've stood with me. We could've stood together. I would've covered for you and this would never have happened.*

Zach called Rebecca Abraham-Hartwell.

"Well, what did you expect?" she said. She, at least, paid him the courtesy of sounding regretful. "After you walked out on them like that. Like some big-shot screw-you *federale*? What did you think they'd do?"

"I thought they said it was a wild animal killed her," said Zach for about the fifth time.

"Well, they can't find a wild animal and the county's in a panic about it and you pissed them off. What did you expect?"

Zach hung up and uttered a single-syllable profanity of his own.

His anger had not abated all through the long drive home, not one bit. His fantasies of taking wolf form and ripping Roth and Washington to pieces became disturbingly repetitive, not to mention satisfying. Even now, as he stood in his living room watching his forlorn wife, the fury seethed within him, tamped down only by his overwhelming sorrow and remorse for the hurt he'd caused the woman he loved more than his own breath. The satin tenderness of Margo Heatherton's skin was gone forever—he could not recall it to his mind in any realistic way—and so he could not imagine for the life of him how on earth he ever could have betrayed this Grace who was the better substance of his soul.

"I guess you better tell me now," she said. She couldn't even ask the question without fighting fresh tears. "Did you love her?"

"Who—Margo?" said Zach. "No, of course not. I didn't even like her."

"Well, did you go to bed with her?"

He hadn't made up his mind whether to tell her the truth or not, couldn't decide whether it would purge the poison of the lie or hurt her needlessly, which course was the selfish one and which correct. In the event, he found that the lie just came out of him, which gave it a spontaneous, almost plausible sound. "No! Is that what they told you?"

"They said she said you did."

"Oh, she was crazy. No, no, no. That's not how it was."

He went to her. Put his hand on her hair. He could tell she wanted to respond, wanted to bury her face in the comfort of him, but she resisted, still uncertain of the truth. She frowned down at the scratched picture frame: a slash across the photo of her mama and sister waving at the camera.

The glass could be replaced, Zach found himself thinking. The glass could be replaced.

"Why didn't you tell me about her?" Grace asked. She had to force herself to this, he could tell; interrogating her husband was the last thing on earth she wanted to do. There was nothing in Proverbs 31 about that! "When she was at the church, you just said you knew her."

"I know, I know. I screwed up. She was threatening to tell you we'd, you know, been together. And we hadn't, but. . . ."

His wife raised her tearstained face to him. "I would have believed you."

He closed his eyes and sighed. "I know. I should have trusted you." He despised himself for saying this—all of it—but the lies just came and kept coming. And what the hell—he despised himself so much already, it didn't make much difference.

She shifted toward him in her chair. She took his hand off her hair, held it in her two hands. Gazed up at him. "I've been praying about it," she said softly.

This, for some reason, only pissed Zach off more. He wanted to throttle God for interfering in his affairs, same as he wanted to throttle Roth and Washington. He wanted to take Grace's Bible *and* her devotional, throw them both in the fireplace, light the gas. Why couldn't God and everyone else just leave them the hell alone?

"Those men, the policemen, they asked me where you were the night this woman Margo died," Grace said.

Zach tried not to stiffen, but he stiffened all the same. She must have felt it, holding his hand like that.

"I lied to them," she went on. "I told them you were home all night." She must have felt him relax too.

"I know you didn't hurt her. I know you couldn't do that. And they said it was some animal anyway, a bear or something. They know it wasn't you. So I lied and I'm not sorry. To heck with them, anyway."

He looked away from her. He couldn't meet her eyes. Because he knew she *was* sorry—that is, he knew it had cost her in leaden grief to break her Sunday-school precepts, to sin against her God (that damned interfering God!).

"I didn't tell them she came to the church either," she said.

He pulled his hand from her. "You didn't have to . . ." he started to say. But he covered his eyes with his hand and said, instead, "Oh, Grace, I'm so sorry. I'm so sorry."

Outside, the rain was still falling—falling hard. It set up a steady hiss and patter on the roof.

"Zach—baby—" Grace said, looking up at him through her tears. "You listen to me now, okay? No matter what—no matter what—you're the husband of my life. You understand? You know for a fact I've never been with anyone else. We are one flesh, one flesh and blood to me, no matter what. And I know I don't see the things y'all see . . . all the horror and reality. But I'm not stupid. I know what people are and what they do. And I know these things are different for men than for women sometimes. And if maybe this woman . . . came on to you or . . . drew you in somehow . . . I'm not gonna pretend that wouldn't hurt me, but we'll get through it, we'll get by. We'll go before God and he will heal us. I know he will. You're a good man, baby. No one knows that better than I do. You're a good man, just not . . . just not perfect is all. And I will live with that and so will you and we will get by, but . . . I think I've got to know the truth, when all is said and done. That's what God sent me to know when I prayed. I think it'd help me to know there's not just lying between us. You understand? Because that would mean you were just treating me like a fool. So that's why I think it's better you tell me the truth now and get it on over with. So why don't you do that—right now, baby. Right now."

Zach prepared himself with a deep breath before he lowered his hand from his face and looked at her. Ah, but that breath—that wasn't enough preparation, not by half. Because looking at her was different this time than it had ever been before, and the sight of her pierced him to the heart.

He had never really known her; Grace. He had never understood her inner world or workings. He had never even thought that he had. He had taken her as she appeared to him, a Proverbs 31 woman like his mama—his sweet, his simple, his innocent angel, his home girl, his Bible girl—but he had always known that that didn't describe the full depths of her. How could it? No one was like that all the way down—probably not even his mama, though if she wasn't, he didn't want to know. But that was the way she behaved—Grace—that was how she appeared to him, so that was how he took her.

And it wasn't that he suddenly understood her now either. It was just that—in the brutal clarity of his remorse, in the urgency of this crossroad moment—he saw her more fully than perhaps he had before. He sensed her, for that moment, as a woman of considerations. A complete woman who had chosen, out of the complex muddle of her doubts and terrors, despite her temptations and the anxieties that gnawed at her in the lightless hours—had chosen her simplicity, that simplicity that he loved. What to him was her sweetness was, to her, the work of her life, as he was the work of her life, and the children were. She had chosen them, and all the regrets that came with them, all the regrets that come with choosing anything.

That was what he saw. And he didn't know why this made it easier to tell her the truth. Maybe it was just easier to confess to a human being than to an angel. Or maybe it just made more sense to him that way. After all, as she said, she was not stupid, not a fool. And the fact was that she was his woman—his only woman—forever. The fact was he had wronged her. The fact was she had the right to choose whether to forgive him or not. He was a man; he could face the facts. She was a woman; so could she. Maybe it was just that.

"She saw my picture in the paper and made a project out of me. You know, targeted me," he told her.

"Of course she did. Because you were a hero," said Grace. "Some folks have to remake everything into themselves."

It was the kindest thing she could have said, and he realized with a pang that she had chosen this too, chosen to say it, in the midst of what must have been her terrible hurt and sorrow.

"I went up there that night because she threatened to tell you about . . . the one time we were together. Ah, God, Grace, I am so sorry."

"I know."

"I got a thousand reasons, a thousand excuses for it, a thousand lame stories I could tell you. I won't, though. It would be a disrespect to you."

"It would."

"I did wrong, Grace. I was standing there and I could've done right and I did wrong, and if I could take it back . . . I am just so sorry."

"God will heal us," she tried to say, though she was crying hard now, shaking her head, forlorn. "I know he will."

"I went up there that night. I told her I wouldn't be blackmailed. I wouldn't live lying to you. I did tell her that, I swear I did."

"I know you did, baby. I believe you, don't worry."

"She didn't care," he went on. "She had this whole fantasy about me loving her, wanting her. She thought. . . . It was crazy. I don't even know how to tell you."

Grace nodded her understanding. She couldn't speak anymore. The tears had overwhelmed her.

He opened his mouth again, trying to think how he could ever explain to her what had happened next, his metamorphosis, how Margo had died. He was just about to stumble on, just about to try to find a way to break the rest of the terrible truth to her. . . .

But here—as he approached the very core of the matter—as he stepped into the center of the whirlwind he had created for them—a strange thing happened.

He solved the case of Dominic Abend. He realized where he could find the man. And he knew what he had to do.

It was Grace—she was the last piece of the puzzle. It was seeing her in that new light that helped him understand the rest. It was Grace and her choices and the body of Angela Bose, bloodless and withered nearly to the bone, and that shifting thing that had approached him in the forest, in the heart of the storm, a few hours ago, that mutating presence and its incomprehensible mutter, which was a darkness beyond the world speaking into his own mind, and the echo of his own mind answering. He remembered Imogen's words: *A force that can't become real without a human will to embody it.* And that made him think about Goulart, how Goulart had snapped at him: *You think that lowlife Kraut piece of shit has enough money to buy me with?* Which brought him back to Grace, who had said of Goulart: *There comes a time in a person's life when doing wrong just makes perfect sense to him. That's when the Enemy can make his move on him.*

Grace's choices, the will she embodied, the voice in the woods, Goulart's choices . . . in a cascade of simultaneous deductions, Zach realized what Goulart had done and where Abend was waiting for him. He knew what would happen next, and he knew that he, Zach—he alone—was the only person alive who could stop it, the only man on earth who could destroy this near-eternal gangster before the force he had unleashed spread everywhere and corrupted everything.

He understood that the job was his alone to do and that, if he was going to succeed, he had to do it now. There was one more night of the full moon, the final night for Abend to use the dagger before its power deserted him, the final night for Zach to heal the rift in reality through which the evil had come, to bring the wolf and the dagger back together again and finally end them both. He knew where he had to go, and there was only just enough time for him to get there. With the storm, with the traffic, with the rush hour, it might already be too late. But he had to try. Alone. Right now.

He was still looking at Grace, his lips parted, the unbelievable truth of Margo's death on the tip of his tongue. She had lowered her eyes to her picture frame. Her tears were falling onto the glass. They seeped into the crack and ran along the line of it. Outside, the rain fell harder. A gust of wind made it splatter against the windows.

Time was passing. Night was coming. The moon. He had to go.

He sat down at the table beside her. He took her hand again, held it in both his hands this time, as she'd held his.

"Listen to me, Grace. There's more to say between us, I know. A lot more. But I can't say it now."

Sobbing, she looked up at him. She shook her head again, bewildered, forlorn.

"I have to leave here," he said. "I know where Dominic Abend is—or where he's going to be."

Grace drew herself up, taking a large breath, steadying.

"If I'm lucky and fast, I'm going to meet him there," Zach went on. "If I'm very lucky and very fast, I'm going to kill him."

Fighting back her tears, Grace managed to nod.

He went on: "And if I don't come back—"

"Zach!" she said, her voice shuddering.

"If I don't come back. . . . There's only one thing you need to know, okay? One thing you always have to remember." He held her hand in his. She waited, crying. He swallowed hard. "I don't have the words to tell you what you are to me, all you are. But it's everything," he said. "If I could reach into the past. . . ." He shook his head, choked up. That wasn't what he wanted to say. He continued: "Just . . . don't ever for a second . . . if you're alone, or if it's the night and you're awake, thinking about things . . . if I'm not here anymore—"

"No. . . ."

"If I'm not here. Don't you ever for a second believe that I ever loved any other woman but you. You understand me? Don't you believe that, Grace. Because that would be a damned lie. That would be. . . ." He couldn't continue. He merely gripped her hand harder.

Then he stood up. "I'm so sorry," he managed to say again.

Without another word, he turned away from her and walked through the living room to the door.

"Don't you let that man hurt you, baby!" Grace cried out behind him, her voice ravaged with tears. She stood up so fast, her chair fell over with a clatter. She raised her fist at him. "Don't you let that bad man hurt you!"

Zach walked out of the house into the rain.

30

WINDWARD

n the Crown Vic, behind the wheel, Zach fed Goulart's number into the tracking app on his phone. It was no good. Goulart was offline. That figured. But it didn't matter. He knew where his partner was going.

Windward Mansion. It was a ruin north of the city, in the woods above the Hudson River. Rebecca Abraham-Hartwell had told him about it back when all this started. Goulart had made several trips there in the middle of the night, she said. She had thought he was using it as a message drop. But that wasn't it. And nothing Goulart had said about his illness could explain those visits either.

Because he was going there to meet Abend. It was their contact place, their rendezvous. That was the only scenario that made sense. And if that's where they met, if that was their spot, then that was where Abend would be tonight—because tonight the gangster would be meeting Goulart one last time to pay him what he owed.

The moon would come up about forty minutes later tonight than last night. That meant there were about two and half hours until moonrise. On a good day, with no traffic, the drive to Windward would be two hours long at least. But the storm had snarled the highways—Zach had seen it on the drive back from Connecticut. He wasn't sure he could make the journey in time. And he felt a strangling fear of what would happen if the moon caught him before he got there.

He used the traffic gizmo on his phone to chart his course. He used the Kojak light and the siren to clear the way. The flasher and the noise carved out stretches of space for him on the passing lane of the Throgs Neck Bridge. The East River and Long Island Sound clashed black and turbulent below him as the Crown Vic raced past the trudging parade of home-bound cars. Not as bad as he'd feared it would be. Still another half hour before the rush began in earnest. He had that much going for him, at least.

Out of the city, the traffic got better, but the storm grew worse. The lightning and thunder returned full force, and for long stretches the rain dropped in enormous gobbets that exploded on the windshield and seemed to melt the view into a blurred, running mess. Zach kept his foot heavy on the gas. He never touched the brake. On the Hutchinson River Parkway, he hit puddles of flood where the water arced up from either side of the car like silver wings and the tires hydroplaned and lost all traction. He felt the car sledding out of control, but he never slowed. Somehow, the tires caught again before the winding road wound away from him. The light flashing, the siren screaming, the Crown Vic raced on.

His phone buzzed where it lay on the passenger seat. The readout told him it was Rebecca Abraham-Hartwell. He didn't answer. Rebecca was redeemed in his eyes now. She was self-serious and political, but honest, untouched by Abend. She had sniffed out Goulart's corruption and tried to bring him down. She'd had plenty of personal grudges to spur her on, but she'd been in the right of it and that's what counted in the end. Still, he let the phone buzz on. Only he could do this. Anyone else would only be in the way. It was better to trust no one now. Better, in fact, to stay off the air.

He reached to turn his phone off so he couldn't be tracked, but before he did, it buzzed again. Goulart this time. Back online. That surprised him. His partner must be getting nervous, wondering where Zach was.

Zach picked the phone up. Keeping half an eye on the rain-drenched windshield, he called up his own tracking app. It found Goulart—on the same highway, about twenty miles behind him. *Good*, he thought. He turned his phone off, even as Goulart tried to call him again. He thought: *We'll meet soon enough, face to face.*

By this time, the lightning was striking over and over rapidly. The sky lit up everywhere, flickered and went dark, and flickered again. The thunder crashed so massively, it made the car rattle. And the rain, which already seemed to be falling harder than rain could ever fall, fell harder yet. Now too, after a while, when the lightning struck, when the flickering ended, the sky was darker than it had been before. Night was near.

And now the ghosts returned.

He saw them out there in the darkening rain. Dim figures, barely discernible through the dusk and downpour. They watched him pass with mournful expressions and haunted eyes. Once, as the dusk imperceptibly died into the night, as the car's interior, lit only by the dashboard's green-blue lights, became difficult to see, he sensed a presence near him. He smelled that nauseating mingled stench of rotting meat and cigarette smoke. He glanced up in the mirror, expecting to see dead eyes staring back at him. Instead, he saw nothing but the backseat shadows. He glanced over at the passenger seat. Nothing but the shadows there as well.

And just then, the lightning struck and Gretchen Dankl was beside him. She was visible only for an instant but, in that instant, he saw her gaze at him with tragic sorrow. She was confessing with her eyes what he had already guessed out in the woods earlier that day: that she had failed—that all the werewolves over the last three and a half centuries had failed—because they feared to succeed. They did not want to reclaim the dagger. They did not want to end the curse. The consequences were too terrible. They were too afraid to face them.

And so they had left the job unfinished. They had left it for him.

Then the flickering lightning snapped out, and there was nothing in the passenger seat but the shadows again.

267

He drove on through the rain and the darkness.

As he left the Taconic State Parkway, he turned off his siren. He buzzed down the window, reached out into the rain, and pulled his flasher in, tossing it on the floor. He wanted to travel the last miles inconspicuously, approach the mansion in secret. He drove along one wooded two-lane, then another. His headlights turned the downpour silver. Lightning etched the tangled shapes of naked autumn trees, their branches tormented by the high winds.

There were no signs leading to the mansion, but he knew the way. He turned off the last two-lane onto a rutted road. The road wound upward, deeper and deeper into the storm-tossed forest. Nothing here but trees around him—swaying trees and rain and lightning—and the climbing macadam full of cracks and divots. The Crown Vic bounced and rattled over the broken pavement, making its way upward.

In the black and chaos of it all, he nearly missed the trailhead, but a violent flash picked it out of the darkness just before he passed it.

There was a wide dirt fire road that led off the damaged macadam and up into the woods. A diamond-link fence blocked the way. The fence was held shut with a padlocked chain. Zach drove past it and continued a few dozen yards, traveling slowly until he spotted a turnout. He stopped then. He brought the Crown Vic around in a three-point turn until he was facing back the way he'd come. Then he slid into the turnout, edging the car as close to the tree line as he could get it.

The turnout was overhung by swaying oak branches. The car huddled under them and under the darkness of the night. Zach killed the lights. Killed the engine. He did not think Goulart would see him there, not unless he was on the lookout for him.

He took off his seatbelt. Twisted around to reach into the back seat. He got ahold of his plastic raincoat. In the tight space behind the wheel, he had to struggle to get the coat on. When he was done, he fetched a flashlight out of the glove compartment. He held the flashlight on his lap and waited.

The rain thundered on the Crown Vic's roof. He had gotten here in good time. He still had more than twenty minutes left before the crisis. He sat and felt the minutes going by in an electric silence. The silence was worse to him—more suspenseful—than a ticking clock.

It was as if the seconds were sneaking past him unseen. Sixteen minutes to moonrise. Fifteen. Zach sat still. As the minutes dwindled, his heartbeat grew louder and kept the time for him, but that was just as bad as the silence, maybe worse.

A rumble of thunder and then, finally, a double smear of white on the Crown Vic's rain-drenched windshield. Headlights. Goulart. Zach watched him approach. He couldn't see the make of the oncoming car, but he guessed it was his partner's own Camaro. It slowed as it reached the trailhead. Stopped.

Zach held his breath. Had Goulart spotted him? No, he just had to get out of the car to unlock the gate, that's all. Zach sat very still and watched. Goulart's headlights illuminated the wash and play of rainfall on the windshield. Through the moving sheet of water, Zach saw the driver's door of the Camaro swing open. The lights inside the car went on. He could make out Goulart's shadow, washed to liquid by the running liquid on the glass. And he saw too the blurry shadow of his passenger.

The fact that Goulart had not come here alone surprised him for only a second. Then, with a subtle wave of nausea, he understood. This was Goulart's offering, his part of the bargain. This was what he was bringing to the sacrifice: the dagger's next victim.

A second more, and Zach knew who it was—or, that is, he guessed who it was and then he saw and knew for sure. Because now she lit a cigarette—and at the same moment, the rain ran heavily down the Crown Vic's windshield and for that moment the view half-cleared and the orange flame of the lighter clarified her face behind the Camaro's ticking wipers.

Imogen Storm. Of course. That was why Goulart had moved so quickly to seduce her. Not just because she was so young, her life force so powerful—unlike the homeless men and women Abend had settled for up till now—but she was dangerous too, a smart reporter who was getting close to the truth. Abend could silence her and refresh himself at the same time, keep his secret and go on living.

And Goulart would be healed by her blood. That's what it was all about in the end. Life. Time. More life, more time. Goulart had spoken the truth: he would never have sold himself for money. He was too good a cop for that. But he was sick. He was terminal. He was desperate. And he believed in nothing, nothing that was worth dying for anyway. Why should he not then live? It was as Grace had said. In his hour of darkness, when doing what was wrong made perfect sense, he had had nothing to keep him from corruption.

Zach sat still in the deep shadows behind the Crown Vic's wheel. The match-light played over Imogen's pixie features, her turned-up nose, her short, nearly blue-black hair. Zach was touched by how young she was, how unconcerned and unafraid even here, even now, convinced and pacified by whatever Goulart had told her, probably already half in love with him, the only man who had ever believed her. Zach felt again how much he liked her, and it made his heart hurt.

Then she had her cigarette lit and the flame winked out and a fresh wave of rain poured down Zach's windshield. Zach squinted through the rippling tide as Goulart returned to the car, as he dropped in next to Imogen and shut the door. The Camaro's interior lights went off and both passengers vanished into the shadows. The car's headlights began to move again. They turned and started up the dirt lane into the forest.

Zach sat for another moment. He watched as the glow of the car sank away into the bowing and sweeping trees—watched until it was swallowed by the blackness of the storm.

Then he stepped out into the rain and followed on foot.

31

SACRIFICE

Even now, after all he'd seen of it, the force of the tempest surprised him. The wind drove at him hard from the side, nearly knocking him off balance. The rain lashed and stung his face and instantly drenched his clothes everywhere they weren't covered by his raincoat: his shoes, the bottoms of his pants, the exposed cuff of his suit jacket. Soon, even his shirt was somehow clammy.

All the same, conscious of the time, he moved quickly. Goulart hadn't relocked the gate. Zach went through, bent his body against the storm, and pushed into the woods.

The going was tough. The dirt road rose steadily. The hard-packed surface was soft with water, nearly mud. All around him, the wind gasped and howled with a voice like phantoms and pushed against him with phantom hands. The rain that soaked him thundered on the bare branches and on the fallen leaves. It left deep, dirty puddles all along the way, and brown streams that flooded the gutters. Lightning tore the sky. It showed the trees towering all around him, bending and swaying violently like orgiastic dancers. Thunder followed and shook the air as if with wrath. It drowned out every other sound—then died, and left only the thunder of the rain.

Head bent, teeth gritted, Zach followed the weak yellow beam of his flashlight up the road. It wasn't a long way. The hill was not high. A few more minutes of bullying through the storm, and he broke out of the tree line into a scraggly clearing.

Though the night seemed black in these last minutes before moonrise, he could, in fact, make out the even darker shape of the ruin against the sky. Big—the mansion was really big and hulking and ominous. With a melodrama that melodrama wouldn't dare to imitate, a single zigzagging bolt of lightning knifed the air behind the structure, and the whole scene was revealed: the surrounding of broken trees and half-grown scrub; the remains of fences standing slanted in the mud; the turrets and gables, arches and broken windows of the massive building itself—the whole ghostly array.

When the lightning flickered out—and as a crash of thunder broke over the following darkness—Zach spotted the dim candle-glow within the ruin, a wavering yellow in the black depths of a window. The thunder drifted down like dust and into silence. In that rain-spattered silence, Zach heard Imogen scream.

She screamed just once. Such a hopeless cry. A sound at first filled with the anguish of betrayal, and then simply desolate. After that, there was only the noise of the wind and rain.

Zach moved quickly across the muddy clearing.

Soon, the mansion loomed blackly over him. Its soaring brick walls and peaked towers gave him some shelter from the lash and buffet of the storm. Afraid of being spotted, he kept his flashlight pointed to the ground. He couldn't see much that way, but he could still make out the yellow candlelight at a window up ahead of him. He edged along the mansion's base in the direction of the glow, peering hard through the downpour, looking for an entry.

Lightning struck again, and in the silver flash he saw the covered portico only a few yards away.

His feet sinking in mud, his socks soaked through with it, he reached the porch. He stepped into the deeper darkness beneath its roof. There was the mansion doorway directly in front of him, wide open except for two boards that had been nailed up some time ago to keep out intruders. There was one board slanting across the top and another across the bottom. The others—the boards that had blocked the middle of the door—had been torn off and casually tossed to the floor against the porch wall.

Zach killed his flashlight and slipped it into his pocket. He ducked down beneath the top board and stepped over the bottom board and entered Windward.

With that single step across the threshold, Zach seemed to leave the violence of the storm far behind. The ceaseless drench and drumbeat of the rain grew distant and was replaced by the drip-drip-dripping audible here and there in the quiet recesses of the broken-down house. The punishing wind dropped to nothing. The thunder was muffled. The chill in the air seemed to soften. Tense as he was—and he was very tense, his whole inner self feeling like a bowstring stretched to its firing limit—it was a relief to come in out of the rain.

Zach pushed back the hood of his coat. Consciously breathing in a long, slow rhythm, he peered into the darkness. He could see little more than vague patches of gray, suggestions of nooks, corners, corridors, and turnings. He edged forward—forward some more—and soon felt the space open wider before him. Then lightning crackled at a window, and for a moment he saw a broad foyer littered with rubble, a wide, broken staircase winding up into nothingness. Then the lightning died.

Zach let out a trembling breath. How long till moonrise now? he wondered. He didn't know. He had lost his sense of time.

He scanned the blackness. There was the candle-glow again, off to his left. He pinned his gaze on it and started that way.

He tried to walk softly, slowly, silently, but the rubble crunched beneath his feet with every step. Creatures scrambled away from him in unseen corners. Rats, probably—but they made him think of the waterbugs that had attacked him in Long Island City. He shuddered—then nearly cried aloud as cobwebs seized his face and clung to it. Fighting panic, he stopped to claw them out of his eyes and spit them from his mouth. When he was free of them, he had to reorient himself, looking around again to re-locate the candle-glow.

There it was—at the end of a short hallway. He went toward it, the walls closing in on either side of him. Halfway down the corridor, he began to hear a murmur of voices.

He reached inside his jacket now and drew out his gun.

The wind rose and the rain rose, but there was no lightning and the way ahead was sunk in deep obscurity. Zach held out his free hand until he felt the wall. Using that as a guide, he edged forward; forward more.

What came to him then, as he inched through the shadows—what came unwanted into his mind—was the memory of Gretchen Dankl—the look in her eyes, her ghost eyes, as she had last appeared to him, in the car as he was driving up. That look—tragic, guilt-ridden, and condemnatory—it was a confession of fear—and an accusation of fear. Well, she was right in that accusation, Zach thought. He was afraid, more afraid than he had ever been, even as a boy. He could feel the sweat of his palm on the handle of the gun. He could hear his own pulse in his ears and feel the airy weakness in his belly. He had to force himself to keep his mind off Grace, to keep from thinking of his children, whom he would never see again. Thoughts of his family could only make him weak and maudlin now. The people he loved could only bind him to the world—this world he had to leave behind. Love was the enemy of death, and it was death he had come for—he knew that now. So yes, he was afraid.

Another step through the darkness—toward the candle-glow—and the general murmur up ahead began to separate itself into voices, each voice growing clearer and more distinct as Zach approached. He heard Goulart speak—not the words, just the tone of it—and he heard Abend answer, then he heard Goulart speak again. But what was awful—what he slowly realized was truly horrifying—was that underneath their voices, there was another sound, a sound that went on continuously while the men chatted, a pitiable counterpoint to their indifferent conversation.

It was Imogen, pleading desperately for mercy. Her words were muffled. She was almost surely gagged. But her sobs were plainly audible, and so was her anguish. Once Zach understood what he was hearing, the straining, strangled rise and fall of it seemed to him all but unbearable. And yet the other men simply ignored it. It was ambient noise to them. They went on talking, and their voices remained—not calm, exactly—Zach could hear the tension in them—but wholly disinterested in what was going on in their victim's heart and mind. As far as they were concerned, she was nothing but a vessel of blood, a carrier of their magic elixir. Goulart, who had been inside her not twenty-four hours ago, chuckled at something Abend told him even as Imogen, in crazed frustration, screamed to him for help through her gag.

This—the woman's cries, the men's indifference—lit something fresh and hot in Zach, a fresh, hot anger. It strengthened him despite his fear. He moved toward the sound through the darkness until he could hear what the men were saying.

"Aren't there some kind of, like, words or something?" he heard Goulart ask. His tone was taut but also dispassionate, curious, as if they were engaged in some sort of experiment.

"Words?" said Abend.

Imogen wept and pleaded.

"Yeah, like, some kind of ceremony. Don't we have to say or do something besides, you know, use the knife?"

"No, no, no. Don't be foolish. That is for stories. There is nothing else to say, nothing else to do. There are no words. There is no ceremony. Only the dagger. And the blood, of course. And the moon."

Imogen babbled at them and sobbed.

"Oh, right, right," said Goulart, "the moon. Should be any minute now, right?"

"Soon. Yes."

"Doesn't matter about the cloud cover?"

"No, no, not at all. We'll feel it, believe me."

Imogen tried to cry out to them for mercy.

"All right," said Goulart. "Well, I'm ready, I can tell you that. As far as I'm concerned. . . ."

Thunder growling like a waking beast came through the broken windows and obscured both the voices and the ceaseless counterpoint of the woman's pleading. Zach was thinking clearly enough, quickly enough, to move faster under cover of the noise, his free hand feeling its way lightly along the wall to his left, his other hand gripping the gun.

The thunder faded away. Zach came to the end of the hall. He stepped into the room beyond and saw the others.

He saw them first by candlelight—by the glow of a single candle burning in a pewter holder on a small table. He saw the shadow-shapes of the two men standing by a doorway on the far wall, and the shadow-shape of the woman dangling slumped between them, her hands above her, cuffed to a bar in the doorway just as Zach had been cuffed to the bar in the beach house. She wasn't struggling or shaking or rattling her bonds. Hopelessness had drained the strength out of her. Even her pleading and her tears sounded weak and empty now. She knew the men weren't listening to her. She was certain that no one was coming to her aid.

The room around the three figures was vast—broad and high—a plain of debris and ruin stretching from the little pool of candlelight into shadow and darkness. Tall windows empty of glass rose on the left wall, showing the tempest-tossed blackness of the night. The rain washed through the openings and spattered the floor. The wind blew in and made the candle's flame gutter.

Goulart's shadow turned to Abend's. "What do we do when we—?"

But before he could finish, a tremendous riving jagged lightning bolt shot across one high window, on the diagonal, corner to corner. The enormous room went silver-white. The shadows turned human. For one strobic second, Zach glimpsed them all. There was Imogen with her hands chained above her, her head fallen forward, her sweater casually ripped halfway open, exposing the small breasts beneath and giving the killers an easy shot at her heart. There was Goulart in an Extraordinary Crimes raincoat just like Zach's, the zipper undone so that his damp suit was visible. His hands were thrust casually in his pockets. His slickly handsome face was likewise casual and relaxed. He glanced at the half-naked girl without any real interest, as if she were a decoration or a piece of furniture.

And there, finally, was Abend.

The gangster's life force was fading. Even the shock of darkness that came off him was weaker now, much weaker. Zach hadn't realized it until this moment, when he felt it—but barely felt it—as he approached. As for Abend's physical form, it was a horror show—worse than it had been when he'd been slicing into Zach at the beach house. His face was alive with decay, the flesh visibly rotting and shriveling around the skull. Squirming bits of something—maggots, maybe?—dropped off him and slithered at his feet. He wore his sword, the longsword of the *Brüderlichkeit* in a belt inside his flowing black coat. In his hand, though, he held the baselard, a thin dark iron dagger.

Zach saw all this in the flickering instant of the lightning bolt.

Then just before the bolt and its light snapped out, he saw Goulart turn and spot him there in the entryway.

The sky went black and, at the same instant, a fresh blast of wind hurled rain through the window—so much rain that it splattered on the floor as if it had been thrown from a bucket—and the candle on the table went out. The room was drenched in darkness—blindness following the flash.

Knowing he was discovered, Zach pointed the gun at Goulart—but he couldn't see him now, and he wouldn't fire without knowing for certain that Goulart had drawn on him as well. The man was his partner, after all. Even now he felt pity for him, for the fear of death that had led him down this road. In that black split second after the lightning strike, when he could see nothing, he wouldn't pull the trigger.

He wouldn't pull the trigger—but he was quick enough to take a leaping sidestep. And good thing too, because Goulart had sunk way beyond any sort of compunction. He had, in fact, drawn his own weapon the moment he spotted Zach and now he fired blindly into the place where he had seen his partner standing.

Zach saw the gout of flame from the gun barrel and felt the whisper of the bullet by his cheek.

In the next instant, both men's vision returned. Zach saw Goulart's dim silhouette and Goulart saw Zach's. Goulart shifted his gun toward the shape of his partner, but Zach's gun was already trained on Goulart's chest. Lightning flashed and the two men saw each other's faces. Goulart's teeth were bared and his eyes narrowed with effort and terror. Zach's expression was calm and certain. It was the face of "the Cowboy," Goulart thought, and he knew he was a dead man.

Goulart's finger began to tighten on the trigger. Zach fired and killed him.

All this took only a second—less. The blast of Goulart's weapon had hardly faded before Zach's weapon blasted back. Goulart's arms flew out at his sides and he stumbled backwards toward the wall. The gun dropped from his slack fingers as he went down, dead.

Zach turned his gun on Abend, on the dim shadow of Abend, which was turned tensely toward him, one hand rising, the hand with the knife.

"Drop it!" Zach shouted, but the thunder crashed and drowned him out.

Zach and Abend faced each other in the darkness, and for another endless moment neither moved. Only the woman in the doorway strained and struggled now as fresh hope—unlooked-for and amazing to her—filled her with electric energy, made her fight against her chains and cry out through her gag with a new fervor.

"Put the dagger down, Abend," Zach said, trying to keep his voice even. "The sword too. Do it now."

Abend shifted, completing his turn until he faced Zach head on, as if presenting himself as a target. Even through the obscurity, Zach saw the gangster smile.

"You will kill me otherwise?" Abend said.

"I'll kill you," said Zach. "I came here to kill you."

"I wonder if you will," said Abend. His left hand came up and flame rose from it, as if by magic. But he had only snapped a cigarette lighter—probably Imogen's, Zach thought. The rising fire sent an orange glow over the shriveling, rotting skin on Abend's skull and the heat made more maggots drop off him to the floor. Abend moved to the small table, only a step away, and held the lighter to the candle and re-lit the wick.

"Put those blades down," said Zach. "I will not ask again."

Abend did not respond. His decaying features still twisting into a smile, he took hold of the pewter candle holder and lifted the candle into the air between them. The flame-light threw a wider circle of glow around the room, deeper shadows wavering.

And Zach slowly became aware of the small firelit eyes staring at him from all around, from every wall and every corner.

"You are the wolf now, I take it," Abend said.

Zach couldn't help but glance to left and right. Rats—rats and spiders—huge, huge spiders big as cats—surrounded him at the edges of the candle-glow. They surrounded him and stared at him and some, one or two, slowly began to creep toward him, step by hesitant step. The sight of them made Zach's heart beat so fast, it left him breathless.

"It is not me you're after, you know that, yes?" said Abend. "I am only the vessel of the thing, the human will of it. Because I have the dagger. The dagger is the doorway. Whoever has the dagger over time becomes the will. There were others before me. The wolves have come for them, even killed them sometimes, but the dagger remains, so the thing itself remains. Why do you think that is, Agent? Why do you think the wolves did not close the door?"

Zach licked his dry lips as the rats and spiders edged his way. He knew the answer and murmured it aloud without thinking. "Because the wolves didn't use the dagger. They didn't end the curse."

"Because they didn't want to die!" said Abend simply, with a small, Germanic shrug. "Even when they could no longer bear what they were, no longer abide the blood they lived by, they didn't want to die, not truly. They passed the curse on, on to you now, yes? And they continued as phantoms. You have seen them, have you not?"

"I have," said Zach.

"So have I. It is a kind of damnation itself, I think."

"It is."

"And yet . . . and yet it is not death." Still holding the candle up in his left hand, he gestured with the dagger in his right. "It is not death."

Zach kept his gun barrel trained on Abend's center. He saw no reason to shout another order, another warning. He either had to pull the trigger now or surrender to the man's logic, which was, in truth, the logic of his own fear.

"What is the point of it then?" Abend asked him. "Coming here? Killing me? What is the purpose? None. Why should you alone destroy yourself when the others haven't? Do you think they want you to? They do not, you know. They do not wish you well in this affair at all. If you do what they could not, you shame them. You shame them and then they die. And not that half-death that they know now, not the death of phantoms, but. . . ."

Abend stopped there, mid-sentence. The expression on his monstrous and shifting countenance changed. His over-round eyes brightened and he cocked his head, as if listening to distant music. Lightning flashed at the window and Zach saw him listening like that and he saw Imogen straining forward in her handcuffs, imploring him with her entire body and all her sobs.

Thunder crashed and ceased suddenly—and in the after-quiet, Zach heard what Abend had heard.

That noise. That voice. That muttering. It was here—that presence—that thing. That beast he had sensed in the forest, that he had seen in the rain, that he had heard murmuring senselessly to him out among the trees—

I AM NOT I AM THAT I AM NOT I AM NOT I

It was here and it was murmuring to him now again, the same incomprehensible susurration rising steadily out of the shadows, out of all the shadows in all the corners of the room, coming through the window and out of the night and out of the fall of the rain and the howl of the wind and out of the deep, mysterious intelligence of the very web and woof of darkness. All, all of it, was muttering and shifting and moving toward him like a closing circle, and the circle of rats and spiders was slowly closing too, empowered by the presence that filled and animated them and was their communal mind and gave them their communal purpose.

"The moon is rising," said Abend with a gentle smile. "The hour has come."

The dagger began to glow in his hand. It turned the color of death—a color Zach had never seen before—a black red light that was indescribable—that seemed to be as dark as it was bright and to grow brighter and darker at the same time. With a grand, sweeping gesture of disdain, Abend hurled the candle away. It turned, burning, through the air one quarter-circle, then the flame went out, and it twirled darkly across the room, landing with a plastic clatter against a far wall. Nearby, an unimaginably enormous tarantula jumped, startled.

Abend didn't need the candle anymore. The dagger glowed and lit the room with that weird red-black bright-dark light. From Abend's right hand, the strange illumination spread in a broadening dome, over the body of Goulart where he lay on his back staring up into the high rafters, over the figure of Imogen where she strained in her bonds, over the rats and giant spiders where they seemed to pause, to hover tensely as if awaiting a command, and finally over the deepest shadows themselves, joining with the shadows until what was in the shadows was also in the light, and what was muttering in the silence was muttering louder and louder throughout the atmosphere.

"Let me go about my business," Abend said, speaking into that terrible music, gesturing toward Imogen and starting to turn to her with the dagger raised. "Let me live and you will live. It's so simple, my boy. All you need to do is nothing."

Zach shot him.

The bullet tore a huge—an unnaturally huge—hole through the center of the man, a hole the size of a fist. Blood exploded backward and forward out of the wound in an enormous red blast. And even so, even so, even with the black-bright air glowing through the middle of him, Abend did not go down. His rotting features contorted with agony, but he still had the strength to keep turning toward Imogen, to keep lifting the knife and to step once in her direction, ready to plunge the glowing blade into the heart of her and drink the healing draught of her existence.

Zach began to pull the trigger again, but he was out of time: the creatures rushed him.

The circle of rats and spiders closed around him instantly, like a noose pulled tight. In a second, the things were swarming over and up him, covering every inch of his body, clawing their ways onto his face, smothering him beneath their huge, furred, wriggling forms, tearing and biting at him with tooth and fang. His arms were forced up. His finger spasmed on the trigger. Flame shot out of the gun barrel straight upward as the bullet went wild. Then the gun was torn from his hands and fell into the glowing dark, he didn't know where. He didn't know anything but the agony and nauseating horror of the rats and spiders crawling over him, tearing into his flesh, so many of them covering him all at once that Zach's mind shut down under the weight of hurt and sheer repugnance. He couldn't think, he could only try to scream—and even the scream was cut off by whatever twisting thing squirmed over his lips to get at him.

He reeled as they devoured him. The loud, dark, thrumming murmur of the Presence filled his head. The lightning flashed and, through the seething beasts, he saw the wounded Abend take another staggering step toward Imogen where she struggled and tried to scream. He saw Abend lift the blade higher, ready to bring it down into her exposed chest.

Then—in the very midst of that abomination: metamorphosis. The transformation exploded inside him and he became the wolf.

A red and wrenching blast went through him, his flesh made fire. His pain became rage and his rage became bloodlust, and all the while his muscles and sinews were bursting their bounds, his bones straining themselves into immensity, his skin pierced from within by the wildly sprouting fur. There was no pleasure in it as there had been the last time. There was almost no man-mind there to experience pleasure. All his thoughts had been consumed by the ravening, disgusting rats and spiders that covered and tore at him—and now even that horror was consumed by this.

And now too, as his jaws were ripped out of their human shape into the form of a snout, as his teeth extended brutally from their very nerve endings into pointed fangs, as his whole form grew enormous in one savage burst, the gnawing beasties flew off him in every direction.

The werewolf roared and, with a paw the size of a boulder, tore one stubborn rodent out of his midsection where it had eaten its way in deep and would not let go. The wolf's razor claws sliced the thing to ribbons as they closed on it, and when he hurled the creature across the room it was nothing but red string knotted with gray fur. A gargantuan spider, mindlessly renewing its attack across the floor, was crushed to twitching sludge by a single lupine footstep.

With that—that quickly—the change was done. And now, howling at the heaven-high rafters, there stood the wolf, the curse's incarnation.

For Zach, for a moment, there was nothing else. He was the creature, and that was all. The incomprehensible murmuring of the darkness was all he knew. It filled his head like the voice of his own imagination. The black light of the dagger filled his gaze till he saw nothing else. For that one second, he looked around him with rolling, yellow eyes and wanted only destruction, only meat, only blood.

But then he saw Dominic Abend—the struggling woman—the upraised dagger—and in a lesser flash—in a still, small but indestructible act of knowing—he remembered who he was.

Abend, weak and bleeding and profoundly wounded, took one final shuffling half step toward Imogen. With his left hand—crawling with rot and maggots now—he seized her black hair to hold her thrashing figure still. Crying out with effort, he jerked the blade up high for the killing stroke.

Zach the wolf leapt at him, swiping with one great claw, and tore his arm off.

The gangster's arm flew through the air, the hand releasing the dagger so that it dropped, clunk, to the floor as the limb kept sailing. Not for another second—not until the bloody appendage itself dropped with a wet thud—not until the surviving rats and spiders swarmed over the fresh feast—not until then did the shocked Abend realize what had happened. Only then did he turn to look at his lost arm with wild-eyed comprehension. Only then did he begin to shriek in horror.

In the next instant, the wolf was on him and the scream was cut short. Zach destroyed Abend. It took mere moments. He was—Abend was—already nothing but rotten flesh, a withering sack of skin holding black blood and maggots. The werewolf's enormous claws ripped him to pieces. What was left sank down to the floor like empty clothes, rags squirming with bugs and viscera, boiling with gore. Whatever else there had once been—the man's substance, his firmer matter—was already long gone.

Growling with confusion and disappointment, the wolf-man stared down at what it had thought to devour. The muck that had been Abend bubbled on the floor and turned to sulfurous steam and then dissipated completely, vanished.

That was not good enough, not half good enough. The wolf needed meat. The wolf needed blood. The wolf raised his enormous head, baring its fangs, and gazed with hungry, yellow eyes at Imogen.

Imogen was now nearly mad with fear, nearly strangling on her gag as she cowered in the shadow of the towering monster that dwarfed her.

To Zach, in his beast state, in his all-compelling hunger, her terror was arousing, a piquant seasoning to his lust for dealing death. The susurration of the shadowy presence that had come into the room through the dagger pounded in him like his own pulse, driving him to attack her, to have her. The dagger itself, the black glow of it, seemed to light his mind with murder.

The beast roared. It moved in for the kill. Lightning flashed. The room went white. Imogen's tear-stained face went white, the shadow of the wolf falling hugely on the wall beside her. The thunder hammered down from heaven, nearly drowning out the mutter of destruction.

Jarred by the flash and clatter, the wolf stopped in his tracks and saw his victim as she was. Zach's heart remembered pity, and what was left of his man-mind cried out to him: *No!*

With that, the mysterious force of human will—like a tiny rudder steering a great ship—turned the hungry werewolf from its prey. Hulking, growling, still drawn back toward the scent and savor of flesh and blood, the beast forced its terrible head to swing round. He looked down at the dagger.

The dagger. Through the noise and desire, it came back to him. The dagger and the curse. They had to be brought together again, the doorway closed, the rift in reality sealed. The room shuddered as the great creature stepped toward the fallen weapon. The sky crackled at the windows, and the shadows muttered their weird incantation and the woman wept, and Zach bent down from his unnatural wolf-height and wrapped his claw around the handle of the baselard.

He lifted the iron dagger clumsily. The black glow of the blade hurt his eyes. The mutter of the Presence that inhabited and ruled the darkness made his head ache. He let out an animal roar of pain and frustration, and as he craned his neck with the effort of making that fearful noise, his eyes swept the dark room—and he saw the phantoms.

They were all there, all around him. Dankl and the executioner and the man in blue and several others whose names and fortunes he had never known. They were standing at the circumference of the shadows, made of the shadows, watching him with their mournful eyes, pleading with him silently not to do this thing, not to destroy them.

How much they wanted to live—even in their ghost-life, how much. And he wanted to live, wanted to go on, even this way, full of blood and violence, wanted so much to continue, a desire beyond telling. His wolf-mind just then was unable to form a clear thought of Grace or Tom or Ann, but he did think of them, did summon the deep sensation of the wife and son and daughter whom he loved above all else. He gazed sadly down into the fathomless dark-light of the dagger blade, and he knew instinctively that this meant separation from them forever. How could he choose that willingly?

But the dagger . . . the curse. . . . It had to be ended.

Lightning flashed once more at the big rain-streaked windows, and the werewolf raised his muzzle to the sky and howled. The mutter of the shadow presence all around him rose in desperate insistence as if it understood that it had lost its power over him. Even the storm seemed to sense what was happening: the thunder that followed was a low, sorrowful moan. Even the woman in her chains seemed to understand: the tone of her sobs changed from one of fear to one of grieving.

Zach's hulking wolf-form straightened, enormous. He wrapped his clawed hand tightly around the handle of the dagger. He lifted the ancient weapon high into the air—hesitated only a second more—then brought the glowing blade down swiftly, and plunged it into his heart.

32

THE DEATH OF
THE WEREWOLF

Christ, how terrible death was! Not the pain of that final moment
or even his shriveling collapse into human form, or his tumbling fall into the spreading puddle of his own blood, or his
last gasping, rattling breath. All that was ugly enough, but it was over
quickly.

But the other death, the great loveless nothing that followed, the
endless torment of blackness—that was terrible beyond imagining. It
was, he saw at once, a cancer in the heart of life. It made life idiotic,
meaningless, and mad. And there was no escape from it.

There was nothing at all here, in fact. There were no words. There
couldn't be: there was nothing to describe. There were no ideas, no

thoughts, not even darkness. There was no pain. There was no else-where. There were no others. There was no time that could end or stretch forever.

There was only this: the inner man in utter isolation, in utter silence, never changing, undifferentiated from his surroundings except by the visceral knowledge that there was such a thing as love that this was not. Love was infinite, but it was not present. This was infinity's end, its defining border. This was solitude—solitude without change. Alone, alone, alone, alone—while love was elsewhere.

Zach's heart stopped. His brain stopped. He ceased to have even himself for company. His body became nothing more than meat. And yet there was still this—this wordless, timeless, loveless brutality of solitude—and it did not even go on forever, because there was no for-ever—it simply remained, constant: there would never be anything else because there was nothing else to be. There was not even false hope.

Christ, oh Christ, it was terrible. This was what the wolves had feared. This was why they had let the curse continue. They had chosen to go on even in the half-life of phantoms rather than face this, this death, the prison of death, that closed around him and held him fast and never ended and would always be the same.

And so that was the end of him—and later, he could not have said what had saved him from it. Even at the time, it was more than myste-rious. It was inconceivable. Here, where there was nothing that could happen, no time for it to happen in, something happened. Somehow something made itself known to him—to him who was even himself no longer there.

That other reality—that unremembered infinity of love—became present to him. He felt a sudden anguish of unquenched desire, an excruciating gesture of the heart toward the impossible. With a bolt of unimaginable being, the endlessness ended.

Zach drew a sharp breath. He coughed. He whispered his wife's name.

He opened his eyes and found that he was a man—a man lying in a pool of his own blood on the floor of a ruined mansion.

He shifted his head. His brow throbbed as if he had been clubbed. He groaned. He rolled over onto one shoulder. He was looking out a window with no glass. He remembered the storm, but the storm was over. How long had he been gone? A long time, it felt like. The clouds were sailing past the moon. The moon was full, and it was still rising.

Still rising, he realized. Still rising, and yet he was a man!

He understood: he had done it. He had done what needed to be done. The curse was over.

In another moment, he became aware that a woman was weeping. Imogen—yes, he remembered her too.

The pain flashed through his head again, and he groaned again as he shifted on the floor until he could see her. She was hanging slack in her chains, exhausted, only barely sobbing. When she saw him move, she gasped into her gag, and her eyes widened—those bright intelligent brown eyes, light brown, almost golden.

"All right," he said, flinching because it hurt to talk. "It's all right."

He sat up slowly. He brought his hand to his brow and rubbed it and shut his eyes tight. When he opened them, he was looking down at himself and he saw that he was naked, his body unscarred, the dagger gone. Still dazed, he searched the room for something he could use to cover himself. He saw the remnants of his plastic Extraordinary Crimes raincoat lying on the floor, not far way. He reached out and pulled it toward him. There was just enough of it left to tie around his waist, a makeshift loincloth.

The wind came through the window and chilled him. He shivered and came wider awake. He climbed painfully to his feet. He searched the floor, somehow knowing he would find Abend's keys—and there they were. He bent down and scooped them up, another shock of pain passing beneath his brow, but a lesser one this time.

He moved to Imogen. She gazed up at him with a sort of helpless wonder, as if she weren't sure whether he had descended to her from heaven, or was about to transform into a murderous beast again.

He tried to smile at her. "It's all right now," he repeated.

He used Abend's key to unlock her wrists and he caught her as she fell into his arms. He supported her with one hand, and with the other he removed her gag. Sneering at the filthy thing, he hurled it to the floor. It fell beside Goulart's body.

Imogen rested her head against him, strangely silent; all cried out. He kissed her black hair to comfort her. But he was looking over her, down at his dead partner. The sight of his friend lying there like that, staring up into the rafters blindly like that—it sent a fresh wave of fear through him. He remembered death. He remembered the unimaginable solitude beyond the edges of infinity. He would never forget it. As he held Imogen against him, he prayed for Broadway Joe Goulart wordlessly. He had always liked the man. He prayed that he wasn't even now in that awful place of death.

When he was done with his prayer, he forced his eyes away. He gazed out the window at the moon.

"Come on," he said hoarsely. "Let's get the hell out of here."

Imogen shifted against him, raised her face to look at him. She looked carefully, a long time, exploring his features. Then, slowly, she nodded.

"Yes. Let's."

EPILOGUE

Half-naked and bedraggled, they made their way hand in hand down through the dripping forest in the moonlight, looking like—feeling like—the first man and woman or the last, as if they'd been expelled from Eden or survived the apocalypse, one or the other. They had recovered Zach's things—his phone, his car keys, and so on—and when they reached the Crown Vic, parked in its little tree-shaded turnout, Imogen waited in the passenger seat while he went around back and opened the trunk. As before, he had packed his overnight bag with some clothes: jeans and a Houston PD sweatshirt. He dressed back there while Imogen sat up front, clutching her torn sweater closed over her breasts, staring through the windshield and shivering. When he was done, he brought her a spare Extraordinary Crimes raincoat he'd found wedged in the trunk's corner. He handed it to her through the window, then walked back around the car slowly to give her time to put it on over her nakedness.

The moment he sat down behind the wheel, she turned to him, her pixie face streaked with grime and mascara and dried tears.

"Thank you," she said.

He shook his head. Turned the ignition on. Put the car in gear. She reached out and touched his arm so that he had to look at her.

"No, I mean it. I don't know how you could have. . . . When you were that thing. . . . It must have required. . . . I can't even imagine."

He managed to smile at her. Then he faced front and pulled the car out onto the road and started driving back toward the highway. He called 911 as they went. The dispatcher's voice came in over the speakerphone. He gave her a quick description of Goulart's death.

"I'm taking the vic to get medical care. I'll let you know where to find me," he said. Then he asked her to call Rebecca Abraham-Hart-well. Then he hung up.

"I don't want medical care, thank you," said Imogen crisply. "I'm not injured."

"You're probably in shock," he told her.

"I'll probably be in shock for the rest of my life, but I don't intend to spend it in hospital."

Zach snorted. He kept his eyes on the windshield, watching the road as it wound through the woods and moonlight. "Guess I'll take you home, then," he said.

They drove in silence for a while. Then Imogen asked him, "What will you tell them? They won't believe the truth. Take my word. I've tried it."

Zach slowly shook his head. "We have to tell them something, I guess."

"I was thinking it could be something like: Abend was practicing some sort of insane sorcery and he persuaded Goulart to go along. Goulart was very ill, you know."

"I know."

"So Abend convinced him that he could help by killing me in some weird ceremony or other, only you found them and killed Goulart and shot Abend. You think Abend was mortally wounded, but he got away."

He glanced at her, a bit surprised. "That's very good. You just come up with that?"

She managed a smile. "I'm a professional journalist. Making up lies to fit the facts—it's what we do."

He was surprised to hear himself laugh, but the very sound of it made him stop laughing. He pressed his lips together, watching the road.

After another mile or two, he called his wife. Grace's soft southern voice came over the speakerphone into the car. She cried out his name as if to warn him from the brink of danger.

"Zach!"

"It's all right," he said. "It's over."

She began to cry. "Thank God! Thank God! You come home now, baby. Come home. Everything'll be all right. I know it will. I *know* it will. Come home."

For a moment, he couldn't answer. Then he managed to say, "I love you, baby. I'll talk to you soon."

He disconnected. He bit his lip, driving.

"What is it?" said Imogen.

"I killed Margo," he told her. "Margo Heatherton. I killed her."

She touched his arm again. "Not you, Zach. It wasn't you. It was the wolf."

"I was the wolf. I had the power to stop it. You saw that. It's just . . . that first time. . . . It took me off guard. It swept me away. I don't even remember what happened."

"Then you can't hold yourself responsible. You can't."

"I can," he said. "I do. There's got to be a reckoning."

Again, they drove along the wooded road without speaking. Then, just as Imogen was about to say something else, Zach's phone rang. It was Rebecca Abraham-Hartwell.

"I shot Abend," he told her. "It was a killing shot, I'm almost sure of it. But he staggered off and I had to tend to the victim. I was so shaken up, I forgot to tell 911. Tell them to search the woods. I'm sure they'll find him."

"I'm sorry about Goulart," Rebecca Abraham-Hartwell said. She sounded sincere.

"He was sick. He was dying. Abend used that, got him involved in some kind of weird black magic crap, offering to heal him. Goulart was a good cop. He just got desperate, that's all. He lost his way."

When he disconnected, he did not look at Imogen. "It's a good story," he said.

They got on the Taconic, heading for the city. Zach was glad to step on the gas and speed up.

"Gretchen Dankl sought you out," said Imogen. "She contacted you, just like she did Bernard. She must've intended to pass the curse on to Bernard, but it went wrong somehow. So she sought you out."

"Yes, that's what I figure too."

"Because she was looking for a good man, you see. A good man who would have the strength to control the beast and the courage to do what had to be done."

"I guess so."

"That's why she chose Bernard. And that's why she chose you. Because you're a good man, Zach."

But Zach shook his head. "I killed Margo," he insisted stubbornly. "There has to be a reckoning."

Even over the noise of the car, he heard Imogen swallow hard. There were tears in her voice when she spoke now. "You died tonight, you know," she said. And when he didn't answer, she said, "You did. I saw it."

Finally, he nodded. "I did. I know."

"You were gone for over twenty minutes."

"Was I? Believe me, it seemed like longer."

"It's impossible that you should have returned as you did. You understand that, don't you?"

"I don't know. It sure seemed that way to me too. Impossible."

"Was it very awful?"

"It was." After a moment, he added, "Worse than you can imagine, Imogen. Worse than anyone could ever imagine. I will never get over it."

This time, when she took his arm, she clutched it hard. He could feel her fingernails through the sweatshirt. "Let that be the reckoning, then," she said. "You have to, Zach. It's fair. It's right. You sacrificed your life tonight. You carried out the death sentence. You did not know it would be undone. You did not know it could be. You did not take your life back. It was given to you: like a gift. You have no right to refuse it. It was the wolf that did murder, and you killed the wolf. Let that be the reckoning. You have to."

Zach felt the pressure of her grip on his elbow. The road blurred through the windshield. The road, the night, the moon, all of it. He raised his free arm and swiped it across his eyes.

"I don't understand any of this," he said hoarsely.

Imogen let him go and sat back in her seat, exhausted. "No," she said. "I don't suppose anyone does, really."

When he pulled up outside her apartment, she leaned across the gearshift and kissed him warmly on the cheek.

"Go home," she whispered to him. "Listen to your wife. What she says is true. Everything will be all right."

His eyes met hers. He shook his head again. "How?" he asked her, in all seriousness. "How will it ever be right?"

"Somehow," she told him.

This much was true, at least: as he was driving across the night streets, weaving through the taxi traffic, heading for the bridge, his mood began almost imperceptibly to lighten. He had turned on the radio so as to have some company, to hear somebody singing and feel less alone. Soon, though, the news came on, and now a dim voice was telling him that there were cities on fire somewhere, there were madmen raving in throne rooms and parliaments, and there were riots in the streets so bad that it looked like revolution or civil war. But as he gazed out the window, out the windshield, at the brownstones, at the towers, at the wet, glistening streets, New York seemed peaceful to him—as peaceful as it ever was, at least. He knew it could only have been his imagination, but he began to sense the influence of Dominic Abend dissipating from the underfabric of the great metropolis even now. It was probably all in his mind, but it did seem to him—it really did—as if the muttering voice of that Presence that had come through the dagger was fading—for a while, for tonight, for a moment anyway. It was probably all in his mind, but it really did seem to him that the storm had washed away some swarm of metaphysical monsters that had been boiling up from the pavements, that the mighty city had been cleansed somehow of supernatural evil and was now prepared once again to stage the hilarious tragedy of ordinary human corruption. That corruption—the city's everyday dishonesty, cruelty, and betrayal—ah, it was music to a lawman's ears. Because somehow you dealt with it, didn't you? Day by day. That was the job. You chased some bad guy down some dark alley while some other bad guy somewhere got away, and you felt everything would indeed be all right for a while. For tonight. For a moment. Somehow.

By the time he reached home, he had decided he would go on in that faith, long as he could, best as he could. Imogen was right. It was the wolf that had done murder, and he had killed the wolf. There could not be any greater reckoning than that.

He pulled the Crown Vic into the driveway and, as he stepped out, Grace opened the front door. They met each other midway along the path, as they usually did at the end of the day. He wrapped his arms around her and she pressed her face against his chest. He breathed her in deeply, filling himself with that scent of hers, that atmosphere that inspired in him such impossible yearning. That atmosphere—it had always seemed so mysterious to him, but not anymore. He understood what it was now. It was life.

She lifted her face to him and he kissed her.